A Gift to Cherish

VICTORIA BYLIN

Scripture quotations are taken from the Holy Bible, New Living Translation, copyright ©1996, 2004, 2015 by Tyndale House Foundation. Used by permission of Tyndale House Publishers, a Division of Tyndale House Ministries, Carol Stream, Illinois 60188. All rights reserved.

Cover designed by Jenny Zemanek, Seedlings Design Studio

ISBN-13: 9781704371474

Printed in the United States of America

To Sara Mitchell
Writing Partner and Friend Forever

Daisy belongs to both of us.
Play the tape!

I also want to thank the gifted women who made this book possible.
(Miss Joan would be proud of us.)

Charlene Patterson
Editor Extraordinaire

Jenny Zemanek
Cover Artist

Virginia Smith
Book Design Guru

Judy DeVries
Proofreading Ace
(Any errors are mine)

Deborah Raad
Insightful Beta Reader and Friend

You must each decide in your heart how much to give. And don't give reluctantly or in response to pressure. "For God loves a person who gives cheerfully."

2 Corinthians 9:7 (NLT)

Chapter 1

A woman's scream cut through the night. Sharp. Penetrating. It pierced Rafe Donovan's eardrums and sent him running down the dark alley toward the shrieks. Three stories above, laughter tumbled out of a tenement window backlit by a dull pink bulb. The old brick walls stank of urine and grease. Dumpsters overflowed onto cracked asphalt, and rotting garbage clogged the gutters.

The woman screamed again, louder this time.

No. No. No. He couldn't let Kara die. He ran harder, faster. The soles of his black work boots slapped the pavement, each stride a hammer blow. His Glock rode tight on his hip, his badge heavy and bright on his chest.

She screamed again—a heaving plea for him to save her.

He ran toward the scream, his arms pumping and lungs straining. But instead of growing louder, the scream faded, as if Kara were being dragged away from him.

He imagined her bare heels scraping against the concrete. He blinked and saw her pale arms flailing, her skin mottled with track marks from the addiction she couldn't shake. She had tried. Rafe knew that better than anyone. But the pills and later the needles had a grip so tight that no one—not even wannabe superhero Rafe Donovan—could drag her from those demons of addiction.

Another scream cut through the night. Vile laughter poured out of the windows above him.

"Kara!" he shouted at the top of his lungs. "Kara! I'm coming for you!" His legs bicycled despite his exhaustion. Sweat poured off his body and he smelled his own stench. A cry ripped out of his throat, and then—

"Rafe!" A deep voice sliced through the fog. "Rafe! Wake up!"

"No!"

"Come on, bro."

The voice belonged to Jesse, Rafe's big brother. Somehow it called to him as if they were kids again, and the monster in the house was their dad.

"Wake up. You're having a nightmare."

A bright light popped on but dimmed to a tolerable glow. With the shift in contrast, Rafe's head cleared. He was in Jesse's house in Refuge, Wyoming, a log cabin with dimmer switches on every wall, hardwood floors that didn't squeak, and almost no furniture because his brother was too busy building houses to furnish them.

Rafe swung his feet over the side of the bed, scrubbed his face with his sweaty hands, then raked his fingers through his hair. His head didn't feel like his own. He'd been on leave from the Cincinnati Police Department for a week now and hadn't bothered to get a haircut or shave.

When he was in uniform, he kept his hair short and used a razor at least once a day, sometimes twice.

Jesse stayed in the doorway. "That sounded like a bad one."

"Yeah. Stupid, too."

"Want to talk about it?"

"No." Rafe snatched up his phone. "What time is it anyway?" The white numbers showed 3:42 a.m. "Crud." Too early to get up. Not enough time to calm down and go back to sleep. It was Sunday morning, so he didn't need to think about getting to work. It was an easy job, just pounding nails for Jesse's construction business, but Rafe took it seriously.

Jesse didn't budge. "Coffee?"

Rafe waved off the offer with a flick of his hand. "Go back to bed. I'm fine."

Except they both knew he wasn't. A few days ago, Rafe had pulled his red Camaro into his brother's driveway, hauled his duffel out of the trunk, and rapped on the door like the cop he'd been until a week ago—the cop he wanted to be again, but first he had to shake the nightmares.

The dreams tormented him, but they weren't new. He'd dreamed of Kara, his high school sweetheart, on and off since her death eight years ago. What had sent him to Dr. Tobani, the department shrink, was two-fold: a drug bust where a teenage girl died seconds before Rafe could administer Narcan, followed the next week by a weird panicky moment in an alley like the one in his dream.

If he couldn't trust himself to be solid, he couldn't be on the street. It was that simple—and that complicated.

Rather than be assigned to a desk, Rafe had asked to take the vacation time he'd stacked up. Dr. Tobani agreed that a change of scenery would be beneficial, added unpaid medical leave, and pulled strings to make it all happen. The plan called for Rafe to get counseling and return to work on August 1 after a twelve-week leave. He'd visited Dr. Susan Patowski before he left home and would continue to see her via FaceTime, a more common practice than he had realized.

A few of his cop buddies asked about the personal leave, but no one thought less of him for taking it. The daily battle against crime, drugs, and ugliness took a toll on everyone.

But leaving Cincinnati put Rafe in a catch-22. Police work gave him a purpose. He was protective by nature, which meant he needed people to protect. People like Kara Howard, the beautiful girl next door who had loved the troubled boy whose father drank too much. Rafe had tried to save her when the pills told their lies. He'd done everything—

"Rafe?"

"Yeah, yeah." Standing abruptly, he snatched yesterday's Levi's off the back of a chair, the belt dangling in the loops. "Go back to bed. I'm all right."

"Sure you are."

"I am." Now they were both lying. "Get out of here. I'm going for a drive."

"It's three a.m."

Rafe scowled out the window. He would have preferred a long, hard run, but Jesse's house sat low in a canyon. No sidewalks. No streetlights. If Rafe went running, he'd be running blind. No way would he risk tripping on a rock and busting his wrist again. Been there, done that. Took the pain pills for a day, then dumped them in a can of stale coffee, duct-taped it shut, and buried it in a Dumpster.

He wished he'd done that for Kara. Icy fingers of sweat dripped down his spine. "I have to get out of here."

Jesse stepped back. "Go for it. Just—"

"I know. Be careful. You sound like Mom."

"Sorry." Jesse grimaced, maybe more at himself than Rafe. Shaking his head, he ambled back down the hall to the master bedroom, leaving Rafe to cinch his belt, punch into a shirt, and snag his key fob.

Two minutes later he slid behind the steering wheel and backed out of the driveway, the headlights slashing through the dark as he drove down a road lined with homes set back in the trees. Only an occasional porchlight hinted at civilization.

Rafe didn't belong here. His heart beat to an urban rhythm—convenience stores open 24/7, the dull hum of cars at all hours, early morning delivery trucks.

Jaw tight, he headed toward downtown Refuge, approximately ten square blocks of restaurants and tourist traps. Every fast food place was buttoned up for the night, so he decided to cruise to Three Corners, a spot twenty miles south where three highways came together, including the east-west link to the interstate system. Something was bound to be open even at this time of night. He'd grab a coffee somewhere and drink it in his car the way he did on patrol back home.

He cruised along the two-lane highway until his gaze snagged on a car pulled over on the other side of the road. The passenger door hung open, and the dome light cast a dull glow inside a late-model Hyundai. The raised trunk lid signaled trouble. So did the slope of the car, listing thanks to a flat tire.

Adrenaline chased away whatever gloom remained from the nightmare. Someone needed help, and he was in the right place at the right time.

Using one hand, he pulled a U-turn just short of a fishtail and parked fifteen feet behind the Hyundai. If the driver was a woman alone, he didn't want to scare her. And if this was some kind of weird setup, he didn't want to be a victim.

The Camaro headlights lit up a Hyundai Elantra with Wyoming plates. So the driver was a local, probably headed to Refuge. Whoever he or she was, they were staying out of sight. After another glance up the hill, Rafe opened the center console and retrieved a mini Maglite. It was the size of a felt-tip marker but could light up the night.

Moving slowly, he climbed out of the car, pushed to his full height, and used the flashlight to scan the darkness on the periphery of the headlight beams.

"Hello there," he called out. "Looks like you need some help."

"Get back in your car! Now!"

Whoa. No doubt he'd ridden to the rescue of a woman alone. She just didn't know it yet and was wise not to trust him. He didn't bother to say he was a cop back in Ohio. Ted Bundy had used that line, too.

Still holding the flashlight, Rafe raised his arms to shoulder level. The beam of light shot skyward, leaving the woman in the dark until footsteps scraped on the sandy apron of the highway. She remained in the shadows but appeared to be Caucasian, in her early twenties, approximately five-foot-six and average weight. She wore a black and white waitress uniform, and a sparkly headband held her short blond hair away from her face. If he wasn't mistaken, she'd assumed a combat stance and was holding a can of pepper spray.

"Don't move!" she said again. "Get in your car and leave."

"Miss—"

"I said *leave.*"

"I can't."

"Yes, you can. It's simple."

Of all the things in life Rafe couldn't do, abandoning a woman in trouble was at the top of the list. He'd rather get pepper-sprayed, even shot, than read about a woman murdered on the side of the highway when he could have saved her. No way could he abandon this woman, which meant he needed to win her trust.

Daisy Walker Riley had been a victim in Los Angeles, and she had no intention whatsoever of letting it happen again.

Even stranded by a flat tire in a dead zone without cell service, she was far from defenseless. Between the pepper spray and her faith, she was ready to stand her ground until her brother came looking for her. Except Shane wouldn't miss her until the sun came up, and fear threatened to swallow her alive.

As for changing the tire herself, she had tried, but the stupid lug nuts wouldn't budge.

The man in front of her kept his hands in the air. She couldn't see more than his silhouette, but she judged him to be in his late twenties, six feet tall, lean but well muscled, and slightly bearded. If it came to fight or flight, she'd be no match for him either way. Her heart dropped with a sickening thud—until she mustered her faith and dug in to protect herself.

"Move it," she said again.

"You're in charge." His voice rang with confidence, as if he were used to giving orders. "But I'm not leaving you here alone. It's not safe, and we both know it."

Maybe he really was a good guy. Or maybe not. Unsure of herself, Daisy answered with a scowl, "I don't trust strangers."

"That's smart. I won't take another step—at least not without your permission." He indicated her slanted car with his chin. "On the other hand, I could change that tire for you right now."

The offer tempted her. But what would happen then? He could follow her, run her off the road, hurt her. She hated feeling so vulnerable, so paranoid, but being beaten half to death by her ex-boyfriend had left her both wise and wary.

She shook her head. "No, thank you."

"Is someone coming for you? A friend, maybe? Or the auto club?"

No way would she tell him they were in a dead zone. "That's none of your business."

The man had the nerve to laugh. "I give up." He lowered his hands to his sides. "I really am a good guy. I'll go wait in my car until someone comes for you."

Daisy sucked air between her teeth. At some point, he'd realize no one was coming.

The man stayed next to his car. "I have another idea. How about if you call my brother? I'm staying with him in Refuge. He'll vouch for me."

The offer struck her as reasonable—unless he and his brother worked together like the Hillside Strangler team. How many women had they murdered in LA in the 1970s? Then again, how paranoid could she be? This man hadn't stalked her or followed her from her job. The flat tire couldn't have been more random.

Still on alert, she lowered the pepper spray. "Actually, I can't call anyone. We're in a dead zone."

"Man, that stinks." He craned his neck to look at the side of the car. Both the flashlight and tire iron were in plain sight. "It looks like you tried to change it yourself."

"I know what to do, but the lug nuts won't budge." She hated to compromise, but he seemed genuine. "Maybe you could help me after all."

He gave a crisp nod, then held his hands to the side. "I'd be glad to, but you're still in charge. Is it okay if I walk over to the car and take a closer look?"

"Yes. Thank you."

Being in control calmed her, but as he moved forward, she backed up. As long as she kept several feet between them, she felt somewhat safe.

He reached the flat tire, crouched, and picked up the tire iron. Daisy heard metal on metal as he matched the pieces, then a deep breath as he sucked in air and held it. The lug nut didn't budge. Muttering something, he tried again. When the nut gave way, he blew out a breath and stood. "Got it."

Curious, Daisy circled around for a better look at him. With the Camaro's headlights at her back, she could see him plainly. Dark hair spiked up from a grown-out buzz cut, and stubble lined his square jaw. She couldn't make out the color of his eyes, but his nose was straight and his mouth formed a relaxed line. There wasn't a tense muscle in his body. In fact, he seemed to be enjoying himself.

He bent down and picked up the flashlight she had abandoned. "I'm going to roll this to you, all right?"

Why not just go and get it? But her nerves prickled under her skin. He held her gaze, waiting for her consent. Finally she nodded and he rolled the black metal flashlight in her direction. It stopped almost at her feet. Taking a step, she bent and picked it up.

Just holding the heavy object made her feel better. If worst came to worst, she could wallop him with it.

The man went back to loosening the next lug nut. "I'm almost ready for the spare. Is it still in the trunk?"

"Yes." She'd already checked it out. "It's one of those little donut things."

"As long as it has air in it, you'll be fine." He spun the loose lug nut with his fingers. "I see where you picked up a nail, but the tire looks good. You might be able to get it patched."

He rambled about tire repair, maybe to distract her, or maybe to put her at ease. She answered back occasionally, but mostly she watched as he loosened the lug nuts but left them in place. When he finished, he faced her. "It's time for the jack and the spare. If you want to step back, I'll get them."

When she nodded permission, he strode to the trunk of her car, turned his back to her, and lifted the jack in one hand and the tire in the other. He hauled the two items to the side of her car.

He didn't say anything more as he worked, and neither did she. In the silence her fear kicked back in, so she turned her head long enough to scrutinize the red Camaro with Ohio plates. She didn't think he was lying about his brother in Refuge, but she couldn't be too careful.

She watched as he put away the jack and flat tire, then closed the trunk. "This will get you to Refuge, but don't drive on it any longer than necessary. It's safe, but just for a short distance."

He sounded just like her brother. Shane was worse than a mother hen since she'd left her old life in Los Angeles and moved into his fiancée's house, but Daisy secretly loved it. They'd been estranged before he found her, and now she cherished their "sibling-ness." When Shane learned about the flat tire, he'd probably tell her again that she didn't need to work right now, that she was still recovering from the assault and could take all the time she needed.

She appreciated his concern, but sitting around made her crazy. She did better with a routine, plus she was determined to move into her own place rather than take over Shane's above-the-garage apartment when he and MJ tied the knot in June. She didn't want to be in the way of the newlyweds, though she loved being Aunt Daisy to MJ's six-year-old son, Cody.

"Miss?" Her personal road warrior peered at her through the glare of the headlights. "You're good to go."

"I really appreciate what you did."

"No problem. If you don't mind, I'd like to follow you back to Refuge just to be sure that spare holds up."

It was a good idea, but she didn't want to inconvenience him any more than she had. "But you were going the other way."

"I was just out driving. It's no big deal."

His words sounded casual enough, but who just went driving at three a.m.? Someone who couldn't sleep. Someone running from the same kinds of thoughts that kept Daisy up at night and made her pace or play too much Candy Crush. It seemed they were kindred spirits, though she wasn't about to follow that line of thought.

Instead she focused on her safety. If he followed her to Refuge, he would find out where she lived. "How far would you follow?"

"Just to downtown. You'll have cell phone reception then."

"All right."

"So," he said, "now we have to change places." He put his hands up where she could see them. "I'm going to walk back to my car. I'll wait there until you're in the driver's seat. How does that sound?"

"Perfect."

With that, he walked to his car. Just like he'd said, he waited until she climbed into the Hyundai and started the engine. Using the rearview mirror, she watched as he eased into the Camaro. When he flashed the headlights, she took off down the highway toward home. As promised, he followed her to Refuge, veering away before she needed to turn toward home.

She wished she'd asked his name. Then again, why would she? She wasn't ready for a relationship. Right now, all she wanted was to stay sober, stay strong in her faith, and stay out of the kind of trouble that came with a good-looking man who made a frightened woman feel safe.

Chapter 2

*R*afe entered the combo into the keypad lock on Jesse's front door, walked silently to the guest room, and stretched out fully clothed on the bed. Sleep came fast and hard.

Four hours later the aroma of coffee tickled his nose, but what most brought him to alertness was the memory of the woman with the flat tire. The way she wielded that can of pepper spray told him a lot about her personality. They hadn't even exchanged names, but he felt a connection to her, a shared understanding of how fragile life could be.

He wanted to see her again.

Jesse had connections—a lot of them between his construction business, church, Twelve-Step meetings, and eating out every night. Maybe he knew something about a woman who drove a 2015 Hyundai Elantra, forest green, with a Life Is Good sticker in the rear window.

Rafe hauled himself off the bed, took a moment to stretch his back and shoulders, then ambled into the kitchen.

Jesse indicated the Keurig. "Help yourself."

Mug in hand, Rafe chose the strongest blend in the tray. "So last night I changed a flat tire for a woman stranded on the road out to Three Corners. A waitress. Blond. Drives a green Hyundai. Do you know anyone who fits the description?"

"You sound like an episode of *Cops.*"

Rafe glanced at Jesse, who raised his mug to his lips and took a long sip. Was he stalling or savoring the coffee? Rafe sipped his own strong brew, decided Jesse was stalling, and challenged him. "So do you know her?"

"Maybe."

That was code for *Don't ask.* With Jesse's history, he was the keeper of a lot of secrets, a trait Rafe respected, though right now he wanted his brother to spill the beans. "What's the big deal?"

"There isn't one, but I'm not talking. How would you like it if I blabbed your business to anyone who asked?" Jesse put on a newscaster-like voice. "Hello, everyone. Meet Rafe Donovan. He's a cop in Cincinnati, but he's here in Refuge because he's having bad dreams—very bad dreams. In fact, he—"

"Yeah, I get it." His neck hair prickled with the memory of the nightmare that had launched him out of bed last night.

Jesse set down his heavy mug. "Rule number one for Donovan Construction is 'Don't run your mouth about other people.' You know that."

Rafe muttered under his breath. "It was just a casual question."

"For people like me, there's no such thing."

Rafe got it. His clean-cut brother hadn't always been a good guy. Jesse had done prison time for drug charges, become a Christian while behind bars, and come to Refuge to start a construction business modeled on the one that had given him a fresh start. The men and women he hired all needed a break, and Jesse gladly provided one.

Rafe admired his brother's efforts, but he didn't share Jesse's ramrod posture about not blabbing. Gossip stank, but legitimate information enabled people to make smart decisions. He wasn't ready to let go of finding out the woman's name—or to let Jesse win. "So let me guess. You know her from prison. She's a mysterious cat burglar released on a technicality."

"Yeah. Right."

"So you won't help me out here?"

"No, I won't."

Rafe held back a snort. Over the past few years, Jesse had morphed from a selfish jerk into St. Jesse, Redeemer of Ex-Cons, Addicts, and Losers of Every Kind. Rafe didn't want to think too hard about the fact that he was living in Jesse's house right now.

The mysterious woman interested him far more, and he didn't really need Jesse's help. He knew she worked the late shift at a restaurant in Three Corners. She wouldn't be hard to find if he wanted to meet her again under safer circumstances, but no way would he act like a weirdo stalker. To Rafe's way of thinking, life was a string of random events. Human beings were like marbles sliding around a great big box. They met, kissed, ricocheted, then rolled away from each other when the box tilted in a new direction.

Jesse glanced at the clock on the microwave. "I'm outta here."

"Where to?"

"Church. You're welcome to come along."

Rafe shrugged off the invitation. "No thanks." Crosses and steeples had been part of his upbringing, but he'd lost his affection for God when Kara died. He didn't mind church on Easter if he wasn't on duty, but he usually worked Christmas so officers with families could be home. As for Sundays, he far preferred sleeping in, watching the Bengals lose, or working on his car.

Jesse rinsed his mug, set it on the sink, then snagged his keys and wallet off the kitchen table. When he put his hand on the doorknob, Rafe thought his brother would leave, but Jesse turned around. "About those nightmares."

Rafe shook his head. "I don't want to talk about them."

"If you don't talk to someone, they'll get worse. Last night you were screaming like a little girl."

He decided to throw Jesse a bone. "I talked to a psychologist before I left home. The department set us up for weekly FaceTime sessions while I'm here."

"FaceTime?" Jesse's brows arched. "Is that legit?"

"Apparently so." Rafe had been surprised too. "Apparently telemedicine is the latest thing. I'm okay with it. The dreams aren't all as bad as last night. That one had Kara in it."

"And how long ago did that all happen?" Jesse had moved to Florida before she died, but he knew perfectly well how much time had passed.

"Eight years," Rafe admitted. "Yeah, I know it's a long time. But—" He didn't want to go there now, so he shook his head. "Get outta here, all right?"

"Fine. But one more thing."

"What?"

"I need you to take over for Brooks starting tomorrow. He bombed out at Cottonwood Acres."

Not a surprise. Brooks was a tough guy with a big

mouth. He'd been assigned to handyman duties at a historic ranch that once served as the set for *Thunder Valley*, an old TV western. The ranch was also home to Miss Joan Prescott, an old lady known for not suffering fools gladly. Brooks had been handyman number three in the past month and had complained heavily about both the lowly job and Miss Joan's perfectionism.

"Great." Rafe faked a groan. "Just what I need—a cranky old lady bossing me around."

Jesse smiled. "Cliff Lopez is the ranch foreman. He'll do the bossing. But be nice. Miss Joan will eat *you* for breakfast and *me* for lunch. We're just getting started on Heritage House. It's a big contract for us."

"I heard you mention it the other day." Rafe had been in the office to fill out employee tax forms. "What exactly is it?"

"A seven-thousand-square-foot building with museum space on the first floor and offices on the second. Miss Joan is a retired history professor and the last of the Prescott family. Apparently she wants to leave a mark of some kind. I don't know anything else."

"Don't worry. I'll be nice." Rafe was glad to help Jesse, and he didn't mind cranky old ladies at all. They were just part of a cop's life—the life he wanted back.

But first he had to beat the nightmares and regain confidence in himself after that weird panicky moment in the alley. Until then, he'd take what pleasure he could find. When it came to the woman with the flat tire, who knew which way their marbles would roll? With a little luck, he'd bump into her again and find out.

Since arriving in Refuge three months ago, Daisy had applied for dozens of jobs but missed out on everything except waitressing. She possessed solid office skills thanks to vocational training at Maggie's House, the women's shelter in Los Angeles that gave her a fresh start, but she lacked experience except for clerking at Mary's Closet, the thrift store associated with that ministry.

The flat tire incident proved without a doubt that she needed a better job. She also needed a break, which came in the form of a Craigslist ad the day after the flat tire. Miss Joan Prescott, owner of Cottonwood Acres, needed a personal assistant. The position required computer and photography skills, a creative mind, and a good driving record. The hours were flexible and the salary negotiable.

What the position *entailed*—the word of the day on Daisy's Grow Your Vocabulary app—fit her skill set perfectly. But landing the job? That was another matter.

Determined to do her best, she dressed professionally for the interview, and left in plenty of time. If she didn't get the job, she'd be disappointed but not defeated. No matter what happened, she refused to lose hope. How could she doubt when God had rescued her so thoroughly? Yet she wrestled with fear as much as ever.

"You can do this." She spoke the words out loud as she turned down the long road to the famous ranch. If talking to herself made her crazy, too bad. Voicing good thoughts muffled the bad ones in her brain.

You'll never get the job. Everyone knows who you really are. You haven't changed, Daisy. You're still the same stupid—

"Stop it." She glared at her evil twin in the rearview mirror. When the twin glared back, Daisy scowled harder. "I mean it!"

To make her point, she added a bear-like growl. It was more Care Bear than grizzly, but it scared away her evil twin.

Pushing up her sunglasses, she refocused on the road

leading to the ranch made famous by *Thunder Valley*. The old show lived on in syndication, and Daisy used to watch it after school. She had loved the horses, the big family meals, and especially the teenage heartthrob who played the oldest son. Back then, she had wanted a horse and a boyfriend. Now she just wanted a decent job.

The interview was scheduled for two o'clock. The dashboard clock showed exactly 1:43. Perfect. For once in her life, she would be on time.

A hundred feet away, something shiny flashed in the green canopy of a cottonwood tree. When the blob jarred loose, a cluster of Mylar and latex balloons shot into the sky. The colorful balloons flew high, higher still, shimmering on this May day so beautiful she wanted to fly, or run away, or—

"Stop it," she muttered.

Sometimes she felt like that dog in the movie *Up*, the one that saw a squirrel and—yes, that dog.

Or maybe she had ADHD, or maybe—never mind. She hated it when her thoughts ran wild, but at least the balloons were pretty and a welcome distraction from her nerves.

But then she saw him—the man who had changed her flat tire.

He was standing by a split-rail fence and gripping the strings of a second cluster of balloons, this one still tied to the top rail. He was looking down, so he didn't see her car, but she saw him plainly. The same dark hair. More beard scruff. The broad shoulders she would never forget. Today an olive green t-shirt with a small logo hugged his chest. It looked like a Donovan Construction shirt, the kind Jesse sometimes wore to AA meetings after a long day at work.

The man looked up, saw her car, and broke into a grin as she sped past. She returned her attention to the road, but her eyes darted defiantly back to the mirror, where she saw him raise his hand in a casual wave.

"Stop staring!" She didn't know if she was talking to him, herself, or her evil twin.

Irked by the distraction, she shoved him out of her mind. But every twenty feet or so, yet another cluster of balloons bounced and bopped on the railing.

The balloon trail didn't end until she reached the scrolled-metal arch marking the entrance to Cottonwood Acres. A banner at the top declared *Welcome!* in primary colors that matched the balloons. Smaller print spelled out *Horses, Hay, & History! Annual Children's Festival* with this past Saturday's date.

Daisy's insides jiggled like one of those inflatable bouncy-houses, and they jiggled even more when she saw a red Camaro in the eight-car parking lot. The man had been careful of her fears when he changed her tire, but in Daisy's experience, fast cars signaled trouble. If she crossed paths with him, she'd be friendly. If she didn't see him at all, even better.

A glance at the clock assured her she was five minutes early, so she dabbed on lipstick, checked her teeth in the mirror, then picked up her gently used Coach bag from Mary's Closet. She had emailed her résumé, but the purse held hard copies, plus three of her seagull photographs and a letter of reference from Lyn Grant, the head of Maggie's House and Daisy's mentor and friend.

Clutching the purse, she strode up the concrete walk to the house. The path ended at a wooden staircase eight steps high and wider than the double doors at the top of the wraparound deck. She took the stairs a step at a time, then used the door knocker to rap twice.

A full minute passed. Or was it a minute? Maybe it had been only seconds—or maybe it was longer? Should she knock again, or—

The door opened wide enough for Daisy to see a black-and-white Great Dane and a woman with stylish gray hair, piercing blue eyes, and perfectly applied lipstick. A tailored white blouse topped a pair of peacock blue capris and worn ballet flats.

Daisy didn't know what she'd been expecting, but it wasn't a Judi Dench look-alike with a slobbery dog. She almost stepped back, but the Great Dane sat and offered its paw. A pink-and-white-checked collar with a heart-shaped ID tag hung from the dog's neck. Daisy couldn't help but smile.

Bending slightly, she accepted the shake and spoke to the dog. Somehow it calmed her. "Well, hello to you too. I'm Daisy Riley, and I'm here for an interview with Ms. Prescott."

"That would be me." The woman patted the dog's head. "And this is Sadie."

"She's huge."

"But friendly." Ms. Prescott opened the door wider. "Please come in. My office is down the hall to the right. May I call you Daisy?"

"Of course."

"I go by Miss Joan."

Daisy stepped into the foyer and glanced around. An arched opening led to what looked like a living room, but the rest of the entry gleamed with memorabilia from *Thunder Valley*. Posters of old *TV Guide* covers adorned the walls, and a display case showed off other souvenirs and props.

Impressed but nervous again, Daisy followed Miss Joan down the hall. Sadie padded behind them, her nails tapping on the wood floor until Miss Joan turned into the last of three doors on the right.

Daisy tried not to gape at the picture-perfect office. Dual computer monitors sat on an L-shaped desk, stacks

of papers lined a credenza, and built-in bookshelves covered an entire wall. Across from the desk, a leather couch
and two chairs formed a casual sitting area near a sliding
glass door.

Miss Joan indicated the couch. "Please. Sit down."

Daisy set her purse on the floor and sat, her fingers
laced together in her lap. Miss Joan took the chair across
from her, and Sadie laid down at her feet in a beam of
sunlight pouring through the window. The view was stunning—distant purplish mountains, glowing blue sky, lush
green meadows, and a rustic barn in the distance.

Just as eye-catching were the photographs on the office walls, especially the one of a younger Miss Joan with
a man in a black cowboy hat. The way they stood, their
heads tipped together and almost touching, put a hitch in
Daisy's heart. Being in love scared her to death, but she
was also female and lonely.

Miss Joan broke the silence. "Welcome to Cottonwood
Acres. This ranch has been in my family for a long time.
Our roots go deep—to 1873 to be precise."

Daisy could hardly imagine. Her own family tree was
more like a tumbleweed. "I used to watch *Thunder Valley*
when I came home from school. I loved it. I never dreamed
I'd be sitting here, or even living in Wyoming."

Was she rambling? Being too informal? Or maybe she
was being confident and assured. Unsure of herself, she
smiled nervously.

Miss Joan tapped one manicured finger on the arm-
rest. "Change is inevitable, and that's why we're here today."

"Yes. I'm very interested in the job."

"And I'm eager to find the right person." A note of frustration leaked into her voice. "Tell me about yourself."

"I moved from Los Angeles three months ago." *I'm not
proud of how I used to live, but I did my best to survive.* "My

brother and his fiancée are here, so I had a soft place to land." *Lord knows, I needed one after Eric assaulted me. I almost died. In fact, I did die. But that's a story for another time.* "Now I'm looking for a job that will use the skills I learned in a training program in LA."

Miss Joan nodded gently, encouraging her. "Tell me about those skills and how you obtained them."

Ah, the tricky part. *I lived in a shelter for women escaping violent situations. I'm an alcoholic—a sober one for eight months now. By the grace of God, I have a brand-new life.* Daisy had made peace with the past, so she ordered herself to sit tall. "I took classes for both Mac- and Windows-based programs. Macs are easier to use, in my opinion, but I'm comfortable on either platform. As for photography, I picked it up for fun and love it."

A used camera from Mary's Closet had given her new eyes to match her new heart.

Miss Joan glanced at the photographs above the sofa, then refocused on Daisy. "I looked at your Instagram. You're an excellent photographer."

"Thank you."

"What specific office experience do you have?"

"Very little." Daisy softened the confession with a smile. "But I'm reliable, willing to learn, and plan to stay in Refuge permanently. This is my home now."

Miss Joan's eyes stayed fixed on Daisy's face, her expression almost stern.

Was she waiting for more? Should Daisy ask one of the questions she had rehearsed? It was important to show interest, so she met Miss Joan's gaze with a direct one of her own. "I'd like to know more about the position. What would an average day look like?"

"Taking phone calls. Driving me into town for appointments—both hair and doctor visits. The cattle operation is handled by my foreman, so you don't need to know anything about the livestock business. Your day would be spent working on the layout and design of a history book I'm writing about Cottonwood Acres."

"That sounds like an exciting project." Daisy wished she could say more. *I designed a book like that for Maggie's House. It's called* The Attic Letters, *and it's for women like me. And MJ. And Lyn.* She wanted to share the details, but that part of her story didn't belong in a job interview. Instead she focused on her skills. "Will the book have photographs?"

"Yes, including several historic ones."

"They'll need to be scanned and edited." Daisy pictured tintypes like the one in *The Attic Letters.* "I've done that kind of work before."

Miss Joan's eyes flared with approval and she smiled. "That's good to know. I'm also interested in your organizational skills. The book is part of a larger project that will require travel arrangements, small event planning, and information management."

"I can do it." She felt confident in this area thanks to helping with Shane and MJ's wedding—a big bash set for the middle of June. "The trick is to use reliable sources, keep a calendar, and send reminders. I'm a firm believer in checking everything twice."

"So am I."

They chatted about planning in general, software preferences, and finally about the driving requirements. Miss Joan explained that she'd let her license lapse because she disliked driving in Refuge during the crowded tourist season.

Daisy's hopes rose with every word. "It all sounds great. I'd really like the job."

Miss Joan locked eyes with her. "I have one more question and it's important."

Daisy couldn't imagine what they hadn't already covered. "Yes?"

"In the past month, I've hired and fired three people for this position. The first young lady couldn't put down her phone, even when mine was ringing. The second turned out to be allergic to dogs—and possibly hard work."

"And the third?" Daisy tried not to cringe.

"I overheard her sharing my personal business with her friends. I value my privacy. And I especially need discretion for the second part of the project you'll be working on. And that, Daisy, is my last question. Can you keep a secret?"

$\mathcal{A}$ larm bells went off in Daisy's head. Should she say, *I'm good at keeping secrets because I have one or two or ten of my own*? But that would raise questions. Instead she pretended to be Lyn. "There's a difference between secrecy and privacy. If you expect me to keep secrets that hurt people, I won't do it. But I can and will respect your privacy, like I expect people to respect mine."

Miss Joan gave a hearty laugh. "Touché, my dear. That's a very wise response."

Daisy blushed. "It's not original. I have a friend who taught me the difference."

"I had to learn that difference myself." Miss Joan's gaze drifted to the array of photographs on the wall—a mix of Hollywood stars and action shots of rodeo riders, plus the one of herself with the man in the black cowboy hat.

"A lot of famous people have come and gone from this place. Most of them had secrets."

"I suppose we all have a few."

"Yes."

That's all she said, leaving Daisy to wonder about the secrets in Miss Joan's life. Sadie, still lying on her side in the sun, began running in her sleep, her tail thumping the floor to the beat of an unheard drummer.

Miss Joan smiled at the dog. "She's chasing a rabbit."

Sadie ran harder, going nowhere in real life but everywhere in her dreams. Daisy could relate.

Finally Miss Joan turned to her. "I assure you there's nothing illegal or hurtful about what I expect you to keep private. The project will eventually go public, but until the decision is final, I want to avoid as much fuss as possible."

"Yes." Daisy didn't like fusses, either. "As long as there's nothing illegal, my lips are sealed."

Miss Joan's face relaxed into a playful grin. "Illegal? No. Unethical or immoral? Not in the least. A little crazy? Perhaps."

"I admit to being curious, but I won't ask."

"Good, because I'd like to offer you the job." Miss Joan crossed the room to her desk, lifted a manila folder, and placed it in front of Daisy. "The position pays twenty dollars an hour with a guaranteed thirty-five hours a week, maybe more, with a flexible schedule. It includes a basic health insurance plan effective in thirty days, plus holiday and vacation pay."

Health insurance? Paid time off? A generous salary? All for the job of her dreams? Daisy's mouth dropped open. "Are you *serious*?"

"Yes. I am." A mischievous twinkle danced in Miss Joan's eyes. "I believe in sharing what I've been given, and to say I've been blessed—yes, *blessed*—is a roaring understatement. Now"—she pointed at the folder—"read the employment agreement carefully. If you're still interested, sign both copies. Sadie and I will be back in a few minutes."

Miss Joan called to Sadie, and the two of them left Daisy alone with the four-page contract. She read every word, paying particular attention to the section she mentally dubbed the keep-your-mouth-shut clause. The language was more legalese than the rest of the document, but she understood it and confidently signed her name.

A few minutes later, Miss Joan and Sadie returned to the office.

Smiling, Daisy indicated the closed folder. "I signed—and I can hardly believe it! This is a wonderful opportunity for me—I can't thank you enough. It's just—just—" She winced. "I'm babbling. Mostly I want to say thank you."

A gentle smile graced Miss Joan's face. "I like your enthusiasm. When can you start?"

"I need to give notice at the restaurant, but they can easily fill my shifts. Would this Thursday be okay?"

"Perfect. Will nine o'clock work for you?"

"Nine is perfect."

Miss Joan stayed on her feet, so Daisy picked up her purse and stood. She schooled her face into a calm smile, but her heart did a Snoopy dance. A job! She had a real job! She could move out of MJ's house before the wedding, go all out on MJ's bridal shower, and even make a donation to Maggie's House. She didn't deserve a job this wonderful—not at all. It was a gift, pure and simple.

A lump pushed into her throat. Swallowing it back, she followed Miss Joan and Sadie down the hall. At the door closest to the entry, Miss Joan stopped and flipped on a light. "This will be your office."

Daisy poked her head into a room unlike any place she had ever worked. A cranberry red sofa sat against the wall to the left, with two matching chairs and a coffee table to make a square. The window matched the view from Miss Joan's office, and the big desk with double monitors was state-of-the-art. Just as impressive to Daisy were the paintings on the wall, a set of four landscapes matching the view through the window, each a different season.

"This is amazing." She told herself not to gush, but a little appreciation was called for. "Having two monitors is ideal for design."

Miss Joan jabbed her finger toward the desk. "Try the chair. It's a Tempur-Pedic. We don't want you getting backaches."

Daisy would have sat on a plastic crate for this job, but she set down her purse and did as Miss Joan asked. After adjusting the height for her long legs, she pulled out the keyboard tray, placed her fingers, and faced the monitors positioned exactly at her eye level. The workspace fit her like a glove.

She spun the chair back to Miss Joan. "It's perfect. I can hardly wait to start."

"Good, because I'm eager to finish the history book and start on the next project."

Daisy took that as her cue to get moving, lifted her purse, and followed Miss Joan to the front door. Excitement bubbled through her entire body—until her evil twin whispered in her ear. *Miss Joan doesn't know who you really are, but I do. You don't deserve any of this. You're a failure, a loser—*

Stop it! She wanted to shout the words out loud but didn't. Miss Joan would think she was crazy if she started talking to herself. Instead Daisy channeled Lyn's advice to replace a bad thought with a good one, then she spoke the truth out loud so she could hear it. "This is a wonderful opportunity for me."

When Miss Joan opened the front door, she wore a

distant smile. "Opportunities come at unexpected times, don't they?"

"Yes."

"And with unexpected consequences."

What did *that* mean? Most of the unexpected events in Daisy's life had been horrific—her mother's death, the sexual molestation by those boys in the garage, Eric's vicious attack that put her at death's door. But that was when she had surrendered fully to Christ. Yes, unexpected consequences. They weren't all bad.

Miss Joan opened the front door, they exchanged good-byes, and Daisy walked down the steps to the path leading to the parking lot. Rounding the corner of the house, she saw her car and stopped, her jaw dropping in surprise. Tied to her windshield wiper was a balloon bouquet with a folded piece of paper pinned beneath the rubber blade.

The balloons had to be from her road warrior. He certainly knew how to get a woman's attention, but under the circumstances, she couldn't afford to respond. She wasn't ready to date again—not even close. She needed time to heal and grow. To be truly independent. Until she could stand firmly—by faith—on her own two feet, she was in danger of repeating the biggest mistake of her life—leaning on a man who didn't deserve her trust.

But her heart didn't want to listen to her common sense, and she couldn't help but smile at the pretty balloons.

Twenty minutes passed between the moment Rafe saw the woman's car and the instant he snipped the ribbons on the last cluster of balloons. He wanted to meet her, so he hurried to the parking lot, tied the bouquet to her windshield wiper, and wrote a note. Hurrying, he drove the ranch pickup to the trash bin behind the garage a hundred feet from the house, tossed in the bulging plastic bags, and returned the truck to the garage.

Before leaving for the day, he needed to check in with Cliff Lopez, ranch foreman, so he strode across the yard to Cliff's office. Lively Spanish music drifted through the screen door, and through the mesh Rafe saw Cliff at his desk, working on a laptop. The foreman was in his fifties, wiry, muscular, and slightly bow-legged from his rodeo days. Silver streaked his black hair, and his brown face testified to both his heritage and decades working in the sun.

Rafe tapped on the screen door. The music coming from the computer faded to nothing. In a single motion, Cliff removed a pair of reading glasses and motioned Rafe to enter. "Come in. Have a seat."

Rafe entered the office but declined the chair. "Do you need me for anything else?"

"You're finished with the balloons, right?"

"They're in the trash—all nineteen thousand of them."

A grin rippled across Cliff's face. "Only nineteen thousand? I thought we put up a million."

"It felt that way." There had been exactly two thousand—one hundred clusters with twenty balloons each. Rafe had cut each bunch off the fence, popped the balloons, and stuffed the remnants into trash bags. One bouquet had made a break for the clouds, and another was tied to the Hyundai.

Cliff gave a nod. "Good work. We'd like you to come back tomorrow."

Between the balloons, sweeping up the hay bale maze, and emptying countless trash cans, Rafe had put in a solid day. "I thought the clean-up was done."

"It is. But Miss Joan wants you back."

Rafe nodded as if the request made sense, but it struck him as odd. He hadn't even met Miss Joan. Why would she ask for him? Not that he minded. He enjoyed working outdoors, and Cliff was a lot friendlier than Jesse's crew. "Do you know what the job involves?"

"Not yet. Joanie called Jesse herself." Only Cliff called Miss Joan by her nickname, a sign they had been friends for decades. He dismissed Rafe with an offhand wave. "*Hasta la vista*, my friend. We'll see you tomorrow."

Rafe offered a wave of his own, then hurried down the concrete path leading to the house and parking lot. In the distance he saw the Hyundai with the balloons bouncing in the breeze.

He was about to cross the entrance road when the front door to the house opened and the woman stepped onto the deck. Dark dress pants showed off her long legs, and a tailored jacket shouted confidence. Her hair, liberated from the waitressy headband, bounced in the sunlight. When she reached the bottom of the staircase, she glanced back at the closed front door, did a little skip, and half danced down the walk to the parking lot.

She looked nothing like the frightened woman who had held him at bay on the side of the road, but appearances could be deceiving. Right now, Rafe looked nothing like a cop. He considered calling out to her, but he wanted to see her reaction to the balloons. If she seemed pleased, he'd ask her out. And if she didn't, he hoped to at least make a friend.

He knew the instant she saw the bouquet because her feet froze in midstride. The sun reflected off the clip in her hair, a wide barrette as sparkly as the Mylar tied to her car. The balloons had stopped her dead in her tracks. A good sign? He hoped so.

He picked up his pace until he reached the parking

lot. "Hello, there," he called, slowing his steps.

The woman faced him, her blue eyes as stormy as an Ohio sky, her lips straight and sealed tight. Was she fighting a smile or restraining a frown? Rafe was good at reading people. He could spot a liar within two sentences, and he could hear the difference between bravado and real courage. He tried to get a read on her reaction but couldn't.

Leaning forward, he extended his hand. "We didn't exchange names the other night. I'm Rafe Donovan."

She looked down at his fingers, hesitated, then offered her hand in return. Her skin felt cool against his, her fingers long and delicate, her grip tentative.

"I'm Daisy Riley. Thank you for putting on the spare."

"Glad to do it." He indicated the front end of her car. "It looks like you bought a new tire."

"Two, actually. My brother thought it was a good idea."

Brother came out a little louder than the rest, a declaration that someone cared about her—and would call the cops if she went missing. That was fine with Rafe. Nothing made him happier than knowing people were safe.

Digging his hands in his pockets, he rocked back on his work boots. "What brings you to Cottonwood Acres?"

"I just interviewed for a job."

"Great. I hope you get it."

"I already did."

A genuine smile lit up her face—the first one he'd seen, and he didn't want it to be the last. "Congratulations. So no more midnight drives?"

"That's right."

"What'll you be doing?"

"Office work. Some driving. Whatever Miss Joan needs."

"So I'll see you around?"

Her eyes went to the Donovan Construction logo on

his shirt. "Do you work for Jesse?"

So she knew his brother. Not a surprise. Jesse's business was well known. "Yes. At least temporarily. We're brothers. I'm out here on a bit of a vacation." Not exactly, but the description was close enough. "He needed an extra guy out here, so I'm filling in."

"Oh."

Rafe hooked an eyebrow. "Is that, 'Oh, great. We'll be seeing each other again.' Or, 'Oh, crud. This guy's a pest?'"

She laughed. "Neither."

"So what would you say if I asked you out to dinner? We could celebrate your new job."

"No. I can't. Definitely not. But thank you." Her words came out like gunfire, one bullet after another. Precise. Prepared. And well aimed.

Something had put her on guard, and it couldn't have been good. Rafe's blood heated the way it had in those final weeks with Kara—the way it still did when he sensed trouble. He had no business worrying about Daisy Riley, but he couldn't help himself.

He decided to keep things light and press at the same time. "If you're seeing someone, he's a lucky guy."

"No. I'm just not dating."

"Ever?"

Daisy laughed. "Well, maybe someday. Like in five years."

Rafe didn't know Daisy at all, but he knew a lot about wounded women. Sometimes they needed to climb out of the pain on their own to prove they could do it. Others needed to be lifted up and carried to safety.

He was more than willing to do some lifting. "How about five days instead?"

Her mouth opened, closed. Opened again.

Good. A crack in her resolve. "Think about it. My number's written down on the note."

Her cheeks flamed pink. "I can't—really—I . . ." She shook her head, letting silence be her answer.

"No problem at all. And no pressure. I'm new in town and just trying to make some friends."

Her pale blue eyes locked on to his brown ones. Was it longing that made them glisten in the silence? Or was it fear?

She glanced at the balloons bobbing in the breeze, then turned to him, her expression wistful. "It's not you. It's just . . ." Her voice trailed off again.

"Bad timing."

"Yes." She turned and opened the back door to her car. Rafe untied the bouquet, stuck the note with his number in his pocket, then handed her the balloons. As she stuffed them into the Hyundai, the balloons fought back, thumping and bumping against her head.

"Do you need help?" he asked.

"I've got it." She popped out of the car and laughed. "They almost won!"

Rafe opened the driver's door for her and stepped back. She slid behind the steering wheel, then looked up at him. "Thank you for the dinner invitation. And the balloons. It's not personal. It's just that I'm new here and still getting settled. My life is . . . what it is."

"Complicated?"

"No." The word came out soft, almost a whisper. "Right now, it's remarkably simple."

"Good. We'll keep it that way." He gave her a smile, then closed the car door with a gentle push.

As she drove away, he pondered her vague words about life being remarkably simple. His cop instincts served him well on the job, and those instincts were pinging now. Unless he missed his guess, Daisy Riley had a past as revealing as skid marks after a car crash.

But he wasn't on the job. He was new in town and

missing his friends in Cincinnati. He'd respect Daisy's boundaries—no question about that. But he also wanted to be her friend, let their marbles do some rolling around, and he would keep an eye out for trouble. That's just who he was.

"Don't look in the mirror," Daisy told herself as she drove away from the parking lot. If she didn't give Rafe Donovan a second look, she wouldn't give him a third one—then her phone number. She needed to stop thinking about that dinner invitation. But despite her resolve, her eyes flicked to the rearview mirror.

To her relief—and admittedly some disappointment—he was already gone.

The joy of her new job flooded back, and she sang her favorite praise songs all the way to MJ's house—until a hatchback with California plates caught her eye. Daisy didn't recognize the vehicle, but nothing good could come from California—at least for her.

Maybe the car belonged to a friend of Shane's. Except Shane had been a professional baseball player. His friends drove Corvettes and luxury SUVs.

Eric . . . Her stomach did a flip, but her common sense kicked in. He'd been sentenced to twelve years in prison for second-degree attempted murder. If he was released early for any reason, her legal aid advocate would contact her. She didn't need to worry. Besides, Eric didn't know where she lived now. Only Lyn knew, and she wouldn't tell anyone without Daisy's permission.

Still nervous, she parked in her usual spot on the left side of the driveway, gathered her belongings including the balloons, and detoured to the hatchback for a peek through the bug-spattered windshield. A child's booster seat, a Barbie doll, and cardboard boxes assured her the car didn't belong to Eric. Most likely it belonged to a friend of MJ's.

Daisy's fear evaporated in a breath, and she walked through the back door and into the kitchen. MJ's laughter drifted down the hall from the living room. Not wanting to intrude, Daisy headed toward the stairs.

A little girl's giggle carried over the conversation. "Mommy? Can you fix my game?"

Daisy knew that voice. Hannah was four years old and the daughter of Chelsea Yeager, a friend of Daisy's from Los Angeles. Daisy's relationship with Chelsea had gone through some ups and downs because of Eric, but there was nothing complicated about her affection for Hannah.

With a big smile and a bunch of balloons for her favorite little girl in the world, Daisy walked into the living room.

Chapter 4

*D*aisy dropped down to a crouch and flung her arms wide. "Hannah-Banana! I can't believe it!"

"Daisy!"

The little girl barreled into her, and they shared one of their famous rock 'n' roll hugs, the kind where they rocked until Hannah rolled onto the floor and Daisy tickled her. Just as Daisy expected, the child flopped down. Daisy obliged with a tickle, then pressed the balloon strings into Hannah's warm palm. "These are for you."

The child tugged on the ribbons to make the balloons bounce. "Mommy, look!"

"Isn't that cool!" Chelsea hurried to Daisy for a hug of her own. "How did you know we were coming?"

"I didn't. The balloons were a stroke of luck." With her initial shock settling into curiosity, Daisy eased back from the hug. "I can't believe this."

Chelsea grinned. "It's a surprise. I know."

"A big one."

The two women had worked together at Shenanigan's, a trendy restaurant in Los Angeles, where they were both servers. They'd been good friends, though the friendship had dimmed when Chelsea brought Eric to Mary's Closet without Daisy's permission. That decision triggered the restraining order, Eric stalking Daisy, and the vicious assault that put Daisy in the ICU.

Chelsea had apologized a thousand times, and Daisy had forgiven her without hesitation. How could she do anything else? Daisy was here now in Refuge—safe and happy—because people like Lyn had been kind, even generous, when she deserved it the least. Hannah, too, tugged at Daisy's heart. The little girl filled the hole left by the abortion Daisy would regret forever. The old guilt raised its head. As always, she silently thanked God for washing away the stains if not the regret.

After a breath, she led the way to the couch. Chelsea dropped down next to her, and Hannah sprawled on the floor with a My Little Pony game on her Kindle Fire. Mother and daughter looked a lot alike with matching dark hair and hazel-green eyes, and they both seemed happy. So why were they here in Refuge? And why hadn't Chelsea bothered to call or text in advance? Daisy needed to find out.

MJ stood up from the love seat and lifted her empty iced tea glass. "I need to pick up Cody. Before I go, I want to know how the interview went."

Fresh excitement bubbled from Daisy's head to her toes. "It was fantastic. I got the job."

MJ let out a squeal. Glass in hand, she gave Daisy an awkward hug. "When do you start?"

"This Thursday." Daisy turned to Chelsea. "I'm officially an administrative assistant at a big ranch." Mindful of Miss Joan's desire for privacy, Daisy held back the details.

"That's great!" Chelsea sounded sincere, but Daisy caught a whiff of envy. It's how *she* would have felt if the situation were reversed.

MJ broke in. "We have to celebrate. Dinner tonight is just taco salad, but Chelsea? You and Hannah are welcome to join us."

Chelsea's face lit up. "After three days of fast food, we'd like that a lot. Thank you."

MJ said good-bye and left to pick up Cody. Daisy slid over to her spot on the love seat so she could see Chelsea without craning her neck. She didn't want Hannah to overhear, so she lowered her voice. "Refuge isn't exactly a ten-minute drive from California. Are you all right?"

"Yes and no. I'm going home."

"To Michigan?"

"To live with my mom and stepdad." Chelsea dragged both hands through her hair, pulling it away from her face as she grimaced. "I hate the idea, but I have to get out of LA. Between rent and daycare, I'm broke all the time. It just never ends, and there's no way out."

Daisy had made decent money at Shenanigan's. Chelsea's earnings had been about the same, even a little higher, plus she received child support from her ex-husband. Money alone didn't explain such a drastic move. Daisy kept her voice low so Hannah wouldn't hear. "Is it just money, or did something else happen?"

"Both." Chelsea exaggerated a shudder. "After you left, a guy from corporate took over as manager. I tried to be"— she made air quotes—"'a team player,' but the new guy put me on lunches. Instead of trading babysitting with a neighbor, I had to put Hannah in preschool. It cost almost as much as my rent."

"Does Brian still help?" Daisy wasn't a fan of Chelsea's ex-husband.

"He pays child support, but he doesn't spend any real time with her. You know how it is."

Daisy's gaze went to Hannah, still absorbed in the game on her tablet, an innocent victim along for a bumpy ride. Sometimes life just wasn't fair. Accidents happened. People died. But sometimes the pendulum swung the other way, and someone who didn't deserve a break got one—like today and Daisy's new job.

Chelsea gazed down at her daughter, her expression tender. "I can't take being broke all the time, so I'm doing what you did."

"Me?" Daisy hardly considered herself a role model.

"I quit my job, packed our things, and hit the road. Hannah and I are starting over."

Daisy puffed up with a hint of pride. If she had inspired Chelsea to make a brave change, some of her own suffering had a purpose. "I'm proud of you, Chels. It's not easy to start over."

"There's just one problem."

Uh-oh. "What is it?"

"I have enough money to get to Michigan, but that's it. My parents are okay with us moving in, but their house is tiny and my mom treats me like I'm fourteen. They want us to stay with them, but I'm going to need my own place. How would you feel if I stayed in Refuge for a few months, found a job, and saved up enough for rent when I get to Michigan?"

"I'd be fine with it, but I'm confused." And still surprised by Chelsea's arrival. A cross-country move required some thought. "If this was the plan, why didn't you tell me you were coming?"

"It wasn't the plan."

"It wasn't? Then how—"

"We were on I-80 when I saw the *Welcome to Wyoming* sign. I said, 'Hannah, look! This is where Daisy lives.' She got so excited that I checked my phone and saw you were only a few hours away. I tried to call, but we were in a dead zone. After that, I just followed the GPS and here we are."

Daisy could see herself making the same impulsive decisions. "I'm glad you're here, but this isn't my house. You're going to need a place to stay."

"Of course," she said quickly. "I wouldn't dream of imposing. I saw a weekly motel that looks reasonable. As for work, I'm sick to death of being a server, but I'm good at it."

Daisy faked a jealous scowl, teasing her. "You always did beat me on tips."

Chelsea grinned. "I just flirted more."

Daisy laughed, but a sad truth lurked beneath it. She'd been living with Eric then, under his thumb, and a victim even if she didn't know it. There were days when she didn't smile at anyone out of the fear that he'd see her and be cruel. Thanks to God, those days were over. Now Chelsea needed help, and Daisy could give it. "You won't have trouble finding a job. It's almost summer. Refuge is already filling up with tourists."

"Do you know anything about daycare? That's a huge problem for me."

Was Hannah listening? Would the four-year-old think *she* was the problem? Daisy hoped not. "I bet MJ will know someone. Of course, I'll help when I can."

Chelsea gave a sad shake of her head. "I love Hannah. I do. But being a mom is *hard.* She comes first, but sometimes I wonder if . . ." The sentence faded into silence.

Daisy couldn't let it go. "Wonder what?"

Chelsea whispered to guard Hannah's ears. "If I'll ever

meet someone special or if this is it." She held out both hands, cupped and empty.

"I won't lie," Daisy murmured. "Life doesn't come with guarantees. You know that because of Brian."

Chelsea's eyes misted. "The divorce nearly destroyed me. I didn't start really dating again until after you left. Do you remember Carol Dixon?"

"Of course." The veteran waitress had been the restaurant's mother hen.

"She talked me into signing up for FriendsFirst."

Daisy recognized the name of an online dating app. "How did it go?"

"Great—until last month." Chelsea reached into her purse for a tissue and dabbed at her eyes. "Nathan and I dated for almost six months, but then it fell apart. I loved him, but he didn't love me—at least not enough."

Daisy knew all about not being enough, so she moved to the couch and gave Chelsea a hug. "I'm so sorry."

"Me too." Chelsea squeezed tight, clinging until she eased back. "I tried so hard to make it work."

"Relationships aren't easy," Daisy replied. "But I'm curious about something."

"What is it?"

"I had no idea you were seeing someone. You didn't text me or call. No pictures on social media. Nothing."

"I wanted to tell you, but Nathan wanted to keep things private until we were sure."

Daisy thought of Miss Joan, the job interview, and her secret project. "That was probably smart. Break-ups are hard enough without having to explain to everyone."

"*And* disappoint people—like my mother." Chelsea rolled her eyes. "If I changed my Facebook status to 'In a relationship,' she'd be planning a wedding."

Chelsea reached for her glass of iced tea, took a sip, then set the glass back down. "I can't believe I'm thirty-one and moving back in with my parents."

Daisy knew enough about Chelsea's upbringing to envy her. "Going home might be just what you need, especially with Hannah. You'll have built-in babysitting, right?"

"Yes, but I don't want to take advantage of my parents. At least if I have some money saved, I won't look like a total failure, which I guess I am."

"Don't say that." Apparently Chelsea had an evil twin of her own. "You're a wonderful mom. Just look at Hannah—she's doing great."

"She's the best thing in my life." Chelsea smiled down at her daughter, then turned back to Daisy. "Are you sure it's okay if I hang around Refuge?"

"Of course. Why wouldn't it be?"

"I don't want to interfere in your life. I did that once with Eric, and I'll never forgive myself."

Daisy made her voice firm. "I forgave you, Chels. You know that."

"Yes, but—"

"No *buts* allowed when it comes to forgiveness. You messed up, but it's over now. If you're going to start fresh, you have to put your old thoughts aside. It's not easy, but you can do it." It wasn't often Daisy gave a pep talk; she was usually the recipient. But today the powerful words came easily.

Chelsea managed a faint smile. "Thanks. I needed that."

"We all need a little help sometimes." Daisy sure did, and she also needed to give of herself whenever she could. "I'll do whatever I can. You know how much I love Hannah-Banana."

Chelsea grinned, and this time it glowed with sincerity. "I love you, Daisy."

"I love you, too." Daisy gave Chelsea a playful fist

bump, and they both grinned.

Hannah announced she needed to go potty, so Daisy took her to the bathroom. They returned to the living room, and Hannah showed her pony-race game to Daisy while Chelsea searched for jobs on her phone.

Shortly before five o'clock, MJ walked in with Cody. He took Hannah under his wing, and they played in the family room. Five minutes later, Shane arrived sweaty and grinning after high school baseball practice. He kissed MJ, high-fived Daisy, and greeted Chelsea with a warm hello. When he insisted they all go to Cowboy's Cantina to celebrate Daisy's new job, she nearly burst with pride.

Could life get any better? Daisy didn't think so.

And then it did. During dinner, MJ pulled her aside and asked if she wanted to invite Chelsea to stay with them until she could find a place of her own. They'd be crowded upstairs, but MJ, like Daisy, knew how it felt to be broke, scared, and in need of a helping hand.

Words of gratitude poured from Chelsea's lips until she was almost babbling. Daisy didn't own the house, but she belonged to the family opening its arms to Chelsea and Hannah. For the first time in her life, she was the person doing the giving instead of the person in need, and it felt good.

Chapter 5

*F*orty minutes after leaving Cottonwood Acres, Rafe pulled into the parking lot behind the high-end log building that housed Donovan Construction. He needed to find out more about tomorrow's assignment, but mostly he wanted to rope Jesse into having dinner with him. It had been a long day, the vast majority of it spent alone, and he was eager to blow off a little steam, tell a few jokes, and chow down on a big meal.

With a little luck, maybe Jesse would spill the beans about Daisy Riley. Rafe hoped so, because he liked her a lot.

He parked a few spaces from Jesse's truck, a steel gray Dodge 3500 with a crew cab. When it came to power, the truck beat Rafe's Camaro hands-down. But for speed and tight turns, the Camaro took the prize.

Not that Rafe was competitive or anything.

Smiling at his own internal joke, he turned off the engine, reached for his phone, and saw a missed call from Dr. Susan Patowski's office. No surprise there. He had a FaceTime appointment tomorrow at nine Eastern time. A text message confirmed it.

He didn't enjoy baring his soul, but when it came to treating trauma, severe PTSD, and milder situations like his, Dr. Susan—she preferred her first name—had serious street cred. An army nurse for over twenty years, with stints in both Iraq and Afghanistan, she had retired, returned to school, and earned her doctorate in psychology.

Rafe didn't want to admit he was suffering from PTSD or anything like it, but he wanted without question to be a solid police officer. In the meantime, he'd give Jesse his best effort. Rafe enjoyed working with his hands, and an assignment at Cottonwood Acres, where he'd run into Daisy Riley, counted as a bonus.

He strode into the building and down a short hall, passing the kitchen and a conference room fit for a Manhattan high-rise. In the lobby, he snagged a couple of mini Snickers bars from the candy dish on the reception desk, then veered to Jesse's office.

Before he reached the open door, his brother called someone a blockhead, and Ben Waters, Jesse's foreman and close friend, broke into his famous baritone laugh.

Rafe tapped on the doorjamb. "Blockhead? Really? You can't do better than that?" Jesse's language used to be far more colorful.

He just shook his head. "Believe me, blockhead fits. Come on in. We were just talking about you."

"So I'm the blockhead?" Rafe hurled one of the Snickers minis to Jesse, and the other one to Ben, a mountain of a man with dark skin, a bald head, and wide-set eyes that didn't miss a thing. A tattoo on his forearm read *For*

Rebecca. No one knew who Rebecca was, but everyone knew not to ask.

Ben slid the candy across the desk and back to Rafe. "Keep it. And for the record, you're not the blockhead."

"Glad to hear it." Rafe sat and ate the candy in one bite. "So what's up?"

Jesse tossed his own candy wrapper into the trashcan under his desk. "You must have impressed Miss Joan, because she wants you back."

Rafe still didn't understand why. "That's what Cliff said, but the cleanup is done."

"She wants you working on Heritage House." Jesse leaned back in his big chair and gave a shrug. "What Miss Joan wants, Miss Joan gets. That's why Ben's here. He's the boss on that project."

Ben draped a creased work boot over his knee, steepled his fingers over his chest, and studied Rafe, his lips pursed into a frown. "We have a problem, because you're Jesse's snot-nosed little brother *and* a cop. Most of my men are ex-cons. They don't like you, don't trust you, and don't want to know you."

Rafe didn't reply. The truth spoke for itself—except the part about being snot-nosed.

"What I say goes out there." Ben's voice boomed and picked up speed. "We work as a *team*. Respect—God bless Aretha—has to be earned. If I put you on the crew, you'll need to hold your own and hold up your brothers—whoever they are. You'll need to take it on the chin, keep your mouth shut, and do the work. How are you with being on the bad end of a bad joke? The guy who gets stuck with the worst jobs?"

Ben had a little "preach" in him, much like the old desk sergeant in Cincy. Rafe considered blustering back, but he kept his tone mild. "I get it. I'm the rookie out there. Believe me, I've been called names before."

Ben and Jesse traded a look. When Ben nodded, Jesse spoke directly to Rafe. "You start tomorrow morning. Breakfast is at seven. Cottonwood Acres is on the back side of nowhere, so we drive out together in company trucks."

Rafe started to say he'd be there, but then he remembered the appointment with Dr. Susan. "I can't make breakfast."

"Why not?" Jesse asked the question, but Ben was staring at him—hard.

Rafe didn't want to share his personal business in front of Ben, so he kept his answer short. "I have a phone appointment at seven our time. Work-related."

"That's fine," Ben said. "It's probably best I warn the guys that SuperCop is joining us."

Let the hazing begin. In some ways, Rafe welcomed it. He missed the brotherhood of the department, especially silly pranks and nicknames.

Ben pushed to his feet. "I'm outta here, gentlemen. See you in the morning."

"One more thing." Rafe was hungry enough to eat two steaks, and he enjoyed Ben's company. "I was about to bribe Jesse into dinner with a steak at Cowboy's Cantina. How about it?"

Ben shook his head. "I'm taking Tamara to see the new Marvel movie. After the week she had, she deserves a break."

Tamara was Ben's girlfriend. She worked as the director of nursing at an assisted living facility. As a cop, Rafe had been summoned to similar places on 911 calls. Between AWOL memory patients and families going Jerry Springer, those calls were among the saddest.

When Ben left, Rafe turned to Jesse. "So how about dinner? I'm buying."

Jesse gave a somber shake of his head. "Man, I wish I

could. But I have a date."

When it came to dating, Rafe had Jesse beat hands-down. Rafe dated easily and often. Jesse, on the other hand, dated often but not easily. He wanted to settle down but couldn't find a woman who held his interest, maybe because of his complicated past.

"So who is she?" Rafe's mind shot back to Daisy. He'd mention her to Jesse in a minute.

"Her name's Emily Todd. She's friendly. Pretty. Dark hair. She works in human resources at one of the resorts."

"How did you meet her?"

"A friend at church set us up. This is date number two, but I don't think we'll make it to three."

"Why not?" Rafe asked.

"I wish I knew. I like her, but so far there's just no chemistry." Jesse shrugged, then rocked forward in his chair. "What's up with you and that appointment tomorrow?"

"It's with Dr. Susan. But right now, I'm more interested in the woman I helped with the flat tire. I met her again at Cottonwood Acres. You know her—Daisy Riley."

"I wondered if it was Daisy."

Rafe waited for more, but Jesse didn't spill. If he knew Daisy from AA, so much the better. Rafe enjoyed an occasional beer, but mostly he avoided alcohol. He strongly preferred to be clearheaded, and he'd seen what alcohol did to his father and Jesse. Rafe knew full well people could relapse into addiction, but he also knew men and women who had stayed straight for years, even decades.

If he shared a bit of info about Daisy, maybe Jesse would, too. "She was at the ranch for a job interview. She got it, so I'll see her again."

"Good, but be nice to her."

Big brother on duty—always. But Rafe didn't mind. "I'm always nice to pretty women."

"In that case, don't be *too* nice."

"Yeah, right." Rafe grinned. "Like I need dating advice from my geek of a big brother."

"Brat." Jesse threw a paper clip at him. "Get out of here. I'm running late thanks to you and Miss Joan. By the way, what did you do to impress her?"

"I don't know. I didn't even meet her."

"Weird. But I'm not complaining. We're under contract to complete the building by October 15, and we're already a few days behind on the framing. Ben could use another hand out there, and I know you have the skills."

Rafe thought back to the house where he and Jesse had grown up. A single story made of bricks, it had provided a roof to the Donovan brothers and not much else. Their father had kicked Jesse out of the house the day he turned eighteen. Two years later, their mother found the courage to kick *him* out of the house after he put her in the hospital.

Rafe would never forget that awful night, but mostly he remembered calling 911, the police breaking down the door, and a female police officer comforting his mom. With their father out of the picture and Jesse living in Florida, Rafe was twelve years old when he learned to fix whatever was broken.

They walked out of the building together, with Jesse locking up behind them. They climbed in their separate vehicles, and Rafe followed the big truck out of the parking lot, considering food options as he drove. He didn't want to sit alone at Cowboy's Cantina. Taco Bell again? No. He'd eaten there three times this week. Maybe a coffee shop in Three Corners? The drive would kill time in what promised to be a long, empty evening.

With rock music blasting, he hit the highway. Forty minutes later, he arrived at a restaurant much like one where he'd stopped on his drive to Wyoming. It had been a bad night. In the grips of a nightmare, he had shouted loud enough for security to pound on his door. Awake and miserable, he bought coffee and drove straight through to Refuge rather than stop again to sleep.

A woman in a pink hostess uniform stepped out from behind the counter, plastic menu in hand. "Just one?"

"Yes."

"This way."

She led him to a booth designed for two. As always, he sat facing the door. The waitress arrived, skipped the chit-chat, and took his order—a double bacon cheeseburger with a double order of fries.

He took out his phone for company until the door chimed and a Wyoming highway patrolman walked in. The man was in his thirties, average height, burly, and re-laxed. The hostess greeted him like an old friend and seated him at a square middle table.

The officer noticed Rafe in a casual way and nodded, but Rafe knew the nod wasn't casual at all. The man was sizing him up and sizing up his surroundings.

The restaurant door opened again, making way for a pair of sheriff's deputies—one male, one female. They carried Glocks along with the other tools of the trade. Like the first officer, they noticed Rafe, nodded what could be a greeting or a warning, then sat with their friend.

Rafe's food arrived, and he dug in. The burger hit the spot, but it didn't fill the silence that came with eating alone. His gaze drifted back to the officers, eating together and trading stories, laughing hard and often.

"Crap," Rafe muttered to himself. He wanted his old life back. He wanted to be on patrol.

The officers finished their meals, bantered again with the waitress, and left without giving Rafe a second glance. Through the window, he watched them climb into their vehicles and drive away in opposite directions.

Rafe left a handful of cold French fries on the plate, paid his bill, and drove back toward Refuge. When he reached the spot where he'd changed Daisy Riley's tire, he slowed enough to take in the spit of gravel where she'd been stranded. He had done a good deed that night. If anything would help him sleep without dreams, it was the satisfaction of a job well done. Tomorrow he'd report to work at Heritage House. Despite the comments he expected to face from the crew, Rafe found himself smiling at the prospect of swinging a hammer, breaking a sweat, and making a difference.

Chapter 6

Forty is the old age of youth; fifty the youth of old age.
Frances Bacon

Joan Prescott didn't mind living alone, though on nights like this, when a deathly quiet filled the house, she wished Sadie could talk.

The dog might have enjoyed it, too. It had been quite a day between attorney calls, hiring Daisy Riley, and most fun of all, seeing Rafe Donovan tie the balloons to Daisy's car. Catching him in the act had been a stroke of luck. After giving Daisy the contract, Joan had purposely gone to a window that faced the parking lot. A car revealed a lot about a person, and she wanted to see what Daisy drove.

The car was unremarkable. The balloons, however,

were not. When Joan saw a young man in a Donovan Construction t-shirt tie the balloons to the wiper blade, she called Cliff and learned the fellow was Rafe Donovan, Jesse's brother. Charmed by the flirting, she called Jesse and asked him to assign Rafe to work on Heritage House. Being old had its privileges, and playing Cupid was one of them.

So was staying up late, but when the grandfather clock chimed midnight, she set down the sweet romance novel she was reading, rose from her spot on the sofa, and put on a light sweater.

"Come on, Sadie-girl." She clapped her hands to wake up the dog. "It's time to go outside."

Sadie pushed up on her long legs, and they walked out to the deck that wrapped around the house. Sadie never went far, so Joan didn't worry when the dog trotted down the steps and wandered into the dark. Even if Sadie scented a rabbit, she wouldn't chase it. Like Joan, she was a senior citizen and content to stick close to home.

While the dog wandered, Joan began her customary lap around the deck. She walked slowly, listening to crickets and night sounds until she reached the side of the house facing the parking lot. Pulling her sweater close, she paused at the railing and gazed up at the stars twinkling unfettered and without apology. There seemed to be a million of them in the Wyoming sky, a place untouched by the light pollution that tainted other places she had lived. The cool air tickled her nose and she inhaled deeply, savoring the piney scent she'd cherished all her life.

Who could worry under a black velvet sky with Polaris, the North Star, pointing the way—with constellations that mapped the galaxies, and a moon that controlled the ocean tides? Not Joan. She trusted God and believed the Bible. But sometimes, on empty nights like this one, memories of the darkest time of her life howled like distant coyotes. There was a beauty in the chorus, a painful one, like the sad songs she and Trey Cochran sang in his truck as if they were Sonny and Cher, both of them off-key and loving it—and loving each other.

"Trey . . ." She didn't say his name often. It was all so long ago, close to fifty years now. Yet tonight it seemed like just yesterday that he had swaggered into her life. Sighing, she wondered if playing Cupid for Daisy and Rafe Donovan had stirred up those old embers.

Joan wasn't overly sentimental. Months, even years, had passed when she didn't think of Trey at all. Over the decades, she dated other men, some of them quite wonderful, but her heart refused to respond the way it did for Trey.

Eventually, she settled for getting a dog. Sadie was her fourth Great Dane and the prettiest with black-and-white harlequin markings. The old gal was taking her sweet time tonight, so Joan continued alone around the deck, fighting memories of Trey. In her mind, she heard the last words he spoke to her.

"I'm sorry, Joanie. So sorry."

"So am I," she said to the stars. How could she have been so naïve?

Memories howled through her. She didn't need to close her eyes to see Trey's face in her mind, or to recall the passion and the lies, the strong beliefs that had empowered her decisions—beliefs she no longer held as true. She had changed, yet love and its demands remained as timeless as the earth itself. Men still tied pretty balloons to cars, and women still fell in love, wise or not.

The past came alive in Joan's mind, and her heart ached for every human being who had walked, stumbled, and fallen in shoes like the ones she wore oh-so-proudly back in 1972 . . .

The first time I saw Trey Cochran, he was covered in blood. Granted, it was fake, but the makeup people for *Thunder Valley* knew their stuff. He'd been gut-shot, left to die in a canyon, and had somehow ridden his horse into the yard of the big house where the widow Becky Monroe lived with her three precocious children. There he'd fallen off like the professional rodeo rider he was, and begged God to let him live.

"Cut!" shouted the director.

Trey jumped to his feet. The crew and guests, including me, broke into applause, and he took a sweeping bow. I almost never cried, but that scene moved me to tears. That's how good an actor he was.

An assistant brought him a towel to wipe away the dirt and fake blood. Rather than head to his dressing room in the bunkhouse, he ambled over to Walter Henning, the director and a man I knew well. Walter motioned me over to meet Trey, something he did with every guest star.

At this point, *Thunder Valley* had been in production for twelve years and was in its final season. Hollywood stars had come and gone, some young and others not, all of them men and women with enough charisma to light up a city. After years of this exposure, I fancied myself immune to raw male charm. I was very much my own woman—thirty years old, an associate history professor at Esther Hobart Morris College for Women, and in control of my romantic choices. This was 1972, a new era of freedom for women a la Mary Tyler Moore tossing her hat in the air every Saturday night.

And then it happened. Trey Cochran lasered me with those smoky brown eyes, and I wasn't nearly as immune as I thought.

"Joan." Walter put a grandfatherly arm around my shoulders. "Meet Trey Cochran. You two have a lot in common."

"We do?" I couldn't imagine what. The man got bucked off horses for a living, and I taught brilliant young women at an elite college.

Trey thrust out his hand, now wiped clean of blood. "It's a pleasure to meet you, Miss Prescott."

"*Miss* Prescott?" I laughed as we shook. Didn't he know what decade it was? At the very least, he should have called me *Ms.* Prescott. "Please, call me Joan."

"My pleasure, Joan." Those eyes . . . somehow they unmasked every lie I believed about *not* being susceptible to male charm. I blushed, and I never blush.

No way would I give Trey Cochran—or any man—that kind of power over me. I stared back as hard as I could. I'm fairly tall, five-foot-seven and proud of it. Trey was a few inches taller, mostly because of his boots. We ended the handshake at the same time, both aware that it lasted a little too long to be businesslike.

Walter finally broke the silence. "Let's get down to business, shall we?"

I tipped my head toward him. "What business?"

Trey broke in. "This is where I come in. Rather than go into it now"—he motioned to his bloody clothes—"I'd like to talk about it over dinner. How about that new place in town?"

"I don't think—"

Walter interrupted me. "She'd love to, Trey."

"Walter!" That was just like him—running the show as if he were on a movie set.

"Do it, Joanie." He winked at me. "You know that conversation we had about what to do with this place?"

Yes, I did. With the show coming to an end and westerns losing popularity, Cottonwood Acres needed a new purpose. None of the old ones fit anymore. My father had loved the cattle operation. Me? Not so much. When he died of a heart attack, I was in college and my mother turned that responsibility over to a ranch manager. Two years later, she passed away from a fast-growing cancer, leaving me, their only child, with the burden and privilege of ownership.

I considered selling the place, but how could I? Seven generations of Prescotts were buried in the family cemetery high on a hill. I loved the land, the river, the grassy meadows, riding the trails at sunrise and dusk. I especially loved the history tucked away in nooks and crannies and wanted to preserve it. But how?

My father had ideas about that. On my twenty-third birthday, he leaned in, poked me in the arm, and winked. "The clock's a-tickin', Joanie. Find a good man. Get married and have some kids. We can't let the Prescotts die out."

I bristled when he said that. I was in grad school at Cornell, the birthplace of women's studies as a discipline, and eager to take on the injustices of sexism. I objected to being treated like a broodmare and told him so. But neither did I want Cottonwood Acres to be handed over to distant cousins.

Walter knew my concerns. He also respected me professionally, so when he clapped Trey on the back, I knew he meant well.

"Take a chance, Joanie. You and Trey have something in common."

"What is it?"

Walter smugly sealed his lips, but Trey looked me straight in the eye. "I'm starting a charity to give worn-out rodeo horses a decent retirement. That's what I want to talk to you about—tonight over dinner."

I loved horses, especially Miss Priss, the chestnut

mare that saw me through adolescence and the pain of losing two parents. She shared the barn with a half dozen other horses left over from the ranch's more active days.

Walter knew how much I loved horses, but I didn't appreciate his gloating, or the cockiness Trey Cochran didn't bother to hide. As a world champion rodeo rider, perhaps he was entitled to that self-confidence, but I saw it as arrogance. Inviting me out to dinner struck me as a power play. Why not suggest a business meeting instead? On the other hand, I was free tonight and interested enough to make a small concession.

"All right," I finally said.

"Perfect. I'll pick you up at seven."

"That's not necessary." I refused to allow him to set the stage. "We can eat at the house. Is six too early for you?"

Trey's eyes glinted. I'd thrown down a gauntlet and he knew it. *My time and my turf. Take it or leave it.*

He nodded once. "Six it is."

I turned to Walter. "Would you like to join us?"

My old friend gave me a look like the one my father used to give—overly patient, as if I were a child missing the point. "Sorry. I already have dinner plans."

I didn't believe him, but the three of us exchanged friendly good-byes. Walter went back to speak to his assistant; Trey took a golf cart to his dressing room in the bunkhouse; and I went into the house to find Graciela, my housekeeper, cook, and self-appointed surrogate mother.

I found her in the kitchen as usual, baking something that smelled delicious.

"Pan dulce?" I pointed to the tray of cinnamon swirls fresh out of the oven.

She waved the spatula at me. "Eat up, Joanie. You're too skinny."

Graciela thought everyone was too skinny. Feeding

people was her mission in life, so I lifted a pastry and took a bite.

A comfortable silence settled between us, with Graciela wiping down the tile counter and me being grateful for her presence in my life. We saw the world through very different lenses, but I loved her—despite her maddening hints that I should get married and have a houseful of children.

Bracing myself for her matchmaking, I told her about Trey Cochran coming to dinner.

She waggled her brows at me. "He must be handsome if he's on TV. Single, I hope?"

"I don't know, and I don't care." I gave her a pointed look. "This is a business dinner—not a date."

"Business! Ha! You should still wear something pretty."

"Graciela, you're unstoppable! Like I said, this is a *business* meeting."

"Whatever you say." Her tone called me a liar. "So what would you like me to cook?"

Trey struck me as a steak-and-potatoes kind of guy. I liked a good steak, too, but something in me rebelled. "Let's go with your vegetable alfredo."

"What? No meat?" Graciela propped her hands on her ample hips and grinned. "So you *do* like him."

"I do not!" Her attitude annoyed me. "Why would you say that?"

"Because you're trying so hard *not* to like him!"

Did she really think I was a six-year-old playing schoolyard games? Far from it. I knew my own mind. If I wanted something, I possessed the confidence to work for it. "Fine," I said to her. "Fix whatever you'd like."

"I will, and it won't be vegetarian!"

She knew me well, but I hated to lose. "If you go with steaks, at least add some broccoli."

Before she could roll her eyes, I headed upstairs. With Trey coming to dinner, I needed to put a dent in the stack of blue exam booklets sitting on my desk. They were from my favorite class to teach, an upper-division seminar that focused on women as motivators of social change. The assignment was to compare and contrast the lives of women in 1872 and 1972, keeping social class in mind.

My own family history was a living testament to that theme, but as much as I admired my female ancestors, I deplored their need to fight battles for things I took for granted, like the right to vote and own property. I loved history, but I had no desire to live in an era when women were limited in their career choices and denied economic power because of their gender.

Three hours later, I marked the last exam with an A-minus and went to my bedroom to change clothes for dinner. I took my time getting dressed—not for Trey, but for myself. Like Ali MacGraw in the movie *Love Story*, I wore my dark hair long, straight, and parted in the middle. High-rise bell-bottoms, a paisley top with a preposterous collar, and clunky platform shoes completed the look.

As bad as that look was, I *owned* it.

Trey arrived promptly at six. I was still upstairs, dabbing on lip gloss, but I heard the doorbell and knew Graciela would let him in. I gave Trey credit for punctuality—and not playing a power game by being late. I honored his effort by coming immediately down the stairs.

When I breezed into the living room, he stood up from the couch and swept me with his eyes. The glance wasn't the least bit wolfish, but when his brows rose a notch, I knew he liked what he saw.

I felt the same way about him. Trey Cochran cleaned up well. A rodeo star to his marrow, he wore dark trousers and a black shirt embroidered with white swirls and arrows across the chest. The sleeves, buttoned at the cuff, pulled tight when he placed his hands on his hips. My platform shoes put us eye-to-eye, but he'd beat me hands-down in an arm-wrestling match.

"Hello, Joan." He extended his hand and we shook. "Thank you for agreeing to meet with me."

"Walter knows me well. I can't resist anything that involves horses." I indicated the sofa. "Please. Sit down."

Trey returned to his spot, and I took the armchair at a right angle to the sofa, the biggest chair in the room and the one my father used to claim.

Graciela walked in with iced tea for me and a bottle of Corona with a wedge of lime for Trey. He thanked her, especially for the lime, which was a surprise to him. Apparently lime went well with Mexican beer.

She told us dinner would be ready in twenty minutes, then smirked at me and smiled at Trey. "Mr. Cochran, how do you like your steak?"

"Medium rare, thank you."

Graciela didn't need to ask me, but I wanted the last word. "Medium for me, please."

She gave me a smug look, and I knew that tomorrow she'd quiz me mercilessly about Trey Cochran.

Graciela returned to the kitchen. Trey bit the lime and took a swig of the Corona, but I left the iced tea on the table. This was a business meeting, so I rested my hands on the arms of the big leather chair, my imitation of a CEO, or maybe my father. "Let's talk about your horse rescue operation. What do you have in mind?"

Trey gave a nod and set the bottle on the coaster, a granite square etched with a *P* for Prescott. "Rodeo has been good to me, very good, in fact. But I wouldn't be where I am without the team that makes it happen. That team includes the horses that made it a point to buck me off. Horses wear out just like people do, and they deserve a good retirement."

I liked what I heard. "That's very kind of you."

The compliment blew right by him. "Some people view rodeo horses as machines. When they break, you send them to the junkyard. I'm not that way. Those horses are beautiful creatures deserving respect, so I'm starting the TC Double R—the Trey Cochran Retirement Ranch. I'm firmly committed to the project, but I don't want to buy property until it's been in operation for a while and I've worked out any kinks."

I thought of my father. "That sounds wise. There's nothing like hands-on to show what works and what doesn't."

"I looked at a couple of places in Texas, plus one in Oklahoma. The Oklahoma site was too small. I planned to lease a place near Amarillo, but the owner died and his wife wants to sell. The second ranch in Texas was a falling-down mess. So here I am with fifteen horses waiting for a new home and a manager ready to start work as soon as I find the right location. Cottonwood Acres would be perfect."

I appreciated Trey's planning. I knew as well as anyone that life took unexpected turns, and he seemed to handle them well. "It sounds like you've done your homework."

"Thanks to Walter, yes. He told me about Cottonwood Acres last week, so I came a few days before my episode started filming. I hope it wasn't presumptuous, but I borrowed a horse from the set, rode around, and camped out by the river. I don't get to do that very often, so it was both business and pleasure."

I didn't mind at all. There was so much activity around the TV production that I hadn't even noticed him. "Where did you camp out?"

"About five miles from here. You know the spot where the river curves and spreads wide? There's a big oak tree that hangs over some rocks."

I knew exactly, because I loved that spot. "The water's calm there. It's perfect for fishing."

"And a quick swim after a long ride. That was the best day I've had in months, maybe years."

His thoughts seemed to drift, something the Refuge River inspired for me as well. More than once, I'd stood on the bank and mentally tossed my cares into the water, everything from grief over my parents to a broken teenage heart, and most recently my worries about the ranch. The river eased my burdens, and it pleased me to share that gift with Trey.

I sipped the iced tea, the glass cold and invigorating against my fingers.

Trey took another swig of the beer, set it down, and relaxed into the couch. "The way your place is laid out, the Double R staff could work out of the bunkhouse and a barn, just like the show does now. You could stay in this big house and not be bothered."

I chuckled softly, letting my eyes twinkle for the fun of it. "Not be bothered? If we reach an agreement, I'll be a hands-on partner. Nothing less."

His eyes twinkled back at mine. "I wouldn't have it any other way."

The cool businesswoman I wanted to be morphed into the little girl who told her daddy she wanted to breed racehorses like the ones in Walter Farley's *The Black Stallion* books. I read Marguerite Henry's pony stories a hundred times and sat glued to the television for *Flicka* reruns. Then there was *Mr. Ed*, the talking horse who caused all sorts of mischief. My father loved that show. I was away at college when it debuted in 1961, but I came home every summer and laughed with him at the reruns.

Those memories put a smile on my face, plus I admired Trey's passion for his cause. Thanks to *Thunder Valley* and the cattle operation, I could afford to indulge in a good cause. "I see why Walter set this up. Cottonwood Acres would be ideal for what you have in mind."

"So you like the idea?"

"Truthfully?"

"Always." His eyes stared into mine, and that night I believed him without question.

I scooted forward in the chair, clasped my hands over my knees, and forgot all about being businesslike. "I love what you're doing, Trey. Not only is Cottonwood Acres the perfect setup for you, the rescue operation is ideal for the ranch. With the show ending, it needs a new purpose. This could be it."

"So you're in?"

"Maybe. We still have a lot to discuss, but I want it to work."

"That's half the battle. Maybe more, because I have a good plan in place and it's ready to go. In the long run, I'd like to see our horses adopted out, but they won't all be fit for new owners. Some will live out their lives here. Once that part of the operation is stable, I'd like to start a rodeo school. An old cowboy taught me a lot when I was a teenager looking for trouble. That's the kind of difference I want the Double R to make."

"I like everything I'm hearing." Actually, I loved it.

Graciela walked in from the kitchen, glanced at me, and indulged in another *I told you so* smirk. "Dinner is ready."

We moved to the dining room, where Trey pulled out my chair. This wasn't 1872, and I was wearing bell-bottoms, not a long dress and starched petticoats, but I enjoyed the attention nonetheless. Not that I'd admit it to Graciela.

Over her delicious meal, Trey and I roughed out a plan for the rescue operation. When we finished eating, we retired to the deck and sat under the stars with coffee and a plate of Graciela's homemade churros. A fire in a chiminea kept us warm, and so did the two blankets Graciela walked out to us when she came to say good night.

Snug as two bugs in our separate rugs, we talked until after midnight.

I learned a lot in those first hours with Trey. He grew up in a small Texas town that profited from the oil boom in the 1920s, then shriveled when the well ran dry. His father worked as a mechanic and owned a gas station. His mother checked groceries at the A&P until Trey earned enough to pay off his parents' mortgage. The youngest of four children, he was the family clown. His two older brothers went to college and worked in business. His sister was everyone's favorite and the true baby of the family. Trey, a third son, was mostly forgotten.

He didn't tell me that he felt forgotten. I saw it in the way he talked about himself, the distance from his brothers, and the fact that he rarely returned home.

The rodeo bug bit when he was fourteen and working at a ranch owned by the richest man in town. When the owner's son dared Trey to ride the meanest horse in the barn, Trey handled the animal like a pro. The foreman, a retired bronc rider, saw his skill and took him under his wing. Instead of bothering with college, Trey hit the circuit and became a star.

I knew enough about rodeo to understand what that meant. Money. Women. Drinking. His life was a country song in the making. No way did I want to become a lyric in that song, so I prepared to ask the question that matters most when a woman notices a man as more than a friend. If Trey was married, I needed to know.

He beat me to the question. "Somehow I've told you all about my life and left out something important."

"What's that?"

"I'm in the middle of a divorce." He swung his gaze away from mine, maybe to hide his pain. "It's over between Kathy and me, and it has been for a while."

"I'm sorry." I meant it. Divorces tore lives and families apart. But my heart thumped with a confusing mix of sadness and hope. Legally, he was still married and off-limits. But emotionally, he appeared to be a free man. Did his wife feel the same way? I needed to know. "How is Kathy taking it?"

"We're both ready to move on. The lawyers are hashing out the details—and making a fortune I might add." Bitterness tinged his voice. "It's been a lot more complicated than I expected."

"How long were you married?"

"Eight years, but we were high school sweethearts before that. She was nineteen when I won my first big competition, and I'd just turned twenty-one. It seemed like the most glorious thing in the world to fly her to Vegas to celebrate. A day later we tied the knot and called our families with the news. Her father wasn't thrilled, but Kathy and I thought we owned the world. Looking back, neither one of us was ready for that step."

"Any children?"

"No. She wanted them, but I didn't. Considering how things fell apart, it's probably for the best."

I nodded but wondered about that *probably*. Did he regret that decision now? I thought of my father admonishing me to carry on the family line. In one of the great inequalities of gender, my biological clock was ticking and Trey didn't have one.

I must have let out a sigh, because he gave me a thoughtful look. "What about you, Joan?"

"Me?"

"Any broken hearts?"

"Just one." Playing Shakespeare's Juliet to the hilt, I

laid a trembling hand over my heart. "I was ten. Kenny was eleven. He liked Bonnie Delco better than me and chose her for square dancing."

A soft chuckle rumbled from his lips. "That's tragic indeed. But it's not what I meant. A woman as . . ." He studied my face for several seconds. "As *accomplished* as you are, has surely broken a few hearts."

"Not really."

"No?"

"No," I repeated. "I was in love with someone in grad school, but his career took him to Chicago and I didn't want to follow him. My dream has always been to teach in Wyoming and to live here as much as possible. Right now, I'm as free as a bird. I like it that way, though my father is probably turning in his grave."

"Why?"

"I'm the last of the true Prescott line. He wanted a houseful of grandkids—little cowboys and cowgirls who would love the ranch like he did."

"And like you do."

"Yes." Closing my eyes, I tilted back my head and inhaled the night air, savoring the smell of the grass, even the livestock. "I can't imagine living anywhere else, especially after being away at school."

"Where did you go?"

"Smith College for undergrad, and Cornell for my Ph.D. Those were good times, and I'm grateful. Women haven't always had the freedom to choose a career."

Trey raised his coffee cup in a toast. "To freedom."

"Yes." I lifted mine in return. "To freedom."

Neither of us sipped. The coffee was either cold or gone, but I didn't want the night to end. Trey hesitated, but then he set the mug down with a soft thud. "It's late. I'm afraid I've overstayed my welcome."

"Far from it."

We both stood, and if not for that *almost* final divorce, I might have kissed him good night—just a peck on the cheek, or even a brush on the lips. Something to say *I am woman, hear me roar* like the new Helen Reddy song. Instead I walked with him to the entry hall, handed him the sport jacket Graciela had hung up when he arrived, and tried not to stare as he shrugged into it, rolling his shoulders for a perfect fit.

Trey's voice came out in a drawl. "You're a wonder, Joan. Do you know that?"

I decided to lighten the mood. "You're a wonder, too. And I think you *do* know it."

He laughed but didn't say anything else. Turning, he trotted down the steps. Twenty steps down the path to the bunkhouse, he turned and raised one arm high in the air, as if he'd just hung on for eight seconds and won the round.

I did the same. Trey Cochran was the start of something good in my life—something big and meaningful. I felt it in my bones. As things turned out, I was right, though the good part turned out to be debatable.

Chapter 7

The phone on Daisy's desk gave two short rings—the signal that Miss Joan wanted to speak with her. She'd been on the job a week now. Some of her nerves had subsided, but she still snapped to attention as she pressed the speaker button.

"Yes?" she answered, sounding professional.

Miss Joan's gruffest voice came over the line. "What shoes are you wearing?"

Daisy glanced down at the Jimmy Choos she'd bought for a song at Mary's Closet. "Heels. But I keep a pair of walking shoes in my car."

"Good. You're going to need them."

"I am?"

"You and I are going for a ride. Change your shoes and meet me on the deck in fifteen minutes."

"Will do."

"And bring your camera."

Miss Joan hung up, leaving no room for questions. That was just like her, but the gruffness no longer made Daisy quake in her shoes. Somehow while working together on the book, and especially during yesterday's drive to Refuge for Miss Joan's hair appointment, the two of them had become friends. Miss Joan loved to teach, and Daisy was a sponge when it came to knowledge of any kind. While they culled through historic photographs of the Prescott family, Miss Joan had told stories that ranged from funny to ribald to heartbreaking.

Her candor put Daisy at ease, so Daisy shared her own stories about growing up with her mom and Shane. For part of each year, they had lived like nomads, traveling the craft fair circuit where her mom sold the metal sculptures she fashioned during the winter. Daisy didn't remember her father; and Shane didn't even know his father's name. But their free-spirited mom had loved them well, until her sudden death shattered Daisy's world.

During yesterday's drive, Daisy had told Miss Joan everything about her teen years, Eric, the assault, her sobriety, and her Christian faith. As she was leaving that afternoon, Miss Joan stopped her at the front door. With her usual brusqueness, she told Daisy to stand tall and be proud of herself for surviving—and thriving.

"I am," Daisy replied. "But I wouldn't be here without my family, good friends, and God."

Miss Joan nodded in agreement. "Yes . . . God. He and I go back quite a few years, though I didn't always believe like I do now."

She waited for more, but Miss Joan told her to have a nice evening and went back inside.

Daisy had no more secrets, but Miss Joan still did— namely the mysterious project she mentioned during the job interview. Daisy knew only that Miss Joan spoke daily to her attorney, Thomas Garrett, and that she had just ended a particularly lengthy call with him. Now she was telling Daisy to change her shoes without revealing why.

Surprises from Miss Joan were usually good, so Daisy was full of happy anticipation when she arrived at her car. She couldn't help but remember finding the balloons from Rafe. She knew he worked at Heritage House. Would she run into him today? Should she thank him again for the balloons? Hannah and Cody had both played with them for hours, taking aim with Nerf guns until the foam darts were all over the room.

When Chelsea asked again where the balloons came from, Daisy told her about Rafe asking her out. Chelsea's words rang in Daisy's ears now. *"You turned him down? Are you nuts?"*

"No," Daisy said out loud now. She just wasn't ready to date again—not even a toe in the water.

Putting thoughts of Rafe aside, she changed her shoes, returned to her office for her camera bag, and walked out the front door. At the bottom of the steps stood a type of vehicle she had never seen before. A cross between an army jeep and a pickup truck, it had two bench seats, wide tires with tooth-like tread, and a plastic top to keep off the sun. Black side panels with gold scrolls gave the vehicle a regal look that didn't match the ruggedness of the rest of it.

Boots tapped on the deck to her right. She turned and saw Cliff carrying a reusable grocery bag and a large plastic cooler. The front door opened, and Miss Joan breezed past her. Dressed in Wranglers, walking shoes, and a red plaid shirt, she waved at Daisy to follow her.

"Hurry up!" Miss Joan called out with a grin. "We're burning daylight."

Following her, Daisy eyed the vehicle with trepidation.

She'd never driven off-road in her life and didn't feel prepared to start now. Miss Joan didn't drive anymore, which left Cliff to play chauffeur. Confident in his abilities, Daisy breathed a little easier.

He stowed the grocery bag and cooler in the truck bed, stepped back, and made a sweeping motion with his arm. "Miss Joan, your Mule awaits."

"Some mule." Daisy shared a smile with Cliff. "What exactly is it?"

"A utility task vehicle made by Kawasaki. 'Mule' is the model name. It's also known as a UTV or side-by-side. We have others, but this one belongs to Joanie."

Miss Joan rested her hand on the hood. "The name fits. She's hard-working and can go anywhere. But driving her—that's different. She's more like a wild mustang, fast and full of spirit."

Cliff propped his hands on his hips. "Joanie's the one full of spirit. Don't let her go too fast."

Daisy swiveled her gaze back to Cliff. "I thought you were driving."

"Me?" He shook his head. "No. I have work to do."

"Then—oh." If Cliff wasn't going and Miss Joan didn't drive, that left Daisy to take the reins, or, more correctly, the steering wheel. Did Miss Joan expect her to drive off-road in the middle of nowhere? What if she crashed the Mule into a tree? Or drove into a ditch? Her stomach dropped to her toes. "Uh—"

"Relax, dear." Miss Joan graced her with a smile. "*You're* not driving. I am."

Daisy gaped at her. "But you don't drive anymore. You let your license expire."

"My ranch. My rules." She put on a haughty look. "I don't need a license to drive on my own land. It's private property."

Relieved, Daisy played along. "In that case, let's go.

We're burning daylight," she quoted back to Miss Joan.

Laughing, the older woman slipped behind the wheel. Daisy set the camera bag at her feet, strapped herself in, and off they went down the asphalt road that connected the ranch's outbuildings. It was a beautiful spring day, just breezy enough to stir the cottonwoods. Daisy inhaled deeply, savoring the loamy smells that were nothing like city grime, car exhaust, and hot asphalt.

At a fork in the road, Miss Joan veered to the right. "Before we start the tour, I want to check the progress on Heritage House."

Daisy nodded as if they were talking business, but her mind slipped back to Rafe's car in the parking lot. Would she see him? More to the point, did she *want* to see him?

Her stomach pulled into a knot, but her eyes shot ahead to the spot where Heritage House was beginning to take shape. She had seen the architect's drawing of the two-story building, but the foundation was even bigger than she'd expected. Eight men were pounding nails into lumber to make the first wall. She knew Ben Waters because he occasionally stopped by the house. The other men were strangers to her, but she recognized Rafe even with his back turned.

Miss Joan stopped on the crest of a hill. "Let's get a few pictures."

"For the book?"

"Maybe. I'll decide when I see the photographs."

Daisy picked up her camera, stepped away from the Mule, and took a wide shot of the foundation. Next she photographed the men working, including one of Rafe just as he turned his head to the side. She caught him in profile—not smiling, maybe listening to someone, but he seemed alone compared to the others. It struck her as a peculiar moment, as if he were a little bit lost.

She didn't want to think about Rafe feeling lost, so she

focused back on Ben looking stern, then on a Willie Nelson lookalike with wrinkles as deep as the tread on the off-road tires. The other men worked in teams, leaving Rafe to stand alone. She took several shots of him driving a nail with an old-fashioned hammer instead of a nail gun.

After three powerful swings, he reached down into a bucket at his feet. Something must have caught his eye, because when he stood, he stared straight at her. Every detail of his face filled the viewfinder—his straight nose, clean-shaven jaw, the knowing glint in his eyes as he matched her gaze.

Her breath hitched at the sight of his widening smile, and she knew he'd caught her looking—and wondering about him. He was too close for comfort, so she snapped a final picture and lowered the camera.

"I'm finished," she said to Miss Joan.

"Did you get some good shots?"

"I think so." She peeked at the last one of Rafe, saw photographic gold, and tried not to smile.

Miss Joan drove down the middle of the road until they reached the sawhorses and yellow tape marking off the worksite. As she and Daisy climbed out of the Mule, Ben approached with long strides. "Miss Joan, good after-noon."

"Benjamin," she said, extending her hand. "You've met Daisy, correct?"

"Yes, ma'am." He gave Daisy a gracious nod, and they traded smiles. She'd spoken to Ben when he dropped off flooring samples at the house.

Miss Joan asked Ben a few questions, then indicated the cooler in the back of the Mule. "We brought lunch for your crew. I'd like to meet them, if you don't mind."

"Of course." Ben let out an ear-piercing whistle. The men stopped working immediately and headed over.

In Daisy's experience as a server, construction crews

were often a rowdy, ragtag bunch. She felt a little intimidated, but these men wore their Donovan t-shirts tucked in and their hair neat. Even Willie Nelson's little brother looked squared-away. So did Rafe, though unlike the others, he had no visible scars or tattoos. The professional look seemed natural to him.

As Ben made introductions, Miss Joan shook each man's hand, called him by name, and thanked him for his hard work. When she finished shaking hands, she spoke to the group. "I brought lunch today to say thank you. Ben? Would it be okay if we all took a lunch break?"

"More than fine." Ben raised his voice to the crew. "It's lunchtime, men. Take thirty and dig in."

Miss Joan led the way back to the Mule, where she opened the lunch bag and the cooler. Daisy didn't know whether to speak to Rafe or not. She didn't want to call attention to herself, or to him, so she stuck close to Miss Joan and helped unpack the thick sandwiches, big bags of chips, chocolate chip cookies, and an assortment of fresh fruit. Bottled water, apple juice, and soda finished off the selection.

When the food was set up, Miss Joan pulled Ben aside for a chat, leaving Daisy to fend for herself. The men helped themselves to the food, then walked over to a picnic table set up under a tree to make a break area. No one said a word to Rafe, and since he went last, there was no room left at the table.

Daisy felt bad for him. She hated eating alone. When their eyes met, she wondered if he felt the same way.

"Hi," she said. "How's it going?"

"Good." He snagged a pastrami on rye, a bag of chips, and a bottle of water. "It looks like the new job's going well for you."

"Oh, it is!" She couldn't help but smile. "I love everything about it."

Miss Joan broke in from ten feet away. "Daisy? I'm going to be a while with Ben. Help yourself to some food, all right? We have a long afternoon ahead of us."

Before Daisy could protest, Miss Joan turned her back and continued the conversation with Ben. There was no getting out of lunch, specifically lunch with Rafe Donovan, and Miss Joan seemed to have engineered it. Mentally, Daisy rolled her eyes over the not-so-subtle matchmaking, but she was glad to keep Rafe company.

He waited for her while she selected a turkey sandwich and a shiny red apple, then aimed his chin at the Donovan Construction pickup parked in the shade of a tree. "How do you feel about tailgating?"

"Just fine."

They walked over to the truck, where Rafe set his food in the bed and lowered the gate. Daisy set down her camera and the food and hopped up. Rafe joined her, and they sat with their legs dangling and sandwiches in hand.

The conversation flowed easily—first about the food and the beautiful weather, then all the things Daisy liked about the job. Before she knew it, she was showing Rafe her phone and a cute picture of Hannah playing with the balloons. He slid a little closer for a better look, and she did the same.

When she set the phone down, he studied her as if considering something important. Was he about to ask her out again? Daisy hoped not. Or maybe she hoped he would. Uncertainty plagued her when it came to Rafe. She had vowed to be fully independent before investing herself in a romantic relationship, but she liked him. Chelsea's urging to take a chance echoed in her ears. So did Lyn's advice to be brave—brave *and* wise, Daisy reminded herself.

Rafe finally spoke. "You know Jesse, right?"

He already knew the answer, so *that* wasn't the real

question. *How* did she know Jesse was what he wanted to know, and that meant bringing up Alcoholics Anonymous. Daisy wasn't shy about sharing her sobriety. That information wasn't a secret, just private. "I know Jesse pretty well. We've been friends for a few months now—since my first AA meeting in Refuge."

Admiration gleamed in his eyes. "I'm glad for you. Was it drugs, booze, or both?"

"Drinking. No drugs. I've been sober for eight months now." But there was more—sleeping around; feeling worthless and being abused; saying *yes* to Eric when she wanted to say *no* and *never.* That part of her story was far too personal to share, even if they were becoming friends, so she told herself to shut up—at least about *that.*

Instead she focused on the bigger picture—and the faith that now defined her. "I thank God every day for getting me out of that mess."

"So does Jesse."

"One day at a time, right?"

"He says that a lot."

"So do I." She didn't tell her story lightly, or buttonhole people in an obnoxious way, but the story defined her now. If Rafe wanted to be her friend, he needed to know where she stood. "AA saved my life. You know the Twelve-Step saying, 'God as I understand him'?"

He nodded. "I've heard it a lot."

"Being open to the possibility of a loving God helped me get sober. Later I became a Christian. My faith is important to me."

"Stay strong." Rafe held up a hand to give her a high-five. "I haven't fought those demons personally, but I had a front-row seat to addiction back home. My high school girlfriend got hooked on pain pills after back surgery. She went all the way down to buying heroin on the street. A lot of us tried to help her, but she OD'd."

Daisy almost reached for his hand but stopped herself. Instead she pressed one hand to her chest, a pledge of sorts to help people recover whenever she could. "I am so sorry."

"Me too. Kara was special. Smart. Upbeat." His mouth hooked into a tender smile. "*And* a great kisser, not that you want to hear about that."

Daisy smiled, too. "I get the picture. What happened?"

"She was in a horrible car accident. Her sister and her sister's kid were okay, but Kara had taken off her seat belt to reach into the back seat for the kid's pacifier. A delivery van ran a stop sign, and Kara ended up with a fractured neck vertebra. Surgery didn't help. She was in pain all the time. Back when this happened, people thought meds like oxy were safe. No one realized how addictive they are, but now we know."

"That's rough."

He offered Daisy the bag of chips. She took a handful and so did he. "Kara is why I became a cop."

"A cop?" No wonder he looked comfortable with his shirt tucked in. "I should have guessed. That haircut—" *It looks good on you.* She settled for giving him a little smirk. "Today you look like a cop."

Rafe ran a hand over his jaw. "Mr. Clean-Cut shows up every now and then."

"So what brought you to Refuge?"

He ate the last chip in his hand, chewed a long time, then answered without looking at her. "I needed a break. I guess you could call it burnout. I hadn't seen Jesse in a while, so I took personal leave. I'm here for three months, then I'll go back."

She thought of his license plates. "To Ohio?"

"Cincinnati. We're in the thick of the opioid crisis."

"Good for you. We need people to fight that war. Addiction is so . . ." She searched for a word. "Insidious."

Thank you, vocab app. It made her sound smart, even if she wasn't.

"Yeah. It sucks."

Daisy laughed. "Sucks? Really? So much for impressing you with my big word of the day!"

Rafe shrugged. "You don't need to use big words to impress me, Daisy. You already did."

"Really?" She found it hard to believe she could impress anyone, especially a squared-away guy like Rafe.

"Yes, really." He smiled at her. "You were smart about that flat tire. One false move, and you would have hosed me down with that pepper spray."

"You bet." The words came out with the vengeance born of her vulnerability. Eric had nearly killed her. *The blood . . . the pain.* And worst of all, the helplessness of being overpowered against her will. Emotions shuddered through her, all of them dark and throbbing.

Rafe laid a hand on her shoulder. "Hey, are you all right?"

She tried to nod, but her neck muscles tensed against the lie. Rafe kept his hand in place—strong, steady, and nothing but protective. The touch calmed her, and she managed to take a breath. "I'm fine. A memory came back—a bad one. It's not something I talk about."

He squeezed her shoulder, then lifted his hand. Daisy breathed a sigh of relief. It felt good to be comforted, but the weight of his arm could have pinned her in place, trapping her, though only in her mind. With space between them, she felt safer, even respected. For a woman who fought to respect herself, that feeling counted for a lot.

She thanked him with a smile. "I bet you're a good cop."

"I try."

"You are. I can tell."

"How?" The question reeked of doubt, as if he really

needed to know.

Daisy thought a moment. "For one thing, you care. It wasn't convenient to change my tire, but you did it anyway. *And* you respected my need for space. You're perceptive. Nothing gets by you, does it?"

Instead of answering, he took a long swig of water. Daisy was about to nudge him with her elbow when Ben whistled to announce that lunch was over. Rafe hopped down from the tailgate and offered Daisy his hand. She gripped his fingers, hopped down, then let go. He gathered their trash, and she put the camera strap around her neck.

They walked toward a trash can, each silent, until Rafe spoke. "Thanks for having lunch with me. I hate eating alone."

"So do I." Her gaze drifted to the picnic table with the rest of the crew. "They ditched you, didn't they?"

He gave her a roguish grin. "Definitely, and I owe them for it. I'd much rather have lunch with you than a bunch of sweaty guys."

"Ewww." She wrinkled her nose. "Thanks for the compliment—I think."

Several feet ahead of them, Miss Joan climbed into the Mule and beeped the horn, a signal for Daisy to hurry up.

"I better go," she said to Rafe.

He waved her off. "Thanks again for having lunch with me."

She hesitated. "I enjoyed it."

Before he could speak again, she hurried to the Mule and climbed in. Miss Joan didn't say a word about Rafe, but a smile flirted with the corners of her mouth as she punched the gas and they continued the tour of the ranch.

Chapter 8

F or the next half hour, Daisy and Miss Joan toured the part of the ranch dedicated to the horse rescue program. They walked around the barn where the last three horses were stabled, and Daisy fed them carrots at the paddock fence. Juggernaut was a big gray known to bite; Comet an elderly Palomino mare with a sweet disposition; and Zip-a-Dee-Doo-Dah, or Zippy for short, a pinto pony with a passion for peppermints.

While feeding the horses, Miss Joan gave Daisy some history. The program started in 1972 and originally included only rodeo horses. Later Miss Joan opened the stable doors to retired thoroughbreds, some of the most neglected horses around. In its heyday, the ranch cared for up to fifty horses at a time, including used-up champions like Jug. A few years ago, Miss Joan had made the hard decision to phase out the program. Other than Jug, Comet, and Zippy, the remaining horses had died of old age or been adopted out.

Next Miss Joan drove Daisy to the 1950s-era bunga-low that had housed the cast and crew of *Thunder Valley*. No one stayed there anymore, but the log building gleamed with a fresh coat of linseed oil and the shrubbery was neatly trimmed.

Miss Joan unlocked the door to the corner suite and motioned for Daisy to enter. What she encountered was a 1970s time capsule with a floral couch, burnt orange arm-chairs, and a wagon wheel lamp hanging from the knotty pine ceiling. An acrylic painting of wild mustangs hung on the wall next to a brick fireplace.

Miss Joan lingered in the doorway, her arms crossed over her chest as she peered into the musty room. "This place already feels like a museum, doesn't it?"

"A little. Yes." Daisy imagined the old television stars who had relaxed on the couch and used the avocado green princess-style phone on the end table, disconnected and reduced to being an artifact.

A sigh whispered from Miss Joan's lips. "Let's move on."

She closed the door behind Daisy, locked it, and they sped away in the Mule without further explanation. Con-sidering the brevity of the visit, Daisy wondered why Miss Joan had bothered to stop.

They rode in silence until the road reached the crest of a gentle hill. In the distance, Daisy glimpsed a stone foundation weathered by time, then a small gray boulder with a bronze plaque displaying the words *Prescott Family Cabin, built 1873*. The vintage photographs she'd seen last week shimmered to life in her mind, along with a series of pen-and-ink drawings done with a delicate hand.

Sweeping her gaze over the tall grass, she imagined

grazing cattle, a vegetable garden, and children romping in the sun. "So this is where it all started."

"It is." Miss Joan tapped her fingers on the steering wheel. "What do you think? Should I ask Jesse to build a replica of the original cabin? It could be a living history exhibit."

Daisy took in the old foundation, the silence, and the row of grave markers a hundred feet away. She tried to imagine museum-style actors in buckskins and bonnets but couldn't. "There's a purity to this spot just the way it is. I'd leave it alone."

"We really are kindred spirits, dear. I feel the same way." A bittersweet note, like the minor tones of birdsong, colored Miss Joan's voice. "Would you mind if I visited my parents' graves?"

"No. Of course not."

Miss Joan drove up the hill to a cluster of stone markers encircled by a low rock wall. She parked and climbed out of the Mule. So did Daisy, but she kept a respectful distance until Miss Joan summoned her with a wave.

When Daisy reached her side, Miss Joan indicated the oldest stone and told her about the life of Major William Jameson Prescott. The fourth son of an English duke and an adventurer, he had come to America and started his own cattle empire.

As they walked from grave to grave, tales of triumph and tragedy rolled off Miss Joan's tongue. Her ancestors came to life in Daisy's mind, but so did the knowledge that life was short. Compared to the mountains, sky, and stars, men and women walked the earth for little more than a blink. Yet the Bible said the hairs on a person's head were numbered. Every human being had a name—and a purpose. *She* had a purpose. For whatever reason, God had brought her to Cottonwood Acres for this very moment.

Miss Joan dragged her wrinkled hand over the top of her mother's gravestone, brushing away a thin coat of dust. Straightening, she bowed her head and stood in silence. So did Daisy, until Miss Joan stepped back, indicating it was time to go.

Instead of heading back to the house like Daisy expected, Miss Joan sped west toward the river. "There's one more place I want to show you."

"More history?"

"You'll see soon enough. Tighten the harness, dear. We're taking a shortcut."

Daisy adjusted the shoulder straps just in time to feel the Mule leap from the smooth asphalt to a rutted dirt trail. Scrub oak and small pines cast lacy shadows on the path, while sagebrush scented the air as the Mule kicked up clouds of dust.

Miss Joan seemed distant, as if she were lost in the past. Daisy followed her own thoughts back to lunch with Rafe, that high-five for her sobriety, and how deeply he had loved Kara . . . who happened to be a great kisser. Not that Daisy was thinking about kissing Rafe. Well, she was. But not seriously. They'd become friends today. That's all. And friends didn't kiss. Except her evil twin whispered in her ear. *Why not take a chance? Why not—*

"Stop it!" she muttered.

Miss Joan tilted her head in Daisy's direction. "Did you say something, dear?"

"No." She changed the subject fast. "This has been an amazing day. How much farther to the next stop?"

"About a mile. We're going to the river."

The Mule bucked and bounced along the rutted road, but the harness held Daisy in place. After a while, she learned to anticipate the bumps and to sway with the vehicle. She was relaxed and enjoying the scenery when the Mule crested a hill and picked up speed.

Miss Joan laughed like a crazy person. "Yeehaw! I love this part!"

The Mule splashed into a stream running fast with winter melt-off. Icy water fanned out from the tires and splashed the hood and windshield. The vehicle tilted forward and Daisy shrieked, but the tires found traction and the Mule shot out on the opposite bank. Or maybe it crawled to the other side, and it just *felt* like they were going a hundred miles an hour. Miss Joan had probably splashed into the stream a thousand times, but Daisy's heart remained wedged in her throat.

She tried to laugh it off, but her voice came out in a squeak. "I don't know if that was fun or terrifying."

"Or both!" Miss Joan grinned from ear to ear. "I used to come down here with a friend. We'd ride through the forest, then gallop our horses through the meadow to the river's edge. The loser had to clean the fish we caught for dinner."

"I bet you won every time."

"Only because he let me." A faint smile lifted her lips, and she craned her neck to see something in the distance. "There's the spot."

Daisy reached down for her camera, but Miss Joan shook her head. "Not yet. You can come back another time and take pictures. Today I have something to tell you."

They drove in silence until Miss Joan stopped the Mule on a sandy apron at the river's edge. The water was wide here, slow enough to reflect the blue sky but strong enough to ripple against the boulders scattered on the banks. A giant oak arched over the water so that its branches made a room of sorts, but what most caught Daisy's eye was a concrete pad with a freshly painted wooden bench.

Miss Joan cut the engine but didn't move. Instead she sat quietly, maybe listening to the gurgle of the river, or maybe to the voices of ghosts from the past. After a moment, she opened the door. "Let's go."

Daisy hopped out and circled the UTV while the older woman stretched a kink out of her back. When Miss Joan settled herself stiffly on the bench, Daisy sat next to her.

Only the soothing ripple of the river broke the silence until Miss Joan cleared her throat. "You must be curious about the secret project I mentioned."

"I am," Daisy admitted. "But I figured you'd tell me when the time was right."

"This is the time." Miss Joan took a short breath. "My attorney finished his part of the project, and I'm ready to move forward with a unique plan to protect the legacy and secure the future of Cottonwood Acres. You know I never married or had a child, so I have no direct heirs."

She paused, stared downstream, then murmured, "There's no one, Daisy. No one at all."

A lonely ache throbbed in Daisy's middle. A year ago, she had felt as alone as Miss Joan, but now she had Shane, MJ, and Cody. *A family.* Love for them welled in her chest. So did a deep caring for this woman who had blessed her so richly in such a short time. "That has to be hard. But you have a good life, right?"

"Oh, yes. Very." The words came out strong. "But that doesn't change the fact that Cottonwood Acres needs someone who will love it and, most importantly, *use it* to do good in the world. That's why I'm giving it away."

"You're . . . *what?*"

"Giving it away." Miss Joan smiled now. "I know it sounds eccentric, maybe even unhinged. But I have a good plan and Tom Garrett is overseeing everything."

Daisy recognized the name of Miss Joan's attorney, though she still couldn't believe her ears. "What exactly is the plan?"

"To pick a charity that will respect the history, purpose, and integrity of Cottonwood Acres, and use its assets to make the world a better place. Tom's office sent letters to a hundred charities of my choosing. The letter gave basic information without revealing the exact location and asked for a one-page letter of intent. The preliminary screening is done, and this morning Tom sent me the letters and his research notes. I'm going to study the letters, pick the final five, and invite them to submit a detailed proposal and visit the ranch."

Daisy was still reeling from the news, but she held back her shock. Miss Joan needed her to be smart and logical, so she kept her voice even. "So the best charity wins?"

"Yes, but this isn't a silly reality show. I want to keep the giveaway as quiet as possible. Once word gets out, I'm liable to be inundated with unwanted attention."

How many people in this world would give away a fortune and keep the gift a secret? Daisy felt both humbled and awed—and privileged to be part of the process. "Do you know how amazing you are?"

Miss Joan huffed air through her nose. "I'm not the least bit amazing. Old, cranky, and rich? Yes. But this gift is small compared to what the Carnegies and Rockefellers gave in the nineteenth century, and to what Bill Gates and others have given in modern times. Compared to Mother Teresa's life of service, it's a pittance."

"Even so—"

"A pittance," Miss Joan repeated firmly. "I don't need to tell you about the greatest Giver of all. You already know what Christ did for us on the cross. Believe me, dear. I don't deserve any of the gifts I've been given—not a single one."

The breeze stirred across the river, riffling through Daisy's short hair. Before Eric's assault, she'd worn it long and loose. But doctors had shaved her head for surgery in an attempt to save her life. The memory of nearly dying, and seeing Jesus in her mind, shot tears of gratitude to her eyes. "I feel the same way."

Miss Joan sat straighter on the bench. "Don't be impressed by what I'm doing. I'm giving from a place of wealth. The real heroes give in spite of their need."

"Like the Bible story about the widow's mite." Daisy felt like that widow when she sent money to Lyn to help Maggie's House. "But what about *you*? Where will you live?"

"I'm looking at a 55-and-over community in Scottsdale. An old friend from my college days lives there and loves it. We're planning some travel too. An Alaskan cruise, to be precise. I'll be fine."

"Even so, it's a big move. You'll have a friend, but you won't know anyone—"

Miss Joan cut her off. "I can afford whatever help I need. What I can't do is live forever."

"Don't say that—"

"It's true." Miss Joan put on her bossiest scowl. "So get a grip. There's a lot of work to do, and I'm counting on you to help."

Chapter 9

Rafe's FaceTime sessions with Dr. Susan brought some relief, and he dared to believe the weird panicky feeling wouldn't return. But then he dreamed about Kara again. Like before, Jesse woke him up and again Rafe went for a drive. After an hour or so, he returned home, collapsed, and slept hard.

Bright sunshine startled him awake. Bolting upright, he grabbed his phone and saw that he'd dismissed the alarm without waking up. He'd missed breakfast with the crew by well over an hour, so he'd have to drive himself to the jobsite instead of riding with the crew as usual. He'd be lucky to make it anywhere close to on time.

Skipping a shower and a shave, he jumped into yesterday's clothes and sped to Heritage House. As he expected, the crew was already pounding nails when he parked next to the work truck. He leaped out of the Camaro, spotted Ben, and approached with an apology ready on his lips. "Man, I'm sorry—"

"You're late," Ben shouted loud enough for the whole crew to hear. "What did you do? Sleep in like a teenager?"

"I messed up." Rafe strapped on his tool belt and cinched it tight. "It won't happen again."

When Ben grunted, the men turned away. Rafe thought he'd dodged a bullet, but Ben motioned him toward the picnic table.

Here comes the lecture. Being Jesse's little brother didn't entitle Rafe to special treatment; if anything, the Donovan name required him to meet higher standards. A sheen of sweat broke out on his neck. He'd failed today. *Failed his brother. Failed Kara. Failed himself.*

When they reached the table, Ben lifted one boot to the bench, crossed his arms over his chest, and gave Rafe the stink eye. But when he spoke, the words came out with kindness. "You look beat. What really happened?"

"I'm fine."

"Yeah, right. We're all *fine.*"

"I am."

"You don't look *fine* to me. Your eyes are bloodshot, and that's yesterday's shirt judging by the wrinkles. So what is it? Hanging out at a bar somewhere?"

No drinking was one of Jesse's rules, and it applied to Rafe as long as he was on the payroll. "No, sir. I had a bad night. Couldn't sleep so I went for a drive. That's all."

Ben waited for more, but Rafe remained silent.

"So that's all," Ben repeated. "One bad night?"

To confess to Ben or not? Rafe had already asked for time off for the phone appointments with Dr. Susan, but he'd been vague. Why open that can of worms now? He decided not to explain to Ben, so what came out of his mouth surprised him. "Sometimes I have nightmares. Bad ones."

Ben lowered his boot from the bench. "Sorry to hear it. Next time you run late, text me." He clapped Rafe on the shoulder and walked away.

That was all. No haranguing. No demands. No probing questions or pitying looks. Just understanding and respect, though Rafe supposed a second offense would lead to a tongue-lashing, and a third infraction might get a man fired.

Still tense, he walked over to the back side of the building and went to work. No one said a word to him—not even a sarcastic jab. He would have welcomed some teasing, even a snide remark, but he didn't take the shunning personally. He was still an outsider, even the enemy, but he could have used some banter to get his mind off last night.

He worked alongside the crew, using a nail gun to shoot nails into the two-by-fours that formed the interior walls. Rafe lost himself as much as he could in the work, but he kept an eye on the road from the house with the hope of spotting Daisy. Lunch with her had been the highlight of his week, and he wanted to see her again. Unless he'd misread her cues, she'd say yes if he asked her out again.

Daisy didn't happen to appear, but Cliff Lopez drove up in a Gator. He approached Ben and they spoke.

Ben whistled to the crew for attention. "My friend Cliff needs a volunteer. Any takers?"

Anyone who'd been in the military or prison knew better than to volunteer without knowing the score.

When no one spoke up, Ben scanned the crew. "Drake? How about you?"

Drake was in his forties, short, and barrel-chested. He never smiled, and his jokes were usually sarcastic. He didn't look pleased to be singled out. "It depends."

Ben arched a brow at him. "On what?"

Drake looked to the side, then tilted his head back toward Ben. Daggers shot from his eyes. "I don't like animals, and they don't like me."

There was a story there, probably an ugly one. Rafe saw a chance to play the good guy and raised his hand. "I'll go."

Approval flickered in Ben's eyes, but he erased it with a blink. "All right, SuperCop. You're it."

The men turned away, but Drake made eye contact with Rafe. Still glaring, he acknowledged Rafe with a curt nod before going back to work. The nod wasn't much, but Rafe counted it as a start.

He shed his tool belt, went to the Gator, and climbed in. "So what's up?" he asked as Cliff headed for the barn.

"Just some general repairs." Cliff ran down a list that included changing out a broken light switch, repairing a leaky faucet, and replacing a busted window pane in the hayloft.

Rafe had made similar repairs to his mom's house in Cincinnati before she moved to Indiana to be close to her sister. "Sounds simple enough."

Cliff parked outside of a two-story barn with three cupolas on the roof, a row of small windows below the weathered eaves, and a high square door that led to what Rafe presumed was a hayloft. Dutch doors lined the side of the building, and a split-rail fence marked off a grassy field. A big gray horse stood on the far side of the pasture, grazing contentedly. Two other horses stood a few feet from him, their heads down as they ate.

Rafe followed Cliff into the barn. To the right was an empty office. To the left he saw a room holding saddles, halters, and other things beyond his city-boy knowledge. The building was cavernous—and sadly empty. Rafe didn't know much about the ranch's history, but the big barn no doubt had stories to tell.

Several of the empty stalls still displayed signs with a horse's name, plus a photograph and a written biography in an 8-by-10 frame. "This place must have been something in its prime."

"It was."

"Were you around then?"

"For some of it. I hired on twenty years ago to take over the horse rescue operation Miss Joan started back in the 1970s with Trey Cochran."

"Who's he?"

"Old rodeo star. Rode broncs." Cliff threw back his shoulders and stood a little straighter. "So did I. But that was a long time ago."

"Were you any good?" Rafe threw down the challenge so Cliff could relive his glory days.

"Good enough for a buckle or two." The foreman shrugged, apparently not wanting to brag. "I held my own, but Trey Cochran—he was a legend. I wish I could have met him. He took home more buckles than any rider in history. Nice guy, too."

Cliff indicated a workroom next to the office. "You'll find tools and parts in there. The bad light switch is here"—he pointed to the wall by the door—"and the leaky faucet is in the wash area. You'll need to replace it. Come on. I'll point you to the hayloft."

Rafe followed him to the opposite side of the barn, where a ladder led to an open area filled with hay bales. Cliff told him to call when he finished, clapped him on the shoulder, and headed for the door. "Call my cell if you need anything."

"Will do," Rafe replied.

As he turned back to the workroom, he paused to look at the photographs on the three stalls filled with hay. The first one was of the big gray now grazing in the field. Juggernaut was a retired thoroughbred and distantly related to the famous Secretariat.

Curious, Rafe glanced at the second stall, home to a palomino mare named Comet. The photograph showed Comet poised for action, her tail and mane waving in the breeze. The bio said she'd been in several A-list movies.

The last stall belonged to Zip-a-Dee-Doo-Dah. Zippy, now thirty years old, had been a rider favorite on the rodeo circuit.

The names made Rafe smile; the smell of manure not so much. But he was glad to be here and pleased to have gotten a nod from Drake.

The handyman work suited him, and it didn't take long to change out the switch. The old faucet was another story. Coated with rust and lime, it took some manpower to remove, then patience to clean the fittings before putting in the new hardware. When he finished, he decided to get some fresh air before tackling the more delicate job of installing glass.

He walked outside and around to the paddock fence to look at the horses. They were on the far side of the pasture, and so was Daisy Riley, standing on the bottom rail of the fence, waving a carrot in the air with her camera dangling from her neck.

This morning's photoshoot wasn't going well at all. Daisy wanted a picture of the horses with the barn in the background for Miss Joan's history book, but Jug, Zippy, and Comet were grazing in the back part of the pasture. If she could lure them closer to the barn, she'd have the angle she wanted.

She didn't need to be close; she just needed the horses

to move. Going to where they were now and shooing them to the middle of the field was an option, but she didn't want to hike around the perimeter of the fence, nor did she want to hop the fence and cross the pasture.

Waving a carrot, she tried to whistle like Miss Joan but failed miserably. The only sound came out of her pocket—the "Here Comes the Bride" text tone she had assigned to MJ. Curious, she stepped off the railing, looked at her phone, and saw a photograph of a bridesmaid's bouquet with the words *What do u think?*

Daisy answered with *Gorgeous!* and added hearts and smileys for good measure.

The wedding was just six weeks away, and MJ and her mom were finalizing the flowers today. The bridal shower was Daisy's undertaking, and she could hardly wait. Now that she had a good job, she could go all-out on food, decorations, and the "sisters forever" necklace she was having custom made. *Thank you, Miss Joan.* It was a privilege to share, and Daisy couldn't have been happier.

She was about to put her phone away when it chirped again, this time with a text from Chelsea. Daisy hoped it was good news about this morning's job interview.

Chelsea's message stream flooded onto the screen and ended with the words Daisy hoped to see. *Interview went great!!! Got the job!*

Daisy shot back *Congrats!!!* with a row of smileys.

Two seconds later, Chelsea responded. *Found an apt too! Two BR-1bath. Want to be my roommate????*

The question wasn't a complete surprise. Daisy and Chelsea had talked about living together and reached an understanding. If Daisy said yes, the apartment would be an alcohol-free zone. Daisy would help with Hannah, but her own commitments to work and family would come first. Any lease would have to be month-to-month, because Chelsea still planned to return to Michigan.

Daisy had given the decision a lot of thought. Paying rent would dent her budget, but once Shane and MJ were married, she didn't want to be in their way.

Neither did she want to be around all that newlywed love. At times, just seeing Shane and MJ together swamped her with envy. She didn't begrudge them a minute of happiness—not even a second of it. She just wanted the same joy for herself. But first she needed to be independent and strong, leaning only on God, before she trusted a man with her heart, even a good man like Rafe. Especially Rafe, because he called Cincinnati home, and Daisy couldn't even spell it.

Moving into her own place struck her as an excellent first step toward independence, so she texted Chelsea, *Address? When can I check it out? Need to see it before I say yes for sure!*

They shot back and forth a few texts that ended with Daisy planning to visit an apartment complex she recognized. It was old but well maintained and affordable.

She put her phone away and went back to waving the carrot. "Hey, horses!"

She tried again to whistle, but she sounded like a tire going flat, which reminded her of Rafe, who she hadn't seen except for his car driving past the house this morning. Her evil twin wanted to find a reason to visit Heritage House, even invite him to the barbecue Shane and MJ planned for this Sunday. Or maybe that wasn't her evil twin—maybe it was just a nice thing to do for a lonely guy—maybe she—

"Stop it," she muttered.

Annoyed with herself, Daisy hopped the fence and walked toward the horses. She was twenty feet away when Jug saw her. Or more correctly, he saw the carrot still in her hand and plodded in her direction. So did Comet and Zippy. Somehow plodding turned into a slow race between the three horses, with Jug kicking out a back leg to keep the other two away.

Jug reached her first, so she fed him the carrot. Zippy crowded to the side, so she reached into the carrot bag and gave him one too. When Comet circled to the other side, Jug shouldered the gentle mare away.

"Hey," Daisy lectured. "Be nice."

She gave Jug the next carrot to keep him settled, then fed Zippy again. Comet hung back, looking sad, so Daisy stepped around Jug to give the mare the next treat. When Comet snapped off a bite, Zippy crowded in. Jug whickered and stomped his foot, then nudged Daisy in the shoulder with his nose.

A wall of horseflesh closed in on her, trapping her with Jug's big head above hers and his eyes glinting with carrot-fever. Fear shot through her—as much for her camera as for herself. Clutching it to her chest, she backpedaled but Jug didn't let up.

"Hey!" a male voice boomed from behind her.

Zippy and Comet wheeled and ran off at a gallop. Jug backed up, whinnied a warning, then ran after them.

She turned and saw Rafe running toward her, his pace slowing from a dead run to a jog. He looked both brave and silly, but there was something even more intense on his face, and that was fear—a feeling Daisy knew all too well.

Rafe couldn't breathe—and not because he'd sprinted fifty yards to save Daisy from the horses. The run was nothing to him. The suffocation came from the danger to Daisy, more imagined than real. He could see that now, but when he first saw Jug crowding her, Rafe had hopped the fence and run toward her without thinking. His imagination was too vivid for his own good, and it was slaying him now.

Daisy trampled . . . her bones broken . . . her body lifeless and bleeding.

Stifling an oath, he put his hands on his knees, hung his head, and sucked in lungfuls of the warm spring air. With a little luck, Daisy would think he was just out of shape.

"Rafe?" She rested her hand on his shoulder, rubbing gently so that the warmth of her hand soaked into his shirt, then his skin. "Are you okay?"

"I'm fine." *Stand up, you idiot!* But he could only shake his head, pulling in air through the straw that used to be his throat. His chest heaved and he almost puked. He was a blink away from a panic attack like that night on the job, and though he wasn't a praying sort of person, he silently cried out to God. If this was what dying felt like, he didn't want to feel it ever again, or see it again.

Kara . . . the needles . . . the dream.

Daisy stayed at his side, her hand light on his back. By now she had to realize he was more than winded. *Pull it together, Donovan.* But his pulse refused to listen, and his lungs demanded more air than he could take in. Daisy didn't speak; neither did he. The quiet gave him a chance to recover on his own, and after a few minutes, some of his usual confidence seeped back into his brain.

When he could breathe without his chest heaving, he stood straight, and Daisy lifted her hand from his back. He opened his mouth to say something, anything to hide his weakness, but he could only hitch up one corner of his mouth in a broken smile.

Concern radiated from her wide blue eyes, the kind he feared because it led to questions he couldn't answer. He braced himself now.

But Daisy just shook her head. "What a crazy moment, huh?"

"Uh, yeah."

"If you wanted to talk about it, you'd talk. So I'm guessing you *don't* want to talk, and you'd probably like it if *I* didn't talk either. Or maybe you'd like it if I talked about something else—like the weather, or what's for dinner, or—or why is the sky blue, anyway?"

That broken smile on his face found its other half. "You nailed it."

"No, you did." She raised the camera with one hand. "I didn't expect the horses to be quite so enthusiastic. You saved me *and* my camera."

Rafe dragged his hand through his hair. "Yeah. Well. I freaked out a little when I saw them crowding you like that."

"So did I. They're a lot bigger than I am."

He needed to change the subject again before they crossed back into the danger zone, but he also needed to face the fear. "It wasn't just the horses," he admitted. "I'm on leave because of some PTSD related to Kara's death. It's weird how it popped up on me."

"It happens." Daisy's words carried authority. "Trauma is a sticky business. Are you getting help?"

"I FaceTime with a psychologist. She's a cross between a drill sergeant and my grandmother. I like her a lot."

"Well, good."

Daisy waited, giving him time to decide how much more to say—if anything at all. To change the subject, he indicated the camera. "Did you get the shots you wanted?"

"No. But it can wait. I'll try again tomorrow." She stunned him by reaching for his hand. "Let's get out of here."

Rafe looked down at her fingers, then into her eyes.

She knows . . . But what exactly did she know? That something was wrong with him? He took her hand in his, and they walked in silence through the swaying grass. Somehow, having her hand warm and snug in his, her fingers delicate yet strong, connected them in a way words couldn't.

They picked their way across the lumpy ground until they reached the gate by the barn. Rafe ushered her through, reluctantly let go of her hand, and latched the gate behind them. Daisy turned back to the paddock, climbed on the lowest rung of the fence, and aimed her camera at the horses on the far side of the field.

She took several shots, then stepped down and swiped through the pictures until she settled on one. After fiddling some more, she showed him the viewfinder. "How's that for an equine mug shot?"

Jug's big head filled the screen in profile, complete with the sour expression of someone who'd just been busted.

Grinning, Rafe pulled out his *Cops'* voice. "Wanted for second-degree carrot robbery: Juggernaut aka Jug. Large gray male, four legs. One tail."

Laughter bubbled out of Daisy's throat, the contagious kind that wrapped itself around a man's soul and lifted him up. He and Daisy cracked a few more jokes, then she graced him with a tender smile.

"My brother and his fiancée are having a barbecue on Sunday. Would you like to come over?"

Relief washed through him. No nosy questions. No worried looks that made him feel like a goof. "I'd like that a lot."

"Good." Daisy gave him the time and her address. "You can meet my friend Chelsea."

"Hold on." Rafe didn't think she was playing matchmaker for Chelsea, but he needed to be sure. Planting his feet a little wider, he put his hands on his hips. "You're not setting me up with Chelsea, are you?"

A rosy glow bloomed on her cheeks. "Do you *want* me to set you up? I could do that, but . . ." She let the sentence dangle, leaving it for him to finish.

"Don't even think about it." His voice came out deep and low, determined, confident, and much more like himself. To prove just how *not* interested in Chelsea he was, he trailed his knuckles down the side of her cheek.

She leaned ever-so-slightly into his touch, her eyes closing as a soft breath whispered from her lips. But when she opened her eyes, he saw a flash of doubt, maybe even fear. He needed to lighten the mood fast, so he lowered his hand and grinned. "How about if I bring Jesse? We can set *him* up with Chelsea. The guy needs all the help he can get."

Just as he hoped, Daisy laughed. "I like that idea. Chelsea is super nice, and she could use a little fun. Is he okay with kids? She has a little girl."

"He's great with kids."

"Then it's settled." They walked together to the Gator she had driven from the house, chatting about their plot to match up two good people. Before she got in the driver's seat, he took his phone out of his pocket. "I'd like to have your number in case I need to reach you before Sunday."

She recited her number, and he called. To finish off the exchange, she snapped his picture for his contact info, and he snapped hers.

To his surprise, she stood on her toes, kissed his cheek, then drove away, picking up speed until she was flying down the road—flying away from him and that tender kiss. If he wasn't mistaken, she'd just scared herself more than the horses had scared him.

Chapter 10

"Fine, you can drive," Rafe said to Jesse as he took shotgun in Jesse's truck. They were headed to Shane and MJ's house for the Sunday barbecue, both spruced up and ready for a good time. "By the way, we need to stop at that grocery store on Pioneer."

"Why?" Jesse pressed the ignition button.

"To pick up flowers."

"Flowers?"

"Yes, *flowers*," Rafe shot back. "Women like them, and I like to buy them. No big deal. Considering your dating history, maybe you should take a few notes."

"Maybe you should too." Jesse punched the gas to climb a hill. "Daisy's a friend. Just how serious are you?"

"The flowers aren't for Daisy, you clod. They're a hostess gift for her brother's fiancée. It's her house." But Daisy would see and enjoy them. "It's good manners to bring something. Didn't they teach you that in prison?"

Jesse laughed out loud. "Social etiquette wasn't high on the list—except to watch your back."

Rafe admired his brother for a lot of reasons. The way Jesse handled his past topped the list—not that he'd ever tell Jesse how he felt, or that he respected him tremendously. Brothers picked on each other, and that's what they did until Jesse pulled into the supermarket parking lot. Rafe went inside and selected a mixed bouquet that included several colorful daisies. Not the cheap dyed kind—these were big, exotic, and richly hued in shades of pink, red, orange, and yellow.

Back in the truck, he texted Daisy that they were on their way. She replied with *In the backyard* and a smiley face.

Twenty minutes later, Jesse parked in front of a boxy two-story house in an old but nice neighborhood. They walked up the driveway, passing Daisy's Hyundai and a Chevy Tahoe as they approached the yard.

With Jesse in the lead, they rounded the corner of the house to a flagstone patio with built-in brick planters. A table shaded by an umbrella was set up for eight and laden with veggies, fresh cut fruit, and bowls of chips. A propane barbecue was open and ready to go, and a blue cooler held soft drinks and bottled water.

Out on the lawn, a man Rafe presumed to be Daisy's brother was throwing a baseball to a young boy, probably Cody, while underhanding a Wiffle ball to a little girl wearing a frilly dress, red sparkly shoes, and a plastic tiara. Rafe recognized Hannah from the picture on Daisy's phone.

"Hey, there." Daisy stood up from one of the patio chairs arranged in a haphazard circle.

So did the brunette next to her. Chelsea was a little

shorter than Daisy, clad in a flowery sundress, more curvy than lean, and cute in a friendly sort of way. An easy smile graced her lips, and she gave them a small wave of acknowledgment—or more precisely, she waved at Jesse. If Rafe wasn't mistaken, Chelsea's eyes had popped at the sight of his big brother.

A woman holding two bowls of dip came around the corner. She greeted Rafe and Jesse with a smile. "Hey, Jesse. It's good to see you. This must be Rafe. I'm MJ."

Daisy and Chelsea joined the group, and all three women eyed the flowers—Daisy with her brows raised, Chelsea with a gasp of longing, and MJ with a quiet look of approval. Her hands were full with the bowls, but Rafe still offered them to her. "Thanks for inviting us. I'm sick of Jesse's cooking, and he won't eat mine."

"With good reason," Jesse shot back.

MJ oohed and aahed over the bouquet, welcomed them again, then held up the bowls to show her full hands. "Daisy, would you put the flowers in water? The vases are over the fridge."

Daisy cupped the bouquet with both hands. Her pinkie fingers grazed his hand fisted on the stems, and for a split second they froze with their fingers touching. Their gazes met and he smiled.

So did Daisy, but she looked down almost immediately. She lifted the flowers so fast the cellophane crackled. "These are beautiful."

Chelsea fingered the petal of a big red flower. "Aren't these gerberas?"

Rafe didn't know what a gerbera was, but Daisy's face lit up like Christmas. "Yes, they are." She admired them for a long moment, then raised her eyes to meet his. "Gerbera daisies were my mom's favorite flower. She named me after them."

Score one for Team Rafe! He shot a glance at Jesse,

who gave him a look of grudging respect.

Daisy stepped back to include everyone in a circle. "Let's get the introductions out of the way. You all know me. This is Chelsea, my friend from Los Angeles. Chelsea, this is Rafe and his brother, Jesse."

Leaning forward, Jesse reached out to shake Chelsea's hand. "It's a pleasure."

Chelsea offered hers in return, bubbled a greeting, and invited Jesse to the cooler to get something to drink. They walked away, chatting easily about the beautiful weather.

Rafe watched them amble off. It was too soon to tell if sparks would fly or fizzle, but when he glanced at Daisy, they shared a look that ignited sparks of their own. A small smile danced on her lips—an undercover smile, because it could have been for Chelsea and Jesse, or just for Rafe.

A throat-clearing rumble caught his attention and he turned. There was no mistaking Shane Riley for anyone but Daisy's brother. They looked alike, but the real "tell" was the protective glint in the man's eyes. *Hurt my sister and die.* Shane might not realize it yet, but she had nothing at all to fear from Rafe.

The men extended their hands at the same time, but Shane spoke first. "I'm Shane Riley. It's nice to meet you."

"Rafe Donovan. Thanks for inviting me today."

They both turned to Daisy, but her gaze was on Shane. She and her brother exchanged a look, then Shane clapped her on the arm. "Go take care of the flowers. I'll entertain Rafe."

Daisy scooted away, glancing once over her shoulder and giving him a nervous smile. They all knew what was going on. This was the start of what Rafe called the "boyfriend interview." It usually involved best friends, sometimes parents, rarely big brothers. Looking at Daisy, he faked a look like the painting called *The Scream.* As he hoped, she chuckled to herself and left with the flowers bobbing in her hands.

Rafe turned back to Shane. Should he talk baseball? Keep it casual? It was way too soon for the *I care about your sister* speech, but the air felt oddly heavy.

Shane motioned to the ice chest on the far corner of the patio. Rafe followed, both slightly irked to feel like he'd been summoned, and respectful because if he were in Shane's shoes, he'd be just as protective—maybe more so.

Shane snagged a bottle of water and invited Rafe to help himself. He selected a Coke, popped the top, and raised the can to say thanks. *Let the interview begin.*

Shane lifted his bottle in response. "Thanks for changing Daisy's tire the other night."

"I was glad to do it."

"Drives me nuts how tire stores use those air guns. She knows how to put on a spare, but those lug nuts were ridiculously tight. Two of the bolts on my truck are stripped because of that."

"Man, that's a pain."

Car-talk was Rafe's second language, and he settled into the jargon. For the next five minutes, they talked about horsepower, Rafe's drive from Ohio, and a little about baseball. Shane said he forgave Rafe for being a Reds fan—the archrivals to the Cougars—and Rafe told him he was forgiven for actually wearing Cougar blue. They raised a mock toast to each other, a sign of respect and the start of a friendship.

The back door opened and Daisy came out with the flowers in a ceramic vase. She put them on the table, looked in his direction, and smiled—at him, not at her brother. Rafe took it as a sign of approval.

Shane clapped him on the arm, then spoke quietly. "Be good to her, Rafe. She's had a hard time."

"I wondered, but she hasn't said anything."

"She will when she's ready."

"That's the only way." But sometimes a person needed to be asked—the way Jesse asked Rafe about the nightmares, the way Rafe wished he had asked Kara about her glittery eyes and all those pills. He wouldn't push Daisy for her story, but when the time was right, he wanted to hear it.

Shane excused himself to fire up the grill. As he walked away, Daisy approached. When she passed her brother, he said something and she laughed.

Rafe took a long swallow of Coke. When he lowered the can, Daisy was at his side.

"Hi," she murmured.

"Hi."

He wanted to reach for her hand, even brush a kiss on her cheek, but he held those feelings inside. Today was about getting to know her as a person—her likes and dislikes, her favorite foods, colors, and movies; what made her laugh, what made her cry; and how had she survived, even thrived, in spite of whatever heartache had come her way.

Her eyes, as bright and blue as the sky, locked with his. Somehow in the midst of the conversations around them, the sizzle of meat hitting the grill, and the kids giggling on the lawn, he felt as if they were in their own private universe.

He gave in to the mood and took her hand. "I hope I passed your brother's inspection."

"You did—with flying colors."

He wrapped his arm around her shoulders and hugged her to his side. When he felt her relax into him, he lightened his tone. "So what are you doing next Saturday?"

She studied him with a hint of shyness, a reminder of how nervous she'd been when he changed the flat tire. But a brave smile slowly formed on her lips. "I'm free all day."

"Me too," he replied. "Let's do something fun."

"I'd like that."

He thought of what he knew about Daisy's past, and how fearful she could be. "Just us? Or would you like to invite—"

"Just us. But you should know something." She looked him in the eye, her gaze both steady and vulnerable.

"What is it?"

"One word from me and my brother will claw you to death with the hot dog tongs."

"Yeah, I figured. I'll be on my best behavior, but you should know something, too."

She looked up at him expectantly.

"My best behavior just might include a kiss or two. In fact, I can pretty well guarantee it."

Her eyes twinkled with mischief, but a loud laugh from Chelsea broke the mood. He and Daisy both turned and saw Chelsea doubled up with laughter, as if Jesse had told the world's funniest joke. Considering his brother's dry sense of humor, Rafe doubted he'd told anything close to a knee-slapper.

Daisy leaned closer to him. "I hope they hit it off."

The plastic look on Jesse's face didn't give Rafe a lot of hope, but his brother often surprised him. "Come on. Let's find out what's so funny."

He looped his arm around Daisy's waist, and they crossed the patio with matching strides. Rafe pulled two chairs around so the four of them could talk more easily, then he sat close to Daisy. Whatever the joke was, it had already been forgotten. The four of them bantered, with Chelsea talking twice as much as anyone else.

After five minutes, Rafe wanted hearing protection like he wore at the firing range. If there was a gap in the conversation, Chelsea filled it. If Jesse told a story, she nodded at every word. She answered questions every bit as enthusiastically as she asked them. Where Daisy played defense, Chelsea played offense.

MJ came out of the house with another bowl, called to the kids to wash up, and made room for the platter of hot dogs and hamburgers. Everyone sat down, leaving Chelsea on one side between Hannah and Jesse, and Daisy wedged between Rafe and Cody, with Shane and MJ on the ends.

After Shane said grace, the conversation took off. Baseball. Church. Jobs. The apartment Chelsea and Daisy planned to share starting next month.

Rafe nudged Daisy with his elbow. "Want some help moving? I volunteer Jesse."

His brother glared at him from across the table. "Thanks a lot."

Daisy started to speak, but Chelsea interrupted. "That would be great! We'll pay you guys back with a home-cooked meal when we're settled. I make the *best* chicken and noodles. It's my grandmother's recipe. You guys will *love* it."

Rafe was pretty sure Jesse wouldn't love anything Chelsea cooked, especially if it came with a side dish of mindless chatter.

Daisy didn't seem to notice Jesse's reluctance, maybe because she had turned her head and was focused on Rafe. "Are you sure you're up for it? MJ's loaning us some furniture. It's—"

"Heavy!" Chelsea gazed up at Jesse. "But you can handle it, right?"

"Uh, yeah." He took a bite of the cheeseburger without batting the conversation to someone else. He wanted it to die, and it did.

Rafe felt sorry for him—and for Chelsea. *Awkward*

didn't begin to describe the bad chemistry between them.

The afternoon wound down, and Rafe and Jesse said their good-byes. Daisy walked with them to Jesse's truck, and Rafe firmed up their date for Saturday. He needed to come up with an idea, so he told her he'd text her later and they hugged good-bye.

The instant he shut the truck door, Jesse took off like a cop in pursuit, whipped around the corner, and gave him a look befitting Johnny Depp as Captain Jack Sparrow—a little crazed, vaguely amused, and ready to make someone walk the plank.

Rafe knew what was coming. "So Chelsea's not your type, huh?"

Jesse's mouth twisted into a demented snarl. "If you ever—*ever*—set me up on a date again, I'm going to punch you in the face."

Rafe broke out laughing. "I won't. I promise."

"Good." Jesse hung a right and hit the main drag to his house. "She's a human word-cannon."

"Yeah, I noticed."

"I feel bad for her." Jesse blew out a long breath, a sign he was practicing what he called "the pause"—a moment where he remained silent when he wanted to cuss, yell, drink, or break things. When he spoke, his voice came out steady. "I just wish women wouldn't try so hard. People click, or they don't."

"No kidding."

"Guys do the same stupid thing." Jesse pressed the gas pedal a little harder. "Only instead of talking too much, they brag and spend too much, or drive a car they can't afford. Why can't people just relax and get to know each other? Now you and Daisy . . ." He let the words hang. "What's going on?"

Rafe grinned in the dark. "She's amazing." Funny.

Brave. And attractive in every way—especially in those leggings.

"Be careful, bro. She doesn't need you to break her heart. You're headed home in a few months, right?"

"That's the plan."

Rafe had been in Refuge for over three weeks. His feelings for Daisy aside, he liked Refuge a lot. But enough to give up the career and city he loved? Not a chance. The realization put a knot in his belly. He and Daisy weren't anywhere close to having an official geography problem, but the potential couldn't be ignored. He liked her, and if the fierce hug was any indication, her feelings were just as potent.

Was Refuge her home or just a safe place to rest and to heal from what she had experienced in LA? Rafe couldn't see himself permanently in Wyoming. Only time—and taking a chance with a first date—would reveal the answers.

He focused back on the present. He didn't know Refuge well, so he decided to ask Jesse for date suggestions. "I'm taking Daisy out on Saturday. Any ideas?"

"Let's see . . . How about Dairy Queen? You can't go wrong with a Blizzard."

"You have *got* to be kidding me." Then again, this was Jesse—King of First and Only Dates. "If you're recommending fast food on a first date, you need more dating help than I thought."

Jesse chuckled, more to himself than Rafe. "I'm just giving you a hard time. Take her to the Riverbend Steakhouse. It's pretty. Lights in the trees. Dark inside with candles. Plus, it's quiet."

"For a first date? No way. That's a third date. Maybe the second if the first is rock-star quality."

"I don't get it." Jesse cruised through a yellow light. "What's wrong with a nice dinner for a first date?"

"Two words, bro. *Awkward. Conversation.* On a first date, you need something to do, so you can talk about it." For Daisy, he wanted to plan something fun and a little wild. But not too wild, because she needed to feel safe. "What's good for a Saturday?"

"Hiking. A river cruise. Fishing is popular." Jesse tossed him a look. "You could be really crazy and take her bowling."

Rafe laughed. "Maybe I will."

Jesse pulled into his driveway and pressed the garage door opener. The overhead light popped on and the panels rolled back to reveal a workbench, tools on a pegboard, and a snowmobile on blocks for the summer. Rafe expected to be long gone before the seasons changed, but the desire to return home didn't burn quite as hot as it had a few minutes ago.

They climbed out of the truck and went into the house. Jesse turned on ESPN, kicked back in his big recliner, and reached for his iPad. Rafe watched sports scores, but his mind returned to Daisy, that first date, and the excitement of getting to know this smart, sweet, beautiful woman who made him want to stand tall.

Chapter 11

*W*hen Daisy went inside after saying good-bye to Rafe, she caught Shane and MJ kissing by the kitchen sink. Not at all surprised, she made a show of rolling her eyes. "Again? You two are ridiculous."

Shane looped his arm around MJ's waist and squeezed her to his side. "Ridiculously in love. By the way, we both like Rafe."

Warmth rushed to Daisy's cheeks, and she had to bite her lips to keep from smiling. Somehow she schooled her voice. "He's nice."

"*Nice?*" MJ grinned like a fiend—a fiend with wedding-brain. "He's *almost* as good looking as your brother, *and* he brought flowers, which we all know were really for you."

"He asked me out for Saturday. I said yes."

Shane played it down with a nod, and MJ smiled.

"You're welcome to invite him to the wedding, but only if you want."

A wiggle of excitement pulsed through Daisy. She'd been a little nervous at the start of the barbecue, but once her nerves settled, she'd had a wonderful time. "Maybe I will."

MJ looked up at Shane and smiled. "You never know what might happen. I'm still amazed your brother walked into my life the way he did."

"More like limped," Shane added.

The tender look in his eyes—and MJ's answering smile—shot arrows of longing into Daisy's heart. She wanted those looks, the private jokes, the soul-deep tenderness—but not until she felt stronger as an individual. She moved toward the door, but Shane called out.

"Hey." He waved her over with his free arm. "Get over here, Daize."

She scurried back across the kitchen for a family hug, flung her arms around the two people she loved most in the whole world, and squeezed hard. Still smiling when the hug ended, she went upstairs in search of Chelsea.

The slosh of water, along with Hannah's giggles, led her to the bathroom. Chelsea, already in yoga pants and a comfy old t-shirt, waited with a towel as Hannah climbed out of the tub.

Daisy tapped on the doorjamb. "How's it going?"

"Just fine. We're clean and ready for a story." Chelsea dried Hannah, wrestled her damp body into Hello Kitty pajamas, and sent her to the bedroom. Bending down, she snatched up Hannah's princess dress and held it out to inspect. Drips of chocolate ice cream stained the bodice, and the taffeta skirt sported a blotch of ketchup. Chelsea shook her head. "At least one of us had fun."

"Hannah?"

"Definitely not me." Tucking the dress under her arm,

she bent to put Hannah's bathtub toys in a bucket. "Jesse's nice, but we just didn't click. You know how it is."

"I do." Daisy had dated a lot in Los Angeles, always the wrong guys for the wrong reasons. But she'd found a new life in Christ and clung to it now. Her heart bled for Chelsea, but they'd had the conversation about Jesus, and Chelsea wasn't interested. Daisy worried about her, but all she could do was love and pray the way others had loved and prayed for *her*.

Chelsea straightened the bath mat with her toe. "I tried to keep things light, but he just was so serious—no sense of humor at all."

"He *did* seem quiet." Far quieter than Daisy had expected. When Jesse shared stories at AA meetings, the crowd roared with laughter.

Chelsea gave a shrug. "Enough of that. I can't let it discourage me, right?"

"Right. Learn and move on." It sounded like something Miss Joan would say.

Chelsea turned off the bathroom light and motioned for Daisy to follow her. "I have to read Hannah a story, but then I want your opinion on something."

"What?"

"You'll see."

Daisy followed Chelsea into the bedroom, where Hannah lay under the covers, already half asleep. Chelsea tossed the dress in an overflowing laundry basket, snagged a Peppa Pig book, and read just four pages before Hannah's eyes closed completely. Chelsea set the book down and whispered, "Let's go to your room."

She unplugged her phone from the charger, and they tiptoed down the hall. Leaving the door open, they plopped onto Daisy's double bed, leaned on the pillows piled against the headboard, and sat shoulder to shoulder.

Chelsea swiped the phone screen to show four dating

apps. "What do you think?"

Daisy had tried online dating but that was before Eric. The memory of the assault shot through her, and she unconsciously brushed her fingers over the scar hidden by her short hair. Never mind that she'd met him at a party. Online dating struck her as risky.

She lowered her hand, the bump of the scar still fresh on her fingers. "It's not for me. At least not anymore."

"I thought I was done with it, too." Sadness tinged her voice. "But I don't know what else to do. I'm lonely, Daisy. And bored. If I'm going to be here for three months, I need to have some fun other than taking Hannah to McDonald's."

"Of course you do." Daisy's heart ached for her friend. "But why use an app? Shane and MJ know a lot of people. Maybe they could introduce you—"

"Forget it."

"Why?"

"You just saw why." Chelsea heaved an epic sigh. "Jesse and I couldn't stand each other. Going through an app gives me more control. I can say yes, no, or walk away. I like that."

"Maybe, but I worry about you. Stranger danger isn't just for kids Hannah's age."

"No, it isn't. But I know the rules." Chelsea ticked them off one at a time. "Meet in a public place. Make sure someone knows where I am. Never leave a drink unattended, and if you're walking around with it, keep your hand over the top so some jerk doesn't slip in a roofie."

Daisy shuddered. "I hate the whole idea."

Chelsea leaned closer to her, touching shoulders in a silent show of support. "Eric was a monster. You need to be extra careful because he messed with your mind. But I've met some nice guys this way—including Nathan. If I don't start dating again, I'll never get over him."

Daisy's stomach knotted, but she saw Chelsea's point. How else could she make new friends? Dating guys she met at work was a bad idea. Chelsea didn't have time for hobbies or interests other than raising Hannah, nor did she go to church. As for meeting men in the produce aisle, that happened in rom-coms, not real life.

Leaning in, she studied the four icons. Like a box of chocolates, the apps were each a little different, ranging from notorious to marriage-minded. "You definitely need to put Nathan in the past. This might be just what you need—but nothing too crazy, okay?"

"*Crazy* is the last thing I want." Chelsea put her fingertip on an app Daisy didn't like. "Forget this one. I used it once on a dare. Never again." The icon wobbled and vanished.

Daisy pointed to an app that had been around for years. An older couple she knew at church had met through it and glowed when they shared their story. "What about this one?"

"No. It's too complicated. You have to take a five-hundred question personality test. I'm not looking for a husband. I just want . . ." Chelsea sighed. "I don't know what I want."

Daisy ached for her. "How about a summer romance? Something light and fun?" Images of Rafe spun through her mind, and she decided the plan worked for her, too.

"That would be perfect," Chelsea replied. "Then again, I wouldn't mind if it turned into something more."

Surprised, Daisy tilted her head. "But you're leaving in three months." And Rafe planned to leave even sooner.

Chelsea shrugged. "If I met someone special, I'd stay. That's a no-brainer."

"It wouldn't be that simple for me." Daisy pulled her knees to her chest and hugged them hard. "Don't you want to be close to your mom, especially with Hannah?"

"Sure. But wait—I'll show you." She swiped to an awkward selfie of a middle-aged couple. A bright smile lit up the woman's face, but the man was too close to the camera and scowling in techno-befuddlement.

Daisy couldn't help but laugh. "Old people take the worst selfies. I recognize your mom. Who's the guy?"

"My stepdad. They got together after I moved to LA. Steve's good for her, but I'm not part of their life together. They love Hannah, but I feel like a guest when we visit."

"That's sad."

"It's okay. Really. I'm glad my mom's happy. They'll take me in, but I hate feeling like a failure, you know?"

"I know exactly."

"So I'm open to possibilities." Chelsea opened the FriendsFirst app to her profile page and handed the phone to Daisy. "This is the profile from before I met Nathan. What do you think?"

Daisy had never used the site, but she'd heard about it. People who met on FriendsFirst pledged to be just friends for at least three dates. *Three dates . . .* as if that boundary protected anyone. Sadly, Daisy understood that world, but now it broke her heart. The best dating relationship in the world didn't hold a candle to how much God loved her.

Chelsea leaned closer to Daisy and peered down at the screen. "I wrote this over a year ago. What do you think? But don't think too hard. It's all about first impressions."

Daisy studied the photo with a critical eye. The camera loved Chelsea, but now she wore her hair long. "It's a good picture, but how about something new? In fact—" Daisy lifted her own phone off the nightstand. "I snapped a few pictures at the barbecue." Mostly of Rafe, but she had a good one of Chelsea. She held out the phone. "What do you think?"

Chelsea studied it for a moment. "I like it. I'm smiling

big, but you don't know why. It's a little mysterious."

Daisy sent it to her. "Now let's read what you wrote last time around."

Looking for Love in all the Right Places!

The most important person in my life is my three-year-old daughter, and that will never change. I know that's a deal-breaker for some men, and that's okay. My little girl deserves the best I can give her. If that includes a stepdad, I'm good with it. And if it doesn't, I'm good with that, too. Mostly I want to be honest, and I expect honesty from others.

So about me:

My favorite movie is Christmas Vacation, *because it reminds me of my own family. Don't worry, they live in Michigan!*

I like to laugh, and I like to make people laugh. Life is too short to miss the joke.

Dangly earrings? Yes, please!

This is weird, but I like beets.

My ideal first date is coffee with a thirty-minute time limit. But if we're lost in conversation and forget to check our phones, that's even better.

"That's really sweet." Daisy gave the phone back to Chelsea. "What do you want to change?"

"Just the beginning." She tapped out a new opening and gave the phone to Daisy. "Is this too pathetic?"

Looking for Summer Fun!

Has your life ever gone sideways? Mine did a few months ago (read—broken heart!). Now I'm in the middle of moving from Los Angeles to Michigan. Wyoming is a temporary stop, but I'm ready

to put my toe back in the dating water.
A step at a time, right? But friendship first. No
more broken hearts—either yours or mine. Let's
keep things light, friendly, fun!!!
Now about me . . .
I'm a mom first. My little girl is four and ador-
able. I enjoy funny movies, sunny days at the
park, and blueberry muffins.

The rest of the blurb remained unchanged. Daisy read
the new beginning a second time. "Are you keeping the
part about *Christmas Vacation* and the beets?"

"What do you think?" Chelsea tapped her finger on her
knee. "It's true, but maybe—"

"I like that part." Daisy had to be honest. "But I'm not
sure about the new beginning. It's honest, which is good,
but it makes you sound a little vulnerable."

"So you don't like it." Chelsea sounded disheartened,
as if Daisy didn't like *her.*

"It's really sweet. *It is.* It's just that online dating
makes me nervous. Anything could happen."

"That's part of the fun." Chelsea gave a shiver of excitement. "Who knows? I could meet someone really special, right?"

"Yes, but—"

"Don't worry, okay? I know how to protect myself."

Daisy held in a wince. A year ago she might have made
the same claim. "Just be careful, Chels. I might be a little
paranoid after Eric. Or a lot paranoid—"

"With good reason." Chelsea's words burst out. "That's
why I'm proud of you for inviting Rafe today. His brother's
a dud, but he's one of the good guys."

"I like him," Daisy admitted. "In fact, we're going out
on Saturday."

Chelsea gave a happy squeal. "I'm proud of you, Daize.

This is your first date since Eric, isn't it?"

"Yes. It's a little scary, but I think it's time for me to put a toe in the water like you said. Considering he's going back to Ohio, am I crazy to start something?"

Chelsea's face softened into wistfulness. "I think you'd be crazy *not* to start something. This afternoon—he couldn't take his eyes off you. If you two fall in love, maybe he'd stay in Refuge, or you could move to Cincinnati."

Daisy shook her head. "Ohio? Forget it. You know how much Shane and MJ mean to me."

"I do. But you'd make a new family of your own. That's what Brian and I did when he took the job in LA. Our marriage fell apart, but I'm glad we tried. And now I have Hannah."

Daisy's mind shot down a road that ended way too far in the future—with a little house, Rafe, two kids, and a cat. Did he even like cats? He seemed more like a dog person. Or—Daisy pressed her damp palms to her cheeks. "This is ridiculous. We're talking about one date. Why am I even *thinking* about Ohio?"

Chelsea squared her shoulders. "Let's both take things a day at a time. You're good at that, right?"

The AA saying calmed Daisy's nerves. Relaxing, she told Chelsea more about Rafe—their tailgate lunch, how he'd chased off the horses, and how much he'd impressed Shane.

Chelsea tapped her phone to wake it up, then uploaded the new picture, and accepted the profile changes. Satisfied, she tossed the phone down on the bed. Let's see how many Hello's I get."

In less than ten minutes, five notifications popped up. Daisy and Chelsea checked out the replies together, read profiles, considered photographs, and answered some messages but not others. After an hour or so, Chelsea said

yes to a coffee date on Tuesday afternoon with a nice-look-
ing banker who didn't remind her at all of Nathan.

Chapter 12

On Monday morning, Daisy dressed for work in a peacock blue gypsy skirt that swirled around her legs, a white ruffled top, and her favorite pair of bohemian sandals. She didn't expect to see Rafe today, but since he was working at Heritage House, their paths could cross at any time.

A zing of excitement danced through her as she settled at her desk. Chelsea's reminder to take things a day at a time had calmed her fears, and today she felt in control of herself. The computer screen brightened with the mug shot of Jug she'd picked for the background, and she wondered where Rafe would take her on Saturday.

The photo-editing software was still loading when her intercom buzzed. Daisy answered, and Miss Joan's voice came over the speaker. "I need your help."

"Of course. Your office?"

"No. It's a beautiful day. Let's sit on the deck. It's time to pick the top five charities for the giveaway, and I want your opinion."

Daisy drew back. "*My* opinion? I'm not qualified—"

"You're *more* than qualified." Miss Joan's voice snapped through the phone. "You're young and smart, and that's what I need. Meet me in five minutes."

They ended the call and Daisy gathered her iPad, a yellow legal pad, and two pens. *Young and smart.* Miss Joan's words echoed in her mind as she headed to the Keurig in the kitchen. *Young* was a no-brainer. But smart? Daisy found it hard—impossible—to believe, but maybe it was true.

Determined to honor Miss Joan's trust, she brewed a K-cup and went out the back door, taking a sip as she approached the round glass table shaded by an umbrella. Miss Joan sat with her back to the house and her eyes on the mountains, while Ana, Miss Joan's housekeeper, tilted the umbrella to fend off the sun. A rock held down a stack of papers rustling in the light breeze.

Daisy greeted Ana, set down her things, and pulled up a chair as Ana went back inside.

"This is exciting." She slid the cushioned chair closer to the table.

"It certainly is." Miss Joan flashed a smile, then looked down her nose at the papers under the rock.

A soft breath whispered just over the silence, and her smile sagged—only slightly but Daisy saw it. Giving away her home wasn't as easy as Miss Joan pretended, but Daisy knew better than to offer sympathy—a lesson learned from her own recovery after Eric's assault. Today Miss Joan needed an ally to help with hard, rational decisions, not a cheerleader, and especially not a pity party.

Daisy tilted her head so she could see the first paper

in the stack. "Which one do you like best?"

"I'm not telling."

"Why not?" Daisy liked having clues.

"I want *your* opinion, dear. Unvarnished. Untainted." Miss Joan pushed the stack directly in front of Daisy. "Start reading."

"Out loud?"

"No. I've gone over them."

For the next twenty minutes, Daisy read through the proposals, commenting to Miss Joan about what she liked and didn't like. After much debate, they picked three of the ten proposals for future visits: Camp Good Times for kids with special needs; the Wildlife Preservation Society, even though Daisy thought it sounded stuffy; and The Hyatt-Howard School for Future Leaders. The school was a mini-university for underprivileged kids in urban areas. Their programs promoted STEM and business careers without neglecting history and the arts—all subjects that appealed to Miss Joan.

They ruled out three others: A Boys Town–style facility because the proposal indicated the desire to build large dormitories; a summer camp dedicated to science and technology because it would close during the winter; and a second wildlife program that wasn't as impressive as the first one.

"Six down, four to go," Daisy remarked as she picked up a proposal from Give-A-Goat, a world hunger organization that provided goats, cattle, and other livestock to families in third-world countries. The livestock was raised locally in Africa and Asia, but the organization proposed using Cottonwood Acres for their headquarters, a research facility, and an educational center.

Daisy saw a problem. "I love what this organization does, but it doesn't seem like a good fit. They need money, not buildings and land."

"I agree." Joan set the page aside. "I've donated to them before and will do it again. What's next?"

Daisy lifted the next page, saw a row of clown faces, and almost snickered. How had Coogan's Clowns made the top ten? Granted, the proposal combined the clowns with a nonprofit rodeo school for troubled teens, plus a horse rescue operation, but did anyone actually *like* clowns? Daisy didn't. She knew that rodeo clowns were different from circus clowns, but clowns in general were scary and weird.

"Forget this one," she said with confidence. "Clowns scare people."

Miss Joan huffed through her nose. "Clowns *do not* scare people. *Meanness* scares people. I like this idea, quite a bit, in fact."

Daisy didn't know which startled her more—Miss Joan's snippy tone or her defense of clowns. Either way, Daisy wasn't about to argue. "In that case, it's a keeper."

Miss Joan nodded crisply. "One slot left and two proposals to go."

The next one-sheet came from a well-known megachurch in Texas. The pastor hosted a popular blog and had written a powerful book on prayer. The plan proposed using Cottonwood Acres as a retreat center for families in crisis. The church currently ran a similar program locally and wanted to expand.

Daisy skimmed to the end. "I can see this one working."

"So can I, but I want your thoughts on the final one before we decide."

Daisy flipped to the last proposal and read out loud. "'Annie's Friends is a New York-based charity dedicated to rescuing women and children from human trafficking and the sex trade in our own American cities.'"

The words grabbed Daisy by the throat and refused to

let go. In her teen years, she'd been needy and vulnerable. She easily could have been lured by a trafficker. With her heart stumbling, she read the story of a young woman who had endured terrible abuse—until she found Annie's Friends. Now she lived in a safe place, attended counseling and Bible studies, and worked as a cosmetologist.

Annie's Friends planned to use Cottonwood Acres as a long-term shelter—something akin to Maggie's House—the ministry that had helped Daisy in Los Angeles. On the downside, they lacked history and experience. This was a big reach for a fledgling organization, but Daisy's heart still thumped with the desperate longing to help women like herself.

Somehow she kept her voice level. "I *love* this one."

"So do I." A familiar spark burned in Miss Joan's eyes. "You know I taught history for almost forty years."

Daisy stifled a smile. "Yes. I do." She knew what was coming—an impromptu history lesson peppered with opinions.

Miss Joan laced her hands on the table as if she were at a lectern. "Sadly, there's a long history of women being exploited by the sex trade, including in our own American West. We tend to romanticize that period, at least that's what *Thunder Valley* did, but outside of marriage, women had few options. Prostitution was a last resort with conditions that ranged from tolerable, at least in terms of food and shelter, to the appalling—like the 'hog' ranches that were even worse than that sounds."

"*Hog* ranch?" Daisy felt sick to her stomach. "What an awful phrase. It's so—so—"

"Demeaning." Miss Joan bit off the word. "If I can use Cottonwood Acres to help even one suffering soul, I'll do it gladly. But I'm concerned about this particular proposal."

"What are you worried about?"

"Annie's Friends is just over a year old. They haven't

been tested by time. I'm also concerned about the remote location. Is Wyoming really the best fit?"

"It's a better fit than you might think." Daisy thought of her own experience. "Getting away from the source of a problem is a plus. Plus the mountains and sky are beautiful. The quiet helps a person feel closer to God."

Miss Joan nodded. "I can relate. But if Annie's Friends folds in a year or two, what will happen to Cottonwood Acres?"

"I don't know."

"I don't either, and I can't take that chance. I've considered contacting similar organizations, but—"

"Wait!" Daisy bolted upright in her chair. "I have it!"

"Have what?"

"The perfect organization. Maggie's House! It has a ten-year history, and it's expanded from one house in the beginning to about a dozen throughout California. They help women in trouble—any kind of trouble."

Miss Joan's eyebrows lifted with interest. "So they have a proven track record."

"Yes." Daisy pointed at herself. "And that record includes me."

"That fact alone would convince me, but we need to be practical. Tell me more."

Daisy didn't feel at all qualified to pitch the idea. She wanted to call Lyn, but an internal nudge urged her to be brave. Ideas flooded into her mind, each picture crisp and clear. She snatched up a pen, wrote *Ideas* at the top of the notepad, and underlined the word four times. "Let's start with a name. We'll call it Maggie's Rescue Ranch. That's perfect! So is the house. It's big. Eight women could live here. Or we could turn the bunkhouse into apartments and use the house for a training center, workshops, Bible studies—"

Miss Joan broke in. "I like what I'm hearing."

"There's more." Daisy scribbled notes as she spoke. "The residents need meaningful work. I know, because I was one. If you open Heritage House to the public, it'll need a staff. I don't know exactly how we'd finance it, but we could restart the horse rescue program and make it even bigger. We could take in dogs like Sadie, or stray cats, even guinea pigs."

"Guinea pigs?" Miss Joan laughed out loud—not at Daisy but with enthusiasm. "Did I hear you correctly, dear? You want to use the vast resources of Cottonwood Acres to rescue guinea pigs?"

Choked by emotions, she felt her cheeks burn with embarrassment. Her next words came out in a hush. "I want to rescue everyone."

Miss Joan laid her gnarled hand over Daisy's slender one. She didn't speak; neither did Daisy, until the lump sank back down to her chest and she mustered a smile.

Miss Joan's eyes twinkled. "It's a wonderful idea, dear. But there's a problem."

Daisy's heart started to break. She wanted this. *She did.* She wanted to work at Cottonwood Acres forever. "What is it?"

"Unfortunately . . ." Miss Joan's lips tipped into a smile. "I'm not fond of guinea pigs. Perhaps we could negotiate that point, because I love the rest of what you have in mind."

Grinning, Daisy crossed *guinea pigs* off her list with a thick line. "Done! But broadening the animal rescue is a good idea. Maggie's House had three cats. I liked it when Meathead jumped into my lap and purred."

Miss Joan feigned fresh outrage. "What kind of name is Meathead for a cat?"

"Well, he wasn't very smart." *Kind of like me.* "But it was nice to have him around."

Miss Joan smiled her approval. "How fast can the people at Maggie's House send a proposal?"

Daisy reached for her phone. "I'll call Lyn now."

"Good. If they're interested, I'll put Maggie's House in the top five based on your recommendation."

Daisy's eyes nearly popped out of her head. "*My* recommendation?"

"Yes. I trust your opinion."

No one had ever trusted Daisy with anything this big. "Are you sure you want to do that?"

"I'm very sure. Call your friend."

"The process has to be fair—"

"It will be. But this is a private venture, not a government grant. My ranch. My rules."

"Like the driving."

"Yes, exactly. I assure you, Daisy, I'm perfectly capable of saying no to Maggie's House if it's not a good fit. But if it is, I'd be thrilled to use Cottonwood Acres to ameliorate a problem that's been around since the dawn of man."

"Ameliorate?" Daisy needed her vocab app.

"To make better or more bearable—to improve."

"That's what Maggie's House is all about." Never in Daisy's wildest dreams did she imagine having an impact like the one dawning on the horizon. "I'll call Lyn right now."

Lyn picked up in three rings, and five minutes later plans were in place for an emergency meeting of the Maggie's House board of directors. She was confident the four other board members would jump at the chance to participate. "We've been looking for ways to help trafficking victims for the past year," she told Daisy. "The remote location is just what we had in mind—a place to retreat and heal."

Daisy couldn't stop smiling. "You'll need to visit the ranch in June. If we time it right, you can surprise MJ at her bridal shower."

"That would be wonderful!"

Lyn was confirmed for the wedding, but she couldn't attend the shower as well because it required too much time away from work. Now she could because the trip was for Maggie's House. They ended the call with promises to firm up travel plans in the next few days.

Before Daisy could catch her breath, Miss Joan broke into her thoughts. "I heard you mention a bridal shower. Who's getting married?"

The question startled her. "My brother. He and MJ Townsend are getting married June 19. I'm her maid of honor and giving the shower."

Miss Joan's eyes misted and she smiled. "I love weddings."

"You do?"

"Oh, yes."

Daisy hadn't pegged Miss Joan as the wedding type, but the older woman often surprised her. "I'm happy for my brother—and for me. His fiancée has a little boy, so I get to be the cool aunt who buys noisy toys."

She expected Miss Joan to laugh but she barely smiled.

Daisy started to ask what was wrong, but the question felt nosy and out of place. Instead she opened the calendar app on the iPad. Knowing Miss Joan, she'd want to focus on work instead of whatever had dulled her smile.

Daisy cleared her throat. "We have a lot to do."

Miss Joan startled out of her mood. "Yes . . . yes, we do. You'll need to book plane tickets, hotel rooms, and rental cars. Spare no expense. Our guests are all dedicated to good causes. I want to treat them like royalty."

Together they set dates for the five organizations to visit Cottonwood Acres starting in two weeks. When they finished, Daisy considered the heavy workload as she gathered her things. "I'll work extra hours to get everything done, but I have plans for Saturday."

"Good for you." Miss Joan sounded more like herself. "What are you up to?"

A faint blush crept up Daisy's neck. She couldn't hide it from Miss Joan, but she schooled her voice. "Rafe Donovan asked me out. I didn't plan to start dating yet, but he's nice."

Miss Joan's eyes twinkled. "Ah, the hottie."

Daisy laughed. "I suppose."

"You *suppose*? Dear, get your eyes checked!"

Daisy blushed again. Before she could graciously leave, Miss Joan gave her the kind of tender look Daisy remembered from her own mother.

The feistiness returned to Miss Joan's eyes, along with an even brighter twinkle. "In my day, we would have called Rafe Donovan a hunk. There's nothing wrong with physical attraction. God put it into us for a purpose. He also gave us a plan for enjoying it wisely."

"You mean marriage."

"I do." Miss Joan's words rang with her usual conviction. "Marriage gives us families. Family members take care of each other, young and old alike. At its best, marriage keeps people safe, though we all know human beings sometimes fail each other. Nonetheless, as imperfect as marriage can be, I still believe in it."

Something indecipherable lurked behind Miss Joan's comments—something personal. The breeze mussed her silver hair, but she didn't seem to notice.

Daisy moved to stand, but Miss Joan had more to say. "I don't mean to suggest that women weren't—and aren't—sometimes oppressed. We shouldn't forget or ignore the sorry side of history. But there's something to be said for protecting our daughters and sisters more than we currently do."

Daisy thought of Chelsea obsessively checking her phone for FriendsFirst notifications. "Dating is complicated now. I have a friend who likes meeting guys online. She says it's fun and gives her control, but I worry about her."

"With good reason—at least in my opinion. Though I'm sure that seems quite old-fashioned."

"Not to me. Women have always been vulnerable, but technology puts risk on an all new level."

"If you were writing a paper, I'd give you an A-plus. Do you know when that change started?"

"Not really."

"In the 1920s." Miss Joan laced her hands on the table, resuming her at-a-lectern pose. "With the proliferation of the automobile, courtship left the relative safety of the front porch and turned into a much more private affair. Now teenagers drive off alone, with their phones as the only link to home. That strikes me as a rather fragile safety net."

Daisy had lived that way in high school. "It's just the way it is."

"I used to advocate complete personal freedom for men and women alike. I still believe in that principle. I always will." She got a misty look in her eyes. "But freedom comes with a cost."

Daisy opened her mouth to ask what Miss Joan meant, but the old woman pushed up in her chair. "I'm tired now, and Sadie needs a walk. Let me know if you have any questions about the charity visits."

Daisy had questions—a lot of them. But they were about Miss Joan, the sad look in her eyes, and that last remark about freedom coming at a cost.

Chapter 13

What makes old age hard to bear is not the failing of one's faculties, mental and physical, but the burden of one's memories.

W. Somerset Maugham

Leaving Daisy alone on the deck, Joan walked into the living room, saw Sadie asleep in a beam of sunlight, and continued alone to her bedroom. Between giving away her home and talking about marriage and family, she had tumbled down a rabbit hole into the past. She hadn't been a Christian when Trey swaggered into her life. She'd been her own oracle—a proponent of feminist principles she still fervently believed in: equality under the law, the right to work, equal pay and equal opportunity.

But she had failed to understand the personal side of

the equation—the cost of sexual freedom, the fact that her choices affected others in unexpected ways. Like layers of an onion, every choice she made regarding Trey had peeled away another layer of her soul—until everything fell apart.

She could have fought for him, married him, been a wife and a mother, had grandchildren and great-grandchildren. Instead of giving away her home to strangers, she might have basked in the shade of a family tree. Instead she was a single woman loved by God; a woman redeemed in the darkest moment of her life.

If only . . . The words echoed in her mind, but they were faint now, muffled by time, acceptance, and finally the blessing of forgiveness, both given and received. She didn't want to remember that time in her life, but neither did she want to forget the humbling that came with it. History mattered. With her heart aching, she went into her bedroom, closed the door, and drifted into the past.

Trey and I didn't see each other for a month after his episode of *Thunder Valley* finished filming, but we spoke every day on the phone. The calls all started the same way—with businesslike reports on the formation of the TC Double R. I was responsible for legalities, accounting, and facility preparation. Trey handled the acquisition of the horses.

With rodeo season in full swing, he was busy promoting the truck he drove and the clothes he wore. In June, he filmed a commercial for his favorite boots. On the phone one day, I teased him. "Are they really your favorite?"

"They are now."

We laughed, but now I see beyond the joke. Trey was

a chameleon, the charming little creature that changes colors to match its environment, thus protecting itself by hiding in plain sight.

Our phone calls grew longer and drifted later into the day, until it became our habit to talk late at night. We were eager to see each other, and those calls all ended with Trey promising to bring the first trailer of horses himself.

I wanted an exact date so I could plan. Instead of taking my usual summer research trip, I was languishing at Cottonwood Acres, supposedly overseeing preparations for the rescue program. I say *supposedly* because there was very little for me to do. The legalities of the process entailed calling my attorney, and the barn was already in tip-top condition. The grass in the pasture certainly didn't need my help to grow, which left me with nothing to do— except wonder if I had met someone truly special.

At night I grumbled to Trey over the phone. "I'm bored. What would you say if I flew to Dallas and we met for a weekend?" The big city was only two hours from where he lived.

The silence thickened, until a long breath gusted across hundreds of miles. "I wish I could, Joan. I really do."

"But?"

"It's just not a good time."

We were friends and business partners, even confidantes. If he was in trouble, I needed to know. "Trey, what's wrong?"

He harrumphed into the phone. "It's Kathy. She wants to try counseling again."

Shock pulsed through me, an electrical feeling that both tingled and hurt. "She doesn't want the divorce?"

"Apparently not."

"Oh, Trey—"

"It's rough right now. My attorney says counseling is a

good idea. It'll give him leverage in the negotiations."

"Are you going to do it?"

"I guess. But the marriage is over. Kathy needs to accept the inevitable. Maybe this will help her."

I mustered both my intellect and common sense. "I think it's a good idea."

"You do?"

"Yes." I'd never met Kathy or even seen a photograph, but I felt a loyalty to her as a woman. "Anytime a relationship ends, there's wreckage. If you clean it up now, you can both move on."

"I like that thought."

"So do I."

His voice dropped an octave. "I want the divorce to be final when I see you again. Joan, I . . ." His words disintegrated into silence.

If the miles had melted to nothing, I would have been in his arms. My own voice came out breathy, which wasn't like me at all, except with Trey. "How much longer?"

"Too long." A new strength reverberated over the line, and I heard the determined man who wanted to honor his commitments. "Maybe someone else should bring the first load of horses. I made arrangements to take in four of them at the end of the week."

Taking his lead, I made my voice brusque. "Then let's get those horses on the road." Our conversation shifted to practicalities and stayed there until we said good night.

The instant the phone went dead, questions stormed through my mind: Where did I fit in Trey's life? Did I even have a place? Did I *want* a place? He was in the middle of a divorce but still legally married. No way did I want to be the other woman, or worse, a cliché. My feminism granted me independence but it demanded integrity in return.

I didn't have answers, so I shoved the questions aside with the belief that the divorce would render them moot.

In the meantime, Trey and I returned to the boundaries of friendship, though loneliness gusted through me every time we whispered good-bye across the miles.

Two long weeks passed. Trey said nothing about Kathy or counseling, and I didn't ask. When there was news, he'd tell me and we'd plan for his visit.

Only that didn't happen.

I was upstairs in my office with the window open wide, working on the syllabus for American History 101, when the hum of an approaching vehicle broke my concentration. I peeked out the window and saw a heavy-duty pickup, brand new, hauling a four-horse trailer, also brand new.

There were no deliveries scheduled, no reason anyone would be bringing horses. I'd spoken to Trey just last night, and nothing at all was said about the rescue horses waiting at his ranch in Texas. Squinting to make out details, I saw bug splat on the windshield and white out-of-state license plates. Why hadn't Trey said anything? It didn't make sense—unless the scoundrel planned to surprise me!

I flew out the door and hurried to the barn a quarter mile away. Excitement gave my feet wings—and my heart, too. Was the divorce final? Were we free to be more than friends? To occupy the same space and breathe the same air; to hold hands and kiss and do more than talk on the phone?

In just minutes, the massive barn loomed in front of me. I smelled hay and horses, then exhaust from the hot engine of the pickup. Passing it, I glanced inside and saw an empty McDonald's coffee cup, a dark brown Stetson on the passenger's seat, and an open package of Wrigley's Doublemint gum—all commonplace items, but things Trey liked.

A ranch hand named Bobby strode out of the barn.

"Hello, Miss Prescott. Some of our new guests have arrived."

"Yes, I can see that." I looked past him in search of Trey—or whoever had brought the horses.

Bobby led the last horse out of the trailer, leaving me to walk alone into the barn. Cool air washed over my flushed cheeks, and I blinked a few times to adjust to the dim interior. Trey was nowhere in sight. Maybe he hadn't driven the horses after all. Maybe he was still in Texas— with Kathy.

My heart slowed to a crawl.

But in the next breath, I spotted him twenty feet away, striding toward me with a grin on his face and a glint in his dark eyes. He'd stunned me, and he knew it. I didn't like surprises, but Trey took pride in pulling them off. We stopped short of hugging, but only because of Bobby tending to the horses.

Trey extended his hand. I reached out to him with both of mine and we shook, clinging to each other far longer than was businesslike, or even just friendly.

"Come to dinner tonight," I said, still holding tight. "We have a lot to catch up on."

"Yes, we do."

Stepping closer, I lowered my voice so Bobby couldn't possibly hear my next question. "The divorce. Is it final?"

"Not yet. But I couldn't wait to see you."

So he was still a married man. My conscience squeaked a warning, but I didn't let go of him. "I'm still glad you're here."

"Me too."

Our fingers squeezed even tighter, then we released each other in the same deep breath. Rumors would fly if we weren't careful, so I raised my voice enough for Bobby to hear. "I'll ask Graciela to make sure the bunkhouse is ready for you."

141

Trey made a joke about needing to wash off horses and highway, and we parted with casual waves.

That night, after a wonderful meal thanks to Graciela, we ended up alone on the deck. Instead of being seated and wrapped in blankets like the first time, we stood on the side of the house facing the barn to the northwest. The sun sets late in June, and I remarked about the orange and lavender rays of light.

"Let's take a walk." Trey looped his arm around my waist. "I want to check the horses. It was a long ride for them."

"For you, too."

He turned his head just enough so I could see his eyes. "It was worth every minute to see you again."

Every female circuit in my body lit up, burned hot, and stayed that way. We needed to have a serious conversation about the divorce, but I couldn't bring myself to quench the relaxed mood. Encouraging him, I faked a pout. "Aren't you a smooth talker!"

"You bet." He looked at me again, this time face-to-face. "The past month has been pretty grim. I don't know what I would have done without those phone calls, Joanie."

It was the first time he used the nickname, and I tucked it close to my heart. "I'm glad I could help."

"You did more than that, darlin'. You're my best friend."

Friend. Ha! There was nothing platonic about that tone, or the warmth of his arm around my waist. He pulled me to his side, and we walked that way to the barn, our steps even and perfectly matched as we veered toward the setting sun. The low angle cast the longest shadows of the day, and I knew if I looked over my shoulder, we'd be twenty feet tall.

When we reached the barn, he released me, opened

the door, and turned on the light. The four horses were bedded down in their stalls, no worse for wear after the long trip. Trey told me their stories, and we both took pride in what we were doing for these fine animals.

I was proud of him—proud of us. Maybe that's why I leaned in and kissed his cheek. The instant my lips grazed his skin, he turned. His eyes met mine, a wind stirred through our bodies, and the line we'd drawn blurred in the sands of desire. Trey brought his mouth to mine and we kissed so tenderly that tears pressed behind my eyes.

He needed this comfort, this assurance that he wasn't evil or bad for the divorce, and I needed it, too. But the kiss shifted from tender to hungry, from giving to taking, from asking to telling. I wanted more of him. He wanted more of me. He was staying in the bunkhouse; only this time he was the only person there. No one would see if I followed him inside. Even if someone did, at that moment I didn't care.

My ranch. My rules. Right?

But sleeping together so soon . . . Was I really considering it? I wasn't a virgin, but I didn't take sex casually. I met my first boyfriend as a senior in college. It had been the first time for both of us. My second relationship was with a man in grad school whom I loved but not enough to follow to Chicago.

This was different from either of those experiences. My feelings were deeper, sharp enough to cut, and far more complex because of Kathy and the divorce, but also because of the desire howling through me, and the belief that I was a strong, independent woman, in charge of my own body, and responsible only to myself.

Trey deepened the kiss and so did I. At that moment, I expected him to suggest we go to his room in the bunkhouse. Instead he pulled back. "Go home, Joan."

Joan. Not Joanie. I froze, my pulse pounding and my

body feverish. "I don't want to leave."

"I don't want you to, but this is too soon. The divorce—"

"I know, Trey. I know. It's not final on paper, but it's final in your heart, right?"

"Yes. The marriage is over."

"Then why—"

"Because I don't want *this* to be our first time. I don't want to feel like there's someone else in the room—or even in our lives. It's going to be good between us, darlin'. I feel it. But I don't want just *good.* I want the best."

"Oh, Trey—"

"Go on," he said, his voice gentle now. "You're testing my resolve."

"You're testing mine, too!" I huffed the words and took a step back, far more annoyed than relieved, but also impressed by his integrity. "All right. I'm leaving."

He nodded once, and I walked out the barn door, my back to him as I sauntered toward the house. Would he follow me? What would he do if I veered to the bunkhouse instead?

"Hey, Joanie!" His voice came from forty feet away. I turned and saw him standing below the light fixture mounted above the barn door. "Get used to being tested, darlin'. Because I hope we're testing each other for a long time to come."

Instead of replying, I walked away in the dark, aware of him watching until he called out again that I should blink the porch light to signal I was safely home. Turning, I told him I would. When I reached the house, I blinked the light as I'd promised, then went up to bed alone. Or maybe not alone. Trey was in my every thought.

Chapter 14

*W*hen it came to dates, Daisy used to keep a mental scorecard: Good, Bad, and Never Again. Sitting next to Rafe, their shoulders touching in the eight-passenger rubber raft owned by River Run Adventures, she added a new category: Best Ever!

The boat was docking now, the final moment of an adventure that started six hours ago with a van ride upriver. Along with six other passengers, she and Rafe had donned life jackets and helmets, settled into the raft, and floated into the gentle heart of the Refuge River. The scenery and an occasional glide over Class I rapids had thrilled her.

The only thing missing was that first kiss. She was sure it was coming for one simple reason. If Rafe didn't kiss her, she'd kiss him.

The workers on the dock tied off the boat, and the captain stepped onto the wooden deck. Turning, he helped out the first of three women in their sixties, life-long friends on a bucket-list trip for the one fighting cancer. A couple celebrating their twenty-fifth wedding anniversary went next, followed by a widower traveling cross-country alone in his RV, visiting his kids and grandkids as he went.

The captain extended his hand to Daisy, and she took it. Rafe climbed out on his own, and they both shed their helmets and orange life vests. Daisy paused to finger-comb her hair, then turned to Rafe.

He hooked his arm around her waist and guided her toward the parking lot. "Are you hungry?"

"Starved, actually."

"Good. So am I." He grinned. "Jesse suggested Dairy Queen, but—"

"Excellent!"

Rafe threw back his head and groaned. "I *hate* it when my brother's right. I was going to suggest Cowboy's Cantina, but if you want a Blizzard—"

"I do." Daisy shoulder-bumped him. "This day has been perfect. I can't think of a better way to top it off than with ice cream."

"I can."

"Oh, yeah?"

"Yeah."

In unison they turned to each other, that first kiss shining in their eyes. She smelled earth and river, the scented sunscreen they used, the warm cotton of his black t-shirt. The start of a five-o'clock shadow darkened his jaw, and the breeze tugged at his hair, still mussed from the helmet.

He lowered his head an inch, then waited. Daisy lifted her chin, her pulse racing and—

"Hey, you two! Have a wonderful life!"

Daisy jerked back. The bucket-list lady and her friends were waving from inside a red convertible Mini Cooper.

Rafe shook his head, then raised his arm in a casual salute. "Thank you, ladies. Enjoy the rest of your trip."

Daisy added a big wave of her own. Life was precious. She knew it, and so did the woman with the short-short hair. Chemo had a way of putting life in perspective, both the beauty and the suffering. But the woman's prognosis was good, and that eased Daisy's heart as the Mini Cooper sped off with Bruce Springsteen blasting from the car speakers.

Rafe looped his arm around her waist. "Nice woman. I hope she does okay."

"Me too."

"Come on." He tucked her against his side. Arm in arm, his ribs warming hers, he guided her to his car. "Let's get that ice cream."

Rafe polished off his double cheeseburger, dragged the last French fry through the ketchup, and drained his Coke. The day had been perfect from start to finish, and he gave himself a ten on the first-date meter. No points off for the interrupted kiss. The delay only ramped up the anticipation. And no points off for Dairy Queen, because Daisy was devouring her Oreo Cookie Blizzard.

Whatever she did, she did it with her whole heart. Today on the river, when a golden eagle soared overhead, she had gasped and pressed her hand to her heart. *"God made this! Isn't it amazing?"* Rafe thought so too. The God part wasn't big on his radar, but he appreciated Daisy's sense of wonder and even envied it. She had gasped again during the run through a stretch of Class I rapids, tiny things by river standards but enough to make her cling to his arm.

They were finished eating except for the Blizzard, so he put their trash on the tray and set it near the edge of the table. Daisy dug her spoon into the soft ice cream, sighed contentedly before taking the bite, and gave him a thoughtful look. "You know what's sad?"

He expected her to mention the woman battling cancer or the widower traveling alone in his RV. "What?"

"Chelsea."

Sad wasn't the word that came to Rafe's mind. *Chatterbox* was more like it, along with *annoying, run for cover,* and Jesse's promise to punch him in the face. He knew better than to share that joke—it was admittedly rude—so he merely nodded.

A smile as sweet as the ice cream sparkled in her eyes as she took a bite. "What aren't you saying?"

Wow. She could read him already. Between her sense of humor and insight into people, she kept him on his toes. He loved bantering with her, but a warning bell clanged in his head. Criticizing her best friend was *not* the way to go. But he also wanted to be honest.

He draped his arm over the back of the booth and shrugged. "She and Jesse didn't exactly hit it off."

Daisy nodded in agreement, then scraped up another bite. "They bombed. What I don't understand is why Jesse was so quiet. He hardly said a word all afternoon."

Rafe snorted just as she took the bite—a dumb thing to do, but it just slipped out.

Swallowing fast, she set the cup down with the empty spoon. The look in her eyes no longer held a twinkle. "What did *that* mean?"

He didn't want their first date to go sideways, but Jesse deserved a defense. "Chelsea's nice, but she was trying awfully hard."

"I know she talks a lot, but Jesse didn't make it easy."

"You know how private he is."

"Yes, I do. But he's not shy. He talks easily to people at church, and he's great with his clients. For some reason, he didn't help Chelsea at all. She was just trying to make conversation."

"You have to admit—she talked a lot. It sounded like a sales pitch."

"A sales pitch!"

"Something like that."

"Well, it wasn't." Daisy nudged the ice cream cup to the side. "She's outgoing. What's wrong with that?"

"Nothing. I'm more than okay with a woman letting a man know she's interested, even making the first move. But no one—male or female—likes being chased down like a rabbit. Dating should be like a dance—not a hunt."

Daisy's expression shifted with her thoughts. "*A dance* is a wonderful description, but to say Chelsea is *on a hunt* is an overstatement. I admit she's a talker. But if men were a little less . . . I don't know." She shook her head. "Let's just drop it."

"No. If you have something to say, I want to hear it."

"Fine. I'll say it. A lot of men don't want to commit. Half of them are still little boys, and the other half are users—"

"Whoa!" He arched back, his fingers on the edge of the Formica table. "That's not fair."

"Okay, maybe not *all* men. But—"

"It's *not* fair," he repeated. "Jesse's not immature. He's one of the most *adult* adults I know. So is my best friend on the force. D'Andre Scott took me under his wing my rookie year and is one of the best cops I know. He doesn't date because he has an ex-wife, two kids, and child support that devours his paycheck—not to mention weekend custody of the kids, who both play sports. He's not commitment-phobic. He's *over*-committed."

"He sounds like a good man," Daisy admitted. "So is Jesse. But my experience is different. There are a lot of men who refuse to commit. It's selfish."

"Is it?" Rafe's foot started to tap. "I'm not defending deadbeats here. But women come with as much baggage as D'Andre."

"Yes, but—" She shook her head.

Rafe refused to back down. "But what?"

"I just think dating is harder for women. For one thing, we're physically more vulnerable."

"I can't argue with that."

"Emotionally, I can't say we feel more than men, but I *do* think women have a built-in desire to connect, while men are more focused on external things, like their careers."

Rafe thought of his lonely marble rolling around that box. "I don't know, but careers put food on the table. They matter."

"Yes, they do. Now that I have one—or at least a job—I understand that better."

"But you don't have a family to feed." Irritation leaked into his voice. "D'Andre really struggles to do it all—pay the bills, get to his kids' football games, keep the cars running. And that's just the start—"

"I know," Daisy said quickly. "I'm sorry for what I said earlier. Jesse and your friend are good men." She let her eyes twinkle again. "So are you."

Rafe appreciated the compliment, but his blood was too hot to cool quickly. "It's just that I know what it's like to struggle. I've worked with some great men—*and* some not-so-great men. My own dad was in the not-so-great category."

Daisy's foot came to rest against his under the table.

"My mom and dad split when I was little. Shane and I are half-siblings. Same mom. It's a long story. I'll tell you some other time."

He wanted to hear it now, but before he could respond, the baby in the booth behind them wailed in his ear. Daisy didn't try to talk over the noise. He liked that about her—the way she went with the flow and didn't overreact. The baby's wailing stopped, and he relaxed into a smile.

Daisy waggled her brows at him, signaling a lighter mood. "How about a change of subject?"

"Sure."

"Did you date a lot in Cincinnati?"

He liked the new subject just fine—quite a bit, in fact. "Define *a lot.*"

"Once a week?"

"It's more like once a month, but you know how it is." He lifted his shoulder in an offhand shrug. "You meet someone new. It's exciting for a while, but the interest fades."

"Any serious girlfriends?"

"Other than Kara—just one. She ended it, but I was on the brink of doing the same thing." He didn't mind the quiz from Daisy at all. It was part of getting to know each other. Before he could call for fair play with questions for her, she asked another one.

"How about online?"

He shook his head. "I tried it a few times but didn't like it. What about you?"

"I never had the courage, but Chelsea likes it a lot. She's back on FriendsFirst."

Chatterbox Chelsea gave Rafe a headache; Chatterbox Chelsea meeting up with strangers for coffee, let alone drinks, put a knot in his belly. His brows pulled together with worry. "I hope she's careful."

"That's the first thing I said when she asked me what

I thought. It scares me, but she won't go anywhere without telling me."

"Crud."

"What?"

"I just don't like it." *It* being Daisy chained to Chelsea. "It's the cop in me. People are crazy."

Daisy heaved a shuddering sigh. "Tell me about it."

"Your ex?"

"Yes. It's an awful story."

"Oh, man." Rafe's whole body tightened, ready for a fight. "I already want to slug the guy."

"He's in jail, so don't worry, okay?"

It wasn't okay—and it was even less *okay* if Daisy planned to be Chelsea's wing-girl. His cop instincts went off like a Geiger counter at Chernobyl, but arguing with Daisy would serve no purpose. Her mind was made up. He nudged the tray stacked with napkins and wrappers. "Are you ready?"

"Yes."

He stood and reached for the tray. The baby wailed again. An old man with a cane hobbled past them on the way to the men's room, his face pinched as he tried to hurry. Two tables away, a teenage girl shrieked as a drink spilled into her lap. Everywhere Rafe looked, he saw vulnerability.

A sheen of sweat broke out on his neck. He ignored the ice-cold prickle, but a familiar helplessness overtook him, sucking him down and away. As he guided Daisy through the front door, someone angrily laid on a car horn.

This wasn't the mood he wanted for their first kiss, and it seemed unlikely to change as they crossed the parking lot. He opened the passenger door for her, but instead of climbing in, she turned and hugged him. Her arms tightened like ropes, and she pressed her cheek against his shoulder.

He held her tight—a life jacket if she needed one. Or maybe *she* was rescuing him. Either way, they were a perfect fit.

Daisy nestled closer, her breath warming his neck. "Thank you for today. And for worrying about Chelsea. That's sweet of you."

He breathed out a sigh. "It's hard to have a friend who takes chances."

"Like Kara . . ." Leaning back, she peered into his eyes. "Who, I believe, you said was a great kisser."

The tension drained out of him, and he relaxed enough to grin. "Did I say that?"

"Yes, you did." Her voice took on a lecturing tone. "Just so you know, men can be great kissers, too—or not."

The gauntlet had been thrown. He lowered his head, matched his mouth to hers, and kissed her for the first time—tenderly, slowly, with curiosity, and the wonder of discovery. He'd kissed a lot of women, but none of those kisses held a candle to this one. Somehow Daisy made him feel strong again, ready to kick down doors and save the day.

When they broke apart, she was flushed and out of breath. Her fingers trailed down from his neck to the front of his shirt. Palms flat on his chest, she swayed on her feet.

Rafe looked into her eyes. "So how did that rate on the kiss scale?" He was pretty sure he knew, but he asked anyway.

She tilted her head to the side. "Top Ten?"

"*What?!*"

"Okay. Top Three. Maybe Top—"

He kissed her again, just as tenderly, but with the insistence of a man who had something to prove. No way would he settle for less than rendering Daisy speechless.

If first kisses asked questions, second kisses answered them. He cared about her—and wanted to care even more.

Daisy eased back from the kiss, breathing hard. "Forget Top Three. That was Top Two, only because I think the best is yet to come."

"Same here," he murmured.

He pressed his cheek to her temple and inhaled the scent of her hair—something flowery with hints of sunshine and the day spent on the river. He breathed in the scent again, held it in his lungs, held on to *her*—not because of the physical attraction between them—though it was there and intense. Something even more special pulsed through him—a connection, a settling of his soul, a burst of energy that refused to be ignored.

But what came next? A second date—yes. But there were some big differences between them, and those differences mattered.

He wanted to go home to Cincinnati; Daisy loved Refuge and her family.

She lived her Christian faith—something he'd seen in action today, both with her care of the boat passengers and how she credited God for the beautiful landscape. Rafe's faith was weak at best, even damaged.

What did her faith mean for physical intimacy? He knew Christians who were waiting for marriage, and others who weren't. He'd respect Daisy's boundaries, of course. He was a physical guy, but he wasn't a beast.

Those questions needed answers, but for now he was content to steal another kiss and be the good man she deserved.

Chapter 15

$\mathscr{A}$fter church on Sunday morning, Daisy followed Shane and MJ up the stairs to his garage apartment to sort through the household items they were giving to her for her new apartment. When they finished selecting furniture, Daisy needed to buy just a twin bed that would fit in the tiny second bedroom of their new apartment. Chelsea and Hannah would share the master when they moved on June 1.

Daisy could hardly believe her good fortune—or her family's generosity. Shane and MJ had a million things to do before the wedding, yet they were giving up their afternoon to help her. For the tenth time that day, her evil twin shouted in her ear.

You don't deserve any of this. You're nothing but a charity case. You're—

Shut up! Daisy silently fought the lies, but when she turned to MJ, old words popped out of her mouth. "I'm so sorry for the timing of the move. With the wedding, you both have a million things to do—"

"Hey." Shane side-armed a throw pillow at her. "Stop apologizing."

Daisy caught the pillow and flung it back. "I'll stop apologizing if you stop worrying about me."

He snagged her bad throw with one hand. "No chance of that. For one thing, I'm your brother. It's my job to look out for you. For another, I love you."

Take that, evil twin! Daisy relaxed enough to smile. "I love you, too."

MJ chimed in from the kitchenette. "Don't think twice about the timing. You're helping *us* by taking this stuff off our hands." She held up a white Corelle dinner plate. "Can you use these? It's a set of four."

"Definitely."

"How about this?" She held up a set of plastic measuring cups. "I don't think Shane ever used them."

"Not even once." He grinned at his fiancée. "You do the cooking and I'll clean up. How does that sound?"

"Like teamwork." MJ blew him a kiss, and they shared one of those special looks that made them a couple.

Envy shot through Daisy, but contentment blossomed in its wake. She belonged here—in Refuge and with her family. She also loved her work and prayed for Maggie's House to be the recipient of the giveaway—and for herself to be chosen as director. Talk about a leap of faith! Who was she to take on such a big responsibility? She was a nobody. But Lyn said God chose *nobodies* to be *somebodies* to share his love with *everybodies*. Daisy could hardly wait for Lyn's visit, and until then she spent every spare moment working on ideas of her own for Maggie's Rescue Ranch.

A jingle from her phone signaled a text from Chelsea checking in after a FriendsFirst date. Daisy read it quickly to herself.

"How did it go?" MJ knew about the date.

Daisy read the text out loud. "'Awesome good time'— with three exclamation points. 'Headed home.'"

"Was this with Chad?" MJ's face lit up. "The outdoorsy guy? Maybe he can be Chelsea's plus-one for the wedding."

"You're obsessed!"

"Just a little," MJ admitted.

Shane gave his wife-to-be a sizzling grin. "So am I."

Daisy had never seen two people more in love—or two people who had met more randomly, though she believed it was God, not coincidence, that brought her brother and MJ together in a laundromat on I-15. She supposed God could use anything to bring two people together, even FriendsFirst.

A question sparked in her mind. "Before you two met, did either of you date online?"

MJ's smile dimmed. "No. Never."

Too late, Daisy remembered that dating had been difficult for MJ. She battled HPV, short for human papillomavirus, the dangerous strain that caused cervical cancer. The fight for her fertility wasn't over, but her most recent pap test was clear.

Sisters shared that sort of thing. Brothers, not so much. But Daisy still wanted Shane's opinion. "What about you?"

"Never." He made a face like a toddler tasting spinach. "To be honest, I thought it was kind of sleazy. You know how I was before MJ."

"You mean obnoxious?" Daisy grinned. "Mr. Goody-Two-Shoes who never made a mistake?"

"Yeah, that guy." Shane rubbed the back of his neck.

"He's gone, but I still don't like online dating. It doesn't have to be sleazy, but an app turns a person into a head-shot and a blurb."

"Maybe," Daisy replied. "But it's also a place to start. You were a famous professional athlete. I doubt you had trouble meeting women."

"None." He propped his hands on his hips, his good looks and confidence on full display. "Being an athlete made dating easy—too easy. I didn't like being chased."

Chased . . . Rafe had used the same word at Dairy Queen. Hearing it twice made Daisy wonder more about what men wanted—and needed. "Maybe the Mars-Venus difference is more real than I thought."

"Oh, it's real." His voice took on an edge. "Men test each other. We naturally compete. Do you know the Bible verse about 'iron sharpening iron'?"

Daisy shook her head. "Not really."

"It's in Proverbs, and it's spot-on. Competition helps a man build muscle and that's good. But women—well, you're different. More caring than competitive, I guess."

MJ and Daisy traded a glance. Daisy loved this kind of talk and wanted to hear more from Shane, even if she didn't fully agree with him. "Women can be competitive, too."

"Of course." He held up his hands, surrendering. "I'm an athlete. I understand that kind of drive."

"Then what did you mean?" MJ asked. "About women being more caring?"

Shane looked into his fiancée's eyes, his own bright with love for her, then he glanced at Daisy to include her. "You ladies might not realize it, but when a woman looks at a man a certain way—when she believes in him—he feels it in here." Shane thumped his chest. "It makes us think that maybe we can climb that mountain after all."

"You do that for me," MJ told him. "But I agree with

you. Men and women are different. God made us that way, and I'm glad he did."

"So am I." Shane held her gaze with an intensity all their own. "We're good together, aren't we?"

"The best." MJ's voice softened to a quaver. She and Shane had both endured trials, come out stronger, and fought hard for each other. They weren't expecting life to be easy, but they knew it would be good.

So did Daisy, but a lump pushed its way into her throat. She couldn't help but think of Rafe and their first kiss. As badly as she needed to be strong and independent, she was also a woman with a big heart, a lot to give, and dreams of sharing her life with someone special. Someone who shared her faith; someone who loved Refuge as much as she did—not a man going back to Cincinnati.

Would Rafe change his mind and stay? *Stop it!* She was talking to herself, not her evil twin. *No future-tripping allowed!* But she couldn't help but soak in Rafe's kindness, his humor, the haunted look that sometimes popped into his eyes—a look she understood well because of her own scars.

Unable to hold in feelings too big to be named, she resorted to blustering at Shane and MJ. "Hey, guys. We have work to do."

Shane swept his arm to indicate the whole apartment. "This place is yours anytime you want it. When Chelsea leaves, you'll be stuck with the full rent. It's a lot."

With Miss Joan's permission, Daisy had told Shane and MJ about the giveaway. But she hadn't mentioned the Maggie's House proposal. She wanted Lyn's visit to be a surprise, but she also wanted to put her brother at ease. "If things go the way I hope, rent won't be a problem. Miss Joan promised to put in a good word for me with whatever charity wins."

MJ raised her eyebrows. "That would be a relief,

wouldn't it?"

Like Daisy, MJ knew the value of a career. In Los Angeles, she had worked retail and barely scraped by. With Shane's income, she could be a stay-at-home mom if she wanted, but she had a heart for women's health issues and planned to enroll in a community college nursing program.

Footsteps tapped up the stairs. A moment later, Chelsea knocked on the screen door. "Hi, there!"

MJ waved her into the apartment. "Come on in. We want to hear about the date."

Shane groaned. "Why don't the three of you head back to the house? I'll finish up here."

MJ gave him a quick kiss, and the women headed down the stairs with Chelsea in the lead, already gushing about Chad, his great sense of humor, and how they planned to have dinner on Tuesday—but only if someone could watch Hannah.

"I'd be glad to watch her," Daisy replied.

"Thanks, Daize. You're the best." Chelsea blew a kiss to Hannah on the other side of the yard. The little girl waved back but didn't come running. She was having too much fun with Cody and the neighbor kids.

Daisy couldn't help but wonder about the future. "Did you tell Chad that you're leaving in the fall?"

"I mentioned the possibility, but who knows? I like it here. Maybe I'll stay."

Now that she had a family, Daisy couldn't imagine living anywhere else. But if Chelsea could change her mind about staying in Refuge, so could Rafe. The thought pleased her far more than was wise, but she secretly hoped that someday soon he'd have a conversation like this one with Jesse.

Chapter 16

"Thanks again, Doc," Rafe said to Dr. Susan at the end of the FaceTime session on Tuesday morning.

With her wavy white hair and red-framed glasses, the psychologist looked more like a grandmother than a battle-hardened army nurse. She smiled at him from the iPad screen. "You're doing the hard part, Rafe. Are you still planning to return to work on August 1?"

"Yes." Daisy's face flashed through his mind. "Yes . . . I am."

"You sound hesitant."

"About getting back to work? No."

Dr. Susan paused for several seconds, giving him time to reply. He liked that about her. She never rushed him or told him what he should think or feel. She simply listened, considered, and shared her knowledge. He'd been night-mare-free for four days now, but he'd lost sleep over Daisy and his feelings for her. If Dr. Susan had advice, he wanted to hear it.

A crooked smile lifted his lips. "You're sharp, Doc. I met someone. It's good—except she's hardwired into Refuge and I'm hardwired into Cincy."

"I won't blow sunshine here." Dr. Susan never did. "Balancing her needs and yours could be a challenge. My only advice is to give it time and, if you're so inclined, to pray about it."

Rafe saw an opportunity and took it. "That's another thing. She's a strong Christian. That's my background, but I'm not sure what I think about God."

"You'll need to figure that out." Dr. Susan paused for a sip of water. "The geography problem is just that—geography. Your religious beliefs are foundational."

"Yeah. I figured. My brother's a Christian. Living with him has been . . . interesting." He'd already told Dr. Susan about Jesse's recovery from addiction. "As much as I hate to admit it, he has it together these days—not that I'm competitive or anything."

Rafe grinned at his joke and so did Dr. Susan. At this point, she knew him well. They confirmed next week's appointment, said good-bye, and ended the call. Rafe snagged his key fob and strode out the door.

With a little luck, he could steal a minute with Daisy before he showed up at Heritage House. She was probably at her desk right now, and he didn't think Miss Joan would mind if he stopped by. The older woman occasionally chatted with him at the worksite and seemed to like him.

The Camaro ate up the asphalt until Rafe turned down the long driveway to the ranch. An approaching sedan caught his eye and he slowed. Through the tinted windshield he made out Daisy in the driver's seat, with Miss Joan riding shotgun. So no joy on that quick hello. Instead he beeped the horn and waved. Daisy honked back and sped by.

It was just as well. Rafe needed to get to work, though Ben knew he'd be late and why. As for the rest of the crew, they didn't know the reason and didn't need to know. Rafe routinely joined them for breakfast because Ben and Jesse insisted on it, but no one bantered with him, not even Drake, the guy Rafe had rescued from shoveling manure.

Expecting the usual cold shoulders, he climbed out of his car, strapped on his tool belt, and walked toward the wooden skeleton of the two-story building. When he didn't spot Ben, he stepped onto the subflooring and headed toward a roughed-out staircase. Ben was probably on the second floor.

A snort caught Rafe's ear. "You're late, Donovan. Glad you could *finally* make it."

Rafe looked over his shoulder and saw Howie, the Willie Nelson lookalike, lined up with Drake in front of two-by-fours laid out on the floor to make an interior wall.

Rafe answered with a shrug. "I cleared it with Ben."

One side of Howie's mouth hooked into a sneer. The scarred side stayed flat, maybe from nerve damage. "Must be nice."

"What?"

"Being the boss's *baby* brother. Coming in late because you need your beauty rest."

Drake glowered at Howie. "Shut up, you idiot."

"Why should I?" Howie hooked his thumbs on a sagging tool belt as leathery as his face. "I got dragged in an hour early because we're two days behind, and Munchkin here slept in."

"Munchkin?" Rafe broke out in a chuckle, knowing full

well it would annoy Howie even more. "That's a new one."

"If the *little* shoe fits, wear it."

Rafe aimed a finger at his work boot. "Size thirteen. There's nothing small about my feet—or anything else."

Howie lunged at him. Rafe had been expecting it, so he sidestepped. The man spun to face him, worked up a mouthful of spit, and let it fly. The glob landed on the toe of Rafe's boot.

His temper flared, but Howie's insults were nothing compared to the hostility he dealt with as a cop. Slinging insults would only make him sound like a brat, but he couldn't let Howie have the last word or he'd be called Munchkin for weeks. There was only one thing to do, and that was lower his shields like Captain Kirk in the *Star Trek* movie he'd watched last night.

Rafe stared at the spit to be sure Howie knew he saw it, then he relaxed his shoulders and shrugged. "I see a shrink. We're working through a mild case of PTSD." Rafe added *mild* out of respect for men and women far more troubled than himself, not out of shame.

Howie's bushy eyebrows collided, then his jaw dropped and he snorted. Finally he laughed without a hint of meanness. "Yeah?"

"Yeah."

"So are you a vet?"

"No. This is personal, but it's affecting my job. I don't talk about it."

"Fine by me." Howie smirked, but the crooked smile seemed more relaxed. "So what do you know? SuperCop has problems like the rest of us."

For a nickname, *SuperCop* beat *Munchkin* by a mile.

Drake stood taller behind Howie, nodded to Rafe, then scowled at them both. "Would you two quit yakking? I have plans tonight, and they don't include hammering nails with you two idiots."

Howie laughed, then shot an insult back at Drake. Grinning, Rafe climbed the stairs and found Ben, who sent him to work alone on the back staircase.

Two hours later, Ben called the lunch break. Drake and Howie walked over to Rafe.

"Come on, SuperCop," Howie called out. "Take a break. You're making us look bad."

Rafe hid a grin. He'd been planning to skip lunch because of his late arrival. "Yeah?"

"Yeah." Drake waved him over. "Hurry up."

Rafe set down the hammer, walked with the two men to the picnic table, and sat. For the first time since lunch with Daisy, he didn't eat alone.

Late that afternoon, when Ben called it a day, Rafe was relaxed, tired, and eager to tell Daisy the Munchkin story. He went home to Jesse's house, showered, then called her. "So what's up?" he asked.

"Not a lot." Her voice sparkled over the phone. "Shane and MJ went grocery shopping. Chelsea's on date number two with Chad, and I'm watching the kids. Cody's upstairs, and Hannah and I are playing Barbies."

"Sounds like fun."

"Oh, it is! Barbie owns a big unicorn ranch." Daisy's voice took on a teasing tone, maybe a dare. "Want to come over?"

Rafe laughed. "Do I have to be Ken?"

"No, you can be Star. He's a blue unicorn with a rainbow tail."

"I'm on my way."

"Really?"

"Yes, really." He lowered his voice. "I had a good day. I want to tell you about it."

"I'd like that."

When Rafe arrived at MJ's house, Cody trotted downstairs and the Barbie-Unicorn game expanded to include Avenger action figures. Rafe took charge of Captain America, Cody chose Thor, and the game morphed into an adventure fit for a Hollywood movie.

When Shane and MJ returned with bags of groceries, the Barbie game ended. Hannah and Cody picked up the toys, and MJ offered to put the kids to bed. She was rounding them up when Chelsea walked in from her FriendsFirst date. She saw Rafe and Daisy and greeted them without a lot of chatter.

"So how was it?" Daisy asked.

"Really nice." Chelsea's voice came out low and slow. "We have a lot in common, and he loves kids. Maybe the four of us can go out sometime? I'd love for you to meet him."

Daisy glanced at Rafe, her brows arched into question marks.

"Sure." He liked the idea. If Daisy was going to play wing-girl for Chelsea, he wanted to be her copilot. "Just let me know when."

"I'll ask Chad," Chelsea replied. "Maybe next week? I have to check my work schedule, plus I need to get ready for the move."

Daisy turned to him, a twinkle in her eyes. "You're already signed up to help. What do you think? Is it too soon to recruit Chad?"

"Probably. Helping a woman move falls under the 'getting serious' category."

Daisy's eyes widened, and he realized what he'd just revealed. *He* was serious about *her.*

Chelsea broke in with a loud laugh. "In that case, it's too soon. I don't want to scare him off!"

The three of them chuckled, though Rafe didn't think

the joke was that funny. "Don't worry about it. Shane and I have it covered." Jesse had offered to help, but they didn't need him—only his truck.

Chelsea excused herself to go upstairs. Rafe needed to call it a night, but he wanted a few minutes alone with Daisy. Before he could speak, she reached for his hand and guided him toward the front door. "Let's sit on the porch. I want to hear about your day."

She opened the front door, turned off the porchlight, and they sat next to each other on the top step. He put his arm around her, and she leaned into him. They sat that way, half hugging, while he told her about the Munchkin incident and eating lunch with the crew.

"I had a good day." He tucked her tight against his side. "Topped off with tonight."

"Barbies and unicorns?" Daisy laughed. "I bet that was a first."

"It was, but don't forget Captain America. He saved the day."

A pleasant silence settled until Daisy broke it. "You're eager to go back to being a cop, aren't you?"

"Yes. I am." He debated how much to say. It was too soon to talk as if they had a future together, but the possibility intrigued him.

Daisy finally spoke. "A day at a time, right?"

"Sounds good to me." He brushed a kiss on top of her head. But what did *a day at a time* really mean? How did a marble take comfort in living a day at a time when all it did was roll around and bounce off the walls? Suddenly the night seemed darker, lonelier, empty except for Daisy warm against his side. His foot tapped in a slow, frustrated cadence.

She pulled away and looked at him, her face lined with concern. "What's wrong?"

"Nothing. I'm fine."

"You tensed up. I felt it."

"I'm all right."

"Did I say something wrong?" Her voice wobbled, a little like Hannah when her Barbie fled from the Avenger villains.

"No." He tucked her tight against his side. "It's not you at all. I'm just—I don't know. A little confused right now."

"About what?"

Great. He was digging an even deeper hole. "It has nothing to do with you—or us." Or maybe it did, because if there was an *us*, it affected Rafe's *I*.

Daisy looked up at him, her eyes wide and bright even in the dark. "Is there an *us*?"

"We're finding out, right?"

"Yes," she murmured. "Since there's an *us*, I need to tell you about my ex and what happened to me."

Relief flooded through him. He far preferred listening to Daisy than talking about himself. "I want to hear it—everything—or at least what you want to tell me."

"Let's go with everything. When I'm finished, you might think I'm nuts and go running back to Cincinnati."

He doubted it but played along. "Oh yeah?"

"Yeah."

"Is it crazier than Barbie having a unicorn farm?"

"I'll let you decide." She scooted a few inches away, pressed her knees together, and laced her hands in her lap. "My ex beat me up pretty badly, but that's not the end of the story. It's not the beginning, either. The beginning goes back to something that happened when I was fourteen—in a garage with some boys."

He knew where this was going—a naïve girl desperate for love, acceptance, caring of any sort; boys full of hormones, charged up by movies and video games, confused about manhood; no adults around, no one to teach and protect. No father in the home, or a weak one who failed to model honor and respect.

As he expected, Daisy told him an ugly tale of sexual abuse, followed by her attempt to escape into booze, relationships, anything that let her hide from the pain. He asked an occasional question, but mostly he listened. By the time she told him about the brutal assault by her ex—how he had stalked her, attacked her, and left her unconscious on the sidewalk—Rafe's arm was around her shoulders, cradling her as he pressed his lips to her temple.

He murmured into her ear. "Please tell me he's in prison for life, because if he's not—"

"He's locked up for twelve years, barring parole. I'm safe here. But that's not the best part of the story—or the real ending."

"Jail works for me." The longer, the better in Rafe's opinion. "What he did to you—"

"Was evil." Daisy slipped another inch away. "But as bad as it was, I'm grateful. Not for the awfulness of it—no one likes hitting bottom or being assaulted or hurting in any way—but the hurting brought me to Lyn. She's amazing and kind—and—" Daisy laughed a little. "I'm babbling, because we're about to get to those purple unicorns."

"I'm confused."

She fluffed her short hair. "This used to be halfway down my back. But the skull fracture required emergency surgery. Afterward, in the ICU, my heart stopped. They did CPR twice, shocked me back to life, but my heart stopped again. Shane signed the DNR, and everyone thought I was gone. But then something amazing happened."

Rafe waited for more, but Daisy remained silent as a tear trickled down her cheek. "I—I can't begin to describe what I saw. What I heard. You know the stories about people who die and come back? Who see amazing things? It's true. I was a Christian before all that happened. But I came out of the hospital even more sure that Jesus is real—and he loves us."

"That's—" He shook his head. Purple unicorns were easy to handle. No one really believed in them. But God? That was different. "I don't know what to say."

"I know people explain those experiences as chemicals released by the brain under stress, but it was so real—every bit as real as sitting next to you now." She took a deep breath. "So, do you think I'm nuts?"

"Not at all." His chin lifted to the dark sky, dragging his gaze to the slice of silver moon surrounded by stars. When it came to talking about God, Rafe didn't have a lot to say. He understood the basics of Christianity thanks to his grandfather, now deceased. They had prayed together when Rafe visited his farm in central Ohio. Christmas trees, Easter baskets, and saying grace on Thanksgiving were all part of his background, but churches were mostly for weddings and funerals—particularly Kara's funeral, where phrases like *she's in a better place* or *she's home now* had eroded what little faith he possessed to a nub.

Daisy rested a hand on his knee. He didn't realize he was tapping his foot until it stilled. She waited until he looked at her, then she wrinkled her nose in a cute way that broke the tension. "You think I'm crazy, right? It's okay if you do. Sometimes *I* think I'm crazy."

He shoulder-bumped her to keep the mood light. "I don't think you're crazy at all. What you experienced was real to you."

"Yes, it was." She shoulder-bumped him back but stayed close. "You can tell me to mind my own business, but I'm curious. Are you a Christian?"

Short and sweetly honest—that was Daisy. But Rafe didn't have an easy answer. "Mostly. I believe God exists, and my mom used to read Bible stories to me. I don't go to church or anything, but living with Jesse makes me wonder."

"About what?"

He gave a faint laugh. "Pretty much everything. I guess I'm somewhere between that song by U2 about not finding what I'm looking for, and Jesse. I admire how he turned his life around."

"He's one of the good guys. So is Shane." Daisy gave a small laugh of her own. "But I have to be honest. I hated God because of how Shane preached at me. He was *so* obnoxious. I won't do that to you. I promise. But my faith defines me. I won't hide it, either."

"I don't want you to hide anything from me, Daisy. No secrets, okay?"

"No secrets," she agreed.

They sat another moment, relaxed and snuggled together. He needed to leave, but his feet refused to move. Being with Daisy calmed him. He didn't fully understand her faith, but being around her was like breathing in an exotic fragrance. There was something there, something real and detectable, yet not concrete.

Visions of purple unicorns dared him to ponder God in a new way. A good way at first, but then a shiver went through him. Believing in God had turned Jesse's life upside down—or right side up. Either way, the changes had been earthshaking. If Rafe dared to make a deeper commitment, would it shake up his life the same way? He didn't know, and the thought scared him. Sometimes it was safer, easier, not to ask questions.

Daisy stood and offered her hand. He took it and felt her lifting him up. It had been a long strange day, one full of surprises, but when she raised her face for a kiss, he knew exactly what to do.

Chapter 17

Don't long for "the good old days." This is not wise.
Ecclesiastes 7:10 (NLT)

*F*riday afternoons were often a lonely time for Joan, and this one troubled her more than most. Seated at her desk with Sadie dozing at her feet, she tried to concentrate on the next chapter of the ranch history book, but she couldn't stop thinking about the three hundred emails flooding her inbox.

News of the giveaway had gone viral, and as she'd feared, pleas for help were unrelenting. The number of them depressed her. It also made her angry, though she wasn't quite sure who to be angry with. Society in general for failing to care for the poor? Individuals for making poor choices? At God for giving human beings free will and the ability to choose badly—with her own bad choices at the top of that list?

Yet her choices—both good and bad—served a purpose. If she hadn't failed herself so profoundly, she wouldn't be a Christian today. Giving away her home wasn't an act of madness like some people thought. It was a gift of her heart in response to the ultimate gift from the ultimate Giver.

Good grief. Now she sounded like Billy Graham.

Sadie sat up and stared, her dark eyes shiny and her tongue lolling to the side of her gray muzzle. Joan rubbed the dog's big head in both hands, commiserated with her about growing old, and wished she could turn back time to when Sadie romped in the grass.

"Now I'm being maudlin," she complained to her dog. "Let's chase away this bad mood with a snack."

Sadie's ears pricked up at the word. In a blink the dog was on her feet and swishing her tail. Joan led the way into the hall and Sadie followed, her nails clicking on the hardwood floor. Those nails needed trimming, so Joan approached Daisy's office, intending to ask her to schedule a vet appointment.

"I will not go nuts! I will not go nuts!" Daisy's muttering spilled through the open door.

Worried, Joan peered into the workspace cluttered with paper, Post-it Notes, purple pens, and photographs of the ranch, both new and old, spread across the side credenza. Daisy was seated at her desk but facing the window instead of the monitor. With her back to the door and earbuds in place, she was pulling her short hair out to the side, her fingers knotted so tight they glistened white.

"I will not go nuts!" she muttered again.

"Daisy?" Joan rapped on the doorjamb. "What's wrong?"

Spinning around, Daisy shook out the earbuds.

"Sorry. I didn't hear you. I was just—just—"

"Having a moment?"

"Yes."

"I know you've been working hard on the giveaway and the book. Do we need to make some adjustments? I don't want you pulling your hair out—figuratively *or* literally."

Daisy finger-combed the blond strands back into place. "It's not the job. I love working here."

"Then what is it?"

The poor girl looked like she'd swallowed a bullfrog. "It's just—just life."

Joan had been around enough young women to know that life's complications, especially ones that caused exasperated hair-pulling, usually involved men. Thanks to Trey Cochran, she had done some exasperated hair-pulling of her own. "Does this involve Rafe Donovan, by any chance?"

"It has *everything* to do with Rafe." The last word she whispered like an endearment.

"I see."

"You do?"

"You like him. Quite a bit, it seems."

Daisy pressed both hands to her cheeks, as if she were trying to hold herself together. "We're going out to dinner tomorrow—to the Riverbend Steakhouse. It's a dress-up date. High heels. The whole bit, and I can't wait. But if playing Barbies counts as date number two, then we have to have the talk. But if it wasn't a date—and dinner is date number two—the talk can wait until date number three. But it can't wait any longer than that, because . . . well, it just can't."

Joan arched a brow. "I'm stuck on 'playing Barbies.' You mean the dolls?"

A sparkle bloomed in Daisy's eyes, making them even bluer and brighter as she practically swooned. "He came over Tuesday while I was babysitting Hannah. Cody came downstairs, and the four of us played with Barbies and Avenger action figures. We had a blast, then Rafe and I had a serious talk about life and what we believe."

"Is he a Christian?"

"I asked him that, and he said 'mostly.'" Daisy's expression turned serious. "He's not strong in this area, but he's searching like I did at first. I prayed about it, and I'm okay with getting to know him. This is a friendship first—with a little romance tossed in." A dreamy look softened her entire countenance, but then she wrinkled her nose. "So does playing with Barbies count as a date?"

"It depends."

"On what?"

"Did he kiss you good night?"

Daisy threw back her head, spun the chair once, and broke out laughing. "Did he ever! I can't even—"

"That settles it. It counts as a date." Joan gave herself a pat on the back for playing Cupid when she asked Jesse to assign Rafe to the ranch. "In fact, it sounds like a very nice date."

"Oh, it was."

"You two have a connection."

"Yes, we do." The words tumbled over themselves. "He makes me laugh, but he can be serious, too. He doesn't push me at all, but I feel brave when I'm with him. Did you know he's a police officer?"

"No, I didn't."

"It's dangerous work," Daisy said quietly. "He's from Cincinnati. He came out to see Jesse and—and to deal with some stuff from his past. There's still a lot I don't know about him, but that's okay. We're getting to know each other. He listens—really listens to me. And he's great with kids— Oh, no!"

"What is it, dear?"

175

"I just said *kids*." Daisy collapsed back in the chair and then slumped forward, as if she'd been shot in the heart. "It's too soon to even *think* that word!"

It was all Joan could do not to laugh. If there was anything more gloriously upsetting than falling in love, she didn't know what it was. Falling *out* of love was a different experience entirely, but that was a topic for another day.

Daisy groaned out loud. "That settles it. We need to have *the talk.* It's not fair to him—or to me."

"I'm not following you, dear. What talk do you need to have?"

Daisy looked her dead in the eye. "The one where we define the relationship—where I tell him that I'm waiting for marriage, if you get my drift."

"Oh, I get it."

Decades had passed since Joan felt that hormonal insanity, but the feelings were as timeless as the pull of the moon on the ocean. On the other hand, social mores had changed drastically—and not all for the better, in her opinion.

She felt a lecture coming on but stifled it. Daisy didn't need a speech from an irritable old college professor. She needed friends like the women Joan had known in grad school—women who listened to each other, supported and challenged each other. Joan and her three housemates in particular had bonded. The memory of their afternoon "toast parties" put a wistful smile on her face, and she silently celebrated that history and the chance to share some of that wisdom with Daisy.

Reaching down, she scratched the top of Sadie's big head. "Sadie and I were about to have a snack. How would you like to continue this conversation in the kitchen?"

"I'd like it a lot."

"Good." Joan pointed a finger at the computer. "Turn that thing off and join us. You're done for the day."

Before Daisy could reply, Joan left for the kitchen. She gave the dog three salmon treats, then gathered bread, butter, and jam. She placed the items on the table along with the spiffy Cuisinart toaster that looked nothing like the one at that first toast party on a stormy November afternoon back at Cornell.

Daisy stepped into the kitchen, saw the toaster on the table, and cocked her head. "We're having toast?"

"Yes. It's a tradition." Joan set down the jar of apricot jam. "It started when I was in grad school and living with my three best friends. We were too busy to cook, but we always had bread and jam on hand. We took to gathering in the kitchen in the late afternoon. Before we knew it, other friends started showing up, and they'd bring their own bread so we always had enough. Some of the best conversations of my life took place in that kitchen."

Daisy headed to the Keurig and selected hot chocolate. "Are you still in touch with your roommates?"

"We all email now and then, and Shirley calls each of us on our birthdays. Jennifer isn't well, but Linda and I are going strong. In fact, the four of us are planning a reunion cruise in the spring."

"That sounds wonderful. Where to?"

"Alaska, I think. But this conversation isn't about me." She indicated the loaves of bread on the table. "Go on. Make some toast and tell me about this conversation you need to have with Rafe."

Daisy picked the cinnamon swirl and popped a slice into the toaster. "I just wish it wasn't necessary."

"Are you sure it is?"

"Definitely."

"And why is that?" Joan knew how *she'd* answer the question. The point was to encourage Daisy.

"Rafe needs to know what to expect—and not expect—from me. And I need to draw lines to protect myself. I can

177

be impulsive—" The toast popped and startled them both. Daisy gasped, then laughed. "I'm ridiculously nervous about the whole conversation."

Joan smiled as she put a slice of sourdough in the toaster for herself. "That's normal, don't you think?"

"Yes, but it's just so . . . confusing. And scary. I'm scared he'll dump me because I won't sleep with him. And I'm scared he won't dump me, and I'll have to be strong enough to stick to what I believe. That's not easy. Sometimes I wish women still had chaperones—well, not really."

"There were pros and cons," Joan replied. "A woman's reputation was everything and had to be protected. On the other hand, why was she judged in a different light than a man?"

Daisy slathered the cinnamon toast with butter, nodding her head vigorously as she wielded the knife. "Definitely a double standard."

"We could talk all day about why that double standard existed, but we live in different times now—as we both well know. I'm proud of what the women's movement has accomplished over the decades, especially regarding property and voting rights, but I fear we solved some problems and created others."

"Like what?"

Joan looked down her nose. "You do realize I taught women's studies for thirty years? I can bore you for hours on the subject of social change, gender roles, and economic power." Forget Billy Graham. Now she sounded like Oprah Winfrey.

"Go for it." Daisy bit into her toast. "This is the closest I'll ever come to going to college. I love learning from you."

Joan's heart warmed with the praise—and with the sweetness of being needed again, especially by Daisy, who felt more like a daughter with every passing day. "You have an education, dear. It didn't result in a college degree, but you have unique and valuable experiences."

"That's true."

"You learned some very tough lessons."

Daisy chewed her toast thoughtfully. "Very tough. I made some awful choices that I can't take back. I'm responsible for those, but some of the bad stuff just happened. I worry about Chelsea. She's pretty serious about a guy she met online. He seems nice, but what if he isn't? MJ struggled with dating, too. So did my brother but in a different way. Why is it so hard?"

"Courtship has always been fraught with challenges, don't you think?"

"I guess."

"The difference now is the level of personal freedom. Thanks to reliable birth control, women have more choices than ever before and so do men. But with freedom comes responsibility—both to one's self and to others. I worry that my generation put too much emphasis on *self* and not enough on *others.* Our focus shifted from moral absolutes to moral relativity, where we each choose our own values. Am I boring you yet?"

"No!" Daisy wiped crumbs off her fingers with a paper napkin. "I know just what you mean. That's what 'defining the relationship' is all about. Different people want different things. Do you think that's bad?"

"Bad? No. But I *do* think that position fails to ask an important question. Which is . . .?"

Daisy thought a minute. "I don't know. What is it?"

"It's this: What makes human beings different from the beasts of the field? Did God create us, or did we evolve from the primordial ooze? If we're created in God's image, we have a spark of the divine. We have souls. We're obligated—even driven—to define ourselves through that knowledge of our Creator. My own spiritual seeking brought me to the foot of the cross."

"Me too." Daisy paused with the toast in hand. "Everything changed when I became a Christian."

"It did for me as well—and rather drastically." An image of Trey swaggered into Joan's mind, but she pushed him away. "Christians choose to define their relationships biblically. But other people won't agree. If human beings are merely the stew produced in Mother Nature's kitchen, it's reasonable to put our individual interests first. And that, I believe, is why 'defining the relationship' has become necessary. We live in a world with a cornucopia of beliefs. Some are compatible; others are not."

"Wow." Daisy put another slice of bread in the toaster. "That pretty much says it."

"So be brave with Rafe, dear. Stand up for what you believe. Physical attraction has a way of making people forget themselves—and the consequences."

Daisy wrinkled her nose in a searching way Joan recognized. "If I've learned one thing, it's that I'm not strong—but God is."

"Yes, he is. And he made you into the wonderful woman you are now." Emotions clogged Joan's throat—good ones that healed one of the fractures in her own heart. "He loves you, Daisy. And so do I."

"Oh, Miss Joan—I love you, too." Daisy reached across the table for Joan's hand.

Joan reached back, but they stood and hugged instead. "I'm grateful for you, dear. You've become far more than my assistant. You're the daughter I never had."

They stood that way, holding tight, until the toast popped, then they sat and finished the last two slices.

The toast party was a huge success, but amid the crumbs and smears of butter and jam, Joan was left alone with her memories of Trey. She couldn't seem to escape him these days.

Daisy's shy voice broke through the mist. "May I ask you something?"

"Yes, of course."

"Trey Cochran . . . Were you in love with him?"

"Madly. Deeply." Joan laughed. "I sound like one of those romance novels with overly muscled men on the cover and too many adjectives. But I confess, I *do* love the clean ones."

Daisy ignored the dodge. "But it ended, didn't it?"

"Yes. It did. It was my doing. It's a tale of woe for another time. I'd much rather hear about what you're wearing for this date."

Taking the cue, Daisy chatted about her favorite dress—a short blue-satin sheath with a scooped neck and a rhinestone belt. They agreed it called for her most sparkly earrings, her highest heels, and gentle pink lipstick.

Despite the distraction, Trey Cochran sauntered back into Joan's mind. Like that 1990s Celine Dion song, the one Joan used to sing alone in her car, it was all coming back to her now.

Trey and I didn't sleep together during that first visit. He stayed strong, and after that heady reunion, I, too, came to my senses. He was still married.

Still. Married.

I must have repeated it to myself a thousand times.

Still. Married.

Over the next couple of visits, those words stopped me from inviting him to the house for dinner, or being alone with him anywhere for too long. Trey flirted in that cowboy way of his, but he didn't press me to cross the line we'd drawn. Instead we drove into Refuge and ate at Cowboy's

Cantina at least three times a week. It was brand new back then, and Trey was still enough of a celebrity to have the manager put his photograph on the Cowboy Wall of Fame.

We also spent a lot of time in the barn with the horses. It was a safe place for us, and we fell into the habit of sharing Graciela's picnic lunches with the ranch hands who happened by. They all loved Trey and his stories. So did I.

Over the course of the summer, he delivered horses four times, with each visit lasting three or four days. They all ended the same way—with a long kiss, hope for the future, and his promise that the divorce would be final soon. Then he'd drive home to Texas, where he lived in an apartment while Kathy stayed on their ranch.

Separated again, we went back to late-night phone calls and talking in the dark—just his voice and mine. I think about that now and wonder what FaceTime would have revealed—if seeing his expression would have clued me in to the ambivalence beginning to brew? I don't know. Trey was a good actor. But even more to the point, I think he believed every word he told me—until those words stopped being true.

At this stage, we were mooning over each other and desperate for the divorce to be final. He complained about going to counseling, and I sympathized with him.

"I can't stand it, Joanie," he told me on a hot September night. My window was open wide, and the crickets were singing their hearts out. Trey's voice dropped to a whisper. "I miss you so much I can hardly stand it."

"I miss you, too." The words were a mere breath, but breath is what sustains life.

"Forget waiting for the next horse delivery. I'm sick of waiting, and I'm sick of the drive. I'm flying up this weekend. No hanky-panky. I want to sit with you by the river and just be us."

"I'd like that."

The crickets kept up their song, but I barely heard them now. My heart was too full of Trey. I loved him. I missed him. I was desperate to move past the divorce and grab hold of the future. Marriage. Children. I wanted it all, and I wanted it with Trey.

We said our good-byes with sweet anticipation, then hung up on the count of three like we always did. The ritual softened the good-bye, but the click of the phone in its cradle plunged me into a hateful silence. Fury pulsed through me—at our situation, at Kathy, at Trey's attorneys. Why couldn't they move faster? Why wouldn't she let him go?

But in the next breath, guilt swamped me. If she really wanted the divorce, why was it taking so long?

Was I stealing her husband?

Was I betraying everything I believed about women supporting each other as sisters? I wasn't responsible for the failure of their marriage. They had fallen apart months before Trey and I met. None of it was my fault, but I felt like an accessory to a crime.

Guilt plagued me day and night—until Trey arrived at the ranch and I saw the deep lines etched on his handsome face. He looked cadaverous, broken, shattered. Couldn't Kathy see the devastation? Why wouldn't she let him go? In that moment, I hated her.

The next day, Trey and I rode to the river. When I asked Graciela to pack a special lunch, she assumed the divorce was final, and I didn't tell her otherwise. The morning sun burned especially bright that day. I rode my favorite mare, and Trey saddled up one of the rescue horses. We checked out the new pastureland, then we rode farther—farther still—until we reached the river's edge.

The silvery water flowed past us at a languid pace. The sun warmed our faces as we ate lunch. When we finished the last of the ripe peaches dripping with juice, I took off my boots, rolled up my Wranglers, and waded into the river. Trey stayed on shore. I sensed him watching me and turned. But it wasn't me he was watching. His eyes were closed, and the look on his face was one of pure pain.

"Trey?"

He opened his eyes. "Yes, darlin'?"

"What are you thinking?"

"That I shouldn't have come up here, because resisting you is harder than I ever imagined."

I stayed in the river.

Trey stayed on the shore.

We stood that way for what seemed like an hour, maybe a lifetime. Finally I turned and stepped deeper into the water—and right into a hole in the sandy bottom. Arms flailing, I went down with a splash, skidded with the current, and went under completely.

Before my bare feet found level ground, Trey lifted me up and into his arms. I was cold, dripping wet, and trembling all over. Holding me tight, he tucked my head against his sun-warmed neck. My wet shirt dampened his dry one, and I felt him trembling as much as I was. I didn't dare move—didn't want to move. He kissed my temple, my cheek, but stopped short of kissing my lips.

Instead his breath caressed the shell of my ear as he murmured in a shaky voice. "Let's go back to the ranch before I forget myself even more than I just did."

"Wait.

"Joanie, I—"

"I love you." The words flowed out of me. Gushed really as I said them again. "I love you—"

"I love you, too." He kissed me then with a passion that tempted us both. But I knew Trey well. He needed his honor, especially in the dishonorable situation of the divorce, so I stepped back first.

We rode home in silence, each alone with our thoughts, but something in our relationship shifted during the ride. When we arrived back at the barn, Trey seemed distant, even nervous. I assumed he was resisting the desire to consummate our relationship. I respected him for it, yet every nerve in my body cried out for him.

Still. Married.

But was he really? In his heart, he was already divorced. He had assured me of that over and over. A mere piece of paper was keeping us apart, and I didn't like it.

The next day, he told me he wanted to camp alone at the river. "Just me and the stars. It's time God and I had a talk."

"Why?" Our time together seemed so precious.

"I promised myself I would."

That wasn't much of an answer, but I understood the need to face one's conscience alone.

I planned to stay away, but the next day, I received a phone call from *Time* magazine. They wanted to interview me for an article on the Equal Rights Amendment soon to be introduced in Congress. I was proud and eager to share the news, but Graciela had the day off. I could have called Shirley or Linda from my grad school days, but the person I most wanted to tell was Trey.

It was late in the day for a long ride, but I didn't care. I saddled up my horse and rode out.

Sunshine poured down from the bluest sky imaginable, and a soft breeze played music in the trees. My mood soared like an eagle in flight. It soared even higher when I reached the rise above the river and saw Trey knee-deep in the current, wearing fishing waders and a white t-shirt that clung to his shoulders and back. The same sunlight pouring into me glistened in his raven-black hair, and I thought of his Indian heritage, that roguish smile that slayed me, and his great love of the land, horses, and creatures in need.

Reining in my horse, I watched as he whipped a fly-fishing line over his head. Back and forth. Back and forth. Until it flew high and plunked into the heart of the river. I'd never seen a more beautiful man, and I haven't seen one since.

Still. Married.

But at that moment, those words struck me as irrelevant and just not true. I loved him, and I wanted to share my life with him. As bold as brass, I rode down to his campsite. He'd set up a tent, hoisted his food up so bears wouldn't get it, and set his horse to graze. That horse whickered and Trey turned. When he saw me, I knew.

I wasn't going home that night.

Chapter 18

The Riverbend Steakhouse was known for its thick steaks, loaded mashed potatoes, and the wandering path that hugged the banks of the Refuge River. Gently lit by a million tiny lights, the path twinkled and glowed as it followed the lazy current around a bend to a secluded lookout on a rocky bluff.

Daisy was smitten—both with the view and with Rafe, who had arrived at her door in a dark suit, a crisp white shirt, and a stylish tie. She'd never been on a date where the man brought her flowers. Even more charming, he had offered his arm as if she were a princess and opened every door for her. If he was trying to melt her heart, he succeeded—and that made *the talk* even more necessary.

Over dinner they shared silly quirks, political views, stories about the best days of their lives—and the worst days. They talked about music and movies, too. Rafe liked dark comedies; Daisy couldn't stand them, but they agreed on the Christmas classics, especially *Polar Express.*

By the time dessert arrived—one plate with two forks— they were content to be silent together, leaning into the candlelight, relaxed and smiling.

The meal was over now, and they were outside and alone, arm in arm at the lookout, peering into the dark night and the darker river. Daisy didn't want to have the talk now—not on this perfect night with Rafe's arm warm around her waist, chasing away every chill in her life. Surely it could wait . . . but then he kissed her gently on the lips, then gentler still behind her ear. His breath warmed her skin, and she trembled as he trailed kisses back to the soft corner of her mouth.

She kissed him back, but alarm bells clanged in her head. Grown-up Daisy, who knew how to draw lines and respect herself, needed to protect the scared, frightened child who would do anything to feel loved. She needed to take control. But God help her . . . Rafe knew how to kiss.

Mustering her rational mind, she eased out of his arms, stepped back, and dropped her hands to her sides without taking her eyes off his face. Shadows hid everything except his square jaw and the glint of the lights in his raven-dark hair.

He opened his mouth to speak, but she stopped him. "Me first. Please."

"Whatever you'd like." His voice came out low, raspy, full of all the feelings she shared but needed to hold inside.

Would he accept the line she needed to draw? Or would the night end with a cool kiss on the cheek and a promise to call, which he wouldn't keep? Or would he mock her, and— *Stop it!*

"We have to talk." Her voice came out husky, not

strong and steady like she'd intended.

He put his hands in his pockets, pulling the suit coat back as he rocked back on one leg. "Something pretty amazing is happening between us, isn't it?"

"Yes . . ." She couldn't deny it—didn't want to deny it. Could this good, steady man really have feelings for her? Could those feelings keep him in Refuge? Tears threatened to flood into her eyes.

Stepping out of the shadows, he offered his hand. "Let's see where it goes."

She longed to cry out, *Yes! Let's find out!* But first she needed to set clear boundaries to protect herself. Trembling inside, she channeled her inner Miss Joan. "I like you a lot, Rafe. I care—but I need to make something clear. I take sex seriously now—"

His eyebrows lifted.

"If you're hoping I'll hop into bed with you, the answer is a big, fat no. I'm waiting for marriage."

He stared at her, his jaw hanging open. She couldn't read his expression at all. *So this is it. It's over. No sweet summer romance.* Humiliation burned through her. She fought it by crossing her arms to look tougher than she felt. For good measure, she squeezed out the strongest glare she could manage.

He raised his arms over his head like a suspect under arrest, but his mouth curved with the hint of a smile. "Guilty as charged when it comes to finding you attractive. You're beautiful, Daisy. But anything physical is your decision. I respect you—as a person and as a woman."

"You do?"

"Yes. I do." He lowered his arms, slowly, then shoved his hands in his pockets. "Just to be clear, seducing you wasn't part of the plan tonight."

A hint of anger hardened his words, and she wondered

if she had insulted him. She'd been braced for anger, emotional pressure, even mockery. But Rafe wasn't Eric—not even close. She was proud of herself for speaking up but felt silly for overreacting. Embarrassed, she pressed her hands to her cheeks.

He reached her in two strides, gently clasped her biceps, and looked her in the eye. "Something good is happening here. I say we be careful with that *something*. Because, Daisy? You're worth waiting for. And I don't mean hopping into bed." He paused, then waggled his eyebrows like Flynn in *Tangled,* her very favorite Disney hero. "Though I wouldn't mind—"

His teasing erased the last of her nervousness, and she played along with her haughtiest look. "Forget it, buster!"

"Yeah, I know. All men are dogs."

"Not all men." *Not Rafe.* Her heart melted even more, and it was already so soft her chest ached. Did his words mean he might stay in Refuge? It was too soon for either of them to make that leap, but the possibility tantalized her. She had learned to trust God by taking baby steps. Were those steps leading to an even bigger leap of faith— falling in love and trusting Rafe with her heart?

He smoothed her short hair back behind her ear. "So kisses only. How does that sound?"

"Good."

He hesitated. "It's not my usual style, but you're not like any woman I've ever dated."

"You're not like anyone I've dated, either." Confident now, she stepped safely into his arms and they kissed— long and slow, tender and wise. And so full of promise she dared to believe that he really did care for her, and maybe—just maybe—he would choose to make Refuge his new home. Her toes curled with that kiss, and they didn't stop curling for the entire weekend.

Chapter 19

On Monday morning, Rafe borrowed Jesse's truck and joined the group helping Daisy and Chelsea move to their new apartment. He didn't know Refuge well, so he'd checked crime stats online. Aside from occasional car break-ins, the complex suffered very little crime. The second-floor location of Daisy's apartment offered another layer of safety.

Even so, before he carried up a single box, he inspected the door locks. They were tarnished and scratched, a sign they hadn't been replaced. Any number of former residents could have copies of the keys.

Shane came up behind him, a box balanced on his shoulder. Like Rafe, he looked at the closed door, then jiggled the knob with his free hand. "What do you think?"

"The locks need to be changed. When we're done here,

I'll head to the hardware store for new ones." He didn't know what Daisy's lease allowed regarding lock changes, but she'd be covered as long as she gave the new key to the manager.

"Go for it." Shane clapped him on the shoulder, a sign of trust and respect, and they went back to work.

The day couldn't have been better. Rafe even enjoyed getting to know Chelsea. When she didn't try so hard, she was fun to be around. Single moms didn't have it easy. While everyone relaxed after the furniture and boxes were unloaded, Chelsea left to work the dinner shift at her server job, leaving Hannah with Daisy.

Rafe should have slept well that night, but despite changing the locks, he tossed and turned with worry for Daisy's safety. The nightmare about Kara lurked on the fringes of his mind, but the milder thoughts Dr. Susan called "squirrels in the attic" plagued him without mercy. According to the psychologist, Kara's death—particularly Rafe finding her alive and failing to save her—had rammed a hole in his subconscious. The therapist compared his mind to a house with a hole in the attic. Squirrels slipped inside and camped out. He tried not to hear them, but sometimes they went berserk, raced in circles, and generally made pests of themselves.

With Dr. Susan's help, he was patching the hole and cleaning out the attic. As much as he disliked those pesky squirrels, the infestation could have been far worse. Some people lived with monsters in the attic.

Rafe felt good about his progress and was confident he'd be ready to go back to police work. But what did that mean for a future with Daisy? He knew how much she loved being close to Shane, MJ, and Cody, and she glowed when she talked about her job, particularly her work on Miss Joan's history book.

Daisy loved Refuge as much as Rafe loved being a city

cop. Could he be happy in Refuge if he joined local enforcement? The thought left him cold inside. He could work for Jesse, but that idea left him even colder. If he wasn't a cop, what purpose did he have? *Purpose* . . . A man needed a mission—at least Rafe did.

By the time he arrived at Waffle World for breakfast with the crew, the squirrels were going full bore. Jaw tight, he headed for the back corner reserved for Donovan Construction.

Howie and Drake greeted him with a wave, and he set his phone down on the table in the middle of six others. Not checking messages was part of the breakfast ritual and a bit of a game. Anyone who picked up his phone during the meal was required to cough up five dollars. The money went into a pot called the Bad Luck Bucket, because it was used to help crew members pay for things like car trouble and root canals.

Rafe pulled out the empty chair across from Drake and Howie. A crumpled five-dollar bill already sat in the pot. "So who's the latest victim?"

Jesse, seated at the head of the table, let out a snort. "Who do you think?"

"Again?" Rafe laughed and so did the guys. Jesse tossed in more five-dollar bills than anyone, only because he owned the business and took every call and text. He could have opted out of the game but didn't. The men respected him for it, and so did Rafe.

Huge plates of food arrived and the men dug in, some quiet but others fussing about this and that. The phones chirped and vibrated several times, and everyone joked about being too broke to check them.

The meal was almost over when Rafe's phone sang out with the breezy tone he'd assigned to Daisy.

A new guy named Webber chortled at him. "Nice ringtone. Must be a woman."

Drake joined in. "I bet it's that cute blonde who works for Miss Joan. What's her name again?"

Rafe laughed. "Come on, guys. Chill."

Ben crossed his arms over his chest, but his eyes held a twinkle. "Are you going to cough up the five bucks or not?"

Rafe was already pulling out his wallet. He tossed down the money, picked up his phone, and saw a text from Daisy.

Dinner tonight with Chelsea and Chad? She wants us to meet him.

A row of cute emojis smiled up at him, but what he most liked was the "us." Rafe tapped back.

Count me in. Anytime after 6. Pick u up?

Every eye at the table stayed on him until he grinned. "Yes, it was Daisy. We're having dinner tonight."

"Woot! Woot!" Howie raised his coffee cup in an awkward toast. "Let's hear it for Romeo!"

Rafe played along, shooting back nicknames as he and Daisy finished texting plans for the night. When she sent the last kiss emoji, they were set to meet Chelsea and Chad at seven o'clock at a restaurant called the Green Light Café. Rafe set his phone back on the table. For now, the squirrels were quiet and he was grinning.

After thirty minutes in the restaurant, Rafe wasn't grinning anymore. He worked with a bunch of ex-cons who insulted each other all day long, but Chad Rodney Whittaker was the most obnoxious person Rafe had encountered in Refuge, possibly in the state of Wyoming— maybe all of America.

Chad-Rod, as he liked to be called, worked as an adventure guide and wore a man-bun. He used the word *vibe* way too much, and Rafe couldn't have cared less about his granola recipe. The guy didn't seem to be firing on all cylinders, and the way he winked at Chelsea was nauseating—even more nauseating than the vegan menu. Cincinnati chili? No joy. A plain old cheeseburger? Not a chance. Even the fries were weird—some kind of squash with a seasoning that tasted like lawn clippings.

At least the corner booth was comfortable. He and Chad were on the ends, with Daisy and Chelsea next to each other. A restaurant worker cleared their plates while Chelsea mooned over Chad-Rod and his over-the-top stories of scaling mountains and living in the wild for a month on fish and berries. Not so humbly, he announced he was preparing for *Naked and Afraid*, the survival show on the Discovery Channel.

"You must have seen it," he said to Rafe with a big grin.

Rafe shook his head, then gulped down some of the organic honey-sweetened tea that wasn't too terrible. He could have told his own stories, but he kept his mouth shut for the rest of the meal. Daisy feigned interest, but early on, she'd given Rafe a couple of secret eye-rolls.

Their server arrived and asked about dessert. To Rafe's dismay, Chelsea insisted they order some berry concoction because life was short and she wanted to savor every minute of it. Rafe declined, but Daisy went along with Chelsea and Chad, though she only ate a few bites. When their server finally returned with the check, Chad signaled for it. Rafe and Daisy protested appropriately, but not too much. Paying for the meal was a nice thing to do, and Rafe figured Chad wanted to impress Chelsea.

"Thank you," Daisy said. "This has been fun."

Not. "Yeah, thanks, man."

Chad set the black bill holder on the table and hiked

up his hip to pull out his wallet. His face wrinkled in con-fusion, then he groaned and dropped back down on the seat. "I can't believe this."

"What is it?" Chelsea's brows crashed together.

"My wallet. I forgot it. Maybe it's in the car." He started to get up, but Chelsea stopped him with a hand on his arm. "Don't worry about it. This is on me tonight."

Relief washed across the man's face. "Thanks, Chels. You're the best. I'll get it next time. I promise."

No way would Rafe let Chelsea pick up the tab. Her chatter drove him nuts, but she was a single mom and a good friend to Daisy. When she wasn't trying so hard, he even liked her. Sliding out of the booth, he half stood, snagged the bill, and sat back down. "I've got this."

Chad's eyes narrowed—out of embarrassment or re-sentment, Rafe couldn't tell. But a sheepish grin quickly overtook the glare. "Thanks, man. I owe you."

Ignoring him, Rafe slipped his Visa into the folder. The server took care of the bill, and the four of them headed to the parking lot. The women hugged good-bye, and Chelsea left with Chad in his ten-year-old Mercedes, a classy car that didn't match Mr. Man-Bun's image.

"Whew!" Daisy said when the car was out of sight. "That was quite an experience, huh?"

Rafe put his arm around her waist. "I can think of a few other words for it."

"Not the best food." She wrinkled her nose as they walked. "In fact—"

"Dairy Queen?" He tugged her tighter to his side. "I could use real food."

Daisy leaned into him. "Sure. I'm good for a Blizzard."

He helped her into the Camaro, and they drove off. He was ready to forget the meal and move on, but when they reached a red light, Daisy finally spoke. "You're awfully quiet. What did you think?"

"About the food? It was awful."

"No, silly!" She pretended to punch his arm. "About Chad. I'm Chelsea's wing-girl. I need to look out for her. This is date number three, and she likes him a lot. By the way, thanks for picking up the check. I'm sure he'll get it next time."

"Uh . . ." *Next time?* He'd prefer bread and water to vegan whatever-it-was.

Before he could formulate the right words, Daisy sighed. "First impressions can be tricky."

They could also be accurate. If he and Daisy were a couple, Rafe needed to freely speak his mind. "To be honest, I wasn't impressed. In fact, I got a bad—"

"Vibe," they said at the same time.

Daisy laughed softly. "He must have used that word a hundred times."

"At least." Rafe wanted to make light of it but couldn't. His cop instincts were too hot to ignore. "How confident are you that he's not some sort of scamster?"

"Pretty confident." She described how she and Chelsea had checked out Chad-Rod's business website and social media after the first date. "We didn't see any red flags."

"I do."

"Really?"

"Yes." Rafe debated how blunt to be. "I understand a guy forgetting his wallet. It happens, but how often does it happen on a date? A guy checks things like that before he leaves the house."

"Well, people make mistakes."

Leave it to Daisy to find an excuse. Most of the time, he admired the way she gave people the benefit of the doubt, but not when it involved her being Chelsea's wing-girl.

He turned left toward DQ. "There's more."

"Like what?"

"Those stories he told—all over-the-top."

"A lot of guys have stories. I worked as a server in LA. You wouldn't believe how many so-called movie stars I've met."

"A lot, I'm sure. We all exaggerate now and then. But I still think Chad's a potential problem. Did you notice his eyes?"

"Not really."

"Bloodshot." Rafe bit off the word. "And all those *vibes* showed mental laziness. Forgetting his wallet? Same thing. Sorry to be blunt, Daize, but Chad-Rod showed signs of being a pothead. Or maybe he was blitzed on pills."

Daisy's jaw dropped. "You don't know that!"

"I'm a cop," he reminded her. "I saw more than enough to be suspicious."

A block away, the DQ sign glowed red in the night. Behind him he saw headlights approaching too fast, then swinging into the next lane. A Corolla missing a taillight blew by the Camaro and picked up even more speed. If Rafe had been in uniform, he would have shot after the car and written a ticket, maybe arrested the driver for reckless driving or OVI—operating a vehicle impaired.

Air hissed through Daisy's nose. He stole a sideways glance just as she sagged against the bucket seat. "This is awful. If you're right about Chad, Chelsea should drop him now. But if you're wrong, that's not fair to Chelsea *or* Chad." She clutched fistfuls of her short hair, pulled hard, and groaned. "I hate this."

Chapter 20

"Hate what?" Rafe didn't understand what Daisy meant.

"Not knowing who to believe and who to trust." She let go of her hair but pulled her knees up and hugged them despite the seat belt.

The position worried him. If someone plowed into them, the airbag would deploy and she'd be hurt. He thought of asking her to sit straight, but DQ was only a block away and traffic was light.

Daisy stared out the window, gnawing her lip. "I'm not ignorant about pot and pills. I see what you mean about all those vibes. But who am I to say Chad's a loser? Maybe that's just his personality."

"Maybe.

"What about his website? It's loaded with pictures and

great reviews. The photos are candids, and he's in them. It can't *all* be made up. Plus he drives a nice car."

Rafe turned into the restaurant parking lot and took a space away from the main door. Daisy's excuses for Chad didn't fit with his cop instincts at all. "How do you know he didn't borrow the car from his mother? For all we know, he lives in someone's basement, smokes pot all day, and is in credit card debt up to his man-bun."

"You can't know that," she insisted. "What happened to 'innocent until proven guilty'?"

"Nothing," Rafe replied. "We're not talking about sending him to prison. We're talking about Chelsea and her safety. You can't be too careful."

"I *know* that." She finger-combed her hair back into place, a reminder of the head injury she'd survived. "But at some point, we have to live. That's what Chelsea is trying to do. I don't think Chad is that bad."

"Maybe not. But—" Rafe clenched his jaw. "Look, I don't want to argue about it. I just don't trust the guy."

"I don't like him, either. But Chelsea does, and she's my friend. For her sake, I'm willing to give him the benefit of the doubt."

"Sorry, Daize. I just can't."

She pulled back, her spine rigid. "Isn't that a little cynical?"

"It'd say it's realistic."

She glared at him even harder, saying nothing, as if she didn't know him at all.

The sudden distance between them stung. Did Daisy understand the cop part of his personality? His gut burned with the need to protect and defend, an instinct that required taking charge, being ready to fight, and even die. If they fell in love, those questions mattered as much as whether or not he returned to Cincinnati, maybe even more.

It was too soon to go down that road—or the 1,600-mile road between Wyoming and Ohio. He reached across the car to give her shoulder a squeeze. "Let's get some real food."

She stared at him, unsmiling and her brow slightly furrowed. "It's late, and I'm not really hungry. Would you mind getting something to go instead?"

"No problem." He put the Camaro in gear, circled to the drive-thru, and ordered his standard burger and fries.

Five minutes later, they were headed to Daisy's apartment with the aroma of hot food filling the car. He reached over the console and gave her shoulder another squeeze. "It's true that I don't like Chad, but Chelsea's your friend and you're trying to help her."

"I am."

"It's just that I worry."

Daisy blew out a slow breath. "It's okay to worry. I worry about Chelsea, too. But I don't have the right to judge anyone—even someone as annoying as Chad."

At least they agreed on *annoying.* "I'm not judging him. I'm looking at the evidence, and what I see is suspicious."

"Maybe," Daisy admitted. "I know how desperate Chelsea is, but she knows the risks. We've talked about it. She's careful."

He opened his mouth to say posers and predators were expert manipulators, but Daisy knew that even better than he did. They both needed to regroup, so he set the radio to a calming Pandora station and drove the last mile to her apartment in silence.

Daisy chewed her lip, then indicated the front of the building rather than the back lot where he usually parked. "I don't want your food to get cold. It's okay to drop me off here."

Was she blowing him off? Or did she really care about

his French fries getting cold? He parked where she indicated, but no way would he let her walk through the complex alone if she didn't have to. The building was well lit and secured with a locked wrought-iron gate, but a person couldn't be too careful, in Rafe's opinion.

Daisy picked up her purse and turned to him. The light from the building entrance lit up her blond hair but silhouetted her face, hiding her emotions, though she seemed relaxed. "Thanks again for tonight, especially picking up the check."

"I was glad to do it. Chelsea works hard and she's your friend."

"*And* roommate," Daisy added, her tone serious. "I'm the only person she has right now. We look out for each other."

"That's good." He meant it, though he suspected Daisy did a lot more *looking out* than Chelsea did.

She reached for his hand, her fingers warm against his cooler ones as she squeezed. Shoulders relaxed, she swayed slightly forward. No blow-off here. Knowing Daisy, she really cared about those cold French fries.

Her voice came out low, soft as silk. "Thank you again, Rafe. I know tonight was—" A text tone from her phone cut off her words. Her hand flew out of his grasp, and she reached into her purse for her phone. "That's Chelsea. I'm sorry, but I have to check it."

The phone chimed again before Daisy could swipe the screen, and then a third time. Wisely, he kept his mouth shut about Chelsea chattering even with text messages.

Daisy read the texts and shot back a reply. "That's her check-in text. She's already upstairs with Hannah."

The phone buzzed a fourth time before Daisy set it down. "I better go."

She leaned in for a kiss. Putting his annoyance aside, he stroked her cheek. "If I don't walk you to your door, I won't sleep tonight. Humor me, okay?"

She gazed into his eyes, blinked twice, then waggled her eyebrows in that playful way that was uniquely Daisy. "I have an idea. How about if you kiss me twice—here and again at the door?"

"I like how you think." He matched his mouth to hers and the kiss came alive. Electricity shot between them— the kind that sizzled and snapped with promise.

Satisfied, he drew back and searched her face. The sparkle in her eyes assured him they were at ease again, so he climbed out of the car and met her on the sidewalk. Hand in hand, they walked to her second-floor apartment, where she opened both locks and turned to him with a look that dared him to make the second kiss even better than the first.

He cupped her face in both hands, leaned in, and— her phone blasted out with yet another text from Chelsea. Rafe dropped his hands to his sides.

Daisy groaned without reaching for the phone. "I should have turned the stupid thing off. Where were we?"

"Kiss number two," he said, but the mood was broken. Instead of a generous kiss that would have topped the one in the car, he brushed a tender one on her lips. "Go on in. Something tells me Chelsea wants to talk."

He tried to keep the irritation out of his voice, but Daisy drew back. "I'm sorry about all the texts. She doesn't realize—"

"It's all right," he assured her. He didn't like Daisy being Chelsea's wing-girl, but he understood the role. Even more to the point, he respected Daisy for looking out for a friend.

They traded another quick kiss and Daisy slipped into the apartment. Rafe waited until the deadbolt clicked into place, then he strode back to the Camaro. He took in his surroundings the way he always did, but his mind drifted back to Daisy. Somehow she made him believe in a better world, calmed the squirrels in his head, and made him laugh even when the dark edges of life pressed in on him. Everything about her called to his blood in the best possible ways.

Did he love her? *Yes . . . Yes, he did.*

The realization washed over him, bringing joy with the force of the mighty Ohio River at flood stage. He punched his fist into the air and almost whooped, but in the next breath, his stomach knotted. Police work was fraught with danger, and she'd been the victim of a violent crime. Even someone without her scars might struggle with the daily risks and uncertainty. The nature of his job took a heavy toll on cops and their families alike. Could Daisy understand and support his career?

The geography problem loomed just as large. If he and Daisy were destined to be together, she'd have to move to Cincinnati—or he'd have to stay in Refuge. One of them would have to make a sacrifice. Rafe didn't want it to be Daisy, but he loved his work and the difference he could make in the city he called home.

But Daisy loved Refuge just as much.

There were no easy answers. Frustrated by it all, he climbed into the driver's seat. A block away from the apartment complex, he turned the radio to classic rock, blasted the volume, and sped into the night, munching cold French fries and missing her already.

Chapter 21

*I*f there was one thing Daisy knew how to do, it was plan a party. When Lyn walked into the bridal shower on Saturday afternoon, MJ squealed with delight. Happy tears streamed down Daisy's cheeks, and she glowed with pride when MJ gushed about the decorations, the adorable custom cake, and the silly games that tied the generations of women together.

When the shower broke up, Shane and MJ took Lyn out for a light dinner while Daisy cleaned up and watched Cody. She owed Rafe a phone call but wanted to be alone when they spoke. He'd been a saint about putting up miles of frilly decorations, and during the shower, he waited outside of MJ's house to greet Lyn when she arrived in her rental car.

Daisy couldn't have pulled off the surprise without

him, but they hadn't seen much of each other over the past week because of her job. The reps from Camp Good Times visited on Wednesday. The organization impressed Miss Joan, but they wanted to put in three swimming pools and a train ride. The Wildlife Preservation Society came on Friday. Their CEO made a strong case, but the focus on endangered species struck Miss Joan as too narrow. Cottonwood Acres was meant to rescue people, too.

Despite her busy work week, Daisy had missed Rafe terribly. They spoke every night, but those conversations were brief and even a little tense. Whenever she mentioned Chelsea and Chad, Rafe warned her about being naïve. Daisy didn't like Chad any more than Rafe did, but who was she to judge?

On the other hand, Rafe was trained to judge situations quickly and to act. Those instincts made him a good cop, but his cynicism worried her.

Shortly after eight, Shane and MJ returned home, and Daisy left for her apartment. When she stepped inside, Chelsea's mommy-voice came down the hall, the words rhyming thanks to Dr. Seuss. No way did Daisy want Chelsea to interrupt her phone call with Rafe even by accident, so she told Chelsea about it, then went out on the balcony.

He answered on the fourth ring. "I just got back"—he gulped in air—"from a run." Another gulp. "How did the shower go?"

"It was perfect. Thanks again for everything, especially meeting Lyn. MJ was ecstatic." She filled him in on the details for five solid minutes, then laughed at herself. "Am I boring you?"

"Hardly." His husky voice convinced her. "It gave me a chance to catch my breath. I'm on the deck cooling off. It's a beautiful night, but it would be even better if you were here. I missed you this week."

"I missed you, too." Her voice came out as earnest as his. "I'd invite you over now, but tomorrow's a big day with Lyn's visit to the ranch."

"What time will she be there?"

"Eleven. She'll give her presentation, then we'll have lunch and go for the big tour."

"I know what that organization means to you. I hope Miss Joan chooses it."

"Me too." She hadn't told him about her personal dream of becoming the director. The week had sped by, and if she voiced that hope, it would become even more real. She'd kept it to herself, but with their feelings for each other growing, what at first seemed private now bordered on secret.

Daisy took a breath. "There's something I haven't mentioned."

"Oh, yeah?"

"If Maggie's House wins the giveaway, I'm going to put in to be the director."

Silence filled the air. "Wow."

Squeezing the phone, she stared out to the parking lot. "It would be a dream come true for me. What do you think?"

More silence, then his breath gusted over the phone. "I think you'd be amazing."

"You do?"

"Yes. Definitely." His confidence cheered her on. "There's always a learning curve, but you have what's most important."

"What's that?"

"Good instincts. You care. You know a lot about Cottonwood Acres, and you understand Maggie's House. You're the perfect choice to pull it all together."

Coming from Rafe, the praise meant a lot. "I'd have to go to LA for training, but it wouldn't be long. Maybe a month."

"When?"

"Late summer? Fall. I don't know exactly." Suddenly the future loomed in front of her. Would Rafe be in Refuge when she returned? Did she dare ask?

Longing washed through her in waves as relentless as a rising tide. Below her, a couple passed through the parking lot holding hands. She pictured Shane walking into the bridal shower at the end, the way he hugged MJ and spun her around.

Daisy wanted it all—a husband, a home of her own, children—and somehow that *all* now included Rafe. The realization stunned her. With her pulse thrumming, she savored the joy that came with wanting this strong, brave, handsome man in her life. But what came next? Did he feel the same way she did? And what did they do about the hundreds of miles between Refuge and Ohio?

Fear pulsed through her, dragging her helplessly away from the peace of mind she'd found in Refuge. Away from Shane and MJ, Cody, and even Miss Joan. Daisy didn't have the courage to face the elephant in the room directly, so she hedged. "A lot can happen in a few months—for either one of us."

Rafe listened to Daisy's trembling voice, the phone slick in his hand as he wrestled with the question neither of them wanted to ask. Was there a chance he'd stay in Refuge? That question had sent him on a five-mile run, and it plagued him now as he walked in circles on Jesse's deck, cooling off in the dry air so unlike the Ohio humidity.

He kept his voice low, the words scraping at his throat. "We have a geography problem, don't we?"

"Do we?" Her voice squeaked, mouse-like, the way it did when she was frightened.

"I know I do," he admitted. "I came here expecting to leave—hoping to go home—"

"I know! That's what you said. You love your job and you're good at it. It's who you are. But you like it here too, right? Jesse's here, and . . ."

"So are you." *I love you, Daisy.* The words begged to be spoken, but it was too soon—and too complicated.

Overhead, a pair of squirrels dashed through the branches of the massive oak tree shading the house. The upper branches slanted down, and a shower of acorns assaulted the deck with a rat-a-tat-tat.

"What was *that*?" Daisy asked.

Rafe looked up, took an acorn to the chest, and muttered at the branches still swaying over his head. "Stupid squirrels are tossing acorns at me."

"They *are* pests. But at least they're cute."

Leave it to Daisy to see the good in a rodent. He laughed, but he didn't think squirrels were the least bit cute—either real ones or the ones in his head. "I like it here, Daize. I like it a lot. But I worked hard to get on the force in Cincy."

"You could be a cop here."

"It's not the same. Besides, the department was great about giving me some time off. They want me back, and I owe them. Plus if I started over somewhere else, I'd have to explain the gap in my work history."

"Of course. But I think it's a positive."

"How?"

"It shows you're not afraid to deal with the stuff in your head. That shows mental strength, right?"

No. It makes me a nut job. Right or wrong, that's how he felt. So did a lot of other people, whether they would admit it or not. His job history aside, her rosy hopes made him wince. He didn't want to hurt her, but staying in Refuge didn't appeal to him at all.

He decided to dodge. "Tomorrow's a big day for you, so let's talk about it later. Okay?"

She paused long enough to breathe a sigh. "Yes. That's best."

"Call me tomorrow, all right? I want to know how things go with Lyn."

"I will."

"Hey . . ." *I love you.* The words shouted louder than the first time, but the complexities silenced him.

"Yes?" she whispered.

"Sleep well, Daize." His voice dipped to a whisper, too. "No matter what the future holds, I want what's best for you."

She murmured in return, her voice an echo of his. "And I want what's best for you."

They traded good-byes, and he went inside to shower, both to wash off the sweat and to clear his head. When he finished, he filled his water bottle and went outside to enjoy the sunset. The deck faced a rippling stream, and sometimes deer came to lap the water. He kept his eyes open, but the deer didn't show up.

Only the chirp of insects filled the air until Jesse's truck rumbled up the driveway. He parked in the garage and trotted up the stairs.

"So where have you been?" Rafe called from the railing.

"Would you believe antiquing? I took your advice about first dates and planned something Angela and I could talk about."

"Angela McCullough?"

"The same."

Rafe had met Angela at the office last week. The interior designer was the daughter of a big client—a multimillionaire building a huge family lodge.

"Antiquing is perfect." Rafe gave his brother a high-five. "So how was it?"

"We had a good time." Jesse swept some of the acorns off the edge of the deck with his boot, gave up, and lifted the push broom leaning against the house. "We're going out again on Wednesday. She likes exotic food. Any ideas?"

"Anywhere but the Green Light Café." Rafe could still taste the lousy fries. "Whatever you do, don't forget your wallet."

Jesse answered with a snort. "Only an idiot does that on a date."

"Or a pothead," Rafe grumbled. "Chelsea's dating some dude named Chad Whittaker. He says he's an adventure guide. Do you know him?"

"Never heard of him."

Rafe took that as a good sign. If Chad was a lowlife, at least he wasn't well known.

Jesse shoved the broom hard. Dust and pine needles flew off the edge of the deck in a cloud while acorns clattered against the planks. "I wish Angela wasn't the daughter of a big client."

"That could get complicated." Rafe knocked back a few gulps of water, wiped his mouth, and scowled. "I hate 'complicated.'"

Jesse kept sweeping. "So what's complicated in your life?"

"Daisy." Rafe downed more water. "We had the geography talk a little while ago."

"That's a tough one. Something has to change, or you both get hurt."

"Have you been through it?" Rafe knew almost nothing about his brother's past relationships.

"The geography problem? No. Being in love? Once. But that's ancient history."

"What happened?"

Jesse stopped sweeping long enough to swat a gnat away from his face. "You remember when I got thrown out of the house."

"Of course."

"I found a job on a farm in Virginia. The woman who owned the place was raising her granddaughter. Smart girl. She was headed to Yale on a full scholarship, and I was doing all the things I wish I hadn't done. One day I just left."

"You didn't say good-bye?"

"No. Nothing." He paused, maybe remembering.

"Man, that's harsh."

"I'm not proud of that summer. The girl was better off without me." He leaned the broom back against the wall and came to stand next to Rafe. "So things are pretty serious between you and Daisy?"

"Yeah, they are."

"Not what you planned, huh?"

"Not even close." Rafe exhaled a weary breath. "When I got here, I just wanted to get my head screwed on right and go home. Dr. Susan's been great. I'm still working on some stuff, but I have new tools in the box."

"I'm glad to hear it."

Rafe mentally tipped his hat to Dr. Susan. "I like Refuge, but I've worked hard for my career."

"So build a career here."

It was an obvious solution but not as simple as it seemed. Refuge had its share of resort town crime, but it lacked the big city atmosphere that called to Rafe's blood. On the other hand, he liked the mountains, enjoyed hanging out with Jesse, and was falling in love with the best woman he'd ever known.

All he could do was shake his head. "This stinks. I just don't know."

"You can always work for me. Ben says you're good, and you handled the SuperCop situation like a pro—"

"Which I am." He reminded Jesse with a smirk. "Conflict resolution—that's what cops do."

"Brat."

They both laughed at the jibes. As brothers, they hadn't always been close, but they were now.

The evening breeze stirred through the pines and knocked down a fresh shower of needles. Jesse reached again for the broom and swept the spot he'd cleared five minutes ago. The extra work would have irked Rafe, but Jesse took everything in stride.

Swish. Swish.

The scraping grated on Rafe's eardrums, and his irritation increased with every patient, controlled swipe of the broom. Jesse hadn't always been the man he was now. Not that he was perfect. He bled and burped like any man. Yet there was a peace about him—a peace Rafe envied. Jesse wouldn't talk about his beliefs unless Rafe asked. That's just how he was—more *walk* than *talk*—so Rafe did the talking. "I give up. How do you do it?"

"Do what?"

"Stay sober. Hold your temper. Not go crazy when life goes off the rails."

Jesse kept sweeping. *Swish. Swish.* "Are you up for some God talk?"

"Between Daisy and thinking about the future, I'm kind of desperate here. Go for it."

Jesse put the broom aside and returned to the railing. Shoulder to shoulder with his brother, Rafe stared into the shadows cast by scattered pinyon pines. The stream gurgled and rushed, a reminder of the river cruise and Daisy singing the praises of God and nature, until Jesse's deep voice rumbled into the quiet.

"Not a day passes that I'm not scared about something, and mad about something else. The calm you think you see? That's me hanging on to what Jesus did on the cross—and I'm usually white-knuckling it with both hands."

"I still don't get it."

"I messed up. You know all about that."

"Sure."

"So in prison, a scrawny college kid with a Bible showed up as part of a prison ministry. Nice guy. I liked him, and we got to be friends. That friendship led to some serious conversations. I have to hand it to him—he had the guts to spell it all out—that Jesus died on the cross to pay for the sins of all mankind. I laughed in his face, but that night I couldn't shake off what he said about eternity. If heaven and hell were real, I knew what I deserved. I'd never been so scared in my life."

Rafe's neck hairs prickled. He didn't know what he thought about heaven and hell, but he understood fear in his marrow. "So what did you do?"

"I tried to shrug it off, but I couldn't. I ended up praying the prayer—accepting Jesus as my savior—then I blubbered like a baby."

Rafe couldn't picture it. "You? Blubbering?"

Jesse scowled at him. "Tell the guys and you're dead meat. But yeah. I was a mess that night. I can't describe it, except after everything, I was at peace. If you want to know where the steadiness you see in me comes from, pray about it. Download a Bible app, or pick up the Bible you see around the house, and read the Gospel of John. What Jesus did on the cross covers it all, bro. It's not me. It's *him*."

Something in Rafe bristled. "There's something I just don't like about religion."

"What?"

"I don't know exactly. Maybe it's the way people talked about God when Kara died—that she was in a better place. I believe that, but why did she have to suffer in the first place?"

"*Why* is a big question. I can't answer it for you."

"That's all right." Rafe could live with the *why*. "But something else bothers me."

"What is it?"

"The notion we're all sinners. That word bothers me."

"Yeah, no one likes to be called names. It comes from the Greek for 'to miss the mark.' To be less than perfect. It's an archery term."

Rafe glared at him. "Since when do you speak Greek?"

"I don't. That scrawny college kid started a Bible study and I paid attention. So what else bugs you about Christianity?"

Rafe thought a moment. "It's a crutch."

"So is counseling." *Score one for Team Jesse.* "Any nightmares recently?"

"Not for a while."

"Yeah, I figured. You snore like a caveman."

"Great." Rafe wished he had a comeback, but he was all out of them.

An empty silence pressed in on him. Not even the squirrels bounced or twittered as he thought about everything his brother had said—and the questions those words inspired in Rafe's own heart. He tried to be a good person, but he had a list of mistakes, failures, and weaknesses of his own. No matter how hard he tried, he often felt like a failure.

Jesse finally broke the silence. "I can shut up and go watch ESPN, or we can talk some more or even pray. It's up to you."

Rafe wasn't close to blubbering like a baby, but a heaviness pressed down on him with even more weight than the silence. He couldn't deny or explain the changes in Jesse, and Daisy had a powerful story of her own. The two people he admired most in this crazy world had one thing in common—their Christian faith.

He wanted what they had—an underlying peace, the courage of their convictions. So what if Rafe felt uncomfortable praying? He was tired of being a marble rolling in a box.

"I'm in," he said to Jesse. "Go for it."

"You mean pray?"

"Yeah."

Jesse looked up at the first star in the evening sky. "Lord, Rafe is looking for you. Show him the way as he makes choices for his life—about trusting you and caring for Daisy. He needs you, Lord. So do I. We're as helpless as sheep. And sheep need a shepherd."

With his eyes on the same star, Rafe offered up a prayer of his own. "Okay, God. Here I am." *I'm tired of the squirrels. Tired of being afraid of failing. Tired of feeling so alone.* "I'm listening again. Show me what's next, Lord. Amen."

There were no shooting stars or sightings of purple unicorns, but Rafe had the distinct feeling he'd just pulled his gun from the holster. When a cop did that, he was ready to use it—even if it cost him his life.

Chapter 22

With Miss Joan behind the wheel of the Mule and Lyn riding shotgun, Daisy sat in the back. They visited Heritage House first, then the historical sites and the bench by the river. The barn was the last stop for the day. As they approached, Daisy saw the horses grazing contentedly in the pasture. A glorious blue sky stretched above them, but storm clouds, dark and heavy with rain, loomed on the horizon.

With the tour nearly complete, the weather didn't worry her at all. Lyn's presentation to Miss Joan couldn't have been more perfect, and the tour had been light-hearted and fun. All Daisy could think about were the endless possibilities for Maggie's Rescue Ranch and the women it was destined to help.

Jug, Comet, and Zippy raised their heads as the vehicle approached. Expecting carrots, they plodded toward the fence. Miss Joan parked and the women climbed out, pausing to stretch their denim-clad legs after the lengthy ride from the river. Lyn removed her sun visor, finger-combed her dark hair, and marveled at the size of the barn and the ranch in general.

A pickup truck loaded with hay bales sat in the shade about fifty feet away. A ranch hand climbed into the bed, lifted a bale, and hefted it to another ranch hand. The man on the ground resembled Rafe, but Rafe was at Heritage House today. Earlier, he had waved to Daisy from the second floor and given her a thumbs-up.

Miss Joan glanced from the ranch hands to Daisy, her eyes twinkling. "I caught that thumbs-up Rafe gave you at Heritage House."

Daisy's face warmed with a blush. Miss Joan played Cupid whenever she could, but right now Daisy wanted to be professional. "He's very nice," she said, her tone neutral

"*Nice?*" Miss Joan leaned toward Lyn, cupped her mouth with one hand, and spoke in a stage whisper. "Our sweet Daisy is rather smitten with Rafe Donovan, and if I'm not mistaken, he's even more smitten with her."

Daisy rolled her eyes. "Miss Joan's been reading too many romance novels. No one says *smitten* anymore."

"Maybe they should!" The older woman stood as tall as her years would allow. "It's a perfectly good word. Check that vocab app you like. *Smitten* comes from *smite*, which means to strike or hit hard, to overwhelm. If that doesn't describe falling in love, I don't know what does."

Lyn pushed her sunglasses to the top of her head, lifted her brows at Daisy, then stage-whispered back to Miss Joan. "What do you think of him?"

"He's a hunk!" Miss Joan whispered back.

Lyn's mouth twitched as she fought a smile. "Yes. I

noticed. When I met him yesterday, we chatted awhile. He's definitely taken with Daisy—and I think she's taken with him."

Daisy groaned. "You two are impossible!" But deep down, she wanted to hug them both for caring about her.

Lyn turned to Daisy, her expression sincere and her voice level. "We haven't had a chance to talk since the bridal shower. Rafe is every bit as charming as you said."

"A perfect gentleman," Miss Joan added. "But Jesse told me he intends to go back to Cincinnati in August. Is that true?"

Daisy's heart tilted sideways. "Yes. Maybe . . . I don't know."

"*You* don't know, or *he* doesn't know?" Concern darkened her eyes. "There's a difference."

"It's confusing." Daisy didn't want to have this conversation now. Her focus needed to be on Maggie's House, but Lyn and Miss Joan were waiting for an explanation. "Rafe and I see a lot of each other. It's good—even great. But he came here because he needed to get over a"—how did she explain without violating his privacy?—"work situation. He likes Refuge, but Cincinnati is his home."

The twinkle in Miss Joan's eyes faded to pewter gray. "So it's complicated."

"Maybe." *No, definitely.* Last night's conversation played through her mind. "We've known each other less than two months. It's too soon for the geography talk, but it came up last night."

Daisy had lain awake for hours, wondering about the future, praying Rafe would stay in Refuge, then taking it back. Who was she to presume on God's will for his life? As for her own, she believed with her whole heart she belonged exactly where she was—here at Cottonwood Acres.

She indicated the barn and pasture with a sweep of her arm. "Maggie's House is the focus today, not me."

Miss Joan refused to budge. "I hate the thought of you being caught between love and a career."

"I'm not caught—"

"Yet." Miss Joan cut her off. "I saw this as a college professor. What does a young couple do when *he's* accepted to a med school in New Jersey and *she's* headed to law school in another part of the country? Who gives in? What does that person give up? Or do they settle for FaceTime, when video chatting is a poor excuse for—oh, never mind." She let out a huff. "I'm being pathetically old-fashioned."

"No." Lyn faced Miss Joan. "You're being realistic. Life is full of compromises—for men and women alike. Family versus career. His career versus her career."

"Exactly!" Joan agreed.

"Finding that balance isn't easy." Lyn turned to Daisy. "Sometimes we have to give up one dream for another, or put the first dream off for a while. But this is where trusting God comes in, isn't it?"

"Yes." Daisy breathed a little easier. She didn't need to worry about the future; her job was simply to trust and follow God.

Miss Joan said she agreed about leaving the future in God's hands, then she fussed about her bad knee acting up and asked Daisy to fetch carrots from the barn.

Daisy walked away, leaving Lyn and Miss Joan to amble toward the paddock. When she reached the barn door, she glanced over her shoulder and saw the two women talking to each other. Miss Joan drew back, then nodded slowly with a solemn look Daisy couldn't interpret. Were they talking about Rafe again? Or maybe Miss Joan was fussing about the arthritis in her knees, how it acted up when the barometric pressure dropped. The storm in the west was moving fast. No rain yet, but Daisy could smell it coming.

She hurried into the barn and went to the stall where carrots were stored in buckets of sand to keep them from getting moldy. Before lifting one of the containers, she silently asked God to bless all the possibilities for Maggie's Rescue Ranch. Excitement flooded through her as she walked back to the paddock, the heavy bucket dragging on her arm.

Miss Joan and Lyn turned to her at the same time, then traded an odd look. Jug was already pawing the ground in anticipation, so Daisy headed for the fence.

Two steps from the railing, Miss Joan laid a hand on her arm and stopped her. "Daisy, Lyn and I need to speak to you."

"More advice about Rafe?" Daisy grinned at the thought of them playing fairy godmother.

"No, dear. It's not about Rafe." Miss Joan's fingers stiffened on Daisy's arm. "We've reached a decision about Maggie's House."

Daisy's heart shot into her throat. She waited for more, but no one said a word. Her gaze darted between them until it settled on Lyn. Compassion glistened in her eyes the way it had nine months ago when Daisy first walked into Mary's Closet, wearing sunglasses to hide her black eye.

"I'm sorry, Daisy," Lyn said. "But Cottonwood Acres isn't a good fit for Maggie's House. I'm withdrawing the proposal."

The bucket tumbled out of Daisy's grasp, spilling carrots and sand onto the sparse grass. "But why? It's perfect. I know it is!" She stared hard at Lyn.

"I know you had high hopes. So did I. But the ranch is just too big for our housing model."

"It can work—it can!" Why hadn't she spoken to Lyn sooner? Why had she assumed Lyn would see the same possibilities? "Give me a chance to change your mind."

Lyn shook her head. "Daisy, I—"

"Please?" No way could she let her dream slip away without a fight. "I was going to talk to you at dinner tonight, but I can talk now. In fact, I can show you. Watch—" Daisy dropped to a crouch, picked up as many carrots as her hands could hold, dumped them into the bucket, and carried it to the fence.

Jug shouldered the two smaller horses out of the way, and Daisy fed him a twisted carrot. "Imagine the women at Maggie's Rescue Ranch caring for these horses and a dozen more. Everyone needs something to love, right? The rescue program provides a perfect opportunity."

She waved a carrot at Comet, who came forward and took the treat like the lady she was. "I love the idea of restarting the horse rescue, and even expanding it to other animals. Heritage House will be open to the public, so it'll need a staff. That'll give our residents solid work experience."

An overly patient sigh leaked from Lyn's lips. "You know our policy on privacy. Heritage House will be open to the public. It's too close to the living quarters for both privacy and security concerns."

Daisy had already considered the situation. "It's not ideal, but we can put a security gate at the front entrance. Overall, Heritage House is a plus. It'll need management, maintenance, plus bookkeeping and ordering if we include a souvenir shop. There won't be a lot of traffic—just occasional tourists. It would function like Mary's Closet—a place for women to work and learn new skills. There's a lot to do on a ranch. We could offer training in other areas, as well."

Lyn's gaze shifted to Miss Joan. Daisy needed an ally, badly. But Miss Joan's lips remained sealed tight.

Fine. Daisy could stand on her own. More determined than ever, she fed the biggest carrot to Zippy, because he was the smallest horse. "Maggie's Rescue Ranch needs to happen. I believe it, and I'm determined to make it work."

Lyn remained silent, and so did Miss Joan. Thunder rolled faintly in the distance. The hint of rain thickened the air, and the wind picked up. Jug stomped his foot, demanding another carrot. Unable to bear his frustration, Daisy fed him a big one, hoping and praying for a reprieve from Lyn.

Miss Joan picked up a carrot for Zippy and stood next to Daisy. "I'm sorry, dear. But I have to agree with Lyn. As I understand Maggie's House, the organization would be better served by several smaller residences, perhaps located throughout the nation."

"Exactly." Lyn joined them at the fence, selected a carrot, and offered it to Comet. "We want our residences to feel like home, not a college dorm, or worse, an institution."

Daisy stepped back, shocked and a little offended. "An institution! I wouldn't let that happen!"

"You can't change human nature." Lyn reached to give Comet another bite, but Jug shouldered the mare out of the way and tried to steal the carrot in Lyn's hand.

"Jug!" Miss Joan scolded him. "You're being a pig!" The carrots were gone, so she waved her arms to shoo the horses away.

Daisy watched them amble off, slowly, their heads down and swaying as they sniffed for grass. She opened her mouth to make a final plea to Lyn, but words evaded her. Ideas turned to dust. So did hope. Her face hardened into a dam holding back tears. "So it's settled."

"Yes," Lyn replied. "But Joan and I would like to talk to you about another possibility."

Daisy thought of the glances they'd shared. They'd been plotting behind her back, talking about her. That was natural, since they were all friends. But to leave her out of the most important conversation of the day? To treat her like a child—to dismiss her ideas without hearing them? It hurt. Terribly. And it made her angry—and scared. A sob threatened to escape from her throat, but she swallowed hard.

Despite her trembling lips, she lifted her chin as professionally as she could. "What possibility?"

"A job offer."

"Where?" She held out her hands and looked around—at nothing. Which was the point.

Lyn, benevolent as always, ignored the gesture. "The board for Maggie's House approved the purchase of five new residences located outside of Los Angeles. Refuge is too small, but we're considering several other cities, including Denver. If you're interested in joining the ministry, we'd love to have you."

Daisy gaped at her. "Denver is five hundred miles from here."

"We're considering other locations, too. Chicago. Las Vegas. Houston. And a city somewhere along the I-75 corridor. Do you know where that is?"

"Not exactly, and I really don't care."

"Daisy?" Miss Joan waited until Daisy looked up. "You know I keep up on issues concerning women."

"Yes."

"Interstate 75 runs from Florida all the way to Michigan. It's one of the busiest drug and human trafficking routes in this country. It also goes straight through Ohio—and Cincinnati."

"Cincinna . . ." The word died on her lips. *Rafe's home.* But a city where she'd be anxious and uneasy, scared all the time, lost on streets with strange names. She *hated* the idea.

She needed to leave—now—before her face crumpled and she burst into tears. But she couldn't find her tongue to make an excuse. Lyn stood in her way, her expression kind as always—and devastatingly hopeful.

Daisy could only shake her head. "I'm—I'm—"

Lyn's expression softened even more. "We know you don't have a formal commitment to Rafe, but if you want to join the Maggie's House staff, you *do* have options. We thought Ohio—"

"Stop!" Daisy's hands flew to her cheeks. "I can't do this now. I can't!"

Lyn reached out to hug her, but Daisy spun away with her pulse pounding in her ears. She hunched her shoulders against the wind coming off the pasture, but she couldn't escape the loamy scent of rain. Thick tears pressed behind her eyes. One leaked out, then another.

Lyn tried again. "Daisy—"

"No!"

The dam snapped, cracked, and finally shattered. Tears gushed from Daisy's eyes, and she ran as if being chased by Eric. Her feet stumbled on ruts. Stray rocks caused her to lurch. She couldn't think—couldn't do anything but run.

Chapter 23

"*D*onovan! Get down here *now*." Ben's voice boomed through Heritage House, up the stairs, and down the hall where Rafe and some of the crew were putting up drywall.

Howie snickered at him. "Sounds like someone's in trouble."

"Hey, I'm innocent." Rafe handed the taping tool to Drake, then shouted down to Ben. "On my way, sir."

He couldn't think of a single reason the foreman would summon him so urgently, unless it had something to do with the storm raging outside. When thunder cracked again, Rafe thought of Daisy touring the ranch with Lyn and Miss Joan. Throughout the afternoon, she had sent short texts and smileys, but he hadn't heard from her in almost two hours.

When he reached the landing in the middle of the staircase, he saw Ben at the bottom, waiting for him with the look of a man who had delivered bad news before.

Bad news . . . Jesse . . . Accidents happened on construction sites. Had Jesse fallen off a ladder? Misjudged a saw blade? Crashed his truck? Rafe had seen his share of bloody messes. Steeling himself, he jogged down the last of the stairs. "What happened?"

Ben clamped his hand on Rafe's shoulder. With the other, he handed Rafe the Donovan Construction cell phone. "Miss Joan wants to talk to you."

"Me? But why?"

"Daisy's missing—"

"*Missing?*"

"Miss Joan will explain. Cliff's bringing a truck for you to use." Ben gave his shoulder another hard-fisted squeeze, then walked away, leaving Rafe with the phone.

Schooling his emotions, he raised the phone to his ear. "Donovan here."

"Rafe. Good." Miss Joan's breath gusted over the connection. "Daisy's missing. We need you to find her."

Worry coursed through him, but professionalism tempered his reaction even as a crack of thunder shook the unfinished building. The more he knew, the better. "What happened?"

Miss Joan told him about the decision regarding Maggie's House. "Daisy took it hard. We thought she'd gone into the barn to collect herself, so we waited before we looked for her. That—that was a mistake."

"I'll find her." Striding toward the door, he unhooked his tool belt with one hand and left it by the door, not caring if someone picked it up or not. "How long has she been missing?"

"About half an hour. Lyn and I searched the barn. She's not there. I don't—" The words broke into disjointed syllables. "Maybe—check the—could you—" More static.

"Miss Joan! Can you hear me?"

"Yes. Can you hear me?"

"For now." The line cleared enough for Rafe to make out the details as he waited in the doorway for Cliff to arrive with the truck. Ana had already checked Daisy's office and the parking lot. Her car was still there.

Miss Joan's voice shook even more. "I—I've never seen her like that—shattered—in pieces."

His heart clenched at the thought of Daisy breaking down so completely. She needed a friend. She needed *him*. "Do you have any idea where she could have gone?"

"All I know is that she's on foot."

Cliff arrived with the pickup truck, jumped out in the pouring rain, but left the engine running. Rafe strode forward, shielding the phone at his ear with his hand as he passed Cliff with a nod. Water trickled down his neck, but he didn't care.

"I'll start looking," he told Miss Joan. "Where are you now?"

"At the house."

"Call me if she shows up. I'm going to check the barn again, then the bunkhouse."

"Yes—" Lightning flashed and the phone went dead.

Rafe climbed into the truck, dropped the phone on the passenger's seat, and sped to the barn.

He'd grown up in the Ohio Valley. He knew what to do when lightning split the sky and wind ripped at trees. Daisy was a California girl. She knew about earthquakes and brush fires—not wind and rain. Had she fled into the meadow to be alone? With lightning bolts forking from clouds to the ground, would she know to find a low spot and stay down?

Considering her state of mind, she could be anywhere. Search and Rescue 101—don't overlook the obvious. Miss

Joan said she searched the barn, but Rafe needed to check for himself. He pulled up to the open door, climbed out, and saw a ranch hand leading a skittish Comet into her stall. Jug and Zippy were already secured, though both appeared nervous.

Rafe called out from across the barn. "I'm looking for Miss Joan's assistant—"

"Daisy, right?"

"Yes."

"I haven't seen her, but some of the guys are looking down by the maintenance yard." The cowhand closed the gate on Comet. "I'm done here. Want some help?"

"Not yet." An all-out search would require some planning. "Just keep your eyes open. If you see anything, call Miss Joan."

"Will do."

Rafe took three precious minutes to check the tack room, the office Cliff sometimes used, and each empty stall. Turning, he spotted a tall ladder leading to the hayloft. With his neck hairs prickling, he climbed the rungs hard and fast, calling to her softly as he stepped into the gloom and took in the hay bales stacked in the middle of the floor. There was no sign of Daisy and no place to hide.

He hurried down the ladder, climbed back in the truck, but didn't drive away. Instead he peered into the rain, putting himself in her shoes—distraught, shattered, maybe afraid. Would she run or hide?

"Where are you, Daisy?" he asked out loud.

If he didn't find her in the next fifteen minutes, he'd call Miss Joan and suggest an official search—but only as a last resort. A search would turn Daisy's private loss into a public spectacle, something she'd find embarrassing.

He drove slowly away from the barn, his head swiveling to the right and left. When he reached the Y in the road that split toward the bunkhouse, his intuition caught fire.

The low building in the distance offered shelter, privacy, and a safe place to hide.

Rafe unrolled the side windows so he could see into the trees and bushes as he drove. The truck swayed with the force of the wind. His foot moved to punch the gas, but his training kicked in and he maintained a constant speed, checking both sides of the road in case Daisy had stumbled and twisted an ankle.

"Daisy!" he shouted. "Daisy! Can you hear me?"

Lightning split the sky, and out of habit he counted the seconds in his head. Before he reached two, thunder cracked and echoed like a rifle shot. Rain soaked his arm through the open window, but he didn't care as he steered toward the bunkhouse. Heavy rain turned it into a blur, but on the covered porch, through the railing, he spotted a smear of bright blue and Daisy's blond head.

She was sitting down, knees to her chest, huddled against a closed door with her neck bent and eyes down. She appeared to be unharmed, though she resembled a rag doll, tossed aside and left in a heap.

If she heard the truck over the pounding rain, she didn't look up. Rafe snagged the phone and called Miss Joan.

"Rafe! Did you find her?"

"She's at the bunkhouse."

"Is she hurt?"

"I don't think so. I just got here. I'll let you know if she needs anything."

"Thank you, Rafe. What she needs most right now is a friend."

"I'm here."

He ended the call and tossed the phone in the console, parked close to the building, and climbed out in the storm, the rain drenching his shirt as he jogged up the three stairs that put him at Daisy's feet. She stayed curled in a ball, leaning against a door, not looking up, though he suspected she'd peeked through her fingers and spotted him in the truck.

He dropped to a crouch but didn't touch her out of fear she'd pull more tightly into herself. "Hey, Daize. I hear you got some bad news. I'm sorry."

She peeked at him from over her knees. "Thanks for looking for me, but I don't want company right now. I have to work this out on my own."

"Work what out?"

"Everything. The future . . . what Lyn said about Ci—" She sucked in a breath and held it, but a squeak leaked from her throat. "I'm sorry, Rafe. But you're making it harder. Please. Go away."

"I can't do that."

"*Please.* This isn't the time—"

"The time for what?"

Frowning and angry, she glared at him through the sheen of watery tears. "I can't talk about it. Not now. And not with you. Please—just go." She sealed her lips so tightly they trembled.

Rafe had seen Daisy afraid when he changed the flat tire; he'd seen her happy playing with Barbie dolls, floating down the river, and eating a Blizzard. They had shared jokes, a quarrel over Chelsea and Chad, and the best kisses of his life. He knew this woman, but he'd never seen her like this—seemingly calm yet trembling; both shattered and angry; and, most confusing of all, dead-set on cutting him off.

No way could he leave without answers. "I thought we were friends—and a lot more. Why are you pushing me away?"

She swung her head to the side, avoiding his gaze. It made no sense to him—and it hurt.

The wind gusted sideways, stinging them both with

needles of rain. He moved closer to the bunkhouse wall for shelter, but the wind still sucked at his wet shirt.

"We're getting soaked," he muttered. "Let's go inside."

"It's locked."

"Not a problem." Using a laminated card he kept in his wallet, he loided the lock on the first try. When the mechanism popped, he helped Daisy to her feet.

Together they walked into a living room straight out of the 1970s. Orange and gold shag carpet covered the floor; a sofa with floral upholstery boasted the same bold colors; and a green princess-style phone sat on a spindly maple table. A brick fireplace formed a middle wall, and an open door led to a hallway. A tiny kitchen occupied the far corner.

Daisy strode inside, whirled, and faced him, her jaw jutting in defiance. Before she could tell him again to get lost, he took control. "I'm not leaving. You're hurting. I want to know why."

Her lips quivered, but she fought the press of fresh tears by crossing her arms over her chest. "It's just not fair!"

He'd take her defiance over despair anytime. "What isn't fair?"

"Everything!" She flung her arms out to the sides. "I had plans! I did everything right and now—" She sealed her lips again, holding in whatever secret had been about to spill. "I'm *safe* here. I *belong* here—in Refuge. *It's my home.*"

Rafe cared about her. Loved her. He wanted to help her, but her jack-knifing emotions left him impossibly confused. The Maggie's House decision had been a big disappointment, a huge one, but losing out on that position didn't explain her rejection of him.

He closed the door behind them, cutting off the storm and most of the light. "Let's start at the beginning. What exactly happened today?"

Daisy grabbed two fistfuls of hair and pulled them up and hard to the side. A ragged sigh hissed from her lips, then her shoulders slumped and her head fell forward.

He couldn't stand her anguish—couldn't bear feeling helpless in the presence of it. Two steps brought him within a breath of her, his arms ready and eager to pull her close. If she pushed him away, fine. He'd respect her choice and step back. But his gut told him she needed to be held—and held tight.

The instant he hugged her, she softened against him— boneless, spineless. Her fingers knotted in his shirt and she clung to him with all her might. He rubbed her back to calm her, grazed her temple with his lips, and held her close despite the dampness of his shirt.

"I've got you, Daize," he murmured.

Her fingers knotted against his back. Her breath came in rasps that tickled his neck. A bolt of desire shot through him, but he held back. Daisy didn't need to be kissed senseless; she needed to be cared for, protected, and carried to safety—all the things he did best.

A whimper spilled from her lips. He expected her to sob against his shoulder. Instead she pressed her mouth against his and dragged him down to the couch. Her hands moved to his chest, then to his torso and under his shirt. Skin to skin. Hers chilled, his burning hot. His brain fogged but instantly cleared.

He didn't know who was kissing him, but it wasn't the woman Daisy wanted to be.

Some people drank to escape. Some did drugs. Some took comfort in sexual pleasure. He knew enough about Daisy's past to realize what she was doing—what he'd done himself a time or two. When she hurt, she wanted to feel loved. And nothing made a person feel loved more than the intimacy of sex. No matter how much he desired her, no way would he take advantage of a weak moment. Loving Daisy meant slamming on the brakes.

After a final soft kiss, he shifted to the middle of the couch and grasped her hand, both to stop her from touching him and to show that he cared.

As gently as he could, he told her the truth. "It won't work, Daize."

"What?"

"Hiding from what hurts."

Chapter 24

*D*aisy gaped at Rafe, her cheeks flushed as the passion drained from her body, leaving her even more lost than when she'd pulled Rafe down to the couch.

Oh, Lord! What have I done?

The last hour was a blur of anger and tears. She hadn't come to the bunkhouse looking for alcohol, but if she'd found a forgotten bottle of gin, she would have thrown away nine months of sobriety. Instead she'd thrown herself at Rafe like the skank she used to be. Shame clawed at her, shredding whatever good feelings about herself she had mustered since finding Jesus. Nausea churned in her belly, shaming her even more. She couldn't even breathe a prayer.

But somehow a guttural cry rose up in her soul and warred with the hateful voices in her head. The fog of lust and desperation cleared from her mind, and she saw the face of her accuser—Satan in the guise of her evil twin. A shocked gasp tore from her throat. Instinctively, she tried to pull herself into a ball, but Rafe tightened his grip on her hand, keeping her in the here and now.

"I'm not letting go," he said. "Stay with me, Daisy."

She could only shake her head. "I can't believe what I just did."

"Forget it."

"You must think—"

"I think you're amazing." He gave her hand another squeeze, then let go. "But I'm also worried about you. What just happened—"

"Was a stupid reaction." She relaxed her knees, swung them off the couch, and sat straight. "I was blindsided by Lyn's decision and—and by something else. I don't really know what exactly happened, except that I fell apart and did what I used to do. Thank you for putting on the brakes."

His mouth quirked into an unhurried grin. "Yeah, I slammed them pretty hard."

They locked eyes, the sparks still flying but no longer a danger.

Outside, the storm had slowed to a drizzle. They could leave anytime, but Daisy owed Rafe an explanation. If they had any kind of future, she needed to be open and honest—no secrets. And no secrets meant telling him about Lyn's offer.

He shifted back on the couch, seemingly relaxed. "I know Lyn withdrew the proposal, but you said something else happened. That's the part I don't understand."

Daisy tried to soften the news with a nonchalant shrug. "Lyn said no to Cottonwood Acres, but she still offered me a job—just not here in Refuge."

"Oh, man." His brows shot up into arches. "Where?

Back in Los Angeles?"

"Just for training." She wanted to hug her knees again but forced herself to sound businesslike. "Maggie's House is opening five new residences in different parts of the country. The locations are TBD, but they're looking at"—she couldn't bring herself to say Cincinnati—"what Lyn called the I-75 corridor."

"That's . . ." His face lit up like Christmas. "Are you serious? I-75 goes straight through Cincy."

"Cincinnati is on the list." She tried not to wince. "In fact, it's high on the list."

His eyes lasered to hers. Her insides melted with that look, and she saw the good man who had rescued her from a flat tire, and now from her evil twin. How could she *not* want to be with him? But at what cost?

The tender sincerity unique to Rafe burned bright in his eyes. "I know this is too soon. But Daisy—you have to know how I feel about you."

All she could do was chew her lip. If she told him she loved him, she'd feel pressured by the circumstances, and feeling pressured made her crazy. On the other hand, where was her faith? She needed to be open to wherever God led—even to a city with a name she couldn't spell.

"Have you ever been to Ohio?" His voice rang with hometown pride.

She held in a cringe. "I think so. My mom traveled a lot when Shane and I were kids." She didn't remember specific details, only that she didn't like being in new places, even with Shane to hold her hand.

Rafe's voice perked up even more. "Cincinnati's not a bad place to live. Before you make a decision, how about coming for a visit? I'll be your personal tour guide. We'll do the Riverwalk, eat food that's not vegan—"

She finally managed a smile, but her heart ached even more.

Rafe's grin turned mischievous. "If you come in September, we'll go to a Reds game. You can send Shane a selfie of you in a Reds cap."

She laughed again, but her chest ached even more. *September . . .* "You're definitely going back, aren't you?"

He didn't speak for several seconds. "That's always been the plan. But this—us—it's pretty amazing. I've thought about staying, but I have to be honest. It's not my first choice."

"Cincinnati is your home. You belong there."

"I do."

"You love it," she murmured. "You love the way it feels, your work, knowing the streets, everything—"

"Yes, but I love you, too."

It was the first time he'd said the words to her. They seared her soul, but the moment turned bittersweet. She loved Rafe with her whole heart—except the part that needed to stay in Refuge. As much as she wanted to say the words back, she couldn't—not unless she could commit to him fully.

Swallowing hard, she broke the silence. "I don't know what to say. You deserve more from me—especially after today. But it's all too much right now. I live a day at a time, because it's all I can handle."

"That works for me."

"Does it?"

"Very much." He shifted his weight again, moving a few inches back to put space between them. "Jesse and I had a little chat the other night. I can't say the earth moved, or that I felt much of anything, but when Jesse prayed for me, I decided to start over—as if I'd never believed in God before."

"Really?"

"Yes, really." He stretched his leg to touch her foot with his. "How could I not want to understand the God that made you the beautiful woman you are—and that's inside and out."

His words lifted her out of the mire of doubt. Why not visit Ohio? Rafe would be there, so she wouldn't be alone. But she knew better than to lean too much on him, or any other human being—which meant she couldn't lean too heavily on Shane and MJ, either.

Oh, Lord. Help me!

Rafe reached again for her hand. "A day at a time, Daize. You set the pace, and I'll follow."

She tried to nod, but her neck locked with uncertainty. When it came to building a healthy relationship, she didn't know what to do. She'd been so focused on herself—staying safe, staying sober—that she hardly knew what loving a man meant. She only knew how Jesus loved *her*, and he'd sacrificed himself on the cross. But Daisy had sacrificed too much of herself for Eric and ended up in the ICU.

But . . . But . . . She was driving herself crazy!

Yet another big question popped into her mind. Could she live with Rafe's career? Police officers faced danger every day. What if she married him and they had three beautiful children and he died in the line of duty? What if—

Stop it! Mentally she slapped her evil twin upside the head. *Enough of that nonsense!*

Glancing around the dimly lit room, Daisy settled back into reality. "The rain's gone. We should go back to the house."

They both stood and headed to the door, but Daisy paused to glance around the room one more time. It held memories for Miss Joan, and now it held memories for Daisy, too. Rafe loved her. The words soaked into her all over again, but so did the stark fear of leaving the life she loved. Lifting her chin, she walked with him to the truck.

Silent but at peace, they drove to the house, where Lyn and Miss Joan were no doubt worried and waiting.

Chapter 25

The glory of the young is their strength; the gray hair of experience is the splendor of the old.

Proverbs 20:29 (NLT)

Joan knew all about mentoring students, but mothering was a new experience for her. When Daisy walked into the house with Rafe at her side, Joan hurried to wrap her in a hug. Lyn followed suit, and the three of them spoke all at once in a mix of apologies, if-onlys, and declarations of love and loyalty. Rafe hung back, but Sadie wiggled her way into the group, poked Daisy with her nose, and woofed a greeting.

Everyone laughed, and the tension broke enough for Joan's practical side to take over. "Stay for dinner. All of you."

Daisy shook her head. "Thank you, but I'm exhausted."

"And wet and bedraggled, I might add." Joan skimmed Daisy from head to foot. "Stay here tonight, dear. We'll find dry clothes for you, then break out the toaster and have a nice long talk."

"It's tempting, but Rafe missed his ride back to Refuge with the crew. We're taking my car home."

"Yes, of course," Joan replied.

Next Daisy turned to Lyn. "We were supposed to have dinner tonight, but I'm not up for it. Could we do breakfast tomorrow before your flight?"

Lyn nodded. "I was going to suggest it myself."

While Daisy and Lyn discussed when and where to meet, Joan watched with a lump in her throat. Disappointment about company for dinner aside, the day was ending well—except for the lonely ache in her own chest.

Rafe came around to her side. "The truck's out front. I left the key on the display case by the door."

"Thank you, Rafe."

Daisy fetched her purse from her office, handed Rafe her car key, and they left. Lyn gathered her things from the living room and returned to the entry. She hugged Joan good-bye, and they promised to keep in touch.

Joan closed the front door with a soft click. The silence depressed her, so she headed to the kitchen to visit with Ana. As she approached, she overheard Ana on the phone with Cliff, telling him she loved him and would be home soon.

So much for a nice chat with her housekeeper. Holding back a sigh, Joan strode into the kitchen with a businesslike air. "It's been a long day," she said to her housekeeper. "Why don't you go home early? I'll make a sandwich for myself."

"Are you sure?" Ana couldn't have sounded more

hopeful.

"I'm positive."

Ana took off her white baker's apron but hesitated. "Before I leave, may I ask you something?"

"Of course."

"With the charity visits, Cliff and I—and the ranch hands—we're all wondering what will happen to our jobs. We're worried."

"Of course you are." Joan paused before opening the refrigerator. "If the new owner doesn't keep you on, I'll help you and Cliff find other positions. Same for the ranch hands. I'm planning a severance package based on seniority. That should help quite a bit."

"You've always been generous."

"I'm only sharing what I've been given." That responsibility weighed heavily on Joan's shoulders. She had thought briefly about leaving the ranch to Daisy but quickly dismissed the idea. Great wealth was both a blessing and a burden. Joan was equipped for the burden; Daisy was not.

When Ana left, Joan ate the sandwich more out of necessity than hunger, took ibuprofen for her aching knees, and decided to wait before she tackled the stairs to her bedroom.

After eyeballing the shelf of old DVDs, she gave in to a fresh wave of loneliness, loaded the disc with the final season of *Thunder Valley*, and settled on the couch. With Sadie at her feet, Joan clicked to the two-part finale that starred Trey.

Episode One opened with a close-up of outlaw Josiah Bent, Trey's character, mounted on a chestnut stallion, his hat low, his duster loose over a pair of pearl-handled Colt revolvers. A week earlier, he had shot a man's son in cold blood. Now the father, Enoch Grant, wanted revenge and rightfully so. Josiah needed a place to hide, and

Becky Monroe's ranch was perfect—as long as he lied to her.

Trey played the part to perfection, reciting dialogue with his natural Texas twang. "I'm a drifter, ma'am . . . headin' west to start over. Looks like you could use some help around here, and I need to earn some travel money."

Joan called him out from the couch. "Liar." Josiah had gold in his saddlebag—a lot of it.

The story unfolded with Becky's children, particularly her fourteen-year-old son, being enthralled with Josiah. Then Becky became enthralled. Despite her grit, she fell for him.

And he fell for her—enough to cry out to God for help. Could Josiah really start over? Could he somehow make amends to the man whose life he had destroyed? Alone on a mountaintop, with the sky blazing as orange as hellfire, Josiah—Trey—hit his knees and begged God to make him a man worthy of Becky's love.

Trey could act. Even now, Joan choked up as he begged God to make him worthy. She choked up again when he vowed to hang up his guns and live honestly from that day on. A changed man, he told Becky everything. He expected her to slap him and call him names.

Instead she wept for him, then held out her hand. "I love you, Josiah. I do."

"I'm not worth the risk," he told her. "My past sniffs me out like a rabid dog. One of these days, it'll kill me. I don't want it to kill you too, so I'm leaving."

Becky grabbed his hand. "No—"

"Yes." He managed a faint smile. "Let me go, darlin'. Think of your children. This may be the only truly heroic thing I ever do."

He kissed her good-bye—the kind of TV kiss that made women swoon—then he climbed onto his horse and rode off, only to be gut-shot a mile away. Somehow he made it back to Becky's house. Near death, he collapsed in the yard.

To Be Continued materialized on the screen in cursive lettering, and violins soared to a tragic crescendo. Joan heard every note, read every word as the credits rolled, then she closed her eyes and remembered.

What does a woman do when the best night of her life results from a choice that shreds her integrity to ribbons? That was my dilemma when I woke up in Trey's arms in a nylon tent down by the river.

I couldn't shake a sense of unease as dawn approached. Did he regret making love? Did I? Not a bit—except I felt sick to my stomach in one breath, yet completely justified in the next. We loved each other. We were both adults. Enough said—except it wasn't nearly enough.

Trey didn't stir as I dressed and slipped outside to watch the sunrise. The eastern sky glowed orange with a layer of lavender clouds. It was lovely, the colors soothing and full of promise. The western sky offered no such comfort. Jagged mountains stood unmoving, silhouetted by a sky more black than navy blue.

Trey didn't say much as he cooked breakfast, and neither did I. Words were unnecessary. I knew what he was thinking, because I was thinking it too.

Still. Married.

But only legally. Soon he'd be free and we could put the guilt behind us.

I consoled myself with that thought as we rode back to the house. I also did some mental calculations about what my ancestors would have called my "monthly." I didn't show up at the river prepared for what Trey and I had done. In other words, we didn't use birth control.

That scared me, but I had made a conscious decision to accept the risk. I knew my body and believed it was a safe time of the month. If I'm even more honest, a primitive force in me wanted Trey's child. A week later, my period started. I breathed a sigh of relief and a sigh of longing, both at the same time.

Trey was scheduled to stay another four days, and he did. We didn't talk about the future in those nights together. What was there to say? I knew he felt guilty about making love and so did I. I tried to console him, but he would have none of it. When he left on a Friday morning, we couldn't find words. It was the hardest good-bye we ever shared—and the shortest.

Over the next two weeks, we went back to late-night phone calls, though we skipped occasionally. He opened up a little. Not a lot, but enough to share his deepening guilt.

"But why?" I insisted. "We're human. I refuse to say it was a mistake—"

"Ah, Joanie. You just don't know."

"Know what?"

"What it's like to be in my shoes right now."

"No, but I know what it's like to be in mine—" I took a breath. "I love you, Trey."

"I love you, too." He sighed. "This is just too hard. I want it to be over."

"Me too." I meant the waiting.

Trey meant something else, but I didn't realize it until three weeks later, when he called earlier than usual. I was in my office when I answered the phone and heard his voice.

"Trey! What a surprise." I turned my chair toward the window so I could enjoy the glorious day.

"I need to tell you something . . . something hard." His

voice dropped low. I heard a quaver in his voice and braced myself.

"What is it?"

"You know Kathy and I are in counseling."

"Yes." *To end the marriage, not to save it.*

"I told her about us."

"I see." Anger swamped me. I felt betrayed, as if Trey had told our secret. Which he had. But can a person betray a betrayal? I wanted to blame Kathy for dragging things out, but I was far angrier with Trey. "So when are you coming back?"

"I don't know. Soon, I hope. But not until the divorce is final."

"Trey—" I bit my tongue.

"I know. Same old song and dance. I gotta go, Joanie. Know that I love you, and I'm doing the best I can. It's not good enough, and for that I'm sorry. I'll talk to you later."

We traded good-byes without the usual banter, then I slammed the phone down as hard as I could.

He didn't call the next night, so the night after that one, I was expecting his call. My anger had cooled, and I was relieved when the phone rang at our usual late hour. I didn't have caller ID like people do now. It never occurred to me that it would be anyone but Trey.

"Miss Prescott?" A female voice.

Every nerve in my body prickled in warning. "Yes?"

"This is Kathy Cochran, Trey's wife."

Shock rocketed through me, settled in my bones, and froze my tongue. Why would she call? Had there been an accident? I swallowed once, twice, then pushed out a few words. "Is—Is Trey all right?"

"He's fine," she replied quickly. "In fact, he's out tonight with a friend—the pastor of our church." *Our* church. "Trey doesn't know I'm calling you. I plan to tell him tomorrow during our counseling session."

"I see." Except I couldn't see anything in the dark. Pressed against the pillows, I stared out the window in search of a shred of light. The moon. Even a single star. But heavy clouds hid the heavens from my sight. All alone, I resorted to my professorial self. "What can I do for you, Kathy?"

"I'm asking you for a favor—woman to woman." She paused again. "I want to save my marriage. I'm fighting for him, Miss Prescott. And I'm fighting for our baby—"

"*Baby?*"

"Yes . . . Trey didn't tell you?"

My silence answered, but I forced myself to say the word—to give voice and life to his betrayal. "No, he didn't tell me. How far along are you?"

"Eight weeks."

My stomach curdled as if I'd swallowed poison. Trey had made love to his wife while claiming he loved me—when the divorce was *almost* final. But it wasn't *almost* final if Trey had slept with Kathy *while calling me* every single night.

Kathy's voice stayed strong. "He cares for you, Miss Prescott. He cried when he told me about you. He's conflicted, and if you know Trey—and I believe you do—you know that sometimes he's two people."

A chameleon. I'd had that thought more than once. Just who was Trey Cochran? Who was this man I thought I loved, slept with, and wanted to marry? Was he a liar and a cheat? Or merely a flawed human being who had failed himself and others?

And who was I? A party to adultery, or another flawed human being eager to love and be loved?

Kathy's voice came back over the line, even steadier than before. "You've been a comfort to him, Miss Prescott. A friend when he needed one badly. For that I'm grateful, but now I need you to be a friend to both of us, and to the baby. I'm asking you to stop seeing him—to give us a chance to be a couple again."

"You're asking me to end it with Trey—because he can't do it himself. Is that it?"

"I suppose. Yes."

Why would any woman want a man that weak? And yet here I was, clinging to him.

Despite the turmoil, I found myself admiring Kathy for the strength it took to call me. Instead of being angry at Trey, I hurt for his wife. If I had been a distant third party instead of a participant, I know whose side I would have taken—and it wasn't Trey's.

The silence was electric until Kathy broke it. "I know this is a difficult request, an unusual one. But I had to call. You needed to know the truth, and I know how Trey is. He believes what he wants to believe. Right now, he's conflicted. I'm asking you to make the decision for him. To end it. At the very least, to give us six months to save our family."

It was a reasonable request, but something in me balked. "Divorced or not, you'll have a family."

"Yes, but you know what I mean. I want Trey to be with his son or daughter every day, not just weekends."

Her words hit like a slap, stunning me into a new clarity. I had wanted children with Trey and had imagined him as a dedicated father, a man who loved and taught his children in small, everyday ways. Geography mattered—more than I wanted to acknowledge. How could Trey be the kind of dad he'd want to be if he moved to Wyoming?

"Will you at least think about it?" Kathy asked.

"Yes." There was no choice. "Yes, Kathy. I will."

"Thank you." With those two humbling words, she hung up.

This time I set the phone down so gently it didn't make

a sound, but my thoughts spun into a whirlwind. As if a tornado had picked me up, I found myself spinning to the point of nausea, helplessly dizzy, and running for the bathroom.

Chapter 26

*B*reakfast with Lyn unfolded exactly how Daisy expected. Lyn told her to take her time, think and pray, and to be brave. A position with Maggie's House, as an assistant manager at one of their safe houses, was Daisy's anytime she wanted it.

Only Daisy didn't want to be brave. She wanted to stay in Refuge forever, but that choice might cost her a future with Rafe. She longed to be with him, but her stomach plummeted at the thought of leaving her nest. God had brought her to Refuge. He'd given her roots. Why would he yank her out of a safe place and replant her now? On the other hand, if she moved to a new city, she'd make new friends, both at church and in AA.

Unable to sleep on Thursday night, she punched her pillow into a ball and worried. Chelsea was out late with

Chad despite saying she'd be home by eleven, and Daisy needed to be at work early tomorrow to help the reps from Coogan's Clowns set up for a rodeo demonstration. Charity number four, the literacy group, had visited yesterday. Though impressive, they wanted to tear down the historic buildings.

That left the clown school. The clowns and Patrick Coogan, the CEO of Coogan Rodeo Enterprises, the parent organization to Coogan's Clowns, were staying in the bunkhouse rather than a hotel. Tomorrow promised to be a full day for everyone and it would start early.

Tiny feet pattered down the hall to Daisy's bedroom. Sitting up, she saw Hannah in the doorway, silhouetted by the plug-in night-light and clutching her ratty stuffed dog.

"Hey, kiddo." Daisy kept her voice worry-free. "What's up?"

"I'm scared-ed."

"Of what?"

"My mommy's not home."

"She'll be home soon." At least Daisy hoped so. It was close to midnight. She patted her own bed and made room for Hannah. "Come and get cozy."

Still clutching her dog, Hannah tumbled into bed and snuggled under the covers. When she settled, Daisy checked her phone for a text from Chelsea. When she saw nothing, she shot off a text of her own. *WHERE ARE YOU?*

While waiting for Chelsea's reply, Daisy rubbed Hannah's back and pondered the situation. Chelsea had told Daisy she loved Chad, but Daisy wondered if Chelsea loved Chad or if she just *wanted* to love him. There was a difference, one that gave Daisy a measure of comfort concerning her feelings for Rafe. She didn't just *want* to love him. Her feelings came from knowing him as a person. Loving him was downright inconvenient, which inspired a frustrated pout.

Her phone finally buzzed with a text from Chelsea. *Horrible night. Am OK. Almost home.*

"That's your mommy," Daisy told Hannah. "She's almost home."

Hannah nodded, sucked her thumb, and relaxed enough to close her eyes. Daisy slipped out of bed and went to the living room to wait. Ten minutes later, Chelsea walked into the apartment, her eyes red-rimmed and puffy. Before either of them could say a word, Daisy wrapped her in a hug.

Chelsea eased back with a shrug. "He dumped me."

"Oh, Chels. I'm so sorry."

"Me too."

"Do you want to talk about it?" Daisy would be exhausted tomorrow for the clowns, but Chelsea needed her now. "How about hot chocolate?" She would have offered to make toast, but they didn't have a toaster.

"Hot chocolate would be nice." Chelsea kicked off the cute shoes that matched her capris and sassy crop top.

"Go put on your jammies," Daisy offered. "The hot chocolate will be ready in a minute."

While Chelsea changed clothes, Daisy warmed milk in the microwave, mixed in chocolate powder, and fetched the bag of mini marshmallows Chelsea kept for Hannah. A few minutes later, they both dropped down on the couch that used to be in Shane's apartment.

"Talk," Daisy said as she lifted her mug of hot chocolate. "What did the jerk do?" Even if Chad had ended the relationship for a good reason, girlfriend-support demanded he be a jerk.

"We've seen a lot of each other, and it's been good." Chelsea paused to sip her hot chocolate.

"You seemed happy."

"So did he, but tonight everything changed. He wanted

to get a lot more physical than I did—and that wasn't fair to me. I told him on our second date I didn't want that kind of relationship without a real commitment."

"Oh, Chels—"

"I guess he didn't believe me." Defeat colored her voice, along with rusty hues of bitterness.

"Did he end it, or did you?"

"I did." Chelsea sipped the hot chocolate again. "I'd rather make a clean break than be ghosted."

To ghost someone meant to block them on social media and disappear without an explanation. No closure allowed. It was devastating to the ghostee—the person left to wonder what they had done wrong or why they weren't enough. Daisy thought ghosting was despicable.

Chelsea set the mug down with a thud, reached for the bag of marshmallows, and put a handful in her mug.

Daisy added a few to her own cup. "It hurts, but you're better off without him."

Chelsea shook her head. "That's easy for you to say. Rafe's a really good guy."

"He's also from Ohio, and he's going back in a few weeks." Daisy hadn't told Chelsea about Lyn's offer in Cincinnati, only that she'd withdrawn the proposal. Now didn't seem like the right time.

Chelsea's mouth pursed into a frown. "You and Rafe seem pretty serious. Have you talked about him leaving—or maybe staying?"

"A little." Maybe a distraction would help Chelsea. "He invited me to visit him."

"Wow. That *does* sound serious."

"It could be. In fact, it is. Rafe used the *L* word."

"Oh, Daize—" Chelsea pressed her hands to her own chest. "Did you say it back?"

"No, but I wanted to."

"Daize! Go for it! I've seen the way Rafe looks at you.

He's head-over-heels. He has a job. He's a decent guy. What in the world is holding you back?"

"Refuge is my home. I don't want to leave."

"Oh, come on!" Chelsea bolted upright. "You tell other people to be brave all the time. I think it's your turn."

Daisy bristled from head to toe. Chelsea *had no idea* how hard it was for Daisy to stand on her own two feet. Even more to the point, she didn't understand Daisy's faith, and that being brave meant trusting God—not her own instincts or desires. She didn't want Chelsea's advice, and she definitely did *not* want to debate. "We can talk about me another time."

"Or now."

"No." Daisy decided to play the distraction card. "By the way—about Chad—Rafe calls him Mr. Man-Bun. They didn't exactly hit it off."

Chelsea laughed, but it sounded hollow. "I'm sure Rafe won't mind not having dinner at the Green Light again."

"No."

"Neither will I." Chelsea picked up the marshmallow bag for the second time and added another handful to her cup. "Bring on the highly processed, artificially flavored junk food. It's more real than Chad." But then she shoved the bag aside, her shoulders slumping again. "I want a relationship. I want to *matter*. Is that too much to ask?"

"No. It's not." Daisy saw an opening and took it. "How about doing something completely different? Come with me to church on Sunday."

"I won't fit in."

"Yes, you will. If I fit, you'll fit."

"It's just not my thing, but you—you're doing fantastic right now."

Daisy shook her head. "It might look that way tonight, but I freaked out over Maggie's House and ended up in the fetal position. You should have seen me. I was a mess."

"I can't picture it."

"It wasn't pretty, but this is where my faith comes in. God helped me get through it. Now we need to get *you* past Chad." But how? A fun idea came to mind—something that didn't happen every day. Daisy played it up with a hint of mystery. "So . . . do you work tomorrow?"

"No. It's my regular day off."

"How would you like to bring Hannah to see a clown show?" She told Chelsea about tomorrow's charity visit. "They need an audience, so Miss Joan invited all her staff and the crew at Heritage House. MJ's bringing Cody and some of his friends."

Chelsea perked up. "Hannah will love it."

"So no 'guy stuff' tomorrow. Just you and your little girl having a good time."

"Well . . ." Chelsea dragged out the word. "That depends."

"On what?"

"If I meet a cute cowboy who calls me 'darlin',' I just might get back in the game—especially if he has beard scruff."

"And smoky brown eyes—"

"*And* he's not a vegetarian!"

They broke out laughing, but the good mood faded quickly. Chelsea eyed her phone sitting by the marshmallow bag. "I don't know, Daize. Maybe I should get back in the game so I don't brood over Chad."

"Forget it. You need time to heal."

"Or maybe it's like getting back on the horse that bucked me off." Leaning forward, Chelsea snagged her phone, swiped and tapped, then set it down. "There. It's done. I'm back on FriendsFirst. I'm not going to let Chad get me down."

"Chels—"

"Don't worry about me, okay? I know what I'm doing."

Rafe eyeballed the big white bull waiting in the pen next to the temporary arena erected where *Thunder Valley* used to be filmed. The beast was huge. And ugly. Kind of dumb-looking, too, though Rafe suspected the bull had more smarts than a lot of the criminals he'd arrested.

The clown show was scheduled to start in just a few minutes. Jesse stood next to him at the fence, while members of the work crew were spread between the fence and the portable bleacher stand. Cliff, Ana, and a half dozen ranch hands were roaming around, distracted by the clowns vying for their attention with balloons and face paint. MJ, Cody, and three of his friends were seated in the bleachers. Rafe expected to see Chelsea and Hannah, but they weren't in his line of sight.

Neither was Daisy, though she had greeted him earlier before going back to play hostess and go-to girl to Patrick Coogan, the clown school owner.

Miss Joan walked up to the fence where a podium and portable loudspeaker were set up. A classic beige Stetson tilted back on her head, and she sported boots and a sequined denim vest like a rodeo queen.

He decided to have a little fun with her. "Hey, Miss Joan." When she turned, he hooked a thumb toward the bull. "Where did that cow come from?"

"Oh, for goodness' sake!" She huffed just like he'd expected. "That's a bull—not a cow. You *are* a city boy, aren't you?"

"I sure am." He grinned at his own joke, but this morning's FaceTime call with Dr. Susan had planted a new seed of concern in his mind. When he told her about his deepening feelings for Daisy, the therapist brought up the danger element of his work and asked how Daisy felt about it.

Rafe couldn't answer. He'd made his peace with the risk when he took the oath, but could Daisy make that same commitment? She understood danger far more intimately than most people.

If he truly loved her—and he did—he needed to put her needs before his own. Being a deputy in Refuge might not be bad . . . not bad at all. Except the salary was lower, and there were fewer opportunities for advancement—which meant less money for a mortgage, decent cars, eventually diapers, family vacations, and maybe college. Love mattered more than money, but he'd grown up without quite enough and wanted to be a good provider. Saying good-bye to the city he loved wouldn't be easy. He'd miss knowing the names of all the streets, seeing longtime friends, and eating Graeter's Ice Cream or a Coney smothered in chili. It felt right to research the possibility of staying in Refuge, but Rafe was a city boy at heart—a city boy in love with an ex-city girl.

"Hey there."

Daisy's voice drifted over his shoulder. He turned, expecting to see her in work attire. Instead his gaze landed on the yellow butterflies painted on her cheeks and the sparkly antennae springing up from a rhinestone headband. Her nose was painted bug-black. Hannah, wearing jeans and a pink t-shirt, sat on Daisy's hip. A silver crown sat crookedly on her head, and pink hearts seemed to dance on the child's cheeks. Since Barbie night, he and Hannah had become friends thanks to the times he'd visited Daisy's apartment.

The child grinned at him as if she expected him to be surprised. Rafe put on a show for her. "Wow! I see a butterfly and a *real princess*."

Hannah giggled. "I have a ti-a-ra."

"I bet you just learned that word."

"I did!"

He gave her a high-five and they cheered with Daisy looking on. If Hannah hadn't already melted his tough-guy heart, the admiration on Daisy's face would have done it like a blow torch.

They were exchanging a long look when Hannah spotted Chelsea and waved. "Mommy! Look at me!"

"You look beautiful, baby!" Chelsea blew a kiss from a seat on the bleachers, then shoulder-bumped the guy sitting next to her. Rafe recognized Brett Lawson, a man Jesse had recently hired. Rafe didn't know Brett well, but Jesse performed thorough background checks. Even so, Chelsea's ease with a man she barely knew concerned him.

Daisy whispered over Hannah's head. "As you can see, it's over with Chad."

"Oh yeah?"

"Yes. Long story. She dropped him."

"Sorry to hear it." He hesitated, then gave Daisy a sheepish look. "Well, not really. Maybe she'll give dating a rest." *And not drag you into her drama.*

"No such luck." Daisy set Hannah down, urged her to go to her mommy, then focused back on Rafe. "She's back on FriendsFirst and talking about another app. I'm worried about her."

"So am I—"

Classic circus music broke out over the portable sound system, signaling the start of the event. Rafe guided Daisy to the bleachers. Jesse followed them, but Miss Joan stayed by the podium. He and Daisy sat next to MJ near the top.

Howie, two rows below, looked over his shoulder and gave Rafe his customary scowl. "Fine, SuperCop. Sit with the pretty ladies instead of us thugs."

"You bet," Rafe replied.

When the music faded, a clown in baggy orange check-ered pants escorted Miss Joan to the podium. She picked up the microphone like a pro, waited for the group to quiet down, and welcomed them all.

"This is a little bit like our old TV days," she remarked. "*Thunder Valley* brought a lot of pleasure to families across America, and the rodeo clown demonstration we're about to see brings personal pleasure to me today. Since 1972, Cottonwood Acres has rescued countless retired ro-deo horses. The men and women who loved and cared for those horses are dear to my heart. So is the sport that tests strength, perseverance, and courage.

"I'm honored to introduce you to Patrick Coogan, a vet-eran rodeo clown and CEO of Coogan Rodeo Enterprises, the parent company to Coogan's Clowns."

Rafe expected a clown in costume to make a big en-trance. Instead a fifty-something man in a tailored suit and wingtip shoes took the microphone with the ease of a CEO.

"Thank you, Miss Joan, for the generous welcome." His baritone voice rang with authority. "And thank you all for coming today. Like Miss Joan said, I'm a retired rodeo clown. I started as a bull rider, and soon gained a deep respect for the role of a rodeo clown. You may not realize it—I see a few city boys here—but clowns put their lives on the line every day. The clown protects the cowboy—"

As a cop, Rafe could relate.

"And he often does it without the respect he deserves. The rodeo clown switches from life-and-death danger to lighthearted entertainment in just minutes, sometimes seconds."

Rafe nodded without thinking. What Coogan described sounded a lot like a domestic violence call. Subdue the perpetrator; comfort the victims. He'd once told knock-knock jokes to a frightened five-year-old boy while his mother was taken into custody.

The CEO swept the crowd with his eyes. "You can joke about clowns all you want, but I'm proud of the rodeo clown heritage, and even more proud of our school and the charitable work we do. We teach riding, roping, and general rodeo skills to adolescents, both male and female, who need to make a change in their lives."

Daisy leaned close and whispered, "Now I know why Miss Joan liked this proposal so much."

Patrick glanced over to the pen holding the bull. A clown signaled with a thumbs-up, and Patrick resumed his talk. "Today's show is just a small taste of what it's like in the ring. But before we let Cotton Ball do his thing, let's have some fun."

Music blasted from the loudspeaker, Coogan left the podium, and a female clown launched into a row of hand-springs while a trumpet played a fanfare. The clowns went to town with gymnastics, a unicycle routine, and a comedy skit with two of them pretending to be a bull and the others subduing it. Cotton Ball made a thunderous entrance with a rider on his back. The rider went flying after eight seconds, the clowns did their job, and the show wrapped up with the bleacher crowd cheering.

Daisy gave Rafe's hand a squeeze where no one would see. "That was wonderful. I have to get back to work, but I'll see you tonight, right?"

"You bet." Between now and then, he planned to do a little research about Wyoming law enforcement. City boy or not, he really could do his job anywhere.

Chapter 27

*W*hile the clowns took their bows, Daisy said good-bye to MJ and Cody, blew Hannah a kiss, and hurried over to Miss Joan and Patrick Coogan. She needed to focus on doing her job, but the picture of Rafe high-fiving Hannah over the word *tiara* lingered in the back of her mind. He'd be a good father—the kind of dad who knew when to enforce rules and when to get on the floor and be silly.

Sweet shivers rippled down her spine. Yesterday she'd googled Cincinnati just to see what it looked like. The skyline at dusk really was pretty, but what most caught her eye was an attraction in nearby Kentucky called The Ark Encounter. Imagine—a full-size replica of Noah's Ark! If Noah could build an ark and face a flood, surely Daisy could manage a visit to Rafe's hometown.

Pleased with her courage, she approached Miss Joan and Patrick with a grin. "That was great!"

When he nodded modestly, Daisy saw a man accustomed to praise but unimpressed by it.

Miss Joan's smile couldn't have been brighter. "Patrick has a plane to catch. Is there anything we need before he leaves?"

Daisy verbalized her close-out list for today's show, ticking off items as she spoke. "I think we're all set—except me saying thanks for a fun day. My nephew and his friends loved it."

"My pleasure," he said. "And thank you too, Daisy. You made this easy. If we're fortunate enough to be chosen for the giveaway, you definitely have a job with Coogan's Clowns."

"I do?" Shock rippled through her. "What would it involve?"

"Pretty much what you do now. Miss Joan told me you coordinated all the charity visits, including the travel arrangements. We'll need someone to schedule classes and events for us, handle meet-and-greets, and generally keep our programs running well."

Daisy could only gape at him. A job . . . in Refuge . . . doing what she loved. Her stomach plummeted to her toes as she shot up a confused prayer. *Oh, Lord! What are you doing?*

Patrick smiled in a way that reminded her of Miss Joan, then excused himself to speak to his manager.

Miss Joan turned to Daisy. "We need to talk—now." Shoulders squared, she marched down the concrete path to the house.

Taking long strides, Daisy barely saw the roses waiting to bloom, spiky juniper shrubs, and patches of pampas grass that lined the walk. The smell of fertilizer irritated her nose, a chemical odor that reminded her of the smells in Los Angeles, and she wondered if Cincinnati smelled that bad.

The women didn't speak until they reached Miss Joan's office and Miss Joan shut the door. Excitement glinted in her eyes as she tossed her Stetson down on the coffee table and turned to meet Daisy's gaze.

"What did you think?" Miss Joan asked.

"I loved today." Daisy sat down on the couch, the same one where she'd interviewed six weeks ago. "I see why you picked them for the top five. Do you think this is the one?"

"It could be." Still tense, Miss Joan walked over to the window and stared through the panes. "Patrick impressed me, and they plan to utilize the ranch to its fullest potential."

"Is there anything you didn't like?"

"It's a perfect fit. I just wish . . ." Her voice faded into a silent shake of her head.

"What is it?"

Miss Joan kept her back turned, but Daisy saw her shoulders slump as she crossed her arms over her midsection. Something was wrong. This woman was like a mother to Daisy. She'd given her comfort and confidence in a way no one else could. Daisy saw a chance to return that kindness and grabbed it. "Would you like to talk about it? We could make toast."

Miss Joan turned with a small smile neatly in place. "Thank you, dear. Just the offer is enough to lift the burden I'm carrying. Today stirred up old memories, particularly about the start-up of the horse rescue."

Daisy knew quite a bit about the early days of the Trey Cochran Rescue Ranch thanks to working on the ranch history book. "The photographs from those days are some of my favorites."

"Mine too. Trey and I were a good team—until we weren't."

Curiosity piqued, Daisy decided to ask a question—
less for herself than for Miss Joan, who seemed to want to
talk. "That photograph of you and Trey on the wall . . . I
can see how much you loved him."

"Oh, I did." Joan turned to the picture, tipped her
head, then wiped off a speck of dust. "If circumstances
had been different, I wouldn't be giving away my home. I'd
have grandchildren like my father wanted."

"Are you in touch with Trey at all?"

"No."

That was all she said. The word struck Daisy as lonely
and unfinished, especially when Miss Joan turned her
back a second time. Daisy started to go to Miss Joan to
hug her, but her gaze snagged on the computer monitor.
Even old people were on Facebook—a lot of them. Plus
Trey was famous enough to have a wiki.

"Have you ever googled him?" she asked.

Miss Joan turned around, looked from Daisy to the
computer, but didn't move. "I did once a few years ago,
but it was . . . uncomfortable. I haven't done it in a while."

"I'm not talking about cyberstalking or anything. But
if you're curious, we can do a search right now."

Miss Joan stared at the blank monitor for five full seconds, then nodded. "Let's do it. At my age, a person won-
ders who's still alive and who kicked the bucket."

Daisy held in a cringe. Jokes about death bothered
her, but maybe that was what old people needed to do.
She jiggled the mouse and typed *Trey Cochran rodeo star*
into the search engine. Links popped onto the screen,
starting with a website to The TKC Cattle Company in central Texas.

Miss Joan stood behind Daisy's chair. When she
spoke, the words came out clipped. "Click the first one,
please."

The link led to a beautiful photograph of desolate

Texas with an announcement on a beige background.

Trey Albert Cochran
1938–2018

Dear Family and Friends,
We thank you from the bottom of our hearts for
your love, prayers, and condolences at the passing of
our beloved husband, father, grandfather, and great-
grandfather.

Miss Joan's hand knotted on Daisy's shoulder. "Oh my word. He's gone."

"I'm so sorry." Reaching back, Daisy covered Miss Joan's fingers with her own and squeezed.

They read the rest of the web obituary in silence. Six months ago, Trey Cochran had suffered a heart attack while riding alone through a canyon he particularly loved. The rest of the article listed his many accomplishments in rodeo, business, and charity work. He was survived by his wife, Kathy, their three children and spouses, seven grandchildren, and two great-grandchildren.

Daisy searched for words, but there was nothing she could say to ease the shock.

Miss Joan finally stepped back. "Well. Now I know. Even after all these years . . ." She pulled a tissue from the box on her desk. "After all these years, I want to cry as if it were just yesterday that we—that he—" Miss Joan turned away, dabbed her eyes, and went to the love seat. "Trey left quite a legacy, didn't he?"

"Yes. But so will you." Daisy swiveled the chair, her hands in her lap. "I know Trey was important to you, but you're important to people, too. Especially me."

"Thank you, dear."

"Giving away Cottonwood Acres is an amazing thing to

do. I admit I'm still a little sad about Maggie's House, but after today, I can see that you and Lyn were right. The rodeo school is a much better fit."

"Perhaps." Her voice held no life. "I'm too shaken to decide this minute. But there's something I very much need to say to you."

"Me?"

"Yes." Miss Joan stared hard through her misty eyes. "Love requires sacrifice. But it can't survive if you compromise your values."

Daisy almost said *huh?* but held it in. Miss Joan was probably talking to herself more than to Daisy.

"Values . . ." Miss Joan continued. "I'm very sorry for what happened with Trey. I loved him. Those feelings were genuine, but what we did was wrong—dreadfully so. But that mistake opened my eyes to my own weaknesses—and how much I need God's grace."

"We all do," Daisy murmured. "What happened? No. Wait—" Daisy's cheeks flamed. "This is so personal. I shouldn't have asked."

"Ask away." Miss Joan's voice steadied. "If anyone can learn from my mistake, I'm glad to share it. It eases my guilt. You see, Trey was a married man."

Daisy winced. "Oh no."

"*Oh no* is right." Miss Joan held her head high. "He was in the middle of a divorce. And I say *middle* with some bitterness. He told me the marriage was over except for the legalities. That proved to be untrue—or inaccurate, depending on one's perspective."

"You're so principled. I can't imagine you as . . ." Daisy didn't want to say it.

Miss Joan arched a brow. "The evil other woman?"

"Not evil. Just . . . I don't know."

"Imperfect?"

"I guess."

"Don't be surprised, dear. Human beings are capable of both great love and great mistakes. With Trey, I experienced both. I'll tell you the whole story another time. Suffice it to say that ending the relationship was the most painful moment of my life—and the best decision I've ever made, because it led me to Christ." Her expression softened as she held Daisy's gaze. "Hiring you is the *second* best decision of my life."

Daisy smiled, mostly because she knew Miss Joan wanted to change the mood. "You know what an impact you've had on me. I'm so grateful."

"And so am I." Miss Joan leaned back against the couch. A long moment passed before she tossed the tissue in the trash can by the desk. "Enough of my personal soap opera. Let's talk about Coogan's Clowns. I overheard Patrick offer you a job."

"Do you think he meant it?"

"I'm sure he did."

"Wow." Daisy could hardly believe it. "I'm grateful, of course. But I've been thinking about visiting Cincinnati. Rafe invited me to go anytime, maybe September. I just don't know."

"Why wouldn't you visit?"

"Because it could make things even harder—for me *and* for Rafe. When I started dating him, I thought it would be a summer romance—not an I-can't-live-without-you romance. It might be easier on both of us to make a clean break when he leaves."

"Do you really want to end it?"

Daisy tried to shrug as if she didn't know the answer, but her shoulders refused to budge. "I love him. *I do.* But Refuge is my home. I've never really had one before now."

Miss Joan's eyes misted with sympathy. "You're a baby bird safe in the nest, aren't you?"

"I suppose."

"You *do* know what birds are made to do?"

"Fly?" Daisy winced at the word.

"Yes. Just how far and how high is up to God. Sometimes we have to make hard decisions, even sacrifices, and trust that God won't nudge us out of the nest before our wings are strong enough to sustain us. Whom the Lord calls, he prepares."

Daisy frowned. "You sound like Lyn. And Shane and MJ. Not to mention the pastor at church."

"We all love you, Daisy." Miss Joan's eyes misted again. "And we all want you to be happy and safe. Whether you want my advice or not, I'm about to give it to you—"

"Yes, I want it."

"Go to Cincinnati. See the sights. But most of all, see Rafe's life. You haven't known each other very long, but I see something special between you two. Give that *something* a chance to grow."

"Maybe I should." Money wasn't a problem. The Maggie's House organization would pay expenses if she did some legwork for them, and she was sure Rafe would help her check out locations for a residence. A visit would be a baby step—something small she could handle with God's help.

"I'll do it," she told Miss Joan. "I'll tell Rafe tonight."

Chapter 28

Old age is no place for sissies.
Bette Davis

Grey . . . dead. It didn't seem possible. In Joan's mind, he was forever thirty-something, handsome with a flat stomach, his hair jet-black and his face as solid as the day she first saw him on the *Thunder Valley* set. He hadn't changed a bit in her memory. Neither had the mountains silhouetted against the starry night sky, pointing upward as she waited on the deck for Sadie to do her business.

Instead of circling the house as usual, Joan stood at the rail facing the barn and bunkhouse. Her arthritic knee appreciated her lack of will to walk, but it was the ache in her chest that kept her anchored to this particular spot.

She hadn't spoken to Trey even once since the end of their affair, but over the years she heard bits of news. He and Kathy had reconciled, and he walked away from his rodeo legacy for the quiet life of a rancher. At Joan's request, her attorney handled the paperwork dissolving their business association, and she changed the name of the horse rescue to something innocuous.

Emotions roiled through her now, much like the ones she'd endured the night of Kathy's phone call. But tonight, with the news of Trey's passing fresh, she didn't want to relive the anger and guilt. She wanted to remember the man who loved horses, took time for others, and tried to be decent despite his flaws.

When Sadie ambled up the steps, Joan headed for the front door. "Come on, old girl. Let's watch some television."

In the living room, Joan picked up the remote, started part two of the episode starring Trey, and settled on the couch with Sadie at her feet.

The show opened where part one left off—with Josiah Bent bleeding in the dirt. Becky and her son, Edward, managed to get him into the house, then Edward raced off to fetch the doctor. The kindly old man removed two bullets, cautioned Becky about infection, and promised to check in.

All three of Becky's children asked hard questions, especially Edward. When she told him Josiah was being pursued by an old enemy, the boy picked up the .22 rifle he used to hunt rabbits, went out to the porch, and sat with the weapon over his knees.

When Becky approached him, he spoke to her like the man he wanted to be.

"I'll protect you, Mama. My sisters too. And Mr. Bent. I know he did bad things. But he's not a bad man. Not anymore."

Becky held in a sob. So did Joan when the actress returned to Josiah's bedside, fell to her knees, and pleaded with God to spare his life. In true Hollywood fashion, she stumbled to her feet and laid her trembling hand on his forehead to check for fever.

The camera zoomed in on his makeup-reddened face, the beads of artificial sweat, and the hair styled to cling to his temples.

For three long days, Becky pressed cold cloths to his fevered skin, spooned broth into his cracked lips, and held him down when he thrashed with delirium. She repeatedly begged God to spare his life, but what would they do if he lived? Alone at his bedside, by the light of a single dying candle, she cried out to God once again. Utterly exhausted, she rested her head on her arms on the side of his bed and wept.

Joan admired the actress who played Becky Monroe. The woman possessed a rare talent. Even so, Trey stole the scene right out from under her. With Becky sobbing, Josiah heaved a deep, shuddering breath and didn't inhale again for five impossibly long seconds. Becky thought he was gone, but instead he opened his eyes, caressed her cheek with a shaky hand, and asked for a sip of water.

Becky leapt to her feet. "I love you, Josiah Bent! Don't you dare leave me again!"

"I won't, darlin'." His voice rasped over his dry lips. "The good Lord spared my life for a reason—and that reason is to love and care for you and the children. If danger comes knockin', we'll face it together."

Whenever Joan felt nostalgic and watched this episode, she battled bitterness. In the light of her own experience, Josiah's promise usually struck her as maudlin and even naïve. But tonight tears welled in her eyes as she watched the final minutes of the final episode of *Thunder Valley.*

With Becky's love and care, Josiah recovered and they planned to marry on Sunday after church, daring to believe Enoch Grant would believe Josiah was dead.

On the day of the wedding, Josiah stood in the parlor, dressed in a black suit, waiting for his bride, and eager to take the family to the church. Becky and the girls were upstairs putting on their finery, while Edward hitched up the wagon in the barn.

Hoofbeats thudded in the yard. Josiah peeked through the curtained window, saw Enoch Grant, and knew what he had to do. Strapping on his guns, he prayed Becky would forgive him and stepped outside.

Grant leveled his rifle at Josiah's chest. "You're like a cat with nine lives, Bent. Get ready, because you're on your last one."

"Not here." Josiah raised his hands over his head. "I don't deserve even a shred of mercy from you, Mr. Grant. I killed your son and I deserve to die. You can hang me for it or shoot me dead. I'm not going to fight you again. But I'm asking for one small mercy. Let's finish this away from the house. There's a woman inside—and children. They don't need to see me die."

Grant's eyes narrowed. "Maybe I should let you live— and kill one of them instead—right in front of your eyes. Then you'd know how I feel."

Josiah lowered his arms. He'd fake going for his gun to draw fire if that's what it took to save Becky and children, but then Edward came out of the barn, leading the horses and wagon. The boy saw Grant, froze, then lifted his little .22 out of the wagon.

"No," Josiah muttered.

The camera zoomed in on Edward taking aim at Grant, then on the boy's finger on the trigger, tense and ready to pull until the camera cut back to Josiah. To his left, the cabin door burst open and Becky's twin daughters chased each other into the yard, oblivious to Edward and Grant.

Josiah did what he had to do. He shot Grant in the leg, sparing his life but saving the girls.

Grant fell to the ground in a heap. Josiah took the man's rifle and holstered his own gun as Becky, ashen-faced, ran through the door.

Grant looked up at Josiah. "You could have killed me, but you didn't. Why?"

"I deserve to die for what I did," Josiah said, his voice cracking. "But God was merciful. I'm a changed man, Grant. Killing you wasn't right."

Grant stared at Josiah, then Becky and the children. The hate drained out of him as he struggled to sit up. "Something in us both died today. I'm done."

"So am I." Josiah turned to Becky and reached for her trembling hand. The children gathered at her sides. Holding her fingers tight, he dropped to one knee. "I love you, Becky Monroe. If you can still see fit to marry me after today, I'll be the happiest man in the world."

Tears of joy flooded her eyes. "Of course, I'll marry you!"

Josiah rose to his full height and drew her into his arms. "How about next Sunday? Right now we need to get Mr. Grant to a doctor."

Grant gave a nod and Josiah helped him to his feet. As the men shook hands, the scene faded into empty blue sky.

The words *A Week Later* rolled on the screen, and the camera zoomed in on Becky and Josiah exchanging wedding vows on a hill dotted with wildflowers. Violin music turned into a jaunty tune full of joy, and as usual Joan didn't know whether to roll her eyes at the sentimentality or to weep with joy for Becky and Josiah.

Tonight, she wept. That last episode of *Thunder Valley* had been filmed decades ago, but when Joan stopped the

DVD, she was trembling with grief, angry at Trey, and back in 1972.

Kathy's voice played in my head as the bathroom spun out of control. Nausea overwhelmed me, and I threw up. Then I collapsed to the floor and buried my face in my hands. The sourness in my mouth mirrored the sickness in my soul.

Trey's wife—*his wife*—was eight weeks pregnant. My mind counted off the weeks. There was no doubt about it. He had made love to Kathy in the middle of telling me it was over between them.

Renewed fury pulsed through me. If he'd walked into that bathroom, I would have slapped him. But even so, my heart longed to make excuses for him. Accidents happen. People get carried away. Sex is a powerful force, and he couldn't help himself.

And yet—there was no way I could justify Trey's behavior. He'd lied to me.

Still. Married.

He. Lied.

Black and white, right? But in the next breath, I was in the fetal position. Weeping. Grieving. Justifying my decisions. Trey loved me. I was sure of it. We belonged together. I could feel it as plainly as the cold tile against my burning cheek. Our love was a grand and living thing—something remarkable to be cherished. A soul connection that trumped every other connection in the human experience.

Maybe that's true for a parent's love of their child. Or for a husband and wife. But with the bathroom stinking of vomit, the cold tile pressing against my cheek, and the hardness of it bruising my hip, the sharp knife of reason cut through my sobs.

If my love for him trumped everything else, what did that say about *Kathy's* feelings for her *husband*?

And what about Trey's feelings for both of us? And the child she was carrying?

I cried for what felt like an eternity. I thought of my father wanting a houseful of grandchildren; my female ancestors breathing life and wisdom into future generations; of my mother fighting the cancer that destroyed her body but not her spirit. *Be brave, Joan.* Her final words to me.

I didn't feel brave at that moment. I felt nothing but anger, hate, and betrayal. Worst of all, I had lied as badly as Trey—I had lied to myself, betrayed my own integrity. Maybe someday I could forgive Trey. But how could I ever forgive myself?

I lay there for over an hour. Eventually the tears eased, and I knew what I had to do. It was after midnight when I splashed cold water on my face, picked up the phone, and dialed Trey's number without caring about the hour.

He answered in a sleepy voice, and I wondered if Kathy was next to him. I hoped so, because I wanted her to know my intention—that I respected her and was honoring her request.

"It's over," I said. "You lied to me. And I lied to myself."

"Joanie—"

"You lied," I repeated, my voice strong. But then something in me quaked and my voice cracked into pieces. "Oh, Trey—it hurts too much. It—"

"Darlin'—"

"Don't call me that!"

"I hate myself right now." Every word he spoke cut me even deeper. "I hate how I hurt you, and how I hurt Kathy. I hate how I lied to you and to myself."

"And to her!"

"To everyone," he murmured. "I don't expect you to

forgive me, Joan. I don't deserve it. But I hope that some-day—maybe—"

Forgive him? Was he crazy? I could barely keep from eviscerating him over the phone. *Liar. Cheat. Fraud. Fake.*

I knew my voice would quaver, but I choked out what needed to be said. "We're done, Trey. Make your marriage work. Be a good husband to Kathy and a good father to your child. I want just one last thing from you."

"Anything, Joanie. *Anything.*"

"Don't ever call me again."

"But, Joan—"

"*Never.* I mean it. Good-bye, Trey."

I hung up. Then prayed that he wouldn't show up on my doorstep in one breath, and hoped that he would in the next. That's the problem with emotions. They can be fickle

"*H*ey, SuperCop." Howie flung a wad of used drywall tape into Rafe's face. "Ben just called it a day and you're standing there like a moron."

Or like a man anticipating a week in his hometown with the most beautiful, most delightful woman in the universe—the woman he loved. Rafe was still looking into law enforcement opportunities in the general vicinity of Refuge, but Daisy's willingness to visit Cincy put a supersized grin on his face.

When she'd told him about checking out the city for Maggie's House, he'd sent up a prayer of gratitude. He knew God wasn't a genie in a bottle, but Rafe had been praying hard for God to work out the situation in a way that gave them both peace of mind.

He picked up the wad of tape and tossed it in the

trash. "Thanks for the wake-up call. My mind wandered."

"Yeah, I bet—right to Daisy, huh?"

"You guessed it."

They cleaned up what needed to be cleaned up, then piled into the crew cab truck with Ben behind the wheel.

No one said much during the ride back to Refuge. It had been a long day, but the project was going well. The instant Ben pulled into the Donovan Construction parking lot, the men were ready to climb out. As the truck doors opened, Rafe checked his phone. It was Wednesday, Daisy's AA night. She wouldn't be around, but he saw a cute message from her. He answered back like he usually did, then decided to go home and work up a sweat on Jesse's exercise equipment. Key fob in hand, he headed to his car.

"Hey, Rafe." Howie called to him from twenty feet away. "What are you up to right now?"

"Not much. Why?"

Howie walked over. "My car's at the tire place on Pioneer. They just texted that it's ready. Could you give me a lift?"

"Climb on in."

Howie hesitated. "No plans with Daisy?"

"Not tonight."

They climbed into the Camaro and took off for the tire store. Ten minutes later, Rafe steered into a parking spot facing a strip mall across the street.

Howie was about to climb out when something caught his eye. "Man, that stinks."

"What?"

"Across the street—that black Honda Civic belongs to a guy named Jax Martin. He's the local pharmacist, if you get my drift."

"I get it just fine."

Rafe followed Howie's gaze to the sports sedan parked

away from the other vehicles in a lot that served a popular café, a trendy secondhand store, the worst Chinese restaurant in Refuge, and a few other businesses. A man sat in the driver's seat, his elbow jutting out of the open window. Maybe he was on his phone. Or maybe he was waiting for someone. Ugly things tended to happen when people lurked in parking lots for no apparent reason. Out of habit, Rafe wrote down the license plate.

Howie's face hardened into steel. "That dude is trouble. You know the pitch. 'First one's free,' and bam—someone falls off the wagon. Jesse caught him hanging around the new worksite. You know your brother. He walked right up to the guy, told him to get lost, and called the cops on him. Jax took off like a scared rabbit."

That sounded like Jesse—bold, in control, and lethal. "I like how Jesse thinks."

"I haven't seen that Jax guy in a while."

"Well, he's here now." Rafe's cop blood heated. Back in Cincy, drug dealers were like gnats with cell phones. A buyer called, and the dealer set up a meeting at a random location. Less than a minute later, everyone was gone.

Air gusted through Howie's nose. "I just don't want to see one of our guys here, you know?"

"Me neither."

A minute later, the door to the thrift shop opened and Chelsea walked out, holding Hannah with one hand and toting a shopping bag with the other. Jax exited the Honda and headed for the coffee place, putting him on a collision course with Chelsea.

Rafe stared through the windshield, taking in Chelsea's pace and direction. "That's Daisy's roommate. If she knows Jax, Daisy could be in trouble."

Howie sat straighter in the seat and stared.

Instead of avoiding Jax, Chelsea greeted him with a big wave and a smile. Jax waved back and approached her.

Every hair on the back of Rafe's neck prickled. Hannah squirmed but stayed by her mother's side. Chelsea and Jax were chatting now. Was she buying narcotics? It seemed unlikely. He'd never once seen her high, and their paths crossed frequently at Daisy's apartment.

Howie broke the silence with a cuss word. "She's got her kid with her and she's meeting up with that piece of trash? If she gets high and drives—"

"She won't." At this point, Rafe was duty-bound to approach her as a friend if there was even a hint of trouble.

Jax and Chelsea exchanged awkward nods, and he went into the café alone. Chelsea veered to her car and put the package in the trunk. Rafe expected her to leave, but she headed back to the café.

Rafe debated on tactics. He could speak to Chelsea later, or he could do it now. He decided to do it now in order to avoid involving Daisy and to be sure Chelsea had all the facts.

"I need to talk to her," he told Howie. "I'm guessing she met Jax on a dating app and doesn't know about his side business."

"Well, she needs to know."

Rafe opened the door locks. "Get out of here. But I'm going across the street for a cup of coffee."

Howie glared at him, his know-it-all smirk firmly in place. "Don't be an idiot. If you walk in there by yourself, she'll think you've been spying on her—which is true."

"Not really."

"Well, you're watching her like a cop, right?"

Rafe couldn't deny it. "Yes, I am. But only because she's flying blind and could get in trouble. I need to talk to her."

"Fine. But I'm going with you," Howie replied. "Stay here while I pay for the tires, then I'm buying you coffee for driving me down here. We'll say hi to her together."

"Thanks. It's a good plan. That'll give me a reason to wait for her without looking like a stalker."

Howie left to settle up on his car, and Rafe drove across the street. A few minutes later, Howie pulled up in his ancient Corolla and they walked into the café together. The space was a mix of half walls, booths, and coffee-doctoring stations. Rafe spotted Jax in the back with a woman rocking spiky blue-tipped hair, maybe on a FriendsFirst date. Chelsea and Hannah were out of Jax's view, seated in a corner booth, waiting for their food to be delivered.

Howie ordered coffee, a couple of sandwiches, and two big cookies. Rafe led the way to a table by the front door. When Chelsea left, he planned to stop her.

He and Howie didn't say much as they ate, though when Jax and the blue-haired girl left, Howie shot daggers at his back. A few minutes later, Chelsea carried her tray to the bussing station, gripped Hannah's hand, and headed their way.

Rafe signaled her with a wave. She approached with a friendly smile, and he stood to greet her. "Hey, Chelsea. Do you have a minute?"

She glanced at Howie, her expression both curious and confused. "I guess. But not too long. The restaurant was slammed today. I'm beat, but at least the tips were good."

"It'll only take a minute." He nodded toward Howie and told Chelsea they worked together. "It seems that you two have a mutual friend."

"Really?" Casual interest sparked in her eyes. "Who?"

"Have a seat." Rafe pulled out a chair for Chelsea, then wrangled one from another table so Hannah could sit next to her mother. Chelsea pulled a Disney princess Barbie out of her big purse, the mermaid with flaming red hair, and gave it to Hannah.

Rafe shifted his chair so he could speak more directly to Chelsea. "How well do you know Jax Martin?"

"Jax?" Honest confusion washed over her face as she glanced from Rafe to Howie.

Howie took the cue. "The guy in the parking lot."

"I know who you mean," she replied, slightly defensive. "I just don't know why it matters. What—were you spying on me?"

"No." Rafe told her about taking Howie to pick up his car. "We were at the tire store when we saw you with Jax."

"I don't understand. I met him online. We went out once. So what?"

Howie and Rafe exchanged a look, then Rafe opened his mouth to speak. In the same instant, Hannah pushed up on her knees. The chair slid back and the doll tumbled to the floor on Howie's side.

"I've got it," he said, bending down. "How about if Hannah and I sit at the next table over? Rafe can tell you about Jax."

She hesitated—not a surprise considering Howie's rough appearance. Rafe started to speak, but Howie broke in. "I'm a grandpa. I know who Ariel is. In fact"—he looked down at Hannah—"did you know that Ariel's favorite food is fish ice cream?"

Hannah's eyes widened, then she laughed. "With chocolate on top!"

"You guessed it." Howie winked at Hannah, then turned to Chelsea to be sure she was okay with him taking Hannah to another table. When she nodded, he indicated the cookie the size of his hand. "A-okay?"

"Yes." Chelsea even smiled. "Thank you."

They went to a nearby table, and Rafe focused back on Chelsea. "I'll make this quick. Howie recognized Jax from an incident at one of Jesse's worksites. The guy's a drug dealer."

"*What!*"

"Yeah, he's dirty." Rafe told her about Jesse running Jax off the jobsite. "I thought you should know."

"I can't believe I went out with him! It was just once—this same coffee place. But still—" She whipped out her phone. "I'm blocking him right now."

Rafe nodded. "That's smart."

She heaved a sigh from deep in her chest. "I know the online world can be deceptive. I'm not stupid—or crazy. I'm careful, Rafe. *I am.* But if I don't take a chance now and then, I'll be alone for the rest of my life."

"And if you take the wrong chance, you could end up in real trouble."

"It's just so frustrating! Why can't I meet someone special?"

Rafe said nothing. He'd learned in his conversations with D'Andre that platitudes—*You'll meet someone someday; it's just not the right time*—only made the situation more awkward.

Chelsea glanced past him to Howie and Hannah. "At least I have my little girl."

"Yes, you do."

"I might not have a date for MJ's wedding, but I have Hannah." A hint of boldness returned to Chelsea's voice. "She's my plus-one for the ceremony. In fact, we just found the cutest dress for her at the secondhand store. It'll be fun."

"She's adorable."

"Who knows? Maybe I'll meet someone fun at the reception."

The reception was at the Riverbend Steakhouse and included dinner, dancing, and all the traditions. Children were invited, but Rafe couldn't see Chelsea flirting with her daughter in tow. "Are you bringing Hannah?"

"No, just to the ceremony. After that, she's spending

the night with her bestie. I just wish"—she looked right at him—"I had someone like you in my life. Daisy's a lucky woman."

"Thank you." The compliment touched him, but her wistful tone grated even worse than her chatter. "Hang in there, Chels. I'm not going to blow sunshine and tell you the right guy will come along, but I will say that life is full of surprises."

"I just hope they're good ones." She gave him a wobbly smile, and they both stood. Howie returned with Hannah, and Chelsea left with her little girl, chattering about how pretty they'd look for MJ's wedding.

Rafe and Howie waved through the window as they passed, then sat back down. Howie broke off some of the second cookie. "So how did it go?"

"Good. She blocked Jax right away." Rafe gave Howie a nod of respect. "Thanks for everything. You stopped a potentially dangerous situation."

Howie grinned. "So, SuperCop, does this make me your sidekick?"

"Nope." Rafe let the cookie sit. "It makes us partners. SuperCop and SuperCon. Sounds like a bad TV show."

"Or a good one." Howie chuckled. "Netflix here we come."

"Works for me." Rafe swigged down the last of his coffee, and they left the café, both proud of a job well done.

Daisy was about to walk into her AA meeting when Chelsea texted. Frustration shot through her. She really needed this meeting—not because she was tempted to drink, but because she was torn up over Rafe and what to do.

She opened the text, and emojis with heart-eyes stared

up at her.

> Chelsea: *If you don't marry Rafe Donovan, I will.*
> Daisy: *Ha ha! What happened?*
> Chelsea: *Details later. But he's a good guy. Seriously, you should marry him.* More heart emojis. *I envy you!!!!*

Daisy glanced at the time on her phone. She had five minutes before the meeting, so she slipped around the corner of the church building and called Chelsea. "So what happened?"

The story unfolded in typical Chelsea style. Daisy remembered Jax's profile—an electrician with insomnia. There had been no clue about his extracurricular activities. Not a surprise, but Daisy worried even more. "Maybe you should stick to people we know in real life."

"Like who?"

"Let me think." None of the men Daisy knew from church were right for Chelsea, or she wasn't right for them. But she wanted to give her friend hope. "Maybe you'll meet someone at the reception. Some of Shane's old baseball friends are coming. I've met his former roommate—"

"A professional ballplayer?"

"You got it."

Chelsea perked up. "In that case, I'm glad I bought a new dress. Well, new to me. It's from the secondhand store, but it's adorable."

They ended the call and Daisy went into the meeting. Her heart ached for Chelsea, but it also ached for herself.

Refuge or Rafe?

She wanted both, and though she was committed to visiting Cincinnati, she could hardly breathe from the fear of leaving her nest.

Chapter 30

On the day of Shane and MJ's wedding, Rafe drove alone to the church for the six o'clock ceremony. He couldn't help but wonder about his future with Daisy. In his experience, weddings were a turning point. Dating couples either fell more in love, or they backed away from each other.

He knew how *he* felt. He loved her and wanted a future with wedding rings, a couple of kids, and a dog. Wherever he worked, that meant asking Daisy to live with the risks of his career, something they hadn't directly discussed. He needed to bring it up, but she'd been somewhat distant since telling him she'd visit Cincinnati. He hoped today would tip the scale in his favor. If it did, they needed to have the *danger* talk.

She was already at the church, doing maid of honor

duties. When he arrived, he texted her and she met him in the hall outside the bridal room for a quick hello.

At the sight of her, his eyes nearly popped out of his head. He'd seen her in denim, dressed to the nines for dinner, and in business casual, but her bridesmaid's dress belonged in a class all its own. The soft rose color made her skin glow, and the strapless top showed off her shoulders and feminine curves. The floor-length skirt fell in soft waves that captured a natural elegance unique to Daisy.

"Whoa." He skimmed her from head to foot, slowly but with respect. Yearning leaked into his voice. "You look amazing."

"Thank you." Her blushing cheeks rivaled the pretty pink of the dress. "I hope I don't trip, or drop the bouquet, or—"

"You'll do great," he assured her. "I'd kiss you right now, but I don't want to mess up your lipstick."

"Smart man! I am so nervous. MJ's calmer than I am!"

Lyn poked her head out from the hallway leading to the dressing room. "Rafe—hello. We need Daisy again. You can have her back after the ceremony."

"I'm counting on it." He gave Daisy's hand a squeeze and stepped back. She scurried away but turned to blow him a kiss before vanishing down the hall.

Rafe walked into the sanctuary, soaked in the air of anticipation, and joined Jesse and Angela McCullough, Jesse's date, in the fourth pew.

A female voice came over his shoulder. "Rafe!"

He turned and saw Chelsea approaching with Hannah. Chelsea looked great in a short, peach-colored dress, but Hannah stole the show in a cloud of matching ruffles.

Chelsea gave him a desperate smile. "Could we sit with you?"

Since the episode at the coffee shop, she'd made a

point of being extra friendly. She even dropped the "if you weren't with Daisy, I'd be even friendlier" bomb again, but she did it in front of Daisy, who, to Rafe's pleasure, had hugged his arm as if to say *mine*.

Jesse and Angela slid over in the pew. Rafe stood and made introductions to Angela. Chelsea scooted in with Hannah, and they all sat with Rafe still on the aisle.

They made small talk while a harpist played Shane and MJ's favorite songs, including a delightfully campy version of "Take Me Out to the Ball Game." The music shifted to something serious, and the formalities began with the minister, Shane, and Shane's best man taking their places at the front of the church.

When Daisy made her entrance, she stole Rafe's breath—every bit of it—as she walked confidently down the aisle, her eyes focused straight ahead except for a glance and a wink just for him. She reached her spot near the altar, traded a smile with Shane, then turned to face the guests.

After a moment of silence, the harpist plucked the first notes of wedding music Rafe had heard before. When the church doors opened again, MJ stood there with Cody at her side, her chin high, flowers trembling ever so slightly, her white gown practically on fire it was so bright. Cody held out his elbow like a pro and walked his mom down the aisle.

When they reached the front of the church, MJ stopped at the front pew and hugged her mother hard. Shane came forward, gave his future mother-in-law an equally long hug, then he helped MJ up the two stairs to the altar, with Cody between them.

The minister's voice boomed through the church. "Ladies and gentlemen, friends, family, and loved ones. We're here today for a joyous event—the marriage of Shane Matthew Riley and Melissa June Townsend. Today they take a sacred step—a step that will unite them in holy matrimony. It will also make Shane a father to Cody."

The minister paused to survey the guests—a crowd of local friends with a few out-of-towners like Lyn. This was Daisy's church, too, and Rafe wondered how many people celebrating today were also her friends. Love and good will radiated from every face, even from the log walls of the church. Rafe felt welcomed, though he knew just a few people.

Light poured through the stained-glass windows as the minister continued. "Marriage is about more than a man and a woman falling in love. It's about forming a family, a foundation that will support generations—young and old, children and grandparents, even siblings and cousins. A family lifts us up when we're hurting and shares our joy when we triumph.

"In more practical terms, we call on family when we need help with anything from childcare to"—he looked at Daisy and grinned—"serving as maid of honor."

The guests chuckled, and so did Rafe. But when Daisy smiled with the pleasure of being included, he tensed. She belonged here. *Belonged.* If their relationship continued to deepen, could he really ask her to leave her home?

The minister scanned the crowd, his expression solemn again. "I'm not naïve. Families are flawed and many are broken. But that doesn't change God's plan—or his great love for his children. That love is the foundation of what Shane and MJ are forming today—a family of their own."

Rafe swallowed hard. Those words hit home, and so did the look on Shane's face as he turned to his bride to speak his vows. There wasn't a doubt in Rafe's mind that Shane would fight for MJ, work hard to support her, and love her as best as he could.

When Shane finished, Rafe stole a glance at Daisy.

Daisy kept her eyes on the couple, but in the middle of MJ's pledge to Shane—where she promised to follow him to the ends of the earth—Daisy looked straight at Rafe, her eyes bright, her lips trembling, and her face full of emotions he hoped matched his own.

Daisy watched as the limo taking Shane and MJ to their hotel pulled away from the restaurant. A few soap bubbles still floated in the air, and birdseed crunched under the feet of the retreating guests, but Daisy's maid of honor duties were complete. Tomorrow Shane and MJ would fly to Hawaii for their honeymoon, leaving Cody with his grandmother and Daisy free to relax after a fun but intense week.

With the last of the crowd drifting away, she turned to Rafe and choked up with love for the hundredth time since the ceremony. During the vows, Daisy had been astonished by how deeply she loved Rafe. Like a flooding river carving new banks, that love for him refused to be contained.

But practicalities were another matter. She couldn't see herself in Cincinnati—she just couldn't. But neither could she see herself without Rafe. On the other hand, could Rafe be happy in Refuge?

Turning to him now, she didn't know what to say or do. She only knew she didn't want this night to end—especially after slow dancing with him to "Unchained Melody," the most classic of classic love songs and her very favorite.

He looped his arm around her waist. "Let's take a walk. I need to tell you something."

Something could mean anything. Daisy decided to play it cool. "Good or bad?"

A half smile lifted his lips. "That depends. Let's go to the lookout."

Arm in arm, they ambled along the same path they'd walked on their third date. The babble of the river competed with the music of crickets, and the cool air soothed her skin. Leaning into Rafe, she rested her head on his shoulder as they walked. The tension in his body seeped into her, and she wondered again what he wanted—needed—to say.

When they reached the lookout, he drew her into his arms. They savored a long kiss until Rafe eased back. "I've wanted to do that since the minute I saw you at the church. Daisy, you amaze me."

"You amaze me, too." She choked out the words. "Rafe, what are we going to do? I told you I'd visit Cincinnati, but—but it's so far away. I'm scared. But it's your home—your job."

"You're right about all of it. Plus there's something else we have to talk about."

"What is it?"

"My job. Being a cop is dangerous work. I don't want to exaggerate the risk, but we can't ignore it either."

"No, of course not."

"I've seen the toll it takes on relationships. It's hard on everyone. That's why I need to say this. If you want to back out of what's happening between us"—he sucked in a deep breath—"I'll understand."

"Back out?" Daisy gawked at him. "After that kiss? Fat chance, buster!"

"Daisy, I—"

"Wait. It's my turn now." She stepped back so she could see his face—and so he could see hers. "I know police work is dangerous. Of course I'd worry about you, but my faith is strong in that area."

"Are you sure?"

"Positive." Those moments in the ICU, when she'd glimpsed Jesus and heaven, flooded back to her. "God alone gives life and takes it away. I don't understand why God does what he does, but that's one area in my life where I'm strong."

"I'm glad, because—"

"Wait." She held up her hand to stop him. "It's not that simple. What I struggle with isn't life and death. I struggle with *living*. I'm okay with you being a cop. What I'm afraid of is being alone and scared in a strange city."

"You wouldn't be alone. I'd be there for you."

"I know you would try. But you're human. Even with the best of intentions, human beings let each other down."

He reached for both her hands, gripped them gently, and lifted them to take the weight. "Partners lean on each other, Daisy. Sometimes they carry each other."

"Yes, they do. But don't you see? I need to be sure *I* can be a good partner *to you*. I have to be strong on my own—with God as my strength. Because like you said, police work is dangerous. Anything can happen to anyone at any time."

"Even in Refuge," he pointed out.

"Yes, even here."

"So you're okay with my career?"

"Yes. I am."

He turned from her, stared out across the river, and jammed his hands in his pockets. After a breath, he faced her again. "There's something I haven't shared with you."

Surprised, she drew back. "What is it?"

"I paid a visit to the local sheriff's office to pass along Jax Martin's car-make and license plate. But I also wanted to get a feel for the department."

Her pulse sped up. "A feel?"

"Yes—a general impression and to see how they felt about a city dude transferring in. The department's a lot smaller than CPD. And I do mean *a lot*. But I met some good people, chatted with the station commander, and told him I was considering a big change."

"You did?" Daisy could hardly breathe.

"Yes—but the keyword here is *considering*."

"Of course! But still—Rafe—I'm stunned." She tried to absorb what he'd just said, but she couldn't get past Rafe staying in Refuge. *Her* nest. *Her* home. *Her* peace of mind. But what about him? *His* dreams. *His* needs. *His* goals. What felt so right suddenly felt all wrong. "Do you want to stay here for yourself or is it just because of me?"

"I like it here, but you're ninety-three percent of the reason."

In spite of her worries, Daisy laughed. "Now that's an odd number." And a sign he'd given the idea a lot of thought. "Is Jesse the other seven percent?"

"He gets five, and the other two percent goes to living in a beautiful place."

"You'd do that for me?"

"I'm *thinking* about it," he reminded her. "It's a big decision—one of the biggest of my life."

"Yes, it is." The gravity of it sobered her, and she suddenly felt overwhelmed and unworthy. "I can't ask that of you."

"You're not. If I make that decision—and it's in the future, not next week or even soon—it'll be my choice. No matter what, I'm going back to work on August 1. If you visit in the fall, we can see what comes next. Who knows?" He gave an offhand shrug, but hope deepened his voice. "You might even like it there."

"Maybe." She tried to shrug the way he did, but her body refused to move. Rafe deserved more than a shrug. He deserved to know how she felt. Stepping closer, she raised her face to his and let her heart do the talking. "Leaving Refuge terrifies me, but there's something I'm not afraid of."

"What's that?"

"Loving you."

A smile formed on his lips, then hooked into a roguish grin. "Oh, yeah?"

A soft trembling erupted in her chest and spread to every cell in her body. "I love you, Rafe. *I do.* After Eric, I thought I'd never feel safe enough to say those words to anyone, but you—you're so good to me. So patient and strong. I feel safe, and—"

He stopped her with a kiss that calmed her fears in one breath and fanned them in the next. Loving Rafe had proved to be surprisingly easy. Matching up the puzzle pieces of their lives was another matter altogether.

The kiss turned into kissing, and kissing spun into a whirlwind of emotions, all of them intense, exquisite, and sharpened by the uncertainty of their future. His world or hers? Was she strong enough to follow him? Would he be happy if—

"Hey, Rafe—Daisy." Jesse's voice shot out of the dark from ten steps away. "Sorry to break this up."

Rafe practically growled at him. "This better be good, bro."

"Yeah, I get it." Humor lightened his voice, but then it dipped again. "It's Chelsea. I'm afraid she needs a friend right now."

Daisy groaned. "Are you kidding me?"

"I wish I were. Angela found her crying her eyes out in the ladies' room. She's been drinking."

Rafe's arm tightened around Daisy's waist. "So she can't get herself home."

"No," Jesse replied. "She's too far gone—even for an Uber."

Daisy turned to Rafe. "I'm so sorry—I have to help her."

"I know you do."

"I just hate that it's ruining our evening."

"So do I." He gave her forehead a quick kiss. "But I'd do the same thing for a friend. Sometimes there's no choice."

The three of them headed for the restaurant with Jesse a few steps ahead. Rafe kept his arm around her waist, holding her close as they entered the lobby.

"I'll wait here," he told her. "You can drive her home in her car, and I'll follow."

Daisy gave his waist a squeeze. "She doesn't usually drink. Something must have set her off."

"I hope it's a one-and-done. But, Daize, I have to be honest. She's so desperate she's taking chances even if she doesn't know it or won't admit it."

"I see it too," Daisy replied. "And it scares me to pieces."

Rafe and Jesse stood in the restaurant lobby, empty now except for a few couples heading for the door. Trickling water from an indoor fountain masked the restaurant hum, but raucous laughter came from somewhere deep in the restaurant.

The situation with Chelsea bothered Rafe far more than he had let on to Daisy. The fact that she'd met up with Jax Martin said everything. And now this—a crying jag fueled by alcohol. If Angela hadn't found her, what would have happened?

Rafe didn't like the circumstances, but he appreciated Jesse's company. "I'm sorry Angela had to get involved. Thanks for hanging around."

Jesse shrugged like it was no big deal. "At least I'm not standing here with a bunch of shopping bags. I always feel sorry for those guys at the mall."

"Yeah, me too." Rafe hated to shop. "I'd rather be the guy with the diaper bag and three kids."

Jesse gave him a sideways look. "If you're talking kids, you've got it bad for Daisy."

"Yeah, I do." Rafe didn't mind admitting it, either. "She's great. I'm ready for more—for everything. But don't ask me about the geography problem."

"Okay, I won't." Jesse started to pull out his phone but stopped. "Forget it. I'm asking. What's up?"

Rafe had already told his brother about his visit to the sheriff's office and how he'd spoken to the station commander. "I like it here, and I think I could fit in. But it's like cutting off my right hand for the sake of my left one."

"Confusing, huh?"

"You bet."

"You have a job with me anytime you want it. It would be a fairly smooth transition—except for the part about not really wanting to be here."

Rafe shook his head. "I laid it all out to Daisy earlier tonight. We're going to take things a step at a time."

Both men sighed in unison, glanced at their watches, then shoved their hands in their pockets. Two minutes after Daisy entered the restroom, Angela came out and focused on Jesse, rolling her eyes as she crossed the lobby. "That girl is a piece of work." She spotted Rafe and put two fingers to her lips. "Oops. Sorry. I shouldn't have badmouthed Daisy's friend."

"I understand." *Piece of work* was probably kind. "Do you know what happened?"

"Only that it involves a guy she just met. He turned out to be"—her manicured fingers formed air quotes—"as boring as all the others."

Rafe didn't need detective skills to guess what had happened. At the reception, Chelsea had sought out

Shane's best man. A pro baseball player nursing an elbow injury, Craig had come to the wedding solo. Chelsea had been interested in him—maybe too interested. If Craig had given her the slip, she might have looked for company in the bar.

There was no reason for Jesse and Angela to wait with him, so he motioned toward the door. "Daisy and I can handle Chelsea. Why don't you two head on out?"

Relief washed over Angela's face, but she gave Jesse a questioning look. "I'm ready if you are."

Jesse nodded, then spoke to Rafe. "Call if you need anything."

"I will." Rafe shared a smile with Angela. "That's my big brother. Always looking out for other people."

Angela grinned—at Jesse, not Rafe. "I like that about him."

Jesse shrugged off the compliment, but Rafe wondered if his brother had finally met someone special. Sparks glowed in Angela's made-up eyes, though Jesse remained as stoic as ever. They left together, holding hands, leaving Rafe to wait alone.

Chapter 31

F or Daisy, the ten days after the wedding dragged on forever. She tried to focus on tasks for Miss Joan, but there wasn't much to do. The charity visits were over, and the remaining effort involved Miss Joan consulting with her attorney before making a final decision. The history book about Cottonwood Acres was finished, and they were waiting for the proof pages from the publisher.

Daisy had far too much time to think about the night of the wedding. Without Rafe's help, she couldn't have gotten Chelsea home. He followed them to the apartment, then carried Chelsea fireman-style after she passed out in the elevator. As for what he called the *vomit comet*, they were both glad it struck in the parking lot and not elsewhere.

It was awful. Every minute of it.

Awful.

And not just because of Chelsea being foolish—which she fully admitted the next day with her head exploding.

The true awfulness came from loving Rafe more each day and being assaulted by doubt. Was he too good to be true? Or was he too good for *her*?

Or was he simply a decent human being who loved her despite her flaws?

Daisy had lost her emotional balance, and she wanted it back. No way would she drink again—*no way.* But she knew that vow for what it was—a confession of her fierce and urgent need for God. People stumbled. They slipped. They *did* things they said they would never do. Or they *didn't* do everything they promised. Daisy was one of those people, and living in Refuge helped to keep her grounded.

She desperately needed a touch from God, but he wasn't exactly holding her hand these days. With Shane and MJ away on their honeymoon, Chelsea obsessed with another dating app, Rafe talking up Cincinnati, and Miss Joan pondering the final decision on the giveaway, Daisy felt alone and even abandoned as she sat at her office computer, scrolling through Instagram.

When the doorbell rang, she gladly popped up from her desk and went to the front door to answer it. The FedEx guy stood there with a bulky padded envelope. He delivered often, so Daisy hoped for a little small talk.

"What's up?" she asked as she signed for the delivery.

"Just a million deliveries thanks to tourist season." He traded the package for the computer tablet. "Gotta run. See you later."

So no small talk, but the package offered a respite from her own thoughts. Daisy took it to her office, sliced it open, saw the proof sheets for the history book. For the first time since the wedding, she genuinely smiled.

Basking in satisfaction, she took the package to her

desk, sat down, and leafed through the stack of pages until she reached a photograph of Jug, Comet, and Zippy grazing in the meadow. The memory of Rafe running to the rescue when the horses crowded her for carrots roared to life and she grimaced.

Why couldn't she have fallen for a man with roots so deep he wouldn't even *think* of leaving Refuge? She leaned back in her chair, closed her eyes, and muttered to the empty office. "Why, God? Why are you doing this to me?"

"Doing what?" God hadn't spoken to her. The voice belonged to Rafe.

Daisy spun the chair, opened her eyes, and saw a bouquet of the most perfect red roses, held by the most perfect man—well, mostly perfect—in the most perfect place where she had a perfect job—and a very imperfect family, which only made Shane and MJ perfect, because they knew they were imperfect and let her be imperfect, too.

Oh, shut up! Daisy was so sick of herself she could hardly stand it. Her evil twin was off duty today, but her evil cousin had arrived in her place with a truckload of self-pity.

Rafe held out the roses. "For you."

Her evil cousin skulked off at the sight of the red velvet petals, and Daisy crossed the room. When she lifted the vase, Rafe's warm fingers brushed hers, with the cold glass of the vase chilling her palms. "They're beautiful."

Leaning over the blooms, she brushed a soft kiss on his lips, lingering just a bit before she placed the flowers on her desk.

Roses were serious flowers. She couldn't deal with all that seriousness today, so she pushed it aside with a playful smile. "Let's see . . . It's not Valentine's Day, and my birthday is in November. What's the occasion?"

She expected him to say he didn't need an occasion to bring beautiful flowers to a beautiful woman. That was the kind of perfect thing Rafe would say. Instead his eyes darkened in a way she didn't often see. The nightmares were gone, and he'd told her Dr. Susan belonged in the Psychologist Hall of Fame, but today something seemed wrong.

He jammed his hands in the pockets of his denim work pants. "This is going to be a bit of a surprise."

She braced herself. "Good or bad?"

"Both." Half his mouth quirked upward. The other half stayed level to create a smile as confusing as his answer. "I'm leaving for Cincinnati on Monday."

"Monday! That's just four days from now!" Her heart plummeted to her toes. "I thought we had more time."

"So did I."

He came forward to hug her, but Daisy didn't want to be hugged. She wanted to kick and scream, and maybe even cuss, which she didn't do anymore. Mostly she wanted to tell God he was dropping the ball and to get his act together—which shocked her to the core. God was, well, God. And Daisy was merely the flower sharing her name—a fragile thing that wilted in the heat and froze in the cold, an ordinary plant not nearly as spectacular as the roses gracing her desk in a perfect array.

It was all too much—too confusing and painful. Hardening herself, she crossed her arms over her chest and lifted her chin as stubbornly as she could. "So what changed?"

Rafe took the hint and stayed three feet away. "I called my sergeant this morning to confirm the August 1 return date. D'Andre's on medical leave with a broken leg. Two other officers are out, plus it's vacation season. He asked if I could possibly make it back by July 10. They've been good to me, Daisy. I had to say yes."

She admired his loyalty, but his choice—as right as it was—frustrated her. Would he always put work first? Was he a crazy workaholic disguised as a laid-back construction worker? What if she took the job with Maggie's House, moved to Cincinnati, and he forgot she existed? After all, they'd known each other only for two months.

Rafe hesitated. "I'll miss you."

"I'll miss you, too." She meant it. But she was also a little mad at him, in part because being mad was a lot easier than being gracious, or mature, or the strong woman she wanted to be.

His gaze went to the flowers on the desk. So did hers. The roses were mostly buds, but they'd open if she placed the vase in the beam of sunshine shooting across the coffee table. For reasons she couldn't quite fathom, she didn't want to move them into the light.

When he looked up, his eyes held an army of questions. "How about visiting in August instead of the fall?"

She glanced at the laminated wall calendar she used to track Miss Joan's schedule. With the charity visits complete, the only things scheduled were Miss Joan's weekly hair appointments and a routine visit to the dentist. It was July 1, but August was next to it—and blank.

Daisy shrugged. "Maybe. I'll have to check with Lyn to see if Maggie's House will be ready for someone to do some scouting." Daisy hadn't accepted the job and Lyn was fine with waiting. The organization had a lot of background work to do before they bought property.

"Let's do this on our own," Rafe suggested. "Come for the fun of it."

"I don't know. Airfare's expensive." Too much to fly back and forth like millionaires going between New York and Los Angeles every weekend.

Rafe shrugged, said the ticket was on him and that she shouldn't worry about the money. "We can figure all that out. Just think about it, okay?"

She nodded, but the evil cousin returned with a

bucket of suspicion. Was Rafe being controlling? Was it *nice* that he wanted to pay her way, or did the money obligate her somehow? Eric had used money to manipulate her. Rafe, on the other hand, paid for things without making a big deal about it, and he let her pay when she insisted. There was no reason to be distrustful of his motives. None. But she couldn't shake old feelings and reactions.

Maybe it didn't matter. She could buy her own plane ticket if she wanted to go to Ohio. She'd been saving so she could pay the full rent when Chelsea left for Michigan. Now it seemed Chelsea was going to stay in Refuge forever—and Daisy was leaving. It wasn't fair or even logical.

Rafe studied her face. "I know this is a surprise, maybe even a shock." He looked down at his feet, then at the roses, and finally back at her face. Questions gleamed in his eyes.

For once, *he* looked insecure. Love for him poured into her, and she put herself in *his* shoes—his black police boots, to be specific. Going back to work after the nightmares and that weird panicky moment might not be as easy as he pretended. Compassion flooded through her. So did the knowledge that he liked having her around. Despite her insecurities, or maybe because of them, she was a support to him and not a burden.

Rafe seemed to be looking right through her—and she felt as if she could see through him as well. Something had to give. Someone had to surrender. Daisy couldn't make the full leap, but she could reach across the chasm with an I'm-here-for-you smile.

"Are you nervous about going back to work?" she asked.

"A little." He gave an offhand shrug. "I'm prepared, but I'll be glad to get the first night under my belt. I haven't lost my situational awareness, but it might be rusty."

"What's situational awareness?"

"Taking in your surroundings. Knowing when a door opens. Staying aware of what's behind you."

As a former victim of violence, Daisy possessed some of those skills. "Like that night you changed my tire. I knew where you were every minute."

"Exactly." A smile pushed away whatever worries remained. "As I recall, you were ready to hose me down with pepper spray. That moment changed our lives."

"Yes, it did." Her voice dropped to a whisper. "Whatever the future holds, you'll do great, Rafe. I know it."

Longing glistened in his eyes. She knew he loved her. Needed her—needed to know she believed in him. With her heart spilling over, she crossed the room, wrapped him in a hug, and squeezed with all her might. They clung to each other for a solid minute, until Rafe loosened his arms. "I have to get to Heritage House. I called Jesse about the departure date, but Ben doesn't know yet."

Rafe glanced out the window, then focused back on her face. "It's been good here, Daisy. I've never been happier."

She opened her mouth but stopped. *Don't say it! Just don't!* But the words squeaked through her lips. "Has it been good enough to stay—or to come back and stay?"

"I don't know." Impatience leaked into his voice. "All I can promise is that I'll think about it. You know what's at stake for me—for us."

"I do." Money. Security. A future. And though he didn't mention it during the talk they'd had a few nights ago, his personal happiness was on the line. She forced air into her lungs. "You need to see Ben, and I need to check in with Miss Joan."

"Has she made a decision about the giveaway?"

"Not yet. But she's been on the phone with Patrick Coogan every day this week. I think she's talking to him now."

"It sounds pretty definite."

"I think it is."

He looked into her eyes. "We have four days. Let's make the most of them."

"Yes."

He trailed his knuckles down her cheek, then gripped her hand and squeezed as if they were about to jump off a cliff together. "I love you, Daisy," he murmured. "I do."

"I love you, too."

He brushed a soft kiss on her lips, let go of her hand, and walked out the door, leaving her alone with a con-flicted heart.

Chapter 32

Now that I am old and gray,
do not abandon me, O God.
Let me proclaim your power to this new generation,
your mighty miracles to all who come after me.

Psalm 71:18 (NLT)

*W*hen I slammed the phone down on Trey Cochran back in 1972, I ended that part of my life as deliberately as a surgeon amputated an arm or a leg. I endured phantom pain for the next several months, at least that's how I thought of it, but the relationship was over—except for the part of me that needed to heal.

Today, when I called Patrick Coogan with the news I'd selected his organization to take over Cottonwood Acres, the experience couldn't have been more different. A bone-deep satisfaction settled into my aging body. I'd healed from the affair decades ago, but the completion of the give-away added a lovely epilogue to my story.

I had expected the moment to be bittersweet, but I couldn't stop grinning as I hurried down the hall to share the news with Daisy.

When I rounded the corner to her office, Daisy was seated on the love seat, slumped over with her head in her hands, and her shoulders pulled so tight I thought her bones might crack.

I sat down and put my arm around her shoulders. "Daisy, honey. What's the matter?"

She leaned into me for a hug. "He's leaving."

"Rafe?" It wasn't really a question, or even a surprise. With Rafe returning to Ohio, they were on a collision course with a painful good-bye, temporary or not.

Daisy cast a stormy look across the room. I followed her gaze to a vase full of glorious red roses and knew something big was up.

"Did you two have a quarrel?" I asked.

"Not even close." She flopped back against the couch and crossed her arms, the picture of how I would imagine her as an adolescent. "If he did something wrong or stupid, I could break up with him. That would be easy. But no—" She sealed her lips but misery squeaked out of her. "He's being completely reasonable; only a little bit self-ish—maybe, and just plain old responsible. I can't stand it."

"What exactly happened?" Frankly, I couldn't see the problem.

"Cincy PD wants him to start work on July 10 instead August 1. He's leaving in just four days."

"I see."

For the next few minutes, I listened while Daisy poured her heart out. She was determined to visit Rafe in the fall, but fear, dread, and more than a little resentment tainted what should have been an exciting time in her life. My news about the giveaway would add to her conundrum, so I decided to save it for later. "Are you sure you still want to visit Cincinnati?"

"Yes. But you know how I feel about leaving Refuge."

"I do." I paused. "I also know that change is inevitable—for both of us."

"I just don't know what to do. Part of me wants to just end it with Rafe now just to make the confusion stop."

"Oh, Daisy—"

"What?"

"If you think ending the relationship will free you from the fallout of loving Rafe, you're dead wrong." I know I sounded pompous, but I was speaking from experience.

She turned to me, her eyes as bleak as winter. "Could we have a toast party?"

I opened my mouth to say yes, but human wisdom wouldn't ease the ache in Daisy's soul. She needed far more than *my* advice to reconcile the demands of her heart. She needed a touch that could only come from God. But God uses people, and I was the only other person in the room.

Whether Daisy could see the big picture or not, God was working in her life, just as he had worked in mine. In that moment, looking at this struggling young woman I loved, I knew what to do, where to go, and exactly what I needed to say.

"A toast party isn't enough." I stood and used the desk phone to call Cliff. "Could you have someone bring the Mule to the house for me? Daisy and I are taking a ride."

When I set down the phone, Daisy looked at me with a plea in her eyes. "Where are we going?"

"To church," I told her, smiling a little. "It's an unconventional one, but a place of worship nonetheless." As I turned to leave, the pages on her desk caught my eye and I stopped. "Oh my. Is that our book?"

"Yes. FedEx just dropped off the proof sheets."

Wonderment flooded through me as I leafed through the first chapter. I'd written the words and seen the photographs on a computer monitor, but seeing the actual pages affected me in a new way. The book was done; my story told. "It's beautiful, Daisy. You did an excellent job."

"Thank you," she said demurely. "But the words are yours."

"The book belongs to both of us." An indescribable contentment left me breathless. "Now we have two reasons to visit the spot I have in mind."

I turned to leave for a second time, but the roses in the corner were terribly out of place. They wouldn't open in the dim light, so I crossed the office, picked up the vase, and set it on the coffee table in front of Daisy. "They need sunlight to open."

She opened her mouth to speak, but I shook my head. "We'll talk when we get to the river."

I went upstairs, changed into outdoor clothes, then went to the kitchen and told Ana I'd be gone all afternoon.

"Would you like me to pack a lunch?" she asked.

"No. I'll get what we need."

I found the insulated bag I hadn't used in ages, packed the two items I needed, and went to meet Daisy at the Mule.

I didn't speak as we drove down the road we'd taken on the day I first told her about the giveaway. Heritage House loomed to the right, on schedule for completion in the fall. We passed the historic homestead and the cemetery without stopping, and I slowed to a crawl for the Yee-Haw Dip, barely making a splash as we crossed the rushing current.

When we crested the hill above the river and the

bench, I slowed to soak in the grandeur of the view. The vastness of the land, the sparkle of the river, and the beauty of the sky turned me into the speck of dust I was. Aware of my human frailty, I prayed for God to meet Daisy in the place where I'd faced my greatest failure and found God's greatest gifts—forgiveness, mercy, and hope.

I parked the Mule several feet from the river, retrieved the insulated bag, and set it on the bench. Daisy stood by the water, her hands behind her back, chin raised to the sky.

"I love it here," she murmured.

"So do I." I stood by the bench. "Come and sit with me."

She turned around and smiled. "I see what you mean about 'church.' It's impossible to stand here and not think about God creating all of this." She swept her arm to indicate the meadows and sky, earth, and clouds.

"He created us, too."

She dropped down next to me. "I believe that, Miss Joan. *I do.* But why does it have to be so hard?"

"I won't lecture you about free will, but I will say we're created in God's image. We have the capacity to think and to reason—and to feel. Christian believers—especially those like me who came to know Christ later in life—often have stories to tell. You know most of mine."

"About Trey."

"Yes. I fully acknowledge the affair was wrong by every standard I wanted to uphold in that time of my life. But that sin—that shame—knocked me off the high horse of thinking I was my own god. The affair was a wrecking ball in more ways than one. But it led to my personal Damascus Road experience. You know the story about Paul, don't you?"

"He killed Christians—a man named Stephen. But then something happened and Paul was in the middle of nowhere when God struck him blind."

"That's right. God struck him blind," I repeated. "Can you imagine how Paul felt for those three days?"

"Scared—no." She shook her head. "He must have been terrified. And maybe angry. And confused."

"I imagine so," I replied. "I relate to Paul rather strongly. God restored my vision, too—not literally, of course—but it was on this very spot that I surrendered my life to the lordship of Jesus Christ. Frankly, that moment was rather brutal."

"How so?" Daisy asked. "My own experience was so different."

I'd heard of conversion stories like Daisy's, where light comes out from behind the clouds and God seems to smile, but mine couldn't have been more opposite.

"I'm glad for you, Daisy." I gave her hand a squeeze. "But for me, the moment was dark. Everything I believed about myself had been proven a lie. All I could do was weep until there were no tears left. I prayed like a pioneer woman lost in a blizzard, begging God for his help and mercy when I deserved none of it."

Daisy spoke for me. "He answered that prayer."

"Yes, he did. And like I feared, it changed me. I thought differently, and it impacted every choice I made. I continued to teach about strong women and the American West because those stories are true and deserve to be told. But I included the faith it took to venture into unknown territory. Our ancestors didn't know what the future held, but they tackled it with great courage and endurance. Those are the most basic elements of faith."

"That was me when I first came to Refuge," Daisy murmured. "I trusted God for *everything* when I came out of the ICU. Why is it so much harder *now*?"

"Because you have something to lose."

"That's it exactly."

"So did I when I finally surrendered my life to God. It was a dreadful day in January when I rode to this spot alone. The wind was howling so loud I couldn't hear anything else, and my face was so cold my cheeks were on fire. But I didn't care. The affair had been over for three months, but I couldn't shake the emotions boiling inside of me—and I do mean *boiling*."

I heaved a sigh, not wanting to think of those days, but Daisy needed to know that she wasn't alone. "In my head I told Trey off a dozen times a day, or I imagined he left Kathy and showed up on my doorstep hat in hand, convincingly remorseful. I watched his episodes of *Thunder Valley* just to torture myself."

Daisy clapped her hand over her mouth, then gasped. "You have an evil twin like I do!"

"An evil twin?" I thought I knew what she meant but wanted to be sure.

"That's what I call the mean voice in my head that just won't shut up."

I couldn't stop a smile. "My evil twin is more of a self-righteous know-it-all. She's convinced the world would be a perfect place if people just took her advice. We both know that's not true."

"No," Daisy agreed diplomatically.

"Human beings need a Savior. You and I are sinners saved by grace. That gift came at great cost, and it's a gift to cherish. That's why I brought the elements for communion."

Daisy pressed her arm against mine. I felt her shaking and realized she had started to cry. "We're having a toast party with God."

"Yes. I suppose we are."

I lifted the insulated bag from under the bench, removed the slice of bread I'd brought and tore it in two. Then I repeated words I'd memorized during the years I

313

went regularly to church.

"This is his body, broken for us." We ate the bread of life in silence.

Next I opened a small bottle of grape juice. "This is his blood, shed for our sins." Daisy sipped, then so did I.

We sat in silence for several seconds, each alone with our thoughts. The bench had been built as an altar in the wilderness—a place of surrender, thanksgiving, and sacrifice. Today it fulfilled its purpose once again.

Daisy had taken communion in church before, but never anywhere else. Yet the moment felt right, even holy. When she swallowed the grape juice, her eyes filled with tears. She didn't know what the future held, but mentally she released her grip on the life she cherished and opened her hand to the future.

Peace settled into her bones, and with it came the awareness of Miss Joan murmuring a quiet "Amen."

The lump in Daisy's throat receded. "Thank you for today. I feel better."

"I'm glad." Miss Joan patted her hand. "Because there's something I have to tell you, and it might rock the boat again."

"The giveaway. You've made a decision."

"Yes. I called Patrick this morning and gave him the good news. He was thrilled, and so am I. As of January 1, Cottonwood Acres will officially belong to Coogan Rodeo Enterprises. He's putting together a transition team, so there will be some activity over the next few months. Plus I'll need your help to finish setting up the displays at Heritage House."

A knot formed in Daisy's belly. Her job would end on January 1. "I'll be here as long as you need me."

"Thank you, dear. But there's one more thing you need to know."

"What is it?"

"Patrick wants to hire you as an administrative assistant to his new manager. The date is of your choosing—if you're interested."

"That's . . . good."

"And confusing," Miss Joan added. "You don't have to decide now, or even in the next few weeks. The transition will be slow and thorough."

Daisy suddenly felt selfish thinking only of herself. "What about you, Miss Joan? Are you still moving to Scottsdale?"

"Yes. In fact, I spoke to my friend Linda for an hour last night. A cute little house near hers is going on the market October 1. I just might fly out there and buy it."

"It'll be a huge change, won't it?" Daisy couldn't imagine Miss Joan living anywhere but Cottonwood Acres.

"Yes, but I'm excited about it—and a little relieved. At my age, a person wants to be close to medical care. Plus the community sounds like a lot of fun. Linda—the old lit professor—runs a book club and plays golf three times a week. Everyone drives around in golf carts, but I'm thinking of bringing the Mule."

Daisy couldn't help but grin. "You'd be a trendsetter."

Chuckling softly, Miss Joan clasped her hands in her lap. "I'm sure I'll make new friends. Linda tells me the community is full of interesting people who like to debate as much as I do, plus she and I plan to do some traveling. Cottonwood Acres was a lively place in its heyday, but that era is gone. It's ready for a fresh start and so am I."

"The new community sounds perfect for you." Daisy couldn't help but think of her own situation with Rafe. "Having a friend waiting makes it easier, doesn't it."

"Yes." Miss Joan's eyes misted. "Stay brave, Daisy.

God will meet your needs, though perhaps in unexpected ways."

"I believe that."

"Good." Miss Joan patted Daisy's knee. "You never know—God just might use Rafe to change your life, and he just might use *you* to bless Rafe. In the end, God will accomplish his purposes. It's a privilege when he allows us to participate."

"I know what you mean." When Daisy shared her story at AA meetings, joy spilled out of her, along with honest tears.

"Are you ready to go?" Miss Joan asked. "I want to be home before dark."

So did Daisy. If she and Rafe had just four days together, she wanted to enjoy every minute, including tonight.

Miss Joan picked up the bag and they got back in the Mule. She took off at full speed, the wind blowing their hair back in tangles. When they reached the Yee-Haw Dip, Miss Joan told Daisy to hang on, then she punched the gas and they flew through the water, shouting "Yee-Haw" at the top of their lungs.

Chapter 33

Rafe's dream on Thursday night stopped short of being the nightmare about Kara, but on Friday morning he woke up nervous and alert in a way that worried him. He avoided the obvious and blamed the dream on the spicy burrito he'd pillaged late last night from Jesse's fridge.

But the dream rattled him enough to walk out on Jesse's deck and pray in the dark.

Lord, guide me. Put me where I belong. Put Daisy where she *belongs.*

Until yesterday, when he told her about the new return date, he hadn't been overly concerned about going back to work. But the dream had nudged the squirrels in his head. How would he react when he ran down that first dark alley?

"You'll be just fine," he said out loud. Mentally, he played out a familiar scenario, planning for it the way Dr. Susan had coached him. Being mindful of his immediate surroundings and emotions kept him grounded in the here and now, and the squirrels in his head settled down. More comfortable, he got ready for work and drove to the coffee shop for his last breakfast with Jesse's crew.

When he walked inside, Jesse and the guys were already seated at their spot in the back. Rafe started to put his phone in the middle of the table, but a three-gallon plastic paint bucket caught his eye. Glancing inside, he saw an assortment of gas station snacks and a shiny new hammer with Post-it notes stuck to it.

He snagged a Post-it and read scrawled names and wishes for good luck. "What's all this?"

Howie spoke up. "That's yours, you idiot. We turned the Bad Luck Bucket into the Good Luck Bucket. Have a safe trip back and be careful when you get there."

A sloppy grin pushed its way to Rafe's face. He glanced at Jesse, who shrugged as if to say, *I didn't know a thing about this.* Rafe picked up the hammer, felt the weight of it in his hand and the weight of being a cop on his shoulders. He raised it up, a little like a sword. "Thanks. I'll use it nail up wanted posters."

The guys all laughed and someone threw a napkin at him. These men had become friends to him. Rafe didn't say it out loud, but he'd miss them—unless he changed his mind and stayed in Refuge.

The day passed quickly. Heritage House was more than half finished and on schedule. As far as Rafe knew, Miss Joan was still deciding on the winner of the giveaway. That decision would impact Daisy, and though it was admittedly selfish of him, he had hoped the end of her job would make Lyn's offer more appealing.

Those were his thoughts when he knocked on her

apartment door at seven that night. Instead of going out, Daisy had invited him for dinner with the caveat that she wasn't much of a cook. Chelsea had a date with someone new, and Hannah was being watched by a neighbor until Chelsea picked her up later tonight.

Rafe couldn't top the two dozen red roses, so when he knocked on the apartment door, he held a pink bakery box instead. When Daisy opened the door, the aroma of something Italian hit his nose. She looked utterly adorable with her hair pushed back from her face and her cheeks red, maybe from slaving over the hot stove.

He kissed her hello and offered the box. "I brought dessert. Death-by-Chocolate Brownies."

"Yum!" She led him past the small table set with plates and candles, then set the brownies on the kitchen counter. "You can't burn spaghetti, right?"

"I don't think so."

"But you can overcook it." She gave the pasta a stir, then looked over her shoulder. "The sauce is from a jar, but I added all sorts of good stuff."

"It smells great."

"MJ makes really good spaghetti sauce. I borrowed her ideas. You can't get any more domestic than spaghetti—except maybe for meatloaf. "

While Daisy rattled on about MJ teaching her to cook, Rafe opened a bagged salad and mixed it. They bumped arms a few times, teased and laughed. It all felt so right. She dished from the stove, and he carried the plates to the table. She lit the candles, he dimmed the overhead lights, and they sat. In unison they bowed their heads. Daisy usually said grace over their meals, but tonight Rafe took the lead. He meant every word of thanks for the food, the caring woman who had prepared it, and the simple pleasure of sharing a meal with someone he loved. Everything about tonight felt natural and right, but so did returning to Cincy.

Daisy offered him the basket of bread. "I haven't told you the big news about the giveaway. Miss Joan made a decision."

"The rodeo clowns?"

"They won hands-down." Daisy took a slice of bread for herself. "As of January 1, Cottonwood Acres will belong to Coogan's Clowns."

"That's great." He decided to take a chance. "So when does your job end?"

She chewed the bite of bread quickly, as if she couldn't wait to speak. Finally, she swallowed. "Miss Joan is moving to Arizona, but she wants me to help set up Heritage House. I told her I'd stay as long as she needs me."

"Of course. Do you think you'll be finished with everything before the end of the year?" In his mind he pictured them together on New Year's Eve, maybe at the party D'Andre usually put on.

"Or . . ." She dragged out the word. ". . . it could be longer. Nothing is definite, but Patrick called me personally to ask if I'd consider staying on as an assistant to the new manager."

"I'm glad for you, Daize. I am." He hoped he sounded convincing, but deep down, he'd been wondering if her need for a new job would nudge her to consider the Maggie's House position in Cincinnati.

"But?"

"You know what I'm thinking."

"I think I do." A candle flickered with her breath. "Right now, everything is on the table. I love Refuge, but I also love Maggie's House and what it does."

"So it's a win-win." For Daisy's sake, he put the best possible face on the choice, though it nearly killed him.

"Yes." She paused. "Just like it's a win-win for you. You could be a cop here or in Cincinnati, right?"

"Maybe. First, they'd have to hire me, and that isn't guaranteed. When I visited the station, the sergeant told me they're running lean right now because of budget cuts. That's a problem with a small department. A big city has more opportunity for career growth. Of course, there's more risk as well."

"Pros and cons, huh?" Daisy put her napkin on the table and pushed back. "I wish it were simpler."

"Me too." He thought of his arrival two months ago, when he felt like a marble rolling around a box. If nothing else had come from his time in Refuge, at least he'd found his faith again. "Maybe it's simpler than we think."

"How so?"

"God has a plan, right? Maybe I'm better off here in Refuge." A hint of uncertainty shaded his voice.

"Better off?" Daisy tipped her head. "You sound worried. Is something wrong?"

Two months ago, he would have shrugged off her concern, or even lied like he had to Jesse the night he went driving and found Daisy with the flat tire. But he never wanted to hide again. Especially from Daisy, who had a way of seeing into his soul.

Rafe manned up. "I didn't sleep well last night. The nightmare didn't come back, but it tried."

She winced on his behalf. "Are you worried about going back to police work?"

"Worried is too strong, but like I said before, it'll be good to get that first night out of the way."

She pressed her foot against his under the table. "I believe in you, Rafe. You were born to help people. From the day we met, you've been there for me, protected me. Plus you're really good at reading people and situations."

"Thanks." He nudged her foot back. "That means a lot to me."

Knowing she believed in him boosted him in ways

nothing else did—not a good word from his sergeant or a clap on the back from a friend. Rafe knew a lot of men who felt the same way about wives and girlfriends. Moms, too. It humbled him to need her, but God had given Eve to Adam for a reason.

They gazed at each other across the flickering candlelight, until a slow smile tugged on her lips. She surprised him by rising up enough to give him a quick kiss. "Let's plan that trip to Cincinnati."

Pleasant anticipation replaced whatever tension remained, and he answered with a confident nod. "The sooner, the better."

They talked dates, checked airfares on their phones, and decided on the middle of September. Relaxed and content, they enjoyed the brownies until Daisy's phone signaled a call.

Daisy picked up her phone, saw the caller ID, and frowned. "It's Chelsea. She almost never calls. We text."

Chelsea also knew about Daisy's home-cooked dinner for Rafe, the candlelight, and the ticking clock to his departure. She wouldn't call without a good reason, though if she'd gotten drunk again, Daisy would need to have a serious talk with her.

Rafe broke into her thoughts. "Maybe it's a butt dial."

"I hope so." Concerned, Daisy accepted the call with a quick swipe. "Hey, Chels. What's up?"

"Daaaize?"

Chelsea didn't sound like herself at all. On alert, Daisy put the call on speaker so Rafe could hear. "Are you all right?"

She laughed at something but didn't answer.

"Chelsea! Talk to me! Where are you?"

"At . . . at that place . . ." She giggled directly into the phone. "The horse . . . on the roof."

"Cowboy's Cantina?" That had been the plan when Chelsea left to meet a guy named Adam White. She'd connected with him on an app called Let's Meet! and they'd been texting. Tonight was their first face-to-face date. As usual, Chelsea showed Daisy the guy's profile. Daisy thought he sounded too good to be true, but he had a warm smile and made fun of himself for being as bald as a smiley face.

When Chelsea giggled without answering the question, every nerve in Daisy's body went on alert. "You're drunk. I'm coming to get you."

Rafe pushed to his feet, reaching for his keys as he stood.

Daisy hurried to her bedroom to put on her shoes. "Talk to me. Are you in the ladies' room?"

"Yeah." Chelsea slurred even more. "I . . . had just one . . . I think . . . oh no."

The sound of her being sick rasped over the phone. Daisy jammed her feet into flat sandals, grabbed her purse, and hurried to join Rafe. Together they raced down the hall with Daisy talking to Chelsea on speaker so Rafe could listen to the disjointed conversation.

Daisy had never heard Chelsea so incoherent. Even during her binge at the wedding, she'd been able to put words together while she cried on Daisy's shoulder. Chelsea drank socially, not habitually, and she was careful about her online dates. To Daisy, Chelsea didn't sound just drunk. She sounded giddy, even euphoric, and bizarrely nonsensical.

With every one of Chelsea's slurred words, Rafe's brow furrowed into deeper ruts. When they reached the parking lot, he motioned for Daisy to give him the phone.

"Chelsea. It's Rafe."

"Hi! I know you!"

"Chelsea. Listen to me." He barked the order as he and Daisy climbed into the Camaro. "I'm calling 911. I think you've been drugged."

The word hit Daisy square between the eyes. She didn't know much about date rape drugs, except that the word "roofie" came from Rohypnol, the name of a drug that caused euphoria, nausea, and then extreme sleepiness and amnesia. One of Daisy's housemates back at Maggie's House had been a victim of it.

Cowboy's Cantina was close by, but Daisy knew full well violence struck fast and hard. Memories of her own assault roared in her head, but only in the form of a memory—nothing like a flashback. An unearthly calm settled into her bones, and she mentally prepared for whatever might unfold.

"Chelsea." Daisy spoke in a strong, clear voice. "Are you with the guy from Let's Meet? His name is Adam."

Chelsea groaned without answering the question. "I . . . had just one drink . . . then a Coke." She started to laugh again. "Not like before."

"Can you describe the guy you're with?" Rafe cut diagonally across the half-empty parking lot and sped onto the street.

Daisy started to say she'd seen Adam White's photograph, but she didn't trust that information. It was best to hear directly from Chelsea.

Chelsea giggled again. "He's . . . cute."

"Tall or short?"

No answer.

"What color is his hair?"

"He's . . . bald!" She laughed like it was the funniest joke in the world.

"Chelsea, listen to me." Authority hammered home Rafe's words. "Do *not* leave the ladies' room. We're calling

911. Do *not* leave with *anyone* except a police officer."

Chelsea just laughed. "This is so weird!"

He handed the phone back to Daisy. "Keep her talking if you can."

Still driving fast, he called 911 through his hands-free car connection. Words Daisy had hoped to never hear again vibrated through the car speakers.

"Nine-one-one. Where's your emergency?"

Daisy spoke to Chelsea but listened to Rafe as he answered the dispatcher without fanfare. "I believe a woman's been drugged at Cowboy's Cantina. She's in the restroom, and there's reason to believe she's in danger."

"Her description, sir?"

"Approximately five feet, six inches. About one hundred thirty pounds. Age thirty-one. Long dark hair. Brown eyes. We believe her companion is a bald man. No other details available at this time."

"Are you aware of any weapons involved?"

"Weapon status is unknown."

"Your relationship to the woman?"

"A friend. I'm off-duty law enforcement. Cincinnati PD."

"Will you be on scene, sir?"

"Yes. My ETA is five minutes."

"Very good, sir. I'll advise accordingly."

Rafe ended the call, sped through a yellow light, then glanced at Daisy. "We'll beat the cops, so we need a plan. Which restroom is she in? Front or back?"

Daisy nodded, then spoke into her phone. "Can you hear me, Chels?"

"Yes . . ."

"Rafe and I are just a few minutes away. Are you in the bathroom in the back or near the front?"

"I don't remember . . . I'm . . . sick."

"Stay there, Chels," Daisy repeated. "Do *not* leave the

bathroom."

"Uh—oh, hi!"

Daisy heard a woman's voice but couldn't make out the words. "Help us!" Daisy shouted. "Help! Chelsea—give her the phone!"

The only answer was a mumble, then the silence of a dead call.

Rafe pressed the accelerator as hard as he dared. The situation called for a siren and flashing lights, but the Camaro provided only speed. Cowboy's Cantina sat in the middle of the block dubbed "Restaurant Row." Popular with locals and tourists alike, the restaurant promised to be crowded.

"We're almost there," he said to himself as much as to Daisy. But then a traffic light flashed to red. Cars spilled into the intersection, leaving him no choice but to come to a dead stop. "If the traffic clears, I'll run the light."

"Yes." Daisy stared hard toward the restaurant. "Every second counts. He could be leaving with her right now—"

"It's possible." *Very possible.*

A block away, the plastic horse on the roof of the restaurant pummeled the air. There were no plastic horses in Cincinnati, but the Friday night glow of restaurants and bars lighting up the night looked the same to him. Rafe wasn't in uniform and his badge held no weight in Wyoming, but he was a police officer down to his marrow. His instincts flared to life.

"We need a plan," he reminded Daisy. "What do you know about Bald Guy?"

"I saw his picture. His name is Adam White, and his profile says he's an IT guy. That's all I know, except he looked big."

"Do you know what he drives?"

"I have no idea."

Precious seconds ticked by. He glanced in the rearview mirror for flashing lights, listened for a siren, but there was no sign of a backup. Not a surprise. Refuge was in the middle of tourist season, and a drugged woman wasn't exactly an active-shooter situation. Cars continued to speed across the intersection, blocking him until the light finally turned green.

Rafe punched the gas. "I'm going to park right out front. I hate to ask this of you—"

Daisy cut him off. "Just tell me what to do."

"Go inside and look for Chelsea. If she's still in the ladies' room, stay with her and call me. If she's with Bald Guy, call me and I'll come in. Don't approach him alone."

"I understand."

Rafe pulled into the packed parking lot. The entrance was in the center of the adobe-style building and set back from the four rows of parked vehicles. "Do you see Chelsea's car?"

Daisy craned her neck and scanned the lot. "It's too crowded to tell."

"I'll look while you go inside. It's a silver Sentra, right? California plates?"

"Exactly."

She reached across the car and squeezed his knee. "I'm so glad you're here."

"Me too. But I hate asking you to go inside alone." Especially with her personal history. His gut tightened at the thought of Daisy being vulnerable, but Chelsea needed her now. Seconds counted. Had she been roofied, or was another drug like GHB involved?

He broke the rules and backed into the handicapped space by the front entrance. As usual, Chelsea had sent

Bald Guy's profile picture to Daisy's phone as a precaution. Daisy took five precious seconds to show Rafe the picture before she hurried inside.

It killed Rafe to watch her walk into the restaurant alone. If another officer had been present, he wouldn't have let her out of his sight.

He opened the glove box and retrieved his off-duty weapon along with the handcuffs he kept with it. He knew the gun was loaded, but he still popped the cylinder of the .38 snubby and checked it. Confident, he climbed out of the Camaro, hid the gun in his waistband under his shirt, and slid the handcuffs into his back pocket.

There was still no sign of the locals, not even a distant siren. Rafe scanned the cars coming and going, the faces of passersby, a row of shrubs. Nothing. A group of adults spilled out of the restaurant. No hats. No bald heads. A middle-aged couple sauntered past him, holding hands the way Rafe wanted to hold Daisy's hand for the next fifty years.

Three full minutes passed. Had she found Chelsea? How far away were the 911 responders?

His neck hairs prickled like they did in his nightmare, but the sensation only sharpened his vision, his awareness of the vehicles in the parking lot, the risks to random passersby if Bald Guy had a gun and used it.

Still no sirens. No sign of the 911 responders.

Daisy raced out of the front door. "She's gone. The hostess saw her leave with a bald guy about five minutes ago."

Five minutes. Long enough for Bald Guy to drive away with Chelsea and disappear into the night. Or long enough to assault her in the back of a van.

Rafe's eyes narrowed to a white van parked near a driveway that exited to Pioneer Boulevard. The brake lights came on, and the van backed out of the space. When it turned, the passenger window lined up with the restaurant. The window was down on the warm night, giving Rafe a glimpse of Chelsea slouched in the seat.

"Let's go!" he shouted.

Chapter 34

*D*aisy flung open her car door, buckled her seat belt, and braced for a wild ride. Her heart pumped at breakneck speed, but her thoughts remained calm, clear, and logical. With Rafe firmly in control, she sent up an urgent prayer for God to keep Chelsea safe, guide their steps, and give them the strength and courage to face whatever lay ahead.

Instead of making a fast getaway, the driver of the van steered down Pioneer Boulevard as if he had all the time in the world. Daisy put the pieces together. "He doesn't want to call attention to himself, does he?"

"Exactly."

"But we're following him, right?"

"Yes. But from a distance. I don't want him to suspect he's being followed and take off." Rafe called 911 for the second time. The same nasally dispatcher answered, and he updated her with the vehicle description, license plate, and location.

"What's your ETA?" he asked her.

"One moment, sir." Silence echoed until the dispatcher came back on the line. "Ten minutes."

Daisy broke in, her voice high. "That's too long!"

"I'm sorry, ma'am," the dispatcher replied. "We're doing our best."

Rafe took over. "We understand. The plan is to keep him in sight and approach only in a case of imminent danger to the victim."

"Your name, sir?"

Rafe fully identified himself and informed the dispatcher he was armed.

That was news to Daisy, but she wasn't surprised. She didn't like guns at all. They usually scared her, but in Rafe's capable hands, the weapon promised protection.

She kept her eyes glued to the van. When it turned on Highway 134—the road to Three Corners twenty miles away—the driver punched the gas.

So did Rafe. Most people did. But it was a road full of dips and curves, and all she could do was pray the van wouldn't notice them, speed up, and crash. Or veer onto a narrow side road even more isolated than the highway. Daisy glanced at the speedometer. They were doing seventy. So was the van. The needle inched toward seventy-five with a curve ahead of them.

Rafe reported the speed to the dispatcher. "This guy's in a hurry. Or he might be trying to lose us."

"Roger that.

Daisy recognized the start of the dead zone. The call would drop any minute.

Rafe continued to report until the dispatcher broke in. "Sir, we're transferring this call to"—static—"however"—

static—"injury accident." Static scraped again at Daisy's ears, then the call dropped completely.

To her left, she saw the turnout where Rafe had changed her flat tire. So much had changed in her life—and in her heart. That night she'd been shaking, alone and armed with pepper spray. Now she trusted Rafe with her life.

He turned off the phone through the hands-free system. "We're on our own for a while. How are you holding up?"

"I'm good." She meant it. "We have to stop him. No matter what—"

"We will."

For the next ten minutes, the van sped along the empty two-lane highway. An occasional car passed going in the opposite direction, ignorant of the drama unfolding on the other side of the double yellow line. Daisy knew the road well. From this point on, there were no turnoffs that led into the hills. No isolated homes. Nowhere to go except the town of Three Corners, where highways crossed on their way to the interstate system.

The interstate . . . Like the I-75 corridor . . . Daisy flashed back to Lyn's words about human trafficking and the new mission of Maggie's House. Her stomach tightened. "Do you think he's kidnapping her?"

"Anything is possible, but Refuge doesn't offer an easy getaway."

"I hope he stops in Three Corners."

"Me too." Rafe kept his eyes on the van. "With a little luck, the locals will pull him over before anything worse happens. If they don't make it, I'll do what needs to be done."

Rafe . . . in danger. Her heart pinched, but she saw honor in his action, and his care and concern for others, even Chelsea, who drove him nuts. Daisy loved this man.

Loved him! And she loved God, who promised to be with her through thick and thin. Her heart hammered even harder against her ribs, but the blood in her veins flowed with a deep inner calm. Much like a river in a violent storm, her faith remained true to its course despite the rain pounding the surface.

Full of courage, she laid her hand on Rafe's shoulder. "We need to pray."

"Go for it."

Daisy spoke in a strong, clear voice. "Lord, be with Chelsea. She's in danger, and I'm afraid for her. Protect her from this evil, Lord. And protect Rafe as he does whatever he needs to do."

"Yes, Lord," he murmured.

"We need you, Lord Jesus. Every day—and especially right now."

When she paused, Rafe's deep voice filled the void. "Thank you, Lord, for Daisy. Keep her safe, too. We're headed into a tough situation, but we're going forward with the knowledge that you're with us—no matter what happens."

They both whispered, "Amen."

Rafe kept his eyes on the van as it swayed around a curve. "Thanks, Daize. I'm closer to God than I've ever been, but right now, I need something from you, too."

"Anything."

"Do *not* leave the car unless I tell you to."

"I won't. I promise."

The local junkyard loomed on Daisy's right, and the van slowed to the speed limit. Ahead of them, the sky took on a neon glow from three fast food joints, the restaurant where Daisy use to work, a country-western bar, two gas stations, and random cars on the road.

Rafe called 911 again. "We should have a connection now. But get ready. If Bald Guy rabbits, we're sticking with him."

A male dispatcher answered in a deep voice. "911. Where's your emergency?"

The instant Rafe identified himself, the dispatcher took over. "Yes, sir. We're aware. ETA is twelve minutes. Unfortunately, there's an injury collision on Highway 185."

Rafe grimaced but responded calmly. "Understood."

"Sir, where are you now?"

"Entering Three Corners. I have the van in sight."

So did Daisy. With her heart in her throat, she watched as it turned left into the parking lot of the motel. Thanks to her time as a waitress, she knew the two-story building was L-shaped, occasionally infested with bed bugs, and staffed by an on-call manager who didn't ask a lot of questions. There were thirty or so rooms, all alike with orange doors. If she and Rafe lost sight of the van, it would be next to impossible to know which room the man entered.

Rafe's brow furrowed. "If I follow too close, the creep will know he's been made, but I can't risk losing him."

They both watched as the van cruised around a corner of the motel.

Rafe punched the gas to catch up but slowed near the back of the building. He spoke to both Daisy and the dispatcher as he swung into a parking space. "The van turned toward the side of the motel facing east. I just parked. You'll see my car—a red Camaro. Daisy Riley is with me. She can point the responding officers in the right direction. I'm approaching alone and on foot."

"Sir, that's unwise. Please wait in your vehicle."

"I can't do that," Rafe replied in an even tone. "The victim is in imminent danger of rape or worse. I'm going in."

Before the dispatcher could protest, he ended the call,

cut the engine, and turned to Daisy. "I mean it, Daisy. No matter what you see or hear, lock the doors and stay in the car until the cops get here. I can handle the situation alone, but I need to know you're safe. I love you. You know that—"

"I love you, too."

Rafe climbed out of the Camaro. He closed the door, motioned for her to hit the locks, then he disappeared around a shadowy corner lit only by the dull glow of a broken overhead light.

Rafe's only advantage was that Bald Guy wouldn't recognize him. Seconds mattered now. With every tick of the clock, the risk to Chelsea escalated. Assault. Rape. Even murder. Anything could happen, and Rafe knew it.

He strode past the identical rooms as if he were just another guest, but his five senses were on full alert. The air smelled like grime; a light fixture buzzed. Ten feet away, he saw the white van parked between two orange doors with matching windows, one dimly lit and flickering as if the television was on, the other dark and private.

Which room?

Which door?

He needed a sign, a break of some kind. A woman's laughter spilled out of an open window on the second floor, almost like in his nightmare but not quite. He wasn't running down a dark alley like in his dream. This situation was real.

Adrenaline surged through him. He moved to pound on the closest door but stopped when he spotted a squinty-eyed man in plaid shorts coming down the walkway with a full ice bucket.

Rafe called out in a friendly voice. "Hey, buddy. I'm

looking for someone. Did you see a bald guy anywhere?"

The man shook his head and kept walking. Rafe would have given a year's vacation to be in uniform. Without the badge, he resorted to the man's good will. "I don't mean to bother you, sir. But a woman's in danger. Did you see anything suspicious?"

The man grunted. "I don't want to get involved."

"You won't be." Rafe lowered his voice. "If you know something, just point to the door. That's all."

The man heaved a breath, glowered at Rafe, then aimed his chin at the door the man had just passed.

Rafe strode forward. Behind him, the reluctant good Samaritan walked into his own room and turned the deadbolt.

The situation called for immediate action, but what kind? Did he kick down the door or go with a ruse? There were no guarantees one good kick would take the door completely down, so Rafe decided on the ruse.

Pulse thrumming, he raised his arm and rapped on the door. "Hey, Rick!" Fake name, fake reason to knock. "I'm here, bro. Open the door." To be convincing, he added a foul word that fit the foul situation.

No answer.

Rafe pounded harder. "I got the beer! Hurry up, man! What are you doing, anyway?"

With a little luck, Bald Guy would open the door wide enough for Rafe to walk in, confirm Chelsea's presence, and take the guy down before he knew what hit him. If that didn't happen in the next five seconds, he'd kick the door.

One . . . Two . . . Three . . . Rafe took a step back.

Before he let loose, the door opened, but only three inches. A flimsy brass chain stopped it, but a sliver of the man's face and his bald head were in plain view. Quick as a cat, Rafe landed a hard kick next to the handle. The wood frame broke with a splintering crack and he burst into the room with his instincts hot. Eyes peeled, he took in his surroundings with a sweeping gaze.

Chelsea prone on the bed. Semi-conscious. Partially undressed. Lit up by studio-style lights.

Video equipment.

Bald Guy. Six feet tall. Shirtless. A snake tattoo on his belly. Barefoot. Lean build. And cursing a blue streak as he hauled back for a roundhouse punch.

Rafe dodged, but the blow still landed near his left eye and broke the skin.

"You're under arrest!" he shouted. With a felony in progress, he could make that call even as a private citizen.

Bald Guy called him a foul name and swung his fist again. Sidestepping, Rafe countered with an uppercut to the man's jaw. The blow spun the suspect backward and into the lights and tripod. The camera smacked the hard linoleum floor. The light stand crashed with it and the bulb shattered into a hundred jagged pieces. Bald Guy stepped on broken glass, cursed, and started to fall.

Rafe moved in, secured the suspect in a wristlock, and took him down to the ground. Bald Guy squirmed like the snake on his belly, but Rafe was now in full control of the situation. With the wristlock in place and his knee to the guy's back, he pulled the handcuffs out of his back pocket.

"Don't move," Rafe ordered as he applied the cuffs. "Stay calm and breathe evenly."

"What the—"

"No talking. Save it for the cops."

"Who the devil are *you*?"

Rafe didn't waste his breath. The man's cursing filled the air, but so did the war cry of an approaching siren.

With the suspect secure, Rafe wiped the blood from the cut on his cheek and turned to Chelsea. Flat on the bed, sprawled bonelessly with her eyes half open, she was the picture of helplessness. Rafe wanted to cover her with a blanket but couldn't. This was a crime scene, and it needed to be preserved.

Only a hospital visit would reveal the extent of the assault, but very little time had passed with Bald Guy in the motel room. Rafe had arrived in time, and Chelsea was alive. Hannah wouldn't lose her mother, and Daisy could take pride in saving a friend.

Rafe had done a good job tonight, but his satisfaction didn't come from saving Chelsea. It came solely from doing his job and doing it well. Cincinnati was still home and his first choice, but he could do that job anywhere, even in Refuge

Chapter 35

*E*ight long minutes ticked by, each more silent than the last, until a lone siren wailed in the distance. Though faint, it freed Daisy from her pledge to stay in the car. Relieved to take action, she flung open the door and hurried to a spot where the responders could see her when they arrived.

She scanned the main road for flashing lights but saw only a stream of cars. "Hurry," she muttered. "*Hurry.*"

The siren howled in the distance, growing louder with each passing second. The motel butted up against the east-west highway, close to the overpass that crossed the north-south route. The grimy smell of exhaust filled her nose. So did the garbage smell of a Dumpster. It was all so unlike Cottonwood Acres, where pine trees scented the air and meadows stretched in languid beauty . . . so unlike

Miss Joan's bench by the river, where God had calmed Daisy's own weary soul.

But God was here too . . . and so was Daisy.

The start of a revelation stirred deep in her chest, pressed upward to her lungs, her throat, seeking air until she inhaled sharply.

What is it, Lord? What can't I see?

She peered up at the moon, saw only reflected light, then lowered her gaze back to the road. The patrol car sped into view, the light bar strobing against the night. A second siren joined the first in a coyote-like song—the kind of song that belonged at Cottonwood Acres—but right now, it belonged here, too.

The harmony of it all hit Daisy square in the chest and she gasped. *Where* she lived didn't matter nearly as much as *why* she lived. And that was to love and to serve others. Geography didn't matter to God—not one bit. He met people where they lived—on mountaintops and in gutters. In Refuge and in Cincinnati.

Suddenly she knew with utter confidence that God hadn't brought her to Refuge to put down roots. He'd given her refuge so she could heal. With a certainty born of faith, hope for a better world, and love for broken people like herself, she knew where she belonged—and where Rafe belonged.

Rafe . . . the man she loved. The good man who had walked into the unknown to save Chelsea from the terror of rape, violence, even death. He'd been out of sight for eleven minutes now.

Please, God. Keep him safe. Please!

A sheriff's car whipped into the parking lot and turned toward her.

"Over here!" she shouted, waving her arms high. "Over here!"

The car slowed, so she pointed frantically for it to go

around the corner. The officer gave a crisp nod and made the turn.

A second car with two officers, one female, followed thirty seconds later.

An ambulance arrived in its wake, lights bright but siren off.

Daisy sagged with relief, but the relief lasted a nanosecond. Every part of her body, mind, and heart yearned to follow the ambulance, but she had promised Rafe she would stay by the car.

"Please, God. *Please.*" It was a plea for mercy, a plea for strength.

A plea for the life and well-being of the man she loved.

A plea for Chelsea to be spared anything worse than she'd already endured.

As tempting as it was to peek around the corner, Daisy knew better. Gunfire could still erupt. Bald Guy could break loose, make a run for it, and take her hostage. That thought sent her scurrying back to the Camaro, where she climbed in, locked the doors, and settled for staring hard at the corner of the building, her heart in her throat.

A small eternity passed before a man's shadow broke the dull glow from the overhead light. The silhouette stretched toward the parking lot, until Rafe rounded the corner with a firm stride.

Overcome with relief, she flung open the door and ran to him. He pulled her tight, and she held him even tighter. The coppery scent of blood reached her nose, and she pulled back to look at his face. A Steri-Strip held the skin on his cheek together, and she saw the start of bruising around his left eye.

"You're hurt—" Her voice cracked.

"It's nothing. What matters is that Bald Guy—aka Douglas Smith—is safely cuffed and enjoying the back seat of a patrol car."

"Thank God." Daisy meant it as a prayer. "Chelsea—did he—was she—"

"I don't think she was raped. The creep had video equipment set up. He was taking his time."

Every cell in Daisy's body recoiled. "Does she know what's going on?"

"She's pretty out of it," Rafe replied. "But she might know if you're there."

Arm in arm, they walked toward the crime scene outlined in yellow tape. The light bars on the vehicles now blinked rather than strobed, less urgent but no less serious. A patrol car left as they approached, and through the window, Daisy saw Douglas Smith seated in the back.

The female officer approached them. Rafe introduced Daisy as Chelsea's friend, and Officer Pettit updated them on Chelsea's condition. The EMTs were with her now and would transport her to a hospital. Tests would be run, but she appeared to be relatively unharmed except for the drugging. She'd be kept at least overnight, or until the drug was out of her system.

Officer Pettit offered them each a business card. "You two did great work tonight. We've been after this guy for a couple of months now. He uses different dating apps to find his victims, picks motels where highways cross, and gets away without a trace. He's clever." She called over to her partner. "Hey, O'Brien. Does this make five or six victims?"

"Six." The male officer joined them, shook Rafe's hand, and thanked him for making their job easy.

The rattle of the gurney caught Daisy's attention and she turned. Chelsea lay covered by a sheet and strapped down for safety, but now she was conscious enough to lift her head.

Daisy hurried to her side. The attendants stopped in the middle of the walkway, below a dim light that reflected in Chelsea's dilated pupils. When she recognized Daisy, she tried to reach for her but the straps held her down. Her mouth worked to form a single word. "Haaannaaah?"

Daisy laid her hand on Chelsea's forehead. "I'll take care of her. I know this is scary for you."

Tears spilled from Chelsea's eyes.

"You're not alone, Chels," Daisy assured her. "Not by a long shot."

Another whimper slipped from Chelsea's lips. With her dark hair tangled against the white sheet, she resembled a discarded doll. Another word slowly formed on her lips. "H-h-hooome."

"To the apartment? I'm sorry, Chels. But you need to go to the hospital."

"No." She tried again. "Mich—Mich—"

"Home to Michigan?"

Fresh tears glistened in Chelsea's dark eyes. Daisy knew exactly how she felt. Tonight Chelsea had become a survivor, someone in need of healing and a new beginning. Silently, Daisy prayed for her friend to invite Jesus into her life, and for God to give Chelsea peace and strength in the arms of her family in Michigan.

Daisy kissed Chelsea's forehead, then stepped back so the EMTs could load her into the ambulance.

Rafe came to Daisy's side. "Do you want to go to the hospital?"

"Yes, but I can't. I told Chelsea I'd take care of Hannah. She's okay with the babysitter for a while longer, but I need to go home. I'll bring Chelsea anything she needs tomorrow."

Rafe took her hand and they walked to his car, both silent until they rounded the corner. The emergency lights faded to reflections on the asphalt, and a calm settled over them both as Rafe opened the passenger door. She started to climb in, but he stopped her with a hand on her arm.

"Hold on a minute." He took the gun out of his waist-band, put it in the glove box, and locked it. Then he paused—his eyes focused on the lock, as if he'd done more than put away the weapon.

Daisy looked up. "What is it?"

He glanced around the parking lot, then at the sleazy motel with the grimy lights, and finally to the Dumpster behind them. "This isn't the place. It can wait."

"No." Concern for him sluiced through her. "A lot just happened—and it couldn't have been easy. Are you all right?"

"Me? I'm fine." Surprise brightened his voice. "In fact, I'm great. I won't say tonight was easy, but it was good. In fact, I realized something important."

"So did I."

"Oh, yeah?"

"Yeah," she echoed. "But you're right, this isn't the place for that conversation."

They stared at each other for ten long seconds, then they spoke at the same time.

"I love you," they said in unison.

Daisy smiled. "There's more."

"Same here. Daisy, I—"

"Wait. Me first." She needed to get the words out before she exploded into a million happy pieces and started to babble, or to cry with joy. Or to— Laughing inwardly, she told herself to stop and just breathe. She inhaled gently, but the joy refused to be contained.

Glowing inside, she focused on Rafe's handsome face. "I know where I belong. I also know where *you* belong—and it's not in Refuge."

"What—wait." His brow furrowed, causing the Steri-Strip on his cheek to wrinkle. If it hurt, he didn't seem to notice. "Hold on, Daize. It's not that simple—"

"It is. I love you."

"I love you, too." His voice deepened into a drawl. "Refuge is your home. I won't ask you to leave. I can do my job anywhere. Tonight proved it."

"Of course you can." Confidence rang in her voice. "But you belong in Cincinnati—and so do I."

He stared into her eyes, giving her time to waffle. "Do you really mean it?"

"Yes. I do."

When she stayed strong, he pulled her into his arms and they kissed. Easing back, he grinned down at her. "You know what this means, don't you?"

"I know exactly what it means." A thousand glorious thoughts pinballed through her mind. "It means I need to tell Lyn I want the job! I have to learn how to spell Cincinnati—"

Rafe chuckled. "Yeah, it's tricky."

"It is!" But Daisy didn't mind at all. "I can't wait to visit! I need a plane ticket, and I have to tell Miss Joan, and—and—" The next thought brought tears to her eyes, because she truly loved Refuge and her family. "And I have to tell Shane and MJ about what I decided."

The bittersweet tears spilled over and streamed down her cheeks, but Rafe held her tight while she cried. After a few soggy minutes, she pulled back and laughed. "I'm a blubbery, lachrymose mess!"

His brows arched. "*Lachrymose?*"

"Vocab app! It means tearful."

"You're also a beautiful mess." He kissed her temple. "What you just said—all that's true, but I was thinking of something else."

"What?"

"This means we have all the time in the world to fall even more in love."

Her heart nearly soared out of her chest. "And to get to know each other even better—"

"A day at a time," he said for her.

She swiped at the tears streaming down her cheeks. "I love you so much."

"I love you, too."

He kissed her then. A simple kiss. A sweet kiss. Daisy kissed him back just as tenderly, then gave him a mischievous smile. "Do you want to guess where *that* ranked on the kiss scale?"

He rubbed the side of his face that didn't have the Steri-Strip. "I'd give it a five."

"A five? No way!"

"Definitely a five. Maybe even a four." Scowling, he glanced around the parking lot. "For one thing, we're standing by a Dumpster. It stinks. How romantic is that?"

Daisy made a show of sniffing the air. "Ewww. You're right. Garbage smell."

"So points off for air quality." He eyed the run-down motel and shook his head. "More points off for the sleaze factor. This place is a dump."

"Yes. It's awful."

"And another point off for—"

Daisy broke out laughing. "Okay, you win. That kiss gets a five. What do you say to trying again later?"

"I'm all for it."

"Me too." With her heart ready to burst, she kissed his cheek.

Rafe smiled into her eyes. "My whole life changed because of you. When I came to Refuge, I couldn't sleep, suffered from nightmares, and wondered if I could keep it together. But Daisy—you showed me the way back to God. So did Jesse, but mostly it was you."

"I'm glad." She hugged him as hard as she could. "It's a two-way street. I love how we take care of each other."

The road back to Refuge lay in front of them, but so

did a future in a faraway city full of challenges, new people, and a job that would test her in ways she couldn't yet fathom. But none of that mattered. God was with her now, and he'd be with her in Cincinnati.

And so would Rafe.

Books by Victoria Bylin

The Road to Refuge Series
When He Found Me
A Gift to Cherish

Contemporary Romance
Until I Found You
Together With You
Someone Like You
The Two of Us

Inspirational Westerns
The Bounty Hunter's Bride
Kansas Courtship
"Home Again" in In a Mother's Arms
"Josie's Wedding Dress" in Brides of the West

The Women of Swan's Nest Series
The Maverick Preacher
Wyoming Lawman
The Outlaw's Return
Marrying the Major

Harlequin Historicals *
Of Men and Angels
West of Heaven
Abbie's Outlaw
Midnight Marriage
"A Son is Given" in Stay for Christmas
"The Christmas Dove" in The Magic of Christmas

* These stories have Christian themes, but they were written
for the mainstream market. They contain scenes, situations,
and language some readers will prefer to avoid.

A Word from Victoria . . .

Dear Readers,

There's a story behind every book I write. For A Gift to Cherish, the story begins on a rooftop near UC Berkeley in 1979. I'll never forget standing on top of the student co-op where I lived at the time, gazing up at the stars, then out to the black hole of the San Francisco Bay. City lights lit up the shore and the hills, but nothing could alleviate the heaviness in my heart.

The social scene at the time was everything you might imagine. The culture focused on personal discovery, self-reliance, self-this and self-that. It also emphasized personal freedom and social conscience—both good things in the proper context. But dangerous things, too.

If you've just finished reading A Gift to Cherish, you know where this is going. Miss Joan's story is rooted in that era. I hope you enjoyed meeting her. The details of her life and mine are light years apart, but our spiritual journeys are parallel—from darkness to light, from sin to salvation, and from fear to faith in our Lord Jesus Christ.

I will be forever grateful for the unique way God worked in my life, and I pray He works in your life, too.

All the best,

Vicki

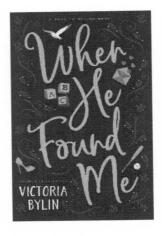

Once a strong Christian, third baseman Shane Riley lost his faith the night he injured his knee in a freak car accident. Determined to return to professional baseball and to find the sister he treated badly, Shane retreats to Refuge, Wyoming. There he meets Melissa June "MJ" Townsend, a single mom battling the virus that causes cervical cancer.

MJ wants nothing to do with the handsome athlete—no doubt a womanizer considering the stories in the news. But when a mistake results in Shane renting her garage apartment, they become friends. That friendship blossoms into something deep and pure, leaving MJ with a painful secret to tell. Even more complicated, she discovers an unexpected tie to Shane's missing sister—a wounded woman who wants nothing to do with the perfect brother who scorned her.

About the Author

Victoria Bylin is known for tackling tough subjects with great compassion. In 2016, *Together With You* won the Inspirational Reader's Choice Award for Best Contemporary Romance. Her other books, including historical westerns, have finaled in the Carol Awards, the RITAs, and RT Magazine's Reviewers' Choice Awards. A native of California, she and her husband now make their home in Lexington, Kentucky.

Manufactured by Amazon.ca
Bolton, ON